PINIONS OF GOLD — AN ANGLO-SAXON ARCHAEOLOGICAL MYSTERY

JAKE CONLEY BOOK 5

JOHN BROUGHTON

Published 2020 by Gumshoe – A Next Chapter Imprint

Cover art by Cover Mint

This book is dedicated to my wife, Maria Antonietta Valente, with thanks for our constant support and love.

Special thanks go to my dear friend John Bentley for his steadfast and indefatigable support. His content checking and suggestions have made an invaluable contribution to Pinions of Gold.

ONE

MINISTRY OF DEFENCE, LONDON, UK

Jake Conley glared at his mobile with venom and a strong temptation to ignore the call. Well aware that it would come sooner or later to disturb his newly-wed bliss, he sighed and accepted the call from his boss, Sir Clive Cochrane. His reluctance was understandable, as previously, this kind of call had led him into situations where he'd been tortured and escaped death by a hair's breadth. Encounters with demonic forces and supernatural entities had all taken place with Sir Clive, a senior civil servant, sitting in comfort behind his plush desk. Feeling little more than a chess piece in the hands of a superspy, Jake wondered whether he was a knight or a castle or nothing more than a pawn in the mind of AA, his boss. Taking a steadying breath, he answered the phone,

"Good morning, sir. Do you have an assignment for me?"

"As ever, you are direct and to the point, old chap. Why don't you slip up to London and see what little treat I have in mind?" The false bonhomie snapped and he reverted to the mode Jake knew and feared so much, "My office 10.30

sharp, there's a good fellow." Before Jake could acquiesce, his chief added, "Ah, and bring the delightful Mrs Conley to the meeting. I'd be pleased to see my former receptionist again. I take it she's well?"

"Very well, thank you. Tomorrow then, goodbye."

The train journey to London into Euston from Warwick was swift but he and Alice spent it in speculation. What did AA want this time? The only ingredients that Jake could promise his wife, in his experience, were danger and mystery with the dosage heavily in favour of the former. Since they were both agents on standby in the pay of the British government, the call was inevitable. But that didn't mean they should be happy about receiving it.

As ever, Jake's approach to the Ministry building was characterised by his mixed emotions: trepidation and curiosity. This was the first time he'd shared them with someone else and glancing at Alice out of the tail of his eye, he saw only the latter emotion. Fighting back the desire to warn her to be ready for extreme peril, he remembered that she too was an agent and had survived the trauma of his last case by a hair's breadth.

Smooth as ever, the lift bore them to the second floor, where the miracle of Sir Clive's hearing played out once more. It intrigued Jake every time. How could the man hear his knock through the layered surfaces of the padded door? He had never heard 'come in' and always entered regardless. Did that account for the inevitable ironical smile that greeted him?

"Ah, my dear fellow and splendid consort. Do be seated."

There followed the usual pleasantries before Sir Clive, duty done, broached the reason for their convocation. Circumspect as ever, he began, "Strictly speaking, neither of you is obliged to accept this job since it is a non-governmental matter. You will effectively remain on standby even if you do take it on. Should a government case arise, you will be expected to give that absolute priority. We should be quite clear. Do you follow?"

Where, down the labyrinthine corridors of your mind!

Thus, thought Jake but nodded and smiled, understanding the *nothing* he'd been given so far.

"Good, as a private matter, in recompense, it should not put you in any danger..."

That'll be the day, crafty old sod.

"...on the other hand, Conley, I suspect this is a matter that's right up your street, as it were, dear boy, involving as it does an element of the inexplicable. Ghosts and all that stuff, so beloved of your very good self." He paused and looked from one to the other with a smug expression on his pinched face, eyes as ever unsmiling and hard as slivers of ice.

"Sir?"

"I have an acquaintance, a nonagenarian, a hero in the Second World War. His son, John Robinson, is a barrister and a close friend of mine – a member of my club, in fact."

He would be.

The long, manicured fingers across the desk from them fiddled with a visiting card, flipping it over and over. "John asked me to find someone who could set his father's mind at rest regarding a long-standing mystery in the family. The old chappie still lives in Lincolnshire in rather grander circumstances than his forebears, by all accounts. Well, there it is. Jake Conley, psychic investigator, summoned to solve a centuries-old mystery once again." This he said, with a certain amount of glee, his predatory smile chilled Jake who watched it change into a practised engaging one as his attention switched to Alice. "Now, as to your role, my dear gal, to keep your husband, how shall I put this? Well, he has, let's say... something of a penchant... for landing himself in trouble. Your job is to baby-sit him." He sniggered.

"Sir!" Jake put as much feeling into the one respectful word as he would have into a familiar Anglo-Saxon expletive. It had effect.

The Head of the Secret Service looked chastened and adopted a mellifluous tone, "Sorry, old man, no offence, but your lady wife's unquestioned abilities should prove invaluable in helping you untangle this intriguing mystery. Two minds being better than one and all that. I foresee no danger. A meeting is arranged for tomorrow in the village of Tealby in Lincolnshire, a pleasant spot. They say the pub's haunted—you'll like it. That by the way, is not the ghost you'll be dealing with. The appointment is at Robinson Senior's house. He has a wonderful garden." He pushed the visiting card across the green-leather-topped desk. "Sir John's details. Give him a call. I expect he'll have you picked up at Lincoln Railway Station. I think train is your best option. With the aplomb of a magician pulling a white rabbit out of a top hat, he produced a cardboard envelope from his desk drawer. "Your tickets, first-class, of course. Most efficient, Ms Brewster; she's your successor in reception, my dear. Tomorrow morning at King's Cross and thank you for taking on the case."

Bloody cheek, we haven't accepted anything—and he knows it.

Outside nearby, perched on a bench overlooking the Thames, Jake let go of Alice's hand.

"The damned cheek of the blighter. Not only does he foist a personal favour on us, he also insults me into the bargain. A bloody baby-sitter. It's all right for him, sitting behind his desk, smarmy as you like, whilst I take all the risks."

"Except, he said this case involves no danger."

"Ooh, look." Jake pointed downriver, "There goes another one."

"What?"

"Can't you see its wings? A flying pig."

She clutched his arm, laughing, "You don't believe him then?"

He shook his head. "I can say that Double-A has never given me a case that didn't involve violence and death, but apart from that, they've been relaxing."

"Fool! But this one sounds intriguing."

"There's nothing in it, just the ramblings of an old man. He's over ninety, for heaven's sake."

Alice frowned and considered, "But his son is one of Her Majesty's Counsel learned in the law. I don't suppose he'd let the old fellow make a fool of himself."

Jake stared at a passing tourist sightseeing boat and pondered. Alice, as usual impressed him with her common sense. She was right to point out that Sir John Robinson QC hadn't arrived at the top of his profession without being in possession of sound judgment.

TWO

TEALBY, WEST LINDSEY, LINCOLNSHIRE. 2021 AD

THE LAND ROVER PITCHED AND RIGHTED AS IT SWEPT through Beck Hill Ford, the road crossing the River Rase at one of the two fords in the village. They drove past the village shop, the Vintage Tea Rooms and the King's Head, the thatched and reputedly haunted ancient public house, out of the picturesque settlement. Their driver, Sir John, pointed out each of the features as they drove by, with a touch of pride in his home county. Jake, having admired the gentle Wolds scenery, could understand the sentiment. He snapped back to attention at the mention of Lord Tennyson, one of his favourite poets.

The barrister was saying, "...and they demolished the manor in the nineteen sixties, a pity, but it was in a dangerous state of neglect and had to go. Lord Tennyson's uncle Charles owned it. There are some memorials to the family in our church. It's largely twelfth-century if you're interested." Jake was. Among his hobbies, he enjoyed visiting country churches. He made a mental note.

"Ah, we're here. The lawyer turned into the drive of an immaculate garden belonging to a splendid detached house of indeterminate style. An eminent architect had designed it in the 1920s, more with blending into the surroundings than with modern creativity in mind. The result was a harmonious, airy, well-lit building that hinted at rural tradition whilst offering every convenience.

The large fireplace with oak lintel, delimited by a stone hearth, dominated the spacious lounge. Sitting in an armchair with a tartan rug over his legs, a white-haired wizened-faced figure looked up with rheumy eyes when his son entered with two newcomers.

"My father, Roy," Sir John indicated the old man. "Father, this is Mr Conley, the gentleman from London I told you about. He's come to attempt to get to the bottom of the Covenham mystery."

Roy Robinson gazed at them, Jake suspected without understanding, when the elderly man wheezed a response, "How I wish he would."

"My father is ninety-four," the lawyer said, "But his mind is active. This affair has troubled him as long as I can remember. I don't want to overtire him, so I'll relate what happened to him since I've heard the tale many times and if I err, he will correct me, won't you dad?"

The senior Robinson chuckled and raised a hand, heavy with blue veins and dark liver-coloured spots. Everyone took this to mean assent, so Sir John pulled three chairs close to the fire, threw another oak log on to add to the others. They settled down to listen.

Sir John began. "His story begins in December 1934 in a village called Covenham St. Mary, beyond Binbrook towards the coast, when he was seven. Father was playing with a tin car and pushing it across the carpet in the living room. He was a sensitive child, and though my grandparents were strict, he enjoyed plenty of affection. His mother, red in the face, came out of the kitchen with a basket full of washing from the wringer. Roy hated washing day because the kitchen was so full of steam from the copper boiler and his mum was so busy that she couldn't give him any attention. It was worse in winter, of course, with damp, steaming washing on the clothes horse in front of the fire.

"My grandmother told him: Roy, don't go into the kitchen. I don't want you anywhere near that boiler, do you hear? I'm just going to peg the washing out, it's a lovely drying day."

My father had no intention of going into the kitchen; he imagined he was Frank Clement with a 4.5 litre Bentley winning the Le Mans race at more than 100 miles an hour... it was just at the moment of his triumph, as he crossed the winning line and took the chequered flag that he felt a strange chill penetrate to his bones..."

At this point in the account, the old man by the fire heaved a wheezing sigh that made Jake and Alice stare at him. They both noticed the strange expression and faraway look in his pale grey eyes. Neither of them doubted that he too was following the story with the same attention as they were. Sir John continued, "...It was a sunny day and up to that instant a draught through the open door cooled the room of the steam from the kitchen. But my father felt a different sensation, numbing and disturbing. He looked up and saw an old woman with a big book in her lap sitting in a rocking chair by the hearth. She had lank, white hair around a wrinkled face. Father felt no fear. It was right. The old woman somehow belonged there. She smiled at him as his teeth began to chatter and he wrapped his arms across his chest to warm up. The woman didn't speak. Instead she raised her right hand and pointed to the stairs. Then she waved him in that direction with the back of her hand. Father stood up and hesitated, still staring into the gentle, reassuring face of the old woman. Smiling, she repeated the gesture and he walked to the stairs, dividing the living room from the kitchen of Rose Cottage. Like an automaton, with no free will, he began to climb the stairs. On the fourth stair he stopped rooted to the spot. He still felt numb and seemed unable to control his body. His head, as if moved by another, turned to face over his left shoulder, until his nose almost touched the wall of the stairs. He didn't know why he was staring at the wall or for how long."

"The old lady must have been a ghost," Jake murmured and as if he could read his mind, the veteran, who was studying his face, nodded in confirmation.

Sir John also looked at Jake and reassured that his guest was following the tale, went on,

"He felt warm again and he turned around and jumped down to the floor. He checked and found his mother still in the garden pegging a linen sheet. Then he skipped back into the living room and found that there was no old woman and no rocking chair. As only a seven-year-old can, he put them both out of his mind at once and concentrated on receiving his cup for winning the Le Mans race.

When his mother came back in, he didn't tell her about the old woman. But what had happened in those few minutes stayed with him for the rest of his life.

Arthur, my grandfather, and his wife Rebecca had moved to Rose Cottage in Covenham St. Mary in the summer of 1933 because they were poor. Arthur was self-employed as a painter and decorator and he kept his paint, brushes and stepladders in a handcart. This he attached to his bicycle, since most of his work was in nearby villages or thirteen miles away in the town of Cleethorpes, which they'd left because they couldn't afford the rent on the houses there. One of his clients mentioned that there was a small cottage that had been empty for a hundred and thirty years in Covenham St. Mary, a village with a population of 270. All the cottage needed was some repairs and a coat of paint. It was available for next to nothing because nobody wanted to live there.

Granddad Arthur laughed off the idea that the cottage was haunted. In fact, he wasn't even interested in hearing about what he called the *whys and wherefores* of the case. Enrolled in the Lincoln Regiment at 16, sent home as too young, joined up at 17 when there were less scruples, wounded twice in the Great War, won the Military Medal twice and made King's Corporal, Arthur wasn't going to be bothered about any ghost nonsense; he'd seen enough carnage to last several lifetimes, but he'd never seen the ghost of a fallen comrade. Ghosts didn't exist as far as he was concerned..."

Sir John excused himself to get a drink, "Need to wet the whistle, old chap. Will you join me... and you, Mrs Conley?" Alice declined, but Jake, on spotting the bottle of Aberfeldy single malt, surrendered to one of his weaknesses. The smooth liquor with a hint of smoke, drunk beside the fire, was the perfect accompaniment to a ghost story in Jake's opinion.

Dabbing his lips with a handkerchief, Sir John, addressing Alice, continued after an apology for the interlude, "...Rose Cottage was suitable for Arthur's small family, with its two rooms downstairs and the bathroom and bedroom upstairs. Now that a second child was on the way grandmother worried that there might be a problem. Already Roy's bed was in the corner of their bedroom, but Arthur had made the cottage very attractive at very little cost. The baby was due in three months, in March, and they'd have to manage. Arthur and Becky were very much in love and that made the difference.

It was a crisp December afternoon and Arthur biked the last few yards to Rose Cottage at around twenty-past twelve. He had a job at Utterby about two and a half miles away and he'd come home for lunch. Arthur was grateful when he was close enough to home to have a cooked meal instead of the packed lunch Becky made him when he was further away. He leant his bicycle against the fence and strode through the gate and up the path to his door.

"I'm home, Bubs." he called, using his pet name for her, because her curls made him think of bubbles. The stairs faced the door and in two bounds he was already mounting them, "I'll just wash my hands." He savoured the delicious aroma from the kitchen. About to turn into the bathroom at the top of the stairs, granddad stopped and the smile vanished. The bedroom door was open and what he saw made him rush downstairs red in the face to the roots of his ginger hair.

"Rebecca!" he barked in the tone of his old company sergeant–and he never called her that unless he was furious. She looked up from stirring the gravy with a sweet smile. She was used to his temper bursting as quick as a spring shower.

"What have you done upstairs, woman? Did you move all the furniture?"

"Yes," she smiled.

Arthur's face became plum red, "Are you crazy? In your state? You're six months gone; you could lose the baby like that. Why didn't you ask me if you wanted the furniture moving?"

Becky moved the gravy to a cold plate on the range and

put her arms around her husband. She kissed his burning cheek. "Well, be honest, Arthur, if I'd asked you, you'd have said no, wouldn't you? Besides, I don't know why, but it was just something I had to do, like it was a feeling stronger than me." She squeezed him tight and gave him another kiss. Becky could feel the tension leave him and he pressed his lips against hers.

"Well, don't have any more of these feelings. Do you hear me? Do you know how much that wardrobe weighs?"

"Oh, come on grumpy, no harm's done, get those hands washed and sit down at table. I've made shepherd's pie. Roy will be home from school in a minute and he'll need the bathroom." At the thought of Roy, she sighed and hoped that her little boy hadn't suffered any bullying today at the Elementary School. It drew from the villages of Fotherby, Utterby and Little Grimsby as well as from the twin village of Covenham St. Bartholomew. Children were often cruel and they teased Roy because of his sensitivity, he was different from them. It was a constant worry.

Arthur's mind was troubled too, but for another reason. As he biked back to work that afternoon he pondered over his wife's strange behaviour. What on earth had possessed her to move the heavy bedroom furniture around in her condition?"

At the same time Becky murmured, "How could I tell him the truth? He'd think me out of my mind." She sat down in the armchair next to the hearth and reflected on the morning's strange events. Roy was at school and Arthur was at work and she decided to have a break from housework with a cup of tea." Sir John looked at his father as if for confirmation that his facts were correct. The old man waved him on. Hesitating for a moment as if he'd lost the thread, he said, "Ah, yes ...she carried it into the living room and that was when she saw an old woman with a black book in her lap seated in a rocking chair by the hearth. Becky felt a chill run up and down her spine. The fine hairs on her arm stood on end and she was rooted to the spot unable to move, while the air around her felt cold."

As for Jake, a familiar dull ache between his eyebrows told him that the tale had psychic importance to him. He rubbed his temples and the old man grinned a toothless smile. Struggling to latch on to the story again, he heard Sir John say, "...Grandma knew at once that this was the old woman who was said to haunt the house, but like Arthur she'd dismissed talk of ghosts as nonsense. Yet she wasn't afraid. There was something kind about the old woman's wrinkly face and its gentle smile. But there was something else in her expression, Becky thought, what was it, concern?"

"As she thought this, the old woman pointed towards the ceiling. Becky's eyes followed the finger upwards. It was in that instant that her head filled with the urgent need to move the bedroom furniture around. When she looked back the old woman had disappeared and in the place of the rocking chair was Becky's familiar armchair. With notable courage, Becky sat down there with her cup of tea. She hadn't imagined the old woman, she knew that —and another thing, the room was warm again. Becky sipped her tea. "*So, I've seen the ghost,*" she thought. She knew that there were people in Covenham who'd believe her, more than once she'd heard the tragic tale of the old woman's death recounted in awed tones by one or other of the villagers; she knew equally well that Arthur would tease her if she uttered even one word about a ghost. When she finished her tea, Becky went into the bedroom. After an hour's exertion, the layout of the bedroom was different, she'd even managed to shift the heavy wardrobe. She couldn't explain why, but she knew this task was urgent. Why it was so pressing, she had no idea."

Alice stared at Jake, who was tense and pale. She knew him well enough by now to see that this tale was having a profound effect on him. Could it be that AA had hit upon something that his old public-school mate had told him and thought it worthy of Jake's attentions? She wondered where all this was leading.

"Father came back from school at half-past four," Sir John continued, "At a quarter-past five Arthur was back home and sniffing the air at the door. "I reckon there's a storm brewing, Bubs, the air's far too still."

"Put the wood in the hole, Arthur," she said, using one of his own favourite expressions for shutting the door, "you're letting all the heat out of the room."

The evening passed much as usual. Roy was asleep by eight o'clock and Becky and Arthur went up to bed around half-past ten. What a gale was blowing! The rain lashed against the sash windows. These were draughty old windows Becky thought as she snuggled down even further under the eiderdown. She worried that Roy wouldn't be warm enough and then thought that if she put any more bedding on him, she'd crush him. Anyway, he had an earthenware hot water bottle in with him. She relaxed, cuddled up to her husband and drifted into an uneasy sleep. Meanwhile, the storm got worse. About one o'clock Becky woke with a start. The wind was howling like a tortured beast in a steel-fanged trap. She gasped as the gale flung something against the rattling window, maybe the branch of a tree.

Thank goodness it didn't break the glass.

Lightning flashed overhead and lit up the curtains that

rose and fell in the draught, like arms raised in anguish. Tense, Grandma lay listening to the small skeleton of the cottage groan and creak under its skin of plaster, while the sounds of water sluicing from the drainpipes and the rain driven against the panes were drowned by the roar of thunder that woke even the deep-sleeping Arthur. Just then the old mortar on the chimney gave way. Like bombardment on the Western Front, there was a deafening crash as the whole stack broke loose and crashed through the tiled roof and through the bedroom ceiling in a cloud of dust and debris. Even in her terrified state Becky realised:

It's come down where our bed would have been if I hadn't moved it.

Roy woke with his heart pounding fit to burst and his face white with dust. Tears washed two flesh-coloured lines down the dust mask as he howled for his mother, but Becky screamed as her contractions began and that morning Roy had a little brother, Kenneth, born three months before his time."

Sir John stood, crossed over to the dresser and poured himself another whisky. Without a word, he waved the bottle at Jake.

"Don't mind if I do. Thank you." When the barrister settled back into his armchair, Jake told him, "You know, that's a fascinating story and whilst I believe that your father," he glanced at the old man, whose head had dropped onto his chest and whose breathing was deep and regular, "saw a ghost, it could be argued that his mother had a premonition. But given the circumstances, I feel sure the ghost saved the family that night."

"By Jove, father has told that story to many people, believe me, but I must say, you are the first that's sounded so convinced." He gave Jake a warm smile and added, "Clive told me you were the chappie to get to the bottom of our mystery and I believe he's right."

"I've had more than a little experience of the supernatural, Sir John, and I feel sure that the ghost was trying to tell your father by gestures that –"

"Yes! Oh sorry to interrupt. My enthusiasm, I'm afraid it gets the better of me. You were going to say that there was something in the stair wall, I think."

"I was. Is that what your father believes?"

"It is."

"Has neither of you been back to find out? I presume the cottage is still standing?"

"Yes, but abandoned for years. The villagers won't go near it. Many still think it's haunted even in this day and age. I imagine it would cost a pretty penny to restore the place and with it being small, pokey by today's standards, who would take it on? Father never did go back, but he's often wondered whether there was something in the wall. Now he's very old, I believe it's become an obsession to unveil the mystery. And, frankly, I'm far too busy."

"It's fascinating. I think you'd better tell me how to find Rose Cottage and anything you think might help an investigation, Sir John."

"Well..."

By the time he'd finished and arranged for them to sleep in his guest room, plus granting them the loan of his Land Rover, both Jake and Alice were happy to retire to discuss what they had heard. The plan was to go to Covenham St. Mary the next morning.

THREE

COVENHAM, LINCOLNSHIRE, 2021 AD

What were Roy Robinson's exact words: *FOUR steps?* Jake climbed to the fourth and stopped. What was he expecting, some kind of odd feeling? Disappointed, he felt nothing, apart from disgust at the damp mustiness of the stale air and a dull ache beginning to his forehead. He faced left and began to tap the dirty white plaster of the stair wall with the butt of his knife, working downwards. It was solid, but after about eighteen inches, he heard a hollow sound. His heart beat faster. Had he imagined it? He tried the same spot again. There was no doubt at all. There was hollowness behind the plaster. Heart pounding fast, he opened the knife and dug in the blade, loosening small pieces of plaster. A whole chunk fell on to the worn and holey stair carpet, revealing a cavity in the wall. It was about four inches deep and contained a small box. It was dirty, white and square. He used his forefinger and thumb to ease it out. Curious, he held it up, turning his wrist to study it.

A key scraped in the lock of the cottage door. What the devil! This place had stood empty for generations. The sound of dull footsteps stirred him into action. Jake spun on his heel and jumped down into the kitchen.

"Hey!"

He lingered enough to glimpse the massive silhouette of a man wearing what seemed to be a chauffer's uniform, a peaked cap on his bull-necked head. Jake plunged the box into his trouser pocket. The feeble light penetrating the filthy windowpanes was enough to make out the man reaching inside his jacket. He pulled out a pistol. With athletic skill he didn't know he possessed Jake dived through the open sash window where he had forced his entry. A shot rang out. It must have disturbed the whole of the sleepy village. He hit the ground outside and rolled with practiced ease, but he felt a searing pain high on his right arm. *The bastard's shot me!* Fear added extra speed to his limbs, so before the man got to the window, he was through a hole in the hedge bordering the small rear garden of Rose Cottage and his legs were pumping across the uneven ground. His disjointed thoughts, trying to make sense of what had happened were overwhelmed by strident warnings to save himself. Thrusting all distractions aside for the moment, he ran for dear life along the edge of a wheat field where a gate gave onto the road in front of the cottage.

He dashed into the road and waved his arms at the Land Rover. He was relieved to find that his arm moved freely enough, a flesh wound, nothing worse than a throbbing pain, but the sleeve of his T-shirt was soaked and rivulets of blood ran to his wrist.

Tyres screeched and he pulled open the passenger door. At the same time, he glanced back at Rose Cottage. There was a grey Mercedes parked outside with smoked glass windows. As soon as he spotted Jake in the road, the brute in a chauffeur's uniform slammed the cottage door and ran down the garden path towards the Mercedes. That was enough for Jake, who jumped into the car and exclaimed to his wife,

"Drive like Hell if you don't want to be shot at!"

She went through the gears at unholy speed and Jake, incredulous, watched the indicator pass 85 mph on the bends out of the village. Far too fast and more by good luck than driving skill, in his opinion, Alice swung the Land Rover into a country lane. He realised with a start that this was the first time he'd been a passenger with his wife driving. The hawthorn hedges were a blur of green along the narrow winding lane. Had this woman never heard of tractors and Land Rovers? Mightn't one appear to create a metal wall for them to die against? Compared to that, a bullet in the back of the head seemed an attractive option.

She braked next to an iron gate where a crushed chalk track led across a field to a barn.

"Don't just sit there, open the gate."

Isn't slow beautiful? he thought while she inched the vehicle behind the barn and cut the engine.

Jake leaned back and closed his eyes. He couldn't believe what had happened to him.

"I think we lost them. Hey! You're bleeding. Let me take a look."

She leant across, her blouse revealing the fullness of her breasts. Jake dragged his gaze away, *I'm a lucky guy*, and his eyes met the concern in hers. For her part, she tried not to show her admiration of the muscular arm under inspection. He'd been working out in the gym to get into shape for the awaited call from Sir Clive.

He pulled up the sleeve, his nose almost touching the wound, "Ach, it's only a scratch." He wasn't going to let her know how scared he was.

This is crazy. Someone's taken a pop at me. Why? And me, I'm more interested in my pretty wife's body. What an idiot!

"It'll need cleaning up as soon as possible, but I don't fancy moving from here just yet."

They tried to understand what on earth was going on.

"It can't be a coincidence," Alice said, "we heard Roy's story and the next day visit the long-abandoned cottage and *just by chance* someone turns up and takes a shot at you?"

"Whoever it is must have had us under surveillance. I'm beginning to think Sir John knows more than he's letting on. I'm going to have it out with him."

Alice frowned, "Do you mean he called on Double-A for help because he was in trouble over this cottage business? And if so, what can it be about? You don't go shooting at people because there's a ghost in a cottage."

"No," Jake murmured, distracted, he was thinking about the little white box in his pocket. Maybe that would tell them something, but it could wait until they got home. Instead, he said, "Whatever this is about, we can forget our impression that it wouldn't be dangerous. I had a lucky escape. It's always a risk when Sir Clive is involved.

Back on the main road, they kept a wary eye open but there was no sign of the Mercedes and Jake found the drive back far more comfortable than the previous breakneck journey, except for his troubled thoughts.

FOUR

The Mercedes parked in a lay-by outside the market town of Louth. The man with the designer glasses pressed a button and the tinted panel separating him from his driver slid down.

"Victor, you are the most confounded idiot. What do you keep in that overripe pumpkin that passes for a head? Whatever it is, it isn't a brain."

Resentful eyes fought to mask a glower with an effort at subservience. The chauffeur assessed his employer's mood. Victor Dogaru owed much to David Briggs QC, a suave, London divorce barrister. Briggs had taken him, an illegal immigrant, from the streets of the English capital, sorted his papers and given him a well-paid job. Of course, he hadn't given Victor the idea that he was legal, preferring to let him think that his residence in England was done by favours. In that way, he ensured the Romanian's insecurity, gratitude and servile obedience: considerable assets in an ex-Olympic wrestler who prided himself on intimidating strength.

The caustic tone continued, "Didn't it occur to what passes for a brain under that cap that you can't use firearms in a Lincolnshire village? My God, man, I have a reputation based on years of hard work. One moment of idiocy could leave it in tatters. Thank heavens it was only one shot and not a very good one at that."

Victor was sweating under his peaked cap, but he didn't dare take his eyes off his employer's face. He studied the eyes in his mirror; they were as cold as adjacent ice floes. There was a hint of something submerged, something dangerous, something the Romanian didn't want to surface. Victor's mean mouth, with hard, cruel sensuous lips compressed even more. Briggs was a generous boss, but not given to supporting fools. Victor sought a means of appeasement.

"Sorry, boss, but he had a white box in his hand and he hid it as soon as he saw me. It must have been important. I only wanted to stop him, not to kill him." Gratified, Victor watched Briggs's expression change. Now he had his complete attention.

"A white box?"

Victor described the hole in the wall and how the box had been hidden there, the crumbs of plaster fresh on the stair carpet and the surprising agility of the intruder.

"I want that box," Briggs murmured more to himself.

"If we find that Land Rover..."

"*We*, Victor, *we*...don't you think you've done enough damage for one day? You can't even catch a bicycle, let alone a Land Rover, not even with a 6.2 litre V8 Mercedes. No," he said, "I'll set a professional on the woman driver's case. Your job is to get me back to London without any further unpleasantness if that's not beyond you."

The partition slid up before Victor could reply. David Briggs opened the fridge door and poured himself a good measure of thirty-year-old Lagavulin, ironically, Jake

Conley's favourite tipple, added ice, then with a sigh sank back in his seat.

All's well that ends well. And despite appearances things had gone better than expected. The mysterious white box would never have come to light without the unexpected intruder. Tracing the Land Rover shouldn't be too difficult for a professional. No, all told, a satisfactory day. As for a gunshot, Victor wasn't to know that in Lincolnshire gunshots were the order of the day. Briggs smirked; small detail, the targets were wood pigeons or crows, not young men. He'd have to sort out the trigger-happy Romanian though. Briggs swirled his whisky around the tinkling ice cubes and murmured: "I want that box, whatever the cost."

FIVE

LOUTH, LINCOLNSHIRE 2021 AD

The conversation with Sir John Robinson was short and inconclusive. Jake and Alice were convinced that the barrister was telling the truth when he reacted with amazement to the events in Rose cottage. This only deepened the mystery, however, since having ruled out coincidence and established Sir John's extraneity meant there was another sinister motive for the attack on Jake. This being the case, he decided that for the moment, he would make no mention of the white box as it might place those who knew about it in danger.

He decided to take temporary lodgings in Louth because Tealby was a little awkward for Covenham, which seemed to be the focal point of the mystery.

"Hang on to the Land Rover, dear boy, it's no use to me in London—not a vehicle suitable for the city centre. I have to get back to Gray's Inn Square. Goodness knows what's awaiting me in Chambers. You have my card. Please keep me informed of developments."

They said their farewells and drove over to the small market town of Louth, dominated by the third highest steeple in England. An obliging estate agent found them pleasant and economical accommodation on Aswell Street. The flat, rented by a music teacher, who was in Wales for three months, was central, had a parking space and was convenient for the roads out of town.

The discovery of the old bone box buried in the stair wall of Rose Cottage was mysterious in every way. How had it got there? And what was the meaning of the contents of the box? In the flat yesterday he prised the lid off and found a piece of paper yellowed with age. It was furled and tied with a tiny strip of ribbon. The neat early-copperplate handwriting made him think that it was very old. Jake flattened it on the table and read it whilst the dull ache between his eyebrows returned to tell him that he was involved with something supernatural. When he overcame the sensation, the words came into focus:

Though ye have lien among the pots, yet shall ye be as the wings
of a dove covered with silver, and her feathers with yellow gold.

He mumbled the words to himself and they struck him as Biblical. Maybe it was a quotation of some sort. He looked around the room, Alice was twirling her dyed blonde hair while studying a cookery magazine – only she could convert a hobby into *haute cuisine*. He loved her for the precision she brought to everything she did. Her attitude was top chefs can do it, so why can't I? Satisfied that she wouldn't take any notice of him, he drifted over to the computer and typed *Bible, wings of a dove* into the search engine and had a hit. The verse was from a psalm: Psalm 68:13 in the King James's Authorized Version of the Bible.

He read the whole psalm, but the context of these two lines left him no wiser. Clicking back to desktop, he rolled up the tiny scroll and put it back in his pocket. It was mid-afternoon and he hadn't achieved anything today. He rubbed the wound in his upper arm over the bandage under his shirt—nothing more than an aching soreness.

"Just going out for a coffee."

He would have added "are you coming?" but he wanted to be alone to think and to get some fresh air for that matter.

He turned into Little Butcher Lane and entered a coffee bar. The owners were a pleasant couple, she made fabulous cakes and he did the best filtered coffee for miles around, to hear his immodest claim. Jake gave his order and reflected. Sometimes he felt that he wasn't born clever enough. He was lucky with his physique: that's why he was such a good mover, but he simply couldn't see how a bit of paper about dove wings could be important enough to make someone attempt murder. Absent-mindedly, he touched the scroll in his pocket and the air in front of his yes and the smiling proprietor began to ripple. By now, he knew what it meant – retrocognition. When he came back to consciousness, he found himself in the Lincolnshire countryside on a damp day, but where and when? He could forget about his coffee unless he could drink it when he got back because time had no relevance in retrocognition. He cursed his cross-wired brain. If only he hadn't been distracted years ago when he walked in front of a Jeep—and changed his life forever.

LINCOLNSHIRE, 11 OCTOBER 1643

SIR JOHN BRIGGS felt the wild heartbeat of his horse as he reined in on Kenwick Top. He had put nineteen miles between himself and the debacle of Winceby. His heart, too, thumped as he stared behind him. Two riders appeared in the distance: parliamentary cavalrymen and the main chasing pack still nowhere in sight. Well, if he had to be the fox, then so be it. Slyness would be his game; he'd go to ground. Sir John turned into the drizzle-laden wind and, knowing this place well, plunged through a gap in the hedge, heedless of the thorns. It was a well-chosen place and not far from where Jake was hiding, unseen, watching him. Blessing his providential nature, the cavalier loaded his pistols with the last of his powder and balls he'd preserved. He soothed his horse with gentle words, for silence was his only hope of surprise. The minutes passed, then his pursuers came over the hill. Jake peered through the branches at them and understood:

My God, he's going to shoot. This is the Civil War.

Sir John took aim and waited until the first rider, just ahead of his fellow, was almost level with him. He squeezed the trigger, causing the second horse to rear at the report, throwing his rider, taken by surprise. His fall was terrible. At a glance, Sir John knew his second ball would serve no purpose. The unnatural angle of the soldier's head showed his neck was broken. The other lay on his back staring at the sky, blood staining his teeth, a hole in the jerkin where the ball had entered.

So, the fox ran on, downhill to the lair he knew so well. Jake watched the killer ride off, calmed the horse of a fallen rider, hauled himself on its back and followed the disappearing rider at a distance. Sir John dismounted before he reached Covenham St. Bartholomew: the village, where he was squire. He led the bay to a gate in a field and slapped him across the rump. The horse skittered off toward the woods and Sir John grimaced. God willing, the Roundheads would find the horse but not the fox. Jake did the same thing and, careful not to betray his presence, shadowed the royalist.

Again, the fugitive thrust through the hedge and slithered along a sheep track, hidden from the road, all the way to the rear of the Vicarage. Jake trailed him with great caution, he had seen what the desperate man was capable of. Ears alert to the sound of hooves, the cavalier heard only the familiar noises of the countryside. Sir John walked round to the front of the house, looked up the road to make sure there were no horsemen and hammered on the door.

"All the fiends of Hell are at my door!" A tall, stooped figure dressed in the black of his calling dragged open the door. "Why, Sir John, in Heaven's name—"

Never had the sight of the reverend figure been so welcome to the squire's eyes,

"Thomas, my dear friend, let be all thy imprecations of Heaven and Hell. There's no time to spare. I'm straight from Winceby with the King's cause lost hereabouts. Soon the whole county will be in rebel hands and Cromwell's hounds are hard on my heels. Find me a safe haven my friend, for pity's sake." Jake, hidden in the darkness by the walls of the building, heard everything through the sash window of the kitchen.

"Ay, well, not here, else they will find thee in a trice." He reached inside the doorframe, his hand reappearing with a ten-inch long iron key. "Come, let's away to the church. There's the place to keep thee safe, but tell me as we walk, what of this news?" In the silence of the surroundings, Jake, keeping low and following within earshot, could hear every word.

Anguish etched the squire's face.

"Our Will has gone to..." his voice faltered, "...a better world. He took a ball full in the chest our first charge." Thomas waited, respecting Sir John's grief at the loss of his only son.

"We were on our way to relieve the besieged garrison at Bolingbroke when we met with the rebels near Horncastle, on the moors at Winceby. The whole battle was over in half an hour. We had three thousand horse and dragoon with Sir William Widdrington in the van. They had more or less the same number under Black Tom Fairfax, but the difference... they must have had two thousand of Cromwell's foot with pikemen well set...my word on it, Thomas...a disaster. We lost some two hundred men at the first charge when Cromwell's horse was shot beneath him. Sir Ingram Hopton went for him, but more's the pity...the arch-rebel seized another horse and saved himself. The second charge was pure folly, with Sir Ingram killed, it turned into a rout. The roundheads chased us down the Wolds, giving no quarter to any they caught."

"And what of our Charlie?" the vicar's voice trembled. His only son was fighting with the king's forces too.

"Safe. He was among those held back at Newark Castle."

Choking back words of relief, Thomas put a hand on his friend's shoulder, "I'm so sorry about Will," he said.

At last the chalk and ironstone tower of St. Mary's loomed, its battlements stark and wet against the sky. Sir John was breathless from talking and walking, while Thomas prayed for the safekeeping of Charles. At last he broke the silence, "Sir John, this way!" The Reverend Thomas Monson inserted the key in the west door and with deceptive ease born of daily practice, proceeded to swing back the heavy, oak door. In no time, Sir John was spirited away and Thomas knelt before the altar. He began his prayers for the soul of William Briggs, only son and heir to Sir John. Thomas also prayed for Will's wife, the lovely Isabel, who had died young in childbirth.

'Here then ends the Briggs line, for I doubt that Sir John, a widower like myself, will remarry should he survive the war.'

Jake, who feared discovery, hadn't dared to enter, instead, hiding behind a headstone in the graveyard. Just as well, because the roundheads arrived. He darted behind a buttress of the church wall and thanked his luck that there was a hole in the leaded window just above his head. He found a foothold in the wall and hauling on the sill, hanging like a bat, was able to peer through it into the gloom of the interior. There was enough light to discern two figures. The cavalier he'd followed was nowhere to be seen.

Thomas's prayers were interrupted as the door creaked open and heavy footsteps resounded on the stone. The vicar forced himself not to move. He continued in what he hoped should pass as deep and reverential devotions. The vicar shuddered as footsteps approached his vulnerable back. A leather-gloved hand hauled him up by the arm. He found himself looking—and this was unusual—straight into the eyes of a man as tall as himself. Thomas studied the round helmet and leather jerkin bound at the waist with a red sash. Voice as cold as his eyes, the soldier asked, "Why art thou in church at this time of day, *father?*" The last word spat out in contempt.

"I might ask the same question of thee, *my son*" Thomas replied in the same tone. "I'm here for private prayer and contemplation, but thy purpose, with sword and armour, seems far from godly in this holy place."

"Let's not bandy words about godliness, lest unseemliness violate the Lord's abode—for I am a god-fearing man as are we all in my company. Captain Michael Bullivant at thy service and at the service of Parliament. There is no time to waste, Vicar. We seek the traitor, Sir John Briggs. Hast thou seen him? Mayhap he hath begged thee for sanctuary?" The grey eyes seemed to bore into the clergyman's soul, "'Tis a crime against the law of the land to harbour a traitor—a crime punishable by death."

Thomas took a deep breath. "As thou canst see," he said, relieved at his voice not betraying his inner turmoil, sweeping his arm around the church, "there are no traitors here. Thou art welcome to search every nook and cranny, but I fear the only living creatures thou "ll find are mice and bats."

The Captain held the clergyman with unblinking eyes seeking the slightest sign of untruth. He grunted, dissatisfied, but turned to stride along the nave, his steps echoing from the barrel-roof above. He stepped outside to bark orders: "Five, inside. Search every inch of this church. Thou, climb the tower and don't miss anything. Fletcher, Smith and Parry, search the churchyard and have an eye for the yews, a man can hide inside them, right enough."

Jake cringed against the wall, deciding whether it was safer to stay frozen there in the shadows or to run. He decided on the former as it wouldn't attract attention.

As the roundhead spoke, he bent down and Jake saw him pick up a smooth river stone, grunting at its weight as he passed it from hand to hand. Determined, he clattered back down the nave and marched past the altar. Before Thomas realised his intention, Captain Bullivant smashed the stone with all his force into the face of the two-hundred-year-old statue of the Virgin Mary. The first blow broke the nose off the statue and the second defaced the area around the right eye. Thomas rushed over to the soldier and grabbed his arm in order to prevent him delivering the third blow.

"Sacrilege."

But the soldier's muscles were as hard as iron. He thrust the vicar aside, into a pew end, knocking the breath out of his body.

"Idolater."

The roundhead smashed the rock down again and now the statue was faceless. "Pray the Lord, Vicar, to see the Light and that the day cometh soon: I swear when this war is won no papist shall defile our faith." A weak beam of light defied the dull day and shone through the stained-glass window. Glancing up, the Captain saw the backlit azure image of the Virgin and heaved the stone at it. It struck the rich tracery and fell to the floor. "Lucky for thee and this temple of idolatry that I have more pressing matters," he scowled at Thomas, who was rubbing what was sure to become a huge bruise. Oblivious to the glare directed at his back, the soldier turned away and gathered his men. Having ensured that there was no sign of the fugitive, they left without a backward glance.

Thomas knelt before the defaced statue and dedicated an *Ave Maria* to Her. Then he began to think. He stood up and again rubbed his painful side. A frown furrowed his brow. He moved with decision to the door and slipped out of the church, locking Sir John inside.

Jake wondered what to do. Retrocognition had brought him for a reason, but what? He decided to follow the vicar as he walked home. The evening was drawing in and the breeze had a cutting edge. Once indoors the vicar had time to lay and light a fire before he heard the sound of hooves.

Jake heard them too and hid at the back of the house, pressing an ear to a window. The vicar had expected them. Crouching, he stretched out his hands to the crackling flames as three parliamentary soldiers burst in. Thomas leapt to his feet. "What in Heaven's name—"

"Check upstairs." Two ironsides mounted the stairs. The officer was young, Jake decided about twenty-five, whose sharp eyes scanned the room before he walked into the kitchen. The Vicarage had a door to a small cellar where the vicar kept some kindling and logs. The officer paused on the threshold. "Fetch a candle." No sooner had Thomas complied than the cornet drew his sword, candle in the other hand, he descended the short flight of stairs. Satisfied that the cellar hid no fugitive, he reappeared, asking the other two soldiers: "Nothing, eh?"

The men shook their heads.

"What is the object of thy search?"

"*Who*...not what," the cornet replied.

"I'll give Captain Bullivant his due, he's nothing if not scrupulous." Said the vicar.

"Ay, Sir John's horse was found nearby, so we must search the church again."

Unsurprised, Thomas pulled a coat over his cassock and unhooked the church key. The three soldiers mounted their horses and kept them at walking pace beside the clergyman, Jake, heart in mouth, trailed the quartet unnoticed before returning to his previous vantage point.

Hidden in the dark in a dank hole, Sir John sat on a stone ledge he'd found before Thomas sealed him into complete blackness. He shivered, drawing his cloak about him, his breathing shallow because he loathed the musty air, but also because his nerves were frayed. The darkness heightened his hearing. After what seemed an eternity, he was startled to hear a key scrape in a lock. Thomas had come back. How he'd berate him for not having thought of a candle—but then, maybe it was a mercy as there was too little air. He froze as steps echoed in the church, too heavy to be Thomas's, some of them passing over his head. The fox was in his lair, but should the hounds sniff him out... there would be no escape. He listened to the steps moving away, aware that he was light-headed from both lack of air and holding his breath. He sucked in the stale air, screwing up his nose while straining to hear. The footsteps were leaving. The Lord be praised the danger had passed. In the name of mercy, he would soon be out of this burrow, breathing pure air again.

Outside, satisfied at their inspection, the soldiers remounted and the cornet spoke in a severe voice belying his youth: "If it comes to thy notice that the traitor Sir John Briggs is lurking hereabouts, "tis thy bounden duty to inform the military, forthwith. On pain o' death, clear, vicar?"

"Quite clear. Have no fear on that score. I bid thee good night, cornet."

Thomas had the satisfaction of turning his back on the three soldiers before enacting the farce of locking up the church again as they looked on. They wheeled their horses and rode off in the direction of Covenham St. Bartholomew.

Jake, from the shadows, watched Thomas Monson sit down on a tree stump, draw his collar up over his neck and wait in the damp and the twilight. He waited for about a quarter of an hour before unlocking the church again. Inside it was now quite dark, but he had no need of light to find his way. Even so, to Jake's satisfaction, he went to the presbytery for a candle and a flint. The flickering candle lit his way along the nave. Resting it on a pew, he heaved against the solid oak of another bench in front, grunted at the stabbing pain in his bruised side, before sliding it forward a yard against the next in line. Kicking aside a kneeler, Thomas exposed a brass handle in a paving stone. Grasping it, he hauled with all his might and the stone lifted, its ancient hinges squealing. Jake could only admire the ingenuity.

So that's how he did it. Brilliant!

The vicar called, "Out with thee, Sir John."

"By all the saints and martyrs, Tom, what kept you? I was beginning to worry about spending the whole night in the company of ghosts. This pit freezes to the marrow." The two friends pushed the pew back in place and replaced the kneeler over the trapdoor handle. "Tom, I could hear them walking back and forth over my head. Had they found me it would have been a sorry end for the both of us. I should never have put an old friend in this position. I beg thy forgiveness."

"The Good Lord kept us safe, John. Think no more on it."

"Is there pen and paper?"

"Ay, in the presbytery, why?"

"Come then, for there are things that must be done."

Jake could not see them but still heard their voices amplified by the silent church.

Sir John Briggs sat down at the table. With his tongue between his teeth and a frown of concentration, he began to draw a map. Satisfied, he sprinkled sand on his effort in order to dry the ink. He ran his left hand through his beard, fixing Thomas with green eyes, and Jake heard, "Listen Tom, damn it, thou hast saved my life and art as good a friend as a man e'er could wish for." He raised his hand. "Hush! Today I lost my son in battle and I am proud that he died for his king. Heed me well; more's the pity," he said, "there is not one righteous and loyal soul in my family to follow me. Tom, I may not be long for this world, there will be more fighting and bloodshed before our blessed King Charles shall restore his realm to peace and prosperity—"

"Amen, to that."

"...I am as mortal as the next man. Place the map in safekeeping Tom. Jake frowned and bit his lip.

He's drawn a map and given it to the vicar.

"...Should news reach thee that I have gone to meet my Maker, then follow the map and it will lead to an object of great worth. I buried it before the battle. Tom, it hath been in my family for time immemorial." Jake caught his breath,

Now, I'm on to something. He strained to hear.

"There is no better man – no, I will not be gainsaid. That's settled. Now I need a horse, I expect those blackguards have taken my Flame." He sighed, "She's a fine horse."

They left the church. As he locked up for the last time that day, the Reverend Thomas Monson pondered on their strange conversation. Fighting a lump in his throat, he watched the golden plume of his friend's hat disappear into the gloom, bobbing to the rhythm of his nag's canter.

He was never to see him again. Of course, neither he nor Jake could know that, at that moment. Sir John Briggs fell, slain at the successful relief of York led by Prince Rupert, eight months later, on 1 July 1644.

Nor was Jake to know, for the time being, as his retrocognition was about to end, that the reverend lived in sorrow through the regicide and the exile of the dead king's son. The clergyman's only son was also in France. As those of many others, Thomas Monson's fortunes changed with the Commonwealth. As a papist sympathiser he was stripped of his living. Therefore, driven by desperation, he used the map to recover the precious heirloom. It was of no use to him. An object of incalculable worth and astounding beauty, it could only bring trouble and probably death in those turbulent times. So, he reburied it under its marker. Of course, he wrote to Charlie in France, but he couldn't tell him of its whereabouts; Cromwell had spies everywhere and there was no doubt that letters, however trustworthy the bearer, were an unacceptable risk. So, he concealed the secret of the treasure's whereabouts in a riddle, in a way most suitable to a man of the cloth. First, he sent word of the buried treasure in a letter to his son couched in general terms. Later, he sent a small package: a box made of bone carved by his own hand; inside, lay a short verse from a psalm indicating the hiding-place of the priceless object. That was the selfsame verse nestling in Jake's pocket. In the spring of 1656, Thomas Monson died and was buried in a pauper's grave.

Louth, Lincolnshire, 2021 AD

The air around Jake stopped vibrating and he reached for his coffee and cake as though nothing had happened. He could remember the fact of the treasure and the name of the vicar so the mystery trail they'd set off on might lead to a fortune in the end. That would provide an explanation of why someone had shot at him. For now, he needed to share what knowledge he had with Alice.

There was a lot to tell, but he showed her the scroll and its box and expounded at some length about the Civil War scenes he had witnessed. When he had finished, Alice, who had listened attentively without once interrupting, drew a logical conclusion.

"You wouldn't have had the retrocognition experience if it hadn't been relevant to your inquiry. You were touching the scroll when it come over you, so it's bound to be the handwriting of that vicar. It looks like he was leaving a clue for someone, perhaps his heir, to find whatever treasure was hidden. Pity you didn't find the map he spoke about—even if it still exists. It's up to us to decipher the Biblical reference."

"It looks like I'll have to buy a Bible then because the context of the verse might be important."

"Why buy one? I've got a copy of the Authorised Version at home."

"Are you suggesting driving down to Warwickshire to pick up a Bible? We can buy one here and it'll be cheaper than the diesel to go there and back." Jake said.

"Look, I'll be honest with you, it's not just for the Bible. When we set off, I forgot to pack my pills and if we're staying in Louth for a while, I'll need more clothes and cosmetics. We can spend one night in our house and then come back. What do you say?"

"Never stand between a woman and her cosmetics."

SIX

LOUTH, LINCOLNSHIRE, 2021 AD

A SCAMPERING CAT AND A MAN IN HIS LATE-FORTIES were the only visible creatures on Aswell Street at four in the morning. Nearby, the soaring steeple of the parish church seemed to seek the stars in vain. The moon, a smudge of white behind a mantle of clouds, leaving the spire unlit, provided the man with the advantage of moving unseen. He was wearing a checked sports jacket that looked as if it came from a charity shop, and crepe-soled shoes, which helped him climb the dark steps to the flat unheard.

It had been child's play tracing the owner of the Land Rover. There were only seven, of that model, registered in the Louth area. It belonged to a London barrister with property in Tealby. He could only conclude that the woman driver was a relative. He had watched her drive away with a youngish-looking man and that they had stowed hand luggage encouraged him to think they were away for the night. He looked around in all directions before sliding a piece of plastic into the mortise lock. He leant against the door that swung open with no trouble. Then he closed it behind him and took a pencil torch from his pocket. The man sat down behind the desk and studied his surroundings. The room was small and tidy and he was happy this wouldn't take long. He began by removing the screwed-up sheets of paper in the waste bin and smoothing them out to read them one by one. Nothing of interest. He emptied the desk drawers on the floor and poked around the contents with the toe of a shoe: another blank. At the bookshelf, he checked each music book in turn, noting that the pages didn't conceal any sheets of paper, before tossing each of them on the floor. He concluded that what he was looking for was sure to be in the computer. A sudden noise made him start. Heart racing, he held his breath. There was someone outside the door. An almighty crash and the yowl of a cat followed frantic barking that receded rapidly. Then silence. He waited.

"I hope it mauls the mangy cur." he grunted. The private detective's heartbeat slowed and he turned his attention to the computer.

The intruder booted up the device and switched on the router. His job, he reflected, was easier twenty years ago, when everything was in documents, diaries or sheets of paper. At worst, it might have been in code, but then you could always go to an expert capable of deciphering. Now, you had to be a qualified hacker to get past passwords. You could struggle for hours and still not get anywhere. He thought for a minute and entered one, with no luck. He failed again a couple of times, but when he typed ALICE85, and he was in. He'd discovered the woman's name and age from her driving license when he'd searched her vehicle and found it in the glove compartment. Some people were very incautious, he sniffed. The man sneered at the ingenuousness of the password; it was as easy as shelling nuts, just her name and year of birth. She'd never had anything to hide and had no idea that her situation had changed, he guessed.

He checked the Internet history and wasn't surprised to see that it hadn't been deleted. In a notebook he jotted down all the links and, when he'd finished, he went into the woman's email. This was ridiculous. The email opened with the same password. The detective snorted at such carelessness. He copied her contacts onto a stick, but it all looked unpromising to him. He would have to follow up each and every one of the names. Disappointed, the private detective stepped around the strewn papers, he didn't want to leave any prints, and picked up a visiting card. He read the name, Jake Conley, and left the premises. Something about the card rang a bell but he couldn't remember, even so, instinct told him that he had found what he was looking for—Stage One completed. The detective had a crooked smile. He used it now even though there was nobody around to impress. Tomorrow morning...no...*this* morning, he would make his first call to his client in London.

SEVEN

LOUTH, LINCOLNSHIRE, 2021 AD

Alice had driven them down to Warwickshire; to even things out, Jake had driven the return journey. When he entered the town centre in Louth, he surprised Alice by pulling up in Little Butcher Lane.

"The owner of this café says he makes the best coffee for miles around. I think we'd better put him to the test, darling."

"Good idea. I'm desperate for a decent coffee."

Having ordered the drinks, his attention strayed to a copy of the local paper the *Louth Leader* lying on the next table. There was going to be a Duck Race down the River Bain in July; it was an annual event. His eyes shifted down to the next article and he snatched up the paper.

Music Teacher's Office Ransacked

There was only going to be one Maria Perri in Louth, no question about that. It was the name of the tenant of their flat now in Wales. A glance at Alice, a gulp of his scalding coffee and they were on their way to their rented property. The mess of books and papers on the floor told him that a search of the property had been made. Alice's portable computer had not been stolen, so he concluded, not a thief, but an investigator prying into their affairs. Jake, who knew about these things, checked her computer to see when it was last opened. As he expected, 4.07 a.m. last night.

Answering a knock on the door, he came face to face with their landlord.

"I hope they haven't taken anything, Mr Copley. I reported the break-in to the police myself and it's already splashed across the local newspaper. I came around this morning to tell you about rubbish collection. When there was no answer, I peered through the window and saw the place had been turned over. I let myself in, but there was no damage. I hope you don't mind?"

"Not at all."

"I wonder if you'd mind calling in at the police station to let them know nothing's been taken?"

"Leave it to me, Mr Bell."

When their fussy landlord had gone, Alice and Jake considered their situation as they put everything back in its place. They agreed that there was no coincidence regarding the shooting at the cottage and this attempt to find...what? Jake was inclined to think that the intruder was looking for the small bone box and its contents that he'd taken to Warwickshire.

When they had finished tidying the flat, they discussed everything that had happened since they entered the Ministry together.

Whilst Jake went to the police station to make his statement, Alice decided to do a little historical research and got to thinking about the old woman and how she could find out something about her. She surfed the Internet to find out about late eighteenth-century newspapers. In those days there were few newspapers in circulation: *The Morning Chronicle*, *The Morning Post*, *The Morning Herald* and an evening paper called *The Star*. Then, there was *The Daily Universal Register*, which lasted from, she discovered, 1785 until 1787, then it became known as *The Times*. So, she searched for archives of that paper and the early years of *The Times*. She could scarcely believe it, but the only way she found to consult one of Britain's historical newspapers was to take out a subscription on her credit card with an American university. Her detective work cost her twenty-five dollars. Then she fed Covenham St. Mary into the internal search engine of *The Daily Universal Register* and ... *Bingo!* On the screen appeared:

No civilized nation has to lament, as we have, the daily commission of the most atrocious crimes, inasmuch as we cannot sleep in our houses without the most imminent danger of thieves and robbers. When vice is tempted by the certainty of gain it will have recourse to every expedient to indulge its depraved propensities: we have the most recent and deplorable instance of an unfortunate defenceless spinster, victim of these plunderers of the public. Miss Agnes Monson, 85 years old, was found on the 20th current, her heart fail'd at the sight of malefactors in her home, Rose Cottage, in Covenham St. Mary in the County of Lincoln. Your humble correspondent can only express his opprobrium at the lack of efficiency on the part of parochial law enforcement, for while our watch committees, commissioners and vestries fail to ensure adequate incentives for diligence, the sleeping watchmen lie beatific in their dormitories. The poor woman's house was ransack'd, little doubt the scoundrels were cognizant of her reputed wealth. A subject *of much wonder and ferment among her neighbours was the finding of the deceased with her finger resting upon a passage of the New Testament: precisely on John 14:3* ***I will come again****. The most fever'd and superstitious imaginings abound, some indeed speculating that the deceased will have no repose until the guilty are apprehended and brought to justice.*

R.H. Covenham St. Mary

Alice read quickly, by now, Jake had returned and she leant on his shoulder, her light perfume going to his head, bittersweet to him. He murmured, "So Agnes Monson was the ghost Roy Robinson saw."

"Which brings us back to the bone box with the little scroll inside." He took the said paper from his pocket and handed it to Alice who re-read the two lines of fading handwriting. As she studied the words, he said, "You, who are so good at detective work. See what you can do with that."

She shook her head. "It's something from the Bible, we said."

"Right, I established it was Psalm 68:13, King James's Version."

"Did you read the whole Psalm?"

"Not yet, I haven't had time, thanks to the intruder, but somehow I don't think it'll help. I'll check it out now."

"Well, it must mean something. And it must be something important if they want it that badly." Alice's tone was cool and logical and he appreciated it.

He closed the Bible and sniffed. "As I thought. Those lines were extrapolated for a purpose. The rest of the psalm holds no significance for me."

"I'll see what I can do with those few lines Jake."

"I agree that the clue is in the verse itself." Jake cupped

his chin in his hand, "We should try to understand what it means. Is it possible that there's a treasure is in the form of a dove made of silver and gold? That wouldn't be a bad find, would it?"

"If it's large, it'd be worth a lot of money and if it's small I'll just wear it as a brooch." Alice laughed. "So, the dove must be lying among some pots then?"

"Yeah, but that's not much to go on is it? Unless there used to be a pottery in Covenham St. Mary, say in the eighteenth century."

"Why the eighteenth? I'd say much earlier. This writing must be at least 1600."

"How do you know that?"

"Because I studied archaeology at university and I know a thing or two about history, and calligraphy if it comes to that. And didn't your retrocognition take you to the Civil War? "

She gazed around the small music school, only big enough to take a piano and a desk, and once more chose not to tell Jake that she had been her father's desperation. That could wait. Despite Mr Harrop's reasoned explanations that archaeology wouldn't put bread on her table, and his long-suffering references to balance sheets, their discussions always ended with him shouting at his daughter and regretting it afterwards. One day, she'd tell Jake how she'd entered the Secret Service; he hadn't been inquisitive about her past and she appreciated it. She snapped out of her reverie and said,

"Maybe there was an excavation and they found some pots and the dove."

Jake thought about that. "Hang on. Perhaps this wasn't a question of finding the dove, more a question of hiding it.

So, the ghost or someone in her family must have hidden the dove among the pots."

As a plan, they searched for potteries in the area of Covenham in the seventeenth century. There were plenty of modern-day potteries in Lincolnshire, even nearby, but nothing came up for the period they were interested in. There were references to the sandy-grey Torksey ware of the Middle Ages or to Lincoln pottery from the same period. They considered both possibilities, but it didn't seem likely that Torksey would be the answer, because it was more than forty miles away from Covenham. Given the difficulties of travelling in the past, it seemed certain that they were looking for a place much nearer to Rose Cottage. Jake read the passage out loud again:

"Though ye have lein..." This must be archaic for *lain*," he said, *...among the pots, yet shall ye be as the wings of a dove covered with silver, and her feathers with yellow gold."*

They talked it over for some time, but made no further progress, before deciding to go to The Golden Fleece just around the corner on Kidgate: convenient since they needed the whole evening ahead to make some inroads into the intractable conundrum. Alice went over to the window and drew back the net curtain. As far as she could tell there was nobody suspicious-looking down there. She locked the flat and they walked the short distance keeping a watchful eye open for an oversized homicidal chauffeur.

In the pub, and lost in thought, Jake chewed his cheese and ham, not really tasting it. She sipped her beer and took another bite of her salmon sandwich, savouring her food. When they went back to the small music school, Jake went straight to the computer, but all he could do was sit and stare at the screen. Alice, instead, sat at the piano and began to play the *Scherzo* from Schubert's *Trout Quintet*. She played it very well before stopping and pointing at Jake.

"What?"

"What was it you said? *Archaic*? Sure, that's it!" She leapt off her stool and joined him at the computer. She clicked the arrow at the top left of the screen and returned to the search engine. "You know what? There are lots of versions of the Bible and this one was written in King James's reign. He came to the throne in 1603, so the English is archaic, let's get a more modern version of the same thing." She clicked on the New American Standard Bible, published in 1995. "I was right," a smile lit up her face and Jake thought she was more beautiful than any woman he knew, apart from Liffi. He smothered the treasonable thought and said, I didn't know you could play the piano so well."

"There's a lot you don't know about me. But let's concentrate on the matter in hand."

She read out:

When you lie down among the sheepfolds,
You are like the wings of a dove covered with silver,
And its pinions with glistening gold.

"*Sheepfolds!* My little genius. That changes everything." He stroked her hair leaving Alice torn between a feminist protest and simple pleasure.

"We've been wasting our time." He added, "We're not looking for old pots anymore; we're looking for a sheepfold that predates 1700, where someone hid the dove. That's more like it!" he enthused, then, quenched, added: "but there must have been quite a lot of them at that time. We'll need an old map of Covenham and a spade. Have you got a spade?"

It was meant to be a facetious remark, but Alice looked troubled. "Listen, I'm not going to do anything illegal. I think the next thing we should do before we go looking for old maps, is to find out what the legal position is. We don't want to end up in court, because we've taken something that isn't ours." She typed *British Law – Treasure Trove* into the search engine and what they read cheered them both. The law had been changed on 24 September, 1997. Thanks to the surge in treasure hunters using metal detectors the government had got rid of the previous provisions, where treasure trove was the property of the monarch if it had been buried with the intention of recovery. "That would have been this case," he said with unfounded certainty, "so the dove would have gone straight to the Queen."

The law now stated that objects at least three hundred years old containing a substantial amount of silver and gold (and hoards of coins) must be reported within fourteen days. There was a penalty of five thousand pounds or three months in jail, or both, for failing to do so. When a museum wished to acquire an item declared treasure by a coroner, the finder would be paid a reward based on its market value.

"Wow." Alice clapped her hands. "If we find the dove, we declare it at once and then we either get to keep it or they give us the money that it's worth. Cool. It's all quite legal. So, all we have to do is find the dove."

"All we have to do. Dead easy, but you didn't notice Article twenty-nine paragraph one. We have to get permission from the landowner; otherwise, anything we find goes to him. We'll have to find out who he is—small detail, once we've found out where the sheepfold is. What now? Old maps of Covenham St. Mary, maybe?"

It was getting late.

"That's about all we can do for this evening. I'll see about the map tomorrow."

"Let's carry on as normal, but take some precautions. Even if someone finds the box, it's empty. Only we know about the psalm. So, I'm going to burn the piece of paper and you're going to clean the chronology on the computer right now."

"I hear and obey oh mighty master." She smirked and turned to the computer.

Jake smiled to himself, but she turned back and caught his expression. He wiped it off his face and her large eyes looked quizzical.

"Nothing." This young woman wasn't just pretty she was smart too and she could play the piano. What else didn't he know about her?

"I was just thinking, maybe I should try to get to know you better, much better."

With less-than-chaste thoughts in his mind, he wandered to the window and drew the curtains. With his head full of thoughts about his wife, the scrupulous Jake didn't notice the man across the road wearing a checked sports jacket and crepe-soled shoes, standing by a car, feigning innocence.

EIGHT

NINE WEEKS EARLIER, MONKEN HADLEY, HERTFORDSHIRE.

David Briggs QC, a London barrister specialising in society divorce cases, was dressed in mourning. His father's funeral had taken place three days before and now, together with his wife Kate, he had to decide whether to move from their expensive riverside flat in the East End of London to this red-bricked Georgian house in the leafy village of Monken Hadley.

Kate looked at David poring over some age-yellowed document found in his father's desk. If anything, she found him more attractive with the passing years. He was tall and slim with a cold, handsome face. There was the slightest trace of grey at the temples of his dark brown hair clipped short and how she loved the contrast with his steel-grey eyes. These were half-closed and a frown of concentration and something else, perplexity, creased his brow.

"In all these years, he didn't speak even once about this."

Kate uncrossed her long legs and leaned forward in her leather armchair, "What is it, darling?"

David held up an old document: its handwriting, even

from where she was sitting, was neat and sloping with many swirls and flourishes - typical quill pen writing. "Do you know, this is dated 15 March, 1655. As far as I can make out it's addressed to a direct ancestor of mine, a certain Sir Henry Briggs." He began to read with difficulty:

To Sir Henry Briggs, Knight

Sir:

I had yours of the 10th current, wherein thou writ of conversing with thy cousin, my old and sometimes much familiar friend Sir John Briggs of blessed memory. Much thought have I given to restoring into thy keeping the object at thy behest. Thou pretendeth that the jewell be morally thine since it is of thy family for centuries. Notwithstanding this and giving scope to my true teacher and guide, the light of God speaking in my soul, I desire to do what is just and righteous in accord with the will of thy dear cousin: namely that this jewell should be mine on his passing away. But one time have I clap"d eyes upon this priceless thing, otherwise it has lain where he placed it. Now I exceedingly long and earnestly desire that the directions to its whereabouts be delivered to my only son, may God keep him faithfull to his King. And acting up on this impulse I sent a mappe to him in a letter. Thou mayst plainly read that I, no more than thy cousin, do hold with thy position which is of Common Lot with the Regicides. It is sad that the Laws of God and the Realm have not deterred Man from Wickedness and Vice. I shall give over wond'ring at anything hereafter, nothing shall seem strange unto me, I will but attend with patience how England will thrive now that she has let the King"s bloud. In short, it is no more my will that the jewell be thine than it was the will of thy dear cousin. Better thousandfold that it pass to a loyall servant of the King far from home. As for myselfe, I have a disease hung lately upon me, proceeding, as the Physician tells me, from my life of penury, which has much wasted my spirits and brought me low. My soul is weary of this prison of flesh and I desire no worldly goods, but a swift and merciful release.

Covenham St. Mary 15 March 1655Thy most humble servitor

Rev. Thomas Monson

"WHAT ABOUT THAT? Do you see, my great great ... whatever...grandfather was robbed of his rightful inheritance by some vicar after the Civil War. And this inheritance just happens to be a priceless jewel buried away somewhere."

Kate pursed her lips, she recognised that tone of voice. It was a mixture of stubbornness and petulance, meaning trouble. She shook her head and opened her blue eyes wide conveying, she hoped, infinite calm and wisdom.

"I doubt very much that the treasure is still buried," she said in a level voice, "and you're a lawyer, you must know that if the jewel were given away, neither your great great... whatever nor yourself have any legitimate claim..."

He avoided eye contact.

"We have a moral right, you heard, it was in our family for centuries."

"Oh, come on darling. Since when have lawyers dealt with moral rights? I hardly have to tell you that. Until five minutes ago you hadn't even heard of it. Your own father can't have thought it worth bothering about. He didn't tell you about this letter, did he? And anyway, you're not strapped for cash, are you?" She smiled, but it froze as she saw the hardness in his pale-grey eyes. He was not for moving. She tried again, but she knew she was wasting her breath; her husband could be exasperating at times. "Look, if we were able to trace the descendants of this vicar, what's his name?"

"Thomas Monson."

"Right," she folded her arms, "and let's say the treasure was found by his son and still exists today," she paused and gave him a stern look, "well, you'd have to commit a crime to get it back, wouldn't you?"

"Maybe, or maybe I could buy it. Let's say restore it to its rightful family."

"Buy it? Are you crazy? If it was priceless in 1655, what will it be worth now? Not even you could afford it – whatever it is."

David put the letter down on the desk and smiled a dangerous smile, the one designed to let him get his own way by melting Kate's resistance. "Listen, love, let's just treat it as a game, eh? We can be detectives and find out what it is and who owns it. It needn't go any further than that if we don't want it to. What do you say?"

"Don't be so bloody patronising," she thought. "I say that's easier said than done, but if you must...." Kate thought that the sheer difficulty of bridging more than three

hundred and fifty years might have more effect on dampening her husband's enthusiasm than anything she might say.

"Now I think that we should get on with sorting out the bills and all the other practical things that we came here to do. You also have to persuade a jury that your client's unfaithful husband deserves to be fleeced, don't you?"

David stood up and pulled Kate out of the armchair. "'*Hell hath no fury like a woman scorned*', but when things hot up, darling, if that woman is married to a rich, philandering actor, who does she turn to? ...yours truly. Anyway, it'll be a piece of cake, my dear girl, I've done my homework, I'll lure the wretched fellow with a few artful questions, which he'll find too delicious to resist and then, his guard down, he'll seal his fate with his own words." He took his wife in his arms and kissed her hard and with longing. He smelled of expensive cologne. "Very well, Miss Efficiency," he said. "*Avanti* with practical matters. Then when we've done, what do you say if I take you out to that Italian restaurant you adore in St. Albans and afterwards, we can inaugurate the master bedroom. What say you?"

LINCOLN, A MONTH LATER

Kate pulled back a wavy lock of blonde hair from her face and her gaze followed a column in the Angel Choir to the famous Lincoln Imp with its wicked grin, one leg crossed over the other at the knee. "Look, darling, isn't it grotesque? You could imagine him hopping down any minute to wreak havoc among innocent tourists."

"Mmm." David Briggs wasn't interested in imps,

cathedrals, churches or any other of his wife's medieval delights. It was the price to pay for getting her to come with him to Lincoln. Last week had been busy at court, but he'd planned ahead and made the necessary bookings for this eastern jaunt. Kate collected cathedrals: that was his impression. He knew the lure of coming here was too strong for her to resist. Even he had to admit that the cathedral was magnificent on its hill, dominating the surrounding lowlands, like an inland Mont St. Michel, but his mind had been on the missing family heirloom since he'd found the letter in his father's desk.

He had to endure the legend of the Imp, see the copy of the Magna Carta and visit Lincoln Castle. Afterwards, they had lunch in an expensive restaurant near the cathedral and the simmering tension between them cooled to a warm bonhomie. At two o'clock they were ready to walk down Steep Hill and Kate linked her arm through David's in mock horror at the well-named road. "Thank goodness we don't have to walk *up* it straight after lunch." Kate liked Lincoln and she was feeling happy. They passed the oldest inhabited house in England, the Crooked House, timbers warped after nine-hundred years as a dwelling. "Can you imagine furnishing that?" Kate, an interior designer, ran a professional eye over the building, "Now there's a challenge, sloping floors and all askew." They passed the picturesque Jew's House with its Norman windows and, going down the steep hill, they were soon past the High Street and in sight of the Stonebow, the southern gateway to the old city.

David stopped, "No, we don't go through there, let's see," he pulled a piece of paper from his jacket pocket and consulted a scribbled map. "We turn left here and then it's off the Monks Road towards the river." Five minutes later they were reading the sign at the door of the Lincolnshire Archives. David had found it on the Internet a few days ago and for a modest sum had booked a space for an hour's research.

They walked into the modern building and Kate nodded her approval of the décor in beech and steel with lime green walls. David walked over to the desk and smiled. "David Briggs, I'm booked in for three o'clock." The clerk gave him a toothy, business smile, and put on a pair of blue-framed reading glasses. She consulted her list, "Ah, here we are sir, table eighteen, it's just over there," she pointed. "Now, what was it you were looking for?"

"The Parish Register for Covenham St. Mary. The Civil War period onwards. Does it go back that far?" he asked, twisting his wedding ring, before rubbing the back of his neck.

"Oh yes, most of the villages have a register dating from the sixteenth century." She came out from behind her desk and Kate studied her.

'Longer skirt with those legs. Square-faced, shouldn't pull her hair back. It stops David eying her up though.'

The young woman led the way to a large, central wooden archive. Ten tables of people concentrating on screens in front of them were arranged on either side.

"These are the microfiche of the Parish Registers, the drawers are in alphabetical order," she tugged one open marked Cha-Cra. "The registers contain births, marriages and deaths. If you need help feel free to ask."

The register began in 1597 and before long David found an entry for 1604, 8 February, a boy, Thomas Mark, born to Richard Monson and Mary Monson, née Walsh.

"That's him," Kate whispered, "he had a son and he

must have been at least twenty then, so skip to 1624 and look at the marriages, year by year."

David reached 1624 and wound on. "Here it is." A couple of people at the next table looked up.

"*Hush.* Or they'll throw us out." She whispered.

"1631, 22 July, a boy, Charles Richard, born to Thomas Monson and Muriel Monson, née Forester."

"Let's move on to Charles's children. Try 1651 onwards."

"I don't think it's a good idea to skip anything," David said, his tone sullen, his lawyer's precision irked as much as his instinct to be in charge.

"We need a *modus operandi,*" Kate hissed through clenched teeth. Her deep, blue eyes flashed; she hated her husband trying to browbeat her.

He ignored her and plodded on year by year. Kate drummed her fingers on the desk, David ignored the provocation, knowing she was right. At last. 1662. "Of course, I should have known," David whispered, "Charles was in France, came back to England at the Restoration. In fact, look, he's a knight as we knew already from the letter. 18 January, a boy, Thomas Richard, born to Sir Charles Monson and Agnès Monson, *née* Chevalier. Probably met a French tart in exile, the dog."

Exasperated, Kate tried once more to convince him of her method. "Skip to 1682."

David acquiesced but there was a problem, he reached 1700 when Kate whispered, "Stop. He'd have been forty by then, too old to get married in those days."

"What if he didn't marry? The end of the line and we draw a blank?"

"Unless, Sir Charles had other children, which it seems he didn't," she mused, "but, in any case, we should try to stick to the firstborn, because they're the ones who inherit. Try something else first, go back to 1678 – that would make any child sixteen years old ..."

"Come on, that's too young even in those days." But David obeyed, he knew all about Kate's hunches. *1678 nothing, 1679 nothing, 1680...*" Look. Dammit, Kate you're right! He was only eighteen: ah, the bawdy days of the Restoration. Another boy, another Charles, born to Thomas Richard Monson and Margaret Monson, *née* Smith. So, not a knight like his father."

"Go to 1700."

Irritated, but compliant, in 1702 David found a girl, Agnes, 27 September to Charles Monson and Alice Monson, *née* Coombs.

"Mmm. Maybe we should check for a male heir."

But the next thirty years didn't throw up any other children to Charles and Alice Monson. "We'd better look through the marriages then, see who Agnes Monson married. Let's see, she was born in 1702. Try from 1718 onwards. That'd make her sixteen."

"Sweet sixteen, eh?" But he wound through the marriages for the next thirty-two years and stopped perplexed in 1750. "She'd have been forty-eight," he said disappointed.

"We'll have to try the deaths now. You know what might have happened, she might have moved to a nearby village and got married there. So, we'll try that after the deaths. But we'll have to go back to the year of her birth, you never know, she could have died in infancy."

David had to admire her logic. He prided himself on his own reasoning, but somehow Kate made things easier. He was getting sore eyes as he studied the deaths, year after year went by and he was just about to give up when he found the entry he was looking for, in 1787.

"This explains everything." There was no mistaking the flatness of his tone, "See here, 19 November 1787, died at the age of eighty-five, Agnes Monson spinster of Rose Cottage, Covenham St. Mary. Spinster. So, she didn't marry and our trail peters out. Damn! If there weren't any descendants, she must have been the last to handle the family treasure," he moaned, "now what do we do?"

"We go to the hotel, have a shower, get changed and have a walk round some of the parts of the city we haven't seen yet and inspiration might come. Then we head back to London for a meal with some decent red wine and you never know your luck, my darling detective."

On his visit to Brayford Pool, he was forced to admire the *"best"* view of the cathedral and where the Fossdyke Canal meets the River Witham, a somewhat distracted David Briggs matured his plan. His grey eyes glinted. Next Sunday, with his driver Victor Dogaru and above all, without Kate, he would come back to Lincolnshire: to Covenham St. Mary's to be exact. With any luck Rose Cottage might still be standing. The trail wasn't stone cold, not yet.

NINE

LOUTH, LINCOLNSHIRE, 2021 AD

ALICE, UP EARLY, EXPLAINED TO HER SLEEPY HUSBAND that there was a website specialising in creating historical mapping products ideal for *meeting present day research needs*. These maps were digitally enhanced, enlarged and matched current Ordnance Survey maps. The company guaranteed that they were immaculately printed and that there *has never been a better way of discovering the landscape of the past*. The earliest map available was 1805 and the cheapest version cost less than ten pounds. On the other hand, the company had its offices in Berkshire with an outlet in London.

"We might as well get it by post," he said, "it should arrive in a couple of days. Today's Wednesday: at worst it should be here on Saturday." He passed Alice his credit card and added, "When are you going to use one of these yourself?" He regretted his attempt at humour as her eyes darkened, her thick eyebrows knotted, she didn't deign him with a reply. Insensitive remarks were added to her private little black book. She ordered the map online while he turned the bone box over in his hands.

"There isn't much else we can do until the map comes," she said. "Shame, we were just—"

"Well as a matter of fact, last night I was running my fingers over the side of this box, and look what I found. There's something carved here. It's faint and covered with dirt. Alice, is there anything suitable in the flat to clean it?"

She found a cloth and spray. He worked on one side of the box. It was tough, because the bone, buried in the wall for so many years, was filthy. The spraying and rubbing seemed to take an eternity and Alice couldn't contain her curiosity. At last he grunted and moved over to the window where he held the box to the light. She hurried over to him and on tiptoe stared up at the etching as he tilted the box to catch the light at an angle so the lines became clearer.

"Isn't it a cup or a chalice and what's this? The cup has a crack drawn in it."

"And there's a branch or a twig with leaves coming out of the chalice, maybe it's an olive branch."

They went to the computer. "Symbols - broken cup?" Typing in the words, she studied a list of links. Clicking on the first, she read aloud:

> ***A group of monks resisting the strict rule of Saint Benedict, tried to poison him. Before raising the cup of poison to his lips, he blessed it, rendering it harmless. A cracked cup in Christian iconography therefore, represents Saint Benedict.***

She clicked on another link and found that the olive branch was another symbol of Saint Benedict, which is why his order was also known as the Olivetans.

Jake gazed at Alice and said, "Are we looking for a Benedictine Abbey near Covenham?"

"I'm sure it isn't just a casual design on the box. It must be a clue – maybe to a sheepfold on Benedictine Abbey lands."

She typed *Covenham Benedictine Abbey* into the search engine bar. *Alien houses – The Priory of Covenham* came up as first link.

"So, it was a priory, not an abbey. Do you know the difference?" She provoked him.

He did, but he thought he'd act the idiot.

"And what's all this about aliens?"

Alice had a tinkling laugh that reminded him of Liffi, "Aliens, Mr Psychic Investigator, are nothing to do with creatures from outer space that eat their way out of your body. They were detached from the main abbey, because the prior was next in rank below the abbot. So, the priory would have been out in the country, but dependent on the abbey."

Jake, who specialised in old churches, knew this but was appreciating the sharp brain helping him to make progress and so flattered her. Their marriage was so fresh that he was only now beginning to appreciate her abilities.

"I bow to your superior learning, madam." and he mock bowed.

Alice scowled and clicked on the link. She read with increasing enthusiasm:

William the Conqueror granted the manor that formed the endowment of the priory of Covenham in 1082 to the abbot and convent of St. Carileph, Le Mans, at the request of the bishop of Durham, who had formerly been a monk of that abbey. A small Benedictine priory was built here soon after, but it is probable that there were never more than two monks, or perhaps only one to take charge of the estate. The advowson remained with the bishops of Durham.

She glanced at him and sure enough, as she suspected, he looked puzzled, but she continued,

> ***In 1303 the cell had become so far unprofitable to the abbey of St. Carileph that licence was sought from the king to sell it to the abbot and convent of Kirkstead. It was then in possession of the original manor of two carucates in Covenham, Grainthorpe, Skidbrook, and Little Grimsby, with the advowson of the church of Covenham, and was charged with a corrody due to Robert Merle of Swinthorpe.***

"It's very technical. We'll need a dictionary, won't we?" he looked at her with a dejected expression.

This time she would impress him. "Well, it means the priory was small and linked to the church of Covenham. Advowson is the right to recommend a member of the clergy for a vacant benefice. So, the priest at St. Mary's had the right to recommend someone to be prior."

"Really? But that doesn't help us find the location of the Priory. Go back to the page with the alien houses. There, click on that other link *Dependent Benedictine Priories*. Let's see what it says."

She didn't like him bossing her, but it made sense, so she did it, biting back a sharp retort.

"Not a lot, look, it just says that there was a small priory dependent on the Priory Church of St. Mary's and, oh no ... nowadays there's no trace of where it used to be. How are we going to find its sheepfold if we don't know where it was?"

"We'll wait for the map to come and then we might be able to make some progress." He leant back in the chair, stretching his arms and yawned unabashed. Alice decided that marriage required some getting used to.

However, her sleepy husband was capable of the most unexpected surprises.

"Alice, whilst we're waiting for the map to come, maybe I can learn something with my psychic powers if I go back to Rose Cottage. I'll take the bone box with me to act as a trigger."

"Be careful. They may be watching the cottage. Do you want me to come with you?"

"No, do you think you could contact Sir John in London? It's best if we keep him updated on our progress. I suspect he sees Sir Clive most evenings in their blessed old boys' club."

"Good idea. I'll do that and I'll need to do some shopping. It'll be fun to look around the market. Small market towns are my favourites. There'll be fresh fruit and vegetables to be had."

He was thinking about more complex matters when he went to the Land Rover. Distracted, he opened the vehicle whilst wrestling with the concept of visibility and invisibility in retrocognition, something he'd never understood. Sometimes when he appeared in the past, people could see him, other times not. He guessed it depended on the psychic potency of the place where he arrived. His lack of attention meant that he didn't notice the man sitting in a grey car parked opposite their flat.

The private detective had been hoping the couple might separate. He decided to follow Jake for the moment, his progress was so poor that he needed a breakthrough before his employer lost patience. Keeping at a discreet distance from the Land Rover, he followed it as far as the road leading to Covenham. The conclusion was that the man was going back to Rose Cottage and since there didn't seem to be much there except a damp abandoned building, he would seize the opportunity of dealing with the woman left alone.

For the second time, Jake entered the cottage through the rear window. His forehead was aching badly, so something supernatural was in the offing. He half-hoped that he would see the ghost, but as he stood on the stairs next to the hole in the wall, clutching the bone box in his pocket, he got much more than he'd bargained for. As ever, the air around him began its vibrations and he knelt on the stairs to stop himself from falling down the steps.

When he recovered his senses, he was surprised to see it was dark outside – night.

COVENHAM ST. MARY, LINCOLNSHIRE, NOVEMBER 1787

JUST AFTER MIDNIGHT, the moon in its third quarter struggled to shed enough light to outline trees and shrubs. Two men crept down the path leading to Rose Cottage. A black cat, slits of eyes glowing, hissed at the man in front. He kicked at it, but too fast for him, the cat scampered into the shrubbery.

"Devil take ye." the man growled, "prob'ly a *familiar*."

Four hundred souls in the village held that Agnes Monson was a witch. She was eighty-five years old and lived alone in Rose Cottage. The few with good sense or learning knew that Agnes, despite her white hair and wrinkled face, was a good woman. She cured all sorts of ailments with herbal remedies. Indeed, she dispensed them mixed in holy water; the medicine to be taken after reciting prescribed prayers. On the other hand, helping out young women who'd got themselves into trouble blighted her reputation. Not that anyone had any real proof of this, but word soon spread around the villages. Besides, this wasn't the only gossip concerning Agnes Monson. There were those who swore that the old woman was rich. Rumour had it that she had some kind of treasure stashed away.

In the Civil War her great great grandfather had been the vicar of St. Mary's. It was well known that his friend the squire, Sir John Briggs, had left something of great value to the Reverend. Some said it was a bag of jewels, but others insisted that it was a bar of gold. Thomas Monson died destitute in the period of the Commonwealth, but facts weren't allowed to get in the way of an appetising tale along these lines.

Sir Charles Monson took up residence in a fine house confiscated from a puritan in the countryside beyond Covenham St. Bartholomew. In spite of the new landowner's fortune, he was tormented by a riddle he couldn't solve and before he died, he told his son Thomas about the treasure, entrusting the box and its verse to him. Thomas gave little attention to the matter, preferring to build up his estate and the family fortune. To no avail, because his son Charles was a wastrel: a gambler, drinker and womaniser, who squandered his inheritance and whose wife, in desperation, abandoned him for another man, leaving him with their young daughter. In dire straits, he was forced to leave the family home and move to a much humbler dwelling. There, he began to rack his brains, dulled by drink, as to the whereabouts of the family treasure. He saw this treasure as his one hope of regaining his station, but his indiscretions and tenuous promises only served to revive half-forgotten memories among the villagers.

Rumours about the hidden treasure began to circulate again, so he hid the box with its verse in a safe place in a wall of the cottage. In spite of his feverish attempts, he couldn't understand the verse and his drinking became worse. On his premature deathbed, when Agnes was seventeen years old, he whispered to her the secret verse and the place where he'd hidden it. He died, still a young man, tormented by demons and debts. So, in Covenham St. Bartholomew everyone believed that Agnes Monson was a rich, old woman even though she appeared to live in poverty in the modest Rose Cottage.

She lived there for the rest of her life and never married, though she was a pretty girl in her youth. She'd been courted by several hopeful suitors, but it seemed she preferred a solitary life, making enough money to get by from her cures, relieving toothache and mending bones, easing fevers and tending sores... and saving some poor girls from scandal and ruin.

Now all the good she had done in her long life was about to be repaid in evil coin. The two men approached the door of Rose Cottage and one of them drew a jemmy from his greatcoat. Jake started, he had company and unpleasant, at that.

What's this? I'd better hide, but where?

"Ye'll not need that, Jud, yon old bat's left the door unlocked."

Surprised and pleased, Jud stole inside after Ned. But a less welcoming surprise awaited them in the small living room. They expected Agnes Monson to be sound asleep in bed at this time of night. But she sat in her rocking chair with a Bible in her lap. Her candle lit her wrinkled face from below, making her look like a witch: an effect heightened by the straggly white hair clinging to her face. Agnes screamed when she saw the intruders, then her face contorted into a horrid grimace and she clutched her chest with her left hand. Her eyes glared in accusation at the two men as she slumped forward in her chair, which began a macabre rocking. Agnes's heart had failed.

" 'ere, I'm off." Ned yelled, unmanned.

Jud grabbed his arm as Ned turned for the door. "Get a grip on yersen man. The old crow's a gonner. She can't harm ye now. An" we've got work to do here."

Jake, who realised that he could not be seen, otherwise, *he* might have caused the poor woman's fatal fright, moved off the stairs, only wide enough for one person to pass at a time.

"I don't want to swing fer this ol' hag," Ned protested.

"An' yer won't. Nobody knows we're here. It's the dead

o' night. I reckon we've plenty of time to turn this place upside down, find the treasure an' then beat it out o' here. Calm down. Think steady-like, there's a good 'un. Take the upstairs. Look at the floor, see if there's any loose boards, 'specially under the bed see. Look under the mattress an' all. An' turn the furniture out, cupboards an' all. Look out for hidey-holes an' the like. I'll do the downstairs, 'cause I ain't afraid o' this owd bat."

After a while Jud found a loose stone under a rug near the hearth and using his jemmy to pry it up, found a white stoneware ointment pot. He scratched his unwashed hair and his sly eyes glanced at the stairs. Ned was still up there, so Jud shook the pot and it jingled. The writing might mean nothing to him, but this was a sound he understood well enough. Snatching off the lid and tossing it back in the hole, he poured five gold sovereigns and some small silver coins into his trembling palm. *Finder's keepers*, he pocketed his loot without calling up to Ned. Replacing the pot under the stone, he adjusted the rug and continued his search. After checking the cellar and drawing a blank he called up to Ned: "Nowt?"

"Nay, an old brooch and a bracelet, but they ain't worth owt."

Jud rushed up the short flight of stairs. "'Ere, let's 'ave a look at 'em, then." He grunted in disappointment, because Ned was right about their worth: paste pearls and coloured glass 'gemstones'. "Nah then," Jud eyed his crony, "yer not keeping owt for yersen, are ye?"

"Nay, lad, we're partners bain't we?" Ned turned out his greatcoat pockets.

"Ay, o' course, Ned, 'scuse me. Let's get out o' 'ere. Waste o' time. Treasure – pah."

The thieves disappeared into the night.

Jake waited until a woman, calling at the cottage for a remedy, found Agnes the next morning. She noticed that the dead woman's right forefinger rested on the Bible at a passage that read: ***I will come again.*** And that, in a small village like Covenham St. Mary, was quite enough to convince people that the ghost of Agnes Monson would haunt Rose Cottage ...

Jake had seen enough. When the woman went away, he concentrated on Alice and found himself standing no longer in the warm cosy cottage but in its damp abandoned interior two hundred and thirty-four years later.

TEN

LOUTH, LINCOLNSHIRE, 2021 AD

On the private detective's mind were his instructions from David Briggs. By any means, fair or foul, he had to gain possession of the box taken from the wall of Rose Cottage. He decided the woman, not the man, was the easiest way. In three days' observation, her weekday routine hadn't varied. The woman was an early riser, by mid-morning she went shopping or did other small errands. Her partner had driven to Covenham, so Bentley had the chance to make progress by using her to persuade Conley to hand over the box.

The detective followed her to the market, turned up his nose at the confusion, and decided to enter her home unobserved to capture her unawares on her return.

At about eleven o'clock, he strolled through Louth straight to the woman's flat. The steps up to the door were oblique to the road, perfect for him to slide back the pin tumbler lock unseen. The road was lacking in movement for the time of day, which helped. He went to his hired Fiesta he had parked opposite the flat confident that he wouldn't be observed. The detective took a black bag out of the boot and climbed the steps. From his pocket he took a pair of rubber gloves and pulled them on. There was no way he would leave any dabs for the boys in blue. Using a credit card to slide open the lock, he caused no damage to the frame. Inside, he closed the door so that it appeared locked.

He went into the kitchen and began to check the drawers. Nothing! But that's what he'd expected. Not even they would leave the box lying around. A pity because it would have saved him a lot of trouble. Still, better to be scrupulous, so he prowled into the bedroom. Taking a pillow off the bed, he carried it back into to the small lounge where he collected three cushions from the sofa and carried them all to the car boot, arranging them to his liking. Again, he stared at the flat door. Would the woman arrive soon? Of course, she would, people were slaves to routine.

Back in the lounge, he took a small bottle together with a cloth pad out of his bag and placed them on the coffee table before settling back on the sofa to wait. He stared at the bottle of chloroform and weighed up the implications. This could cost him twenty-five years in prison, but then again it was hard to get rich without breaking the law. If he got this job right, he could earn more in a few days than most workers were paid in a year.

The sound of footsteps outside the door set his pulse racing. Placing his bag out of sight behind the sofa, he prepared the correct dose of the anaesthetising liquid, too much could be fatal and too little was useless. He darted behind the lounge door.

Alice turned the key in the lock. She tossed her handbag on the small table by the door and walked into the lounge. Someone grabbed her from behind. *Good God, there's a thief!* There was no time for further thought. A strong hand clamped a pad over her mouth and nose. Alice struggled for a couple of seconds as the intruder held her in a strong grip around the waist. Pungent vapour made her head swim and she couldn't breathe. Everything went black.

The woman's legs gave way under her and he had to take her dead weight. He hoisted her on to the sofa and, embarrassed, adjusted her short skirt. It was the work of seconds to blindfold her and to cover her mouth with duct tape. He rolled her over and secured her wrists and ankles with the tape. Lifting her, he carried her through the door, breathing in her subtle scent and admiring her softness and prettiness. Having ensured the coast was clear, he laid her in the boot, taking excessive care to adjust her hair and her head on the pillow and to make her comfortable by padding her with the extra cushions. It was only a short journey, so she wouldn't suffer too much. He checked her breathing was regular. He didn't want her to suffocate. Satisfied, he went back up the stairs to the lounge. There he replaced the pad and bottle in the bag, found her handbag and the door key on the table. The detective locked the door and put the key in her handbag. Then he rooted around in the bag and located her mobile phone. Carrying both bags, he returned to the car and made a perfect unseen getaway.

GRIMSBY, LINCOLNSHIRE, LATER THE SAME DAY

THE PRIVATE DETECTIVE carried the woman to an armchair in the detached rented house and ensured that she was comfortable. He adjusted her head, resting it on the chair back so that she could breathe and then ripped the plaster off her mouth. He felt sure that even if she screamed, nobody would hear her. He had chosen the house well. She was still out, but he calculated that she'd come to before long.

With more trepidation than the first time, he dialled a London number. One of the lawyers he worked for had put him on to this bigwig and had been quite clear about the man's importance and had pointed out that he didn't suffer fools.

"David Briggs."

"Can we speak freely?"

"Just a minute."

He heard the muffled sound of voices and then a door closing, then the controlled, clipped speech of the lawyer:

"There's no problem now. What do you have for me?"

"I've got the woman. Without complications."

There was a short silence at the other end.

"Excellent, make her sing. Use whatever methods you think fit, because I want to know everything. What they found in the cottage wall and what they've done with it. Use the woman to get to her boyfriend and retrieve the box, do you understand Bentley?"

The detective marvelled at and resented the coldness in the lawyer's voice.

"If he doesn't co-operate, be imaginative." The lawyer paused for effect, "I'm sure he'll have the woman's welfare at heart. Don't you agree? Oh, and listen, the next time you call me, use this number ..." Briggs dictated a mobile number. "Yours is the only number on this card and it has top priority. Keep the calls to a minimum, but don't fail to call if there are problems." The phone went dead.

"That's what I like, a free hand," Stephen Bentley muttered, thinking that the lawyer was a ruthless piece of work. "So, we'll get some quick results here," he said half under his breath and glancing at the unconscious woman. He dug inside her handbag and pulled out her mobile phone. It was switched on. He found Jake's number and called it.

"Hey!" a youthful voice greeted him.

"Hey, yourself. I've got the woman and you've got something I need."

"Who is this?"

Bentley was pleased at the note of panic at the other end.

"If you're interested in your girlfriend's wellbeing, you'll do as I tell you. Keep the police out of this. Is that clear?"

There was a moment's silence, then: "Yeah. But how do I know you've got Alice? Is she all right?"

"Later. I'll let you speak to her, all in good time. Listen. Ring whoever might be missing her. Invent something. Tell them she'll be away for two days. Make it good. They will expect her at work soon. Don't fail...and no police. I'll get back to you later."

Jake frowned, the kidnapper knew very little about them, given the nature of his instructions. *Here we go again,* he thought, it wasn't so long ago that Alice had been taken hostage by the Black Elves. This time, it was some treasure hunter or similar. *Sir Clive bloody Cochrane strikes again!*

The detective looked at the phone in his hand, it would be better switched off. He didn't want disturbing. Then Bentley turned his attention to the woman. He went into the kitchen and made a strong filter coffee, unscrewed the cap on a whisky bottle and poured himself a good measure. Switching on the radio, he fiddled around until he found some classical music: Bach. He let the coffee cool down. Testing, he sipped at it. Satisfied that it wasn't scalding, the detective grabbed a towel and carried the coffee through to the woman. Bunching the towel under her chin, Bentley poured the drink into her mouth. Alice spluttered and, dazed, she opened her eyes under the blindfold. He made her sip some more coffee. When she turned her head away from the cup, he withdrew it. In a small, hesitant voice she said, "I think I'm going to be sick."

Putting down the cup he ran into the kitchen and grabbed a plastic bowl from under the sink before thrusting it under the woman's chin. She emptied her stomach, but after wiping her mouth for her and giving her mineral water, she revived.

"Who are you? Why are you doing this to me?"

"Better you don't know who I am. As to why you're here, well, you and your friend have got mixed up in something a lot bigger than yourselves. Now, my boss has a very mean streak." He took her chin in his hand and squeezed hard. "If you tell me everything I need to know and if your precious Jake behaves himself, there's no need for either of you to be hurt," the deep, gravelly voice assured her. "So be a sensible young lady and answer my questions. You know, I don't want to slice that pretty face–" Alice gasped and Bentley let go of her chin stroking her cheek. He stood up and walked over to the table, carried a chair over to the armchair and sat down in front of the woman.

"Let's begin with the stairs wall in Rose Cottage, shall we? What did you find there?"

Alice's mind raced, she realised that these people wanted what they'd found and would stop at nothing. There was no doubt that the man would carry out his threat, so she had to answer him or risk being cut. But how much could she hold back and still seem plausible? At least her eyes wouldn't betray her. "Look, it was only a small bone box," she said, her voice pleading. "I'm sure Jake will let you see it if you ask."

Bentley took a penknife out of his pocket, opened it and leaned forward, pressing the blade flat against the woman's face. She shrank back and blurted, "I've told you the truth—everything."

"Everything? It's not much is it?"

"No, but even Jake doesn't know why the box was there. Please believe me."

"Well, he went and found it, didn't he? It would be a pity to mess up this pretty face." He moved the knife a little.

Her lower lip trembled and Bentley wondered if there were tears under the blindfold. "I'm sure you can do better than that if you put your mind to it."

"Please, I need to go to the toilet," she said almost inaudibly.

"Tough. You're a big girl now, so just control yourself. There's no way I'm untying your hands. The choice is yours, dry and uncomfortable or wet and uncomfortable." His laugh was harsh. "Now, out with it or you'll be known as *Scarface* for the rest of your life." He removed the cold steel and left it to her imagination.

"Please, there is no more ... it's just that—"

"What?"

"Just that there was some kind of design, like...like a broken cup scratched into the bone. Honestly. That's everything now. Please don't cut me."

She heard him walk away. The music stopped. In the silence she could hear traffic faintly in the distance and nearer some birdsong. The footsteps returned.

"It's time to talk to your boyfriend. I'll use your phone and you'll tell him that you're OK, but that he has to do as I say and no police. Got that? Don't try anything silly."

She nodded. The detective passed her the phone and Jake answered the call.

"Jake, it's me. Just listen. I'm OK, but do as this man says...please...and don't go the police..."

Bentley snatched the phone. "I'll be in touch soon," he said and snapped the mobile closed, switching it off again. Leaning forward, he scooped the woman into his arms and carried her upstairs. He laid her on the bed. He ran downstairs, took the large roll of duct tape out of his bag and was back in seconds. He rolled the woman over several times in the quilt, so that just her head was showing. Then he passed the tape several times around the quilt at knee level and at the level of her elbows.

"There," he said, inches from her face. She could smell tobacco on his breath, "I can't take any more risks with these phone calls, in case lover boy isn't behaving himself. I'm going out for ten minutes. Try not to get too hot in there." He repeated the harsh laugh.

She heard him shut the front door and a car drive off. She tried, but she couldn't move, except for wiggling her feet and moving her neck. She bit her lip and thought over what she'd told the man. At least he didn't know about the sheepfold, but would Jake tell him?

Oh God. What have we got ourselves into? If we get out of this in one piece, I'll have nothing more to do with buried treasure.

He hadn't hurt her so far, she thought, but would her luck hold?

ELEVEN

MONKEN HADLEY, HERTFORDSHIRE FIVE DAYS EARLIER

From the front gate Kate regarded their new property with its five bays and pediment, standing facing the green and the triangular common separated by the church. It was befitting for her husband's social status. Besides, this was the house he'd grown up in, where he'd brought her to meet his parents for the first time eighteen years ago. It felt like his house and this was a far stronger attraction than the lure of the money he could bank from its sale. There was a snag, David seemed bothered about the commuting. She'd tried to reassure him, this house was only 15 miles from his office, but they both knew very well that there was traffic and congestion to consider.

A lot was riding on settling here for Kate. She gazed with longing at the house, loving the feel of it—her career could be based anywhere. She was an interior designer with an extensive clientele. At the moment her head was full of ideas for the rooms, as yet unshared with David, because she judged it indelicate to suggest changes so soon after her father-in-law's death. A childless couple in their early forties, Kate hadn't wanted to start a family and with David at best only lukewarm on that score, she was free to throw herself heart and soul into her career. But Kate felt since their wedding each had gone his own way and, though the physical attraction was still strong, the marriage was creaking. They had no interests in common except their appreciation of chic restaurants and there were times when she loathed David for his condescension. Once or twice, the lingering scent of perfume on a shirt collar and a tell-tale hair on his jacket betrayed David's infidelity. Love-hate, she recognised, was the term that best described her feelings for her husband. In fact, she was afraid to analyse her sentiments, sensing an inherent danger in them; she preferred to busy herself with her career. Their new situation with the house, she hoped, might serve as the focal point to re-kindle the flame of their relationship.

Also, as she'd pointed out to her husband more than once, they could well afford to keep the London flat, which meant that they could stay over in the city whenever they felt inclined. In that way, they need not give up on their established social circle. As if a reflex to the thought, Kate adjusted her grey wool business suit. Today she was wearing a somewhat prim, high-necked white blouse offset by three delicate coral buttons. She knew that her appearance could be impressive, indeed for some intimidating, with her delicate brow, high cheekbones and her piercing gaze inherited from her father.

Everything was perfect, but one thing was troubling her. David hadn't mentioned the cottage or the treasure in the last few days. It was a bad sign. She knew him too well to suppose that he'd given up and the fact that he hadn't said anything meant just the opposite, he was brooding about what to do next. She'd talked about this and that, to pass the time with him more or less monosyllabic in his answers or reduced to uncivil grunts. Then he disappeared "on business" all day on Sunday with Victor. No, it didn't bode well at all, Kate thought.

TWELVE

GRIMSBY, LINCOLNSHIRE, 2021 AD

FROM A PUBLIC PHONE BOOTH SOME STREETS AWAY, THE detective dialled Jake's number. He replied at once.

"I want what you found in the wall. You know what I mean. Do you know Weelsby Woods? In Grimsby?"

"Yeah."

"Right, at the entrance there are two stone lions, you with me?"

"Yeah."

"Leave the box under one of the lions and you get the woman."

"When?"

"That's the interesting bit. At four o'clock in the morning. If you're a good boy and don't try any fancy tricks, you'll have your sweetheart back safe and sound straight after. Understood? There's no need for the boys in blue – just the box."

Bentley cut him off, left the booth and drove back to the house.

Jake sat still in front of his wife's computer, his mind racing. The man didn't know about the paper scroll or he'd have mentioned it. Well done, Alice. Good. He couldn't risk going to the police. The man only wanted the box and, damage limitation, he'd be no farther ahead than they were. The important thing was to get his wife out of the man's clutches. He wondered who the devil he was and what Cochrane had got Alice into? If anything happened to her, he would never forgive him. He wondered whether he should go to the police, weighing up the options. He decided; he'd have to obey instructions—what had the man said?—No fancy tricks. Her safety was the main thing.

It was mid-afternoon and Bentley unwound Alice from the quilt. She was red-faced and sweating. The change of temperature made her desperate to go to the toilet again, so Bentley consented, but threatened to beat her if she tried to remove her blindfold. Her hands needed to be free. Once over this little crisis, he bound her hands behind her again, but left her legs loose so that he could lead her around the house to regain circulation. In the evening he even spoon-fed her. At half-past three in the morning, while she was sleeping, he bound her ankles again. This woke her.

"I'm going to cover your mouth again," he told her, "but don't worry, in three-quarters of an hour, you will be free and back with your partner—if there's no silliness. So be a good girl. Just another bit of discomfort, that's all."

"Don't expect me to thank you."

He taped across her mouth and produced his by now familiar harsh laugh, vindictive this time. "There, the perfect woman," he said, "helpless and above all, silent."

She was quiet but her thoughts were racing.

He doesn't know Jake's my husband. Whoever he is, he seems to be muddling along.

Bentley lifted her into the car boot, where he settled her as before. The detective drove the couple of miles to

Weelsby Woods and swung across the road through the entrance, his beam lighting the pair of stone lions that stood there like sentinels. He stopped in the car park just beyond, from where the road and the statues were in his line of sight. He checked his watch and saw that there were still eight minutes to four o'clock. Bentley got out the car. Even though it was June, it wasn't more than two miles to the sea and the night was cool. He walked over to the lions and peered back into the darkness. It was an overcast night, which favoured his plan. Peering into the darkness, he couldn't distinguish the trees of the woodland. From a previous daytime visit he knew of their dense presence beyond a pleasant rolling park. From where he was standing, he couldn't even see the Fiesta. With a crooked smile, he unwrapped a chewing gum and, pleased, strolled back to the car. He checked his watch again. The occasional vehicle passed along Weelsby Road, which was only to be expected, as it was one of the main roads into Cleethorpes, but none of them pulled in.

A car pulled up in front of the lions and the headlights lit the pavement and the fringe of trees that skirted its flagstones. The strong beams went out and by the dimmer streetlamps, Bentley watched a fair-haired man in what he guessed to be his early-thirties get out of the car. The man stood still and peered through the darkness. Bentley tensed; he was looking straight toward him. The seconds passed, but the detective relaxed when the wiry, young man turned and took something out of his pocket. He looked around several times as if he were still alert to any sound of movement. Bentley realised that he was suppressing his breathing and took a couple of controlled breaths. A passing car's headlights lit up the athletic frame of the younger man and Bentley noted how he turned his back to the light as if he didn't want to be recognised. Ironical that. Jake strode over to the statue on the left. Again, he looked around him and once more he peered into the darkness toward the Fiesta as though he knew it was there. The detective shrugged; he was certain he couldn't be seen. In any case, despite the lad's physique, he felt sure that he could handle the younger man in a straight fight unless he was armed. Bentley had police training. He'd served on the Force in Kent for five years before they dispensed with his services for the overblown matter of a sum of money a punter refused to pay to keep his name squeaky clean in a sex scandal. That'd been a serious error of judgement that cost him his police career. Well, water under the bridge, and he had no regrets. He gave his undivided attention to the shadowy figure.

Jake bent down and put the box under the lion's belly. He straightened up and looked round in all directions. He sauntered back to his car. Standing with one hand on the door handle, he cocked his head to one side listening. There was no sign of the kidnapper. Then he got back into the car and let a couple of minutes go by before switching his headlights on and turning the engine on. He pulled away, heading in the same direction from which he had come.

The detective heaved a huge sigh of relief, and realised that his body was aching from maintaining the same immobile position. He thrust his elbows backwards and stuck out his chest for immediate relief to the small of his back. He went over to the statue and under it found a white box. He bent over, feeling a dull ache: he was getting middle-aged. Maybe he wouldn't have come out on top with that young fellow after all. He made a mental note that more gym work was needed as he picked up the box and flipped it open. Empty. So what? It seemed the genuine article and he slipped it into his pocket, pulled out the woman's mobile and switched it on. He called Jake while he walked back towards the Fiesta. The man answered at once.

"Keep going towards Cleethorpes for five minutes. When you get to the roundabout at Grimsby Road, turn around and come back to the lions, respect the speed limit. You will find your girlfriend just past them in the car park, sitting on a bench waiting for you. Don't try anything stupid. Do as you're told and nobody will get hurt. Got that?"

There was no answer at first, then, a reluctant, "OK ... But if you've touched her–"

Bentley snapped the phone shut. The detective ran over to the car and lifted the girl out of the boot before sitting her on a bench near the children's swings.

"Lover boy's coming, so, much as it saddens me, I'll have to leave you. Time to get some shut-eye. Nightie-night."

That horrible laugh grated, but relief flooded through her as she heard him hurry to the car, her whole body relaxed as he drove away. Alive and unhurt: her face hadn't been slashed. She began to struggle to free her hands, but it was useless, the duct tape was strong. Where was Jake? What was keeping him? Tears stung her eyes.

Bentley drove away, his crooked smile revealing his satisfaction at everything going like clockwork. There was a minor irritation though, this couple had only found a white box and he didn't know if the big lawyer-man was going to be best pleased. The hard work of finding the treasure still had to be done, but at least he was up to speed on those two youngsters. He began to whistle "A Wandering Minstrel I" from *The Mikado*.

A few minutes later Jake drove into the car park near the playground and his headlights lit up the trussed figure of

Alice. He rushed over to her, overwhelmed by a feeling of tenderness for his poor wife. He undid the blindfold and pulled the tape away from her mouth.

"Oh Jake, thank God you're here," she said and the threatened tears flowed. He sat down beside her and putting his arm around her pulled her to him, kissing her hair, forehead and the salty tears on her cheeks.

"It's all right, love, you're OK now. That bastard! I could kill him." His voice changed to concern, "He didn't hurt you, did he?"

"No. I'm OK, but can you untie me, please. I'm getting cramp in my legs."

He had trouble undoing the tape, but once free, she rubbed her arms and jiggled her legs.

"Brrr! It's chilly," she said, wiping her eyes with her sweater sleeve, trying to sound braver than she felt. "Let's get out of here."

"Blast." Jake said, "I thought you might want to go into the woods with your rescuer. Some people are ungrateful." He put a hand on her shoulder.

She shrugged him off and glared, "I just want to go home ...*please*." The last word was tremulous.

He felt ashamed at his thoughtlessness. "I'm sorry, darling. Come on." He took her hand and led her to the car. He turned left taking the road for Louth, then looked out of the corner of his eye, "Are you OK?"

She shuddered, "No thanks to that creep. Oh, Jake, it was horrible. He put me out with some chemical—chloroform? I was so sick. There were moments when he threatened to slash my face; he meant it too, but I didn't tell him anything. You didn't give him the paper you found?"

"No, I burned it last night. I figured out that you hadn't mentioned the psalm to him. Clever of you."

"Well done, too. He tried to get me to tell him everything. We're going to have to be careful from now on—"

"*We*. You mean you want to carry on looking for the treasure after what's happened? Alice, these people are dangerous. I think we should go to the police."

The immediate fear passed, vow forgotten, she said: "No. Listen, we were the first on to this treasure and I want to find it. I've no idea how they got on to us, but we'll be more careful from now on. Go on. Think about it. If he'd wanted to, he could have killed me in that house. And... he could have killed you in the woods. There was nobody around. You won't believe this, but he was quite kind to me, I mean, if you ignore the fact that he chloroformed me and tied me up—"

"You're doing my head in. How can you ignore being chloroformed and tied up? Anyway, if we find the treasure before them, they'd have a good reason to kill us, don't you think? I'm going to the police."

THIRTEEN

LONDON, 2012 AD

David Briggs felt his priority mobile phone vibrate in his shirt pocket. Breaking off a dictation, with no explanation to his secretary, he hurried through to his office and shut the door.

"What have you got for me?"

He listened and, unimpressed, treated Bentley to one of his polished cross-examinations; he circled, like a fencer, feinting, waiting to thrust home. He listened as the detective struggled to convince him.

"As I say, I've got the box. No. I'm quite sure the girl had no more to tell me. She was wetting herself with fear. No, I didn't need to use physical methods. Well, not many. No, of course not. Yes, I am sure. I know how to do my job." By now exasperated, Bentley stared at his reflection in the lounge mirror and wasn't pleased at the angry expression he found there. No smooth-tongued London lawyer, however important, could treat him like this.

At the other end, tight-lipped and frowning, Briggs was getting a feel for the man's worth, unwilling as yet to trust the reference given him by Anthony Braithwaite. He pressed on:

"Listen Bentley, I'm paying you a considerable fee and I expect the best possible return on it." He relented a little. "You've done well to get the box. I just have the feeling that you might have squeezed more information out of them when you had the upper hand. I consider it a missed opportunity. I want you sharper understand? I won't tolerate incompetence. Listen. I'll deal with Conley. Don't let him out of your sight. Whatever those two know about my treasure, well, I also want you to know about it, am I making myself clear? Oh, and another thing, are you sure they don't know who you are, what you look like?"

David Briggs took up an ornamental magnifying glass and focused it on his desk calendar, quintupling the size of a half moon, as he listened to Bentley's assurances.

"You did well in that respect. I'm sure a man of your undoubted abilities can avoid alerting his quarry. Ring me when you have anything else. Now see to the courier."

'He's cut me off again.' Bentley lit a cigarette and pulled on a steadying lungful of smoke, breathing it out and obscuring his thunderous expression in the mirror. He didn't like Briggs and if he could find some way of making him pay for his disrespect, he would. Not that it would be easy with a barrister and above all if he didn't want to lose the handsome sum the QC was prepared to pay for his success. He took another long drag on his cigarette. He smiled his crooked smile. Nobody should underrate Stephen Bentley.

Underrating him was what David Briggs was about in that instant. He called for Victor and before long the chauffeur shuffled his massive bulk into the lawyer's office. The barrister told him about Bentley's plans to check out the premises of the young couple while they were out. Conley would be out and about in Louth the next day and it was there that Victor should rough him up to extract all the information the fellow possessed about a Priory: '*every last squeak*'. There were to be no firearms and no deaths. Did Victor think he was up to such a task? The close-set eyes sparkled. This was what he was best at, crushing people into submission. He, Victor Dogaru, had two Olympic wrestling bronze medals that should have been gold but for a cheating Bulgarian and a partial judge. Was he up to such a task? Here was the opportunity he so craved to show his boss the worth of Victor Dogaru.

FOURTEEN

LOUTH, LINCOLNSHIRE, 2021 AD

The sound of a woman's voice, bright and efficient, advising of hold-ups and diversions woke Alice. She experienced an intense wave of pleasure as she realized she'd spent the whole night lying with Jake's arm around her. Now stiff and numb with the immobility and aware of his arm, heavy, across her chest, constricting her breathing she wriggled out, kissing and squeezing his shoulder until he turned to focus on the radio alarm by the bed. He sighed, swung round and sat up, switched off the radio, grabbed a bathrobe and prowled around the bedroom, belt trailing behind like a tail, until he found his mobile under a pile of clothes. Back in bed he curled into her foetal position, arm around her waist, enjoying the scent of her hair. They slept until late morning, made love again and afterwards Alice, on one elbow, her breast pressing against his chest, leant over him and stared into his eyes.

"If we move with care, we can find the treasure before these people, whoever they are, and declare it at once. When we hand it over to the authorities, they won't be able to do anything and we'll get the reward."

He studied the intent, determined eyes, his own betraying a whole range of emotions as he wrestled with his fear, shame at not displaying her same courage until his growing resolve won. His wife interpreted every stage without comment.

"That's better," she smiled and rewarded him with a lingering kiss.

After a shower, she did her best in this small bathroom to adjust her hair, reflecting on the implications of the past night. Now, she put her hand on her chest, lowered her head and smiled at the memory of their lovemaking. Her attraction to him had increased in inexplicable leaps, since truth be told, he irritated her more than any other man she knew. She'd never lost her head like this before. Maybe it was the inexplicable that was so electric, that and his sheer sexiness. She shuddered at the memory of those hard muscles and was dragged out of her reverie by Jake calling from the kitchen where scrambled egg and toasted bagels were waiting for her. They devoured this and gulped mouthfuls of strong tea. As they ate, they discussed their plans after he had agreed not to contact the police.

"The first thing is to locate this sheepfold," she said, "but until the map arrives...."

"I've been thinking about that. What about the vicar of Covenham?"

She was silent for a moment, "Not a bad idea, that article on the web said the abbey was lost, but a priest might have some record, or some idea of where it was."

"Bear in mind it's not the abbey we need to find but the sheepfold that belonged to it."

She gazed at him, her expression tender and anxious, taking his hand across the table, "Now I have something more precious than any treasure; we have to be very careful.

I couldn't bear it if anything happened to you." Even as the words left her mouth, she reddened and wished she could take them back. She didn't want to make him feel overconfident of her love for him. She could not know that an angel had made these worries irrelevant.

He took her in his arms and gazed into her eyes, "We'll be extra careful. They're sure to be watching our every move. We'll just have to outsmart them. I won't let anyone get near you again. That's a promise." He kissed her on her forehead. "Now, let's look for that sheepfold."

It was a fine day, the dense clouds of the night before replaced by high fluffy wisps. Jake took a torturous route through the back streets of Louth until he was quite satisfied that they weren't being followed. Not knowing where to find the Covenham vicarage Jake decided to drive straight to St. Mary's Church. He slowed down for a moment when he glimpsed a likely building made of red brick, but it turned out to be a Community Room with a stone plaque, informing the reader that it was once the United Free Methodist Church. They reached St. Mary's and he parked, the street empty apart from a grey Fiesta further up the road. He was about to get out when Alice laid her hand on his arm. "We have to think up a white lie. We can't just barge in there and say we're looking for hidden treasure. That'll put an end to any co-operation."

"Right." He turned in his seat and looked at her. "What do you think we should tell him?"

"Let's say we're researching Benedictine monasteries."

Jake snorted, "Oh come on, he'd see straight through that. Can you remember any of those strange words? I know I can't, five minutes and the game would be up. No, I'll tell you what, we'll tell him that we're studying medieval farm practices. I can bluff on that. I went on a school trip to see the Saxon open-field system at Haxey in the Isle of Axholme when I was ten."

"Oooh. Did you wear a uniform, with a little cap?"

"Don't be daft, of course we didn't."

"I'd love to have a photo of you in your short trousers."

Smiling, he opened the car door, "Come on, just leave the talking to me."

"Oooh arrr, I'm only a farmer's daughter, but I know my carats from my carrots."

Laughing, they walked down the path to the studded wooden church door. There were notices outside but no mention of the vicarage. Strange, but the next service wasn't for another three Sundays. Alice turned the heavy iron ring on the door and was pleased to find it unlocked. They entered and stopped beside the font. He touched the carved stone, its rim dotted with flowers, and admired the shields bearing crosses, nails, hammers and scourges, the instruments of the Lord's passion. A middle-aged woman walked, smiling, toward them down the nave. She appeared to be in her late forties, with short, mousy hair streaked with grey, pulled straight back from her face into a clumsy knot. Her eyes were hidden in this half-light by a pair of blue plastic-framed glasses. She was holding a cloth and a spray can in her hands.

"It's from the fourteenth century, Perpendicular style, like the windows."

"Yes, I know, I studied history at university," he said. "It's a lovely, little church."

He won a wide smile. "You're lucky to find it open, you know, nowadays we have to keep everything locked with all this vandalism. Before you'd always find a church open at some time for a few minutes each day of silent prayer...."

she shook her head, "...I don't know what things are coming to."

"We were looking for the vicar. But we don't know where the vicarage is."

"Well, there used to be two vicarages – one for each Covenham, but I'm afraid they're private houses now and we don't have our own vicar any more. You see, it isn't economical for the Church. The congregation is small here and St. Bartholomew's is redundant."

"That's why there isn't a service for three weeks, then," Alice said. "Who's the vicar? And how can we talk to him?"

The woman smiled, "It's a *her*, not a *him*. Our vicar is a woman, but I'm afraid you'd have to go to Elkington to find her. It's about seven miles away, but perhaps I can help, I'm the Church Warden."

"We're preparing a book on medieval farm practices," Jake said, "and there used to be a Benedictine Priory in Covenham in the Middle Ages. What we wanted to know is whether there was any record of its whereabouts."

The woman shook her head. "Our church records go back to the beginning of the seventeenth century; they're kept at Lincoln, but I can tell you that there's no mention of a priory hereabouts. I doubt very much that the vicar can help either, she's not a local woman."

"Oh well, it was a bit of a long shot. Never mind. Thanks for your time, anyway." They turned to go.

"Wait a minute though; there might be someone who can help. Two ticks and I'll put these things away," she said, holding up the cloth and spray in front of her. "Then I'll take you to see him."

They stepped outside, squinting in the stronger light and the warden locked the door with an old iron key.

"That must be centuries old," Jake said, nodding at the key.

"Yes, and it weighs a ton. Here try that for size." the woman laughed, handing it to him, who passed it on to Alice, who faked sagging at the knees, puffed out her cheeks and gave it back to the warden.

"There isn't much chance of misplacing it, at any rate. Now come with me, I'll take you to meet old Jacob. He's over ninety and he's lived in Covenham man and boy. If anyone knows local history, it's him. He's still got his wits about him. But I warn you; you'll only understand the half of it. Our Jacob speaks broad Lincolnshire dialect. He's one of the last who does hereabouts. You'd be surprised how many linguists come to see him with their notebooks and recorders. Do you know, there are evening classes to save our dialect? Most of it was wiped out with the mechanisation of farming, but we have a few out of the way farms where it's still hanging on – just in a few words and expressions."

They passed one at a time through the small gate to the road.

"Do we need to take the car?" Jake nodded towards the Land Rover.

"No, lovey. Jacob lives in sheltered housing; it's only two minutes, around the corner."

As they turned the corner the man in the grey Fiesta eased away from the kerb and took the same turning.

Yellow brick bungalows were laid out around a grass quadrangle bordered by a few scrawny lavender plants alive with bees. Four bespectacled elderly men were playing dominoes around a table in front of the first house. The churchwarden asked in passing whether Jim was cheating again. The men cackled, but they all stared at the two young people as if they were Martian invaders. Alice gave them her prettiest smile and one of the men waved at her with a toothless grin. Outside the third bungalow, his walking stick propped against a wicker armchair padded with cushions, sat a wizened old man soaking up the sun. His toothless mouth was nothing more than a compressed line, so that his chin almost reached the tip of his nose. The brown and blue speckled skin of his wrinkled face contrasted with the brushed and parted white hair so out of keeping with his bedraggled clothes.

"How are we today, Jacob?"

"Ah caant mither, tha knows."

"Now then Jacob, if you're not too busy, I've brought these two young people who want to ask you some questions about the history of Covenham."

The old man studied them for a whole minute, staring straight into Jake's eyes, as if he was weighing up whether the young man's character was acceptable. Jake had to suppress a laugh as a gnomish smile lit up Jacob's extraordinary wrinkled face. But then he was surprised when the old man raised himself to his feet leaning on his walking stick and hauling on his armchair. He shuffled off into the bungalow as Jake raised an eyebrow at the churchwarden, who seemed delighted by the whole performance. At the height of his perplexity, Jacob reappeared in his doorway crunching and clicking his dentures in his mouth. The old man had rearranged his face as an act of courtesy to his visitors. His flannel shirt, pale from excessive washing hung on his bony frame, over the shirt was an open cardigan wrong side out, buttons facing inwards, grown long perhaps from Jacob stuffing his hands in the pockets when it was worn the right way.

"Nah then, ah twigged ye wur frim folk. An "'ow can ah "elp 'ee?"

The churchwarden interrupted and turned to the young couple, "If you don't mind, I'd best be getting off home now. There's lunch to prepare for my three men and they won't be happy if it isn't ready. I do hope that you can understand our Jacob, he's a bit broad with the dialect." She added in a low voice. "By the way, "frim folk" are outsiders if you're wondering," she laughed.

They thanked the woman, who hurried off. Alice helped Jacob settle back into his armchair and Jake explained about the Benedictine Priory. Jacob listened, but when his visitor had finished, he shook his head.

"Nay, tha's gotten us reet flummoxed maaister, ah aint 'eard tell o' na priory in these paarts."

"What's he say?" Alice whispered, but Jake had understood him all right.

"Well, we aren't looking for the priory, what we're after is the sheepfold the monks once used."

The old man leant forward in his chair and raised his forefinger, "Nah then tha's inother matter. Tha knows Ings Lane, reet inuf?"

Jake nodded.

"Well now maaister, if tha goes down Ings Lane reet to tuh end tha comes to tuh ings."

"The ings?"

"Ay, tuh oppen meadow. Tha comes to tuh public path, unsneck tuh gate an" ye goes ower tuh noggin thruff tuh woods an" behint it tha'll come to what tuh owd folks sed wur Monks Cote. Ah nivver bin there mysen, but 'appen as there's na smoke wiyout fire."

Jake nodded in agreement, but Alice had no idea what the old man was on about. "Yeah, now I remember from our local studies at school, *cote* is another word for pen or sheepfold, isn't it? You've been a great help."

"Is that how North Cotes and the Somercotes got their names?" Alice interrupted.

"Ay, 'appen," Jacob nodded, then pointed at her feet, "Nah when tha goes ower to Monks Cote, tha doant want them there fancy shoes. Tha'll be clagged an' blathered clomping ower there."

She looked at her feet with a puzzled frown.

"We'll bear it in mind, then" Jake smiled, "By the way, you don't know who the land belongs to by any chance?"

"Oh ay. It be young Teddy Johnson's land tha' there."

They took their leave of the old man. As they walked back to the car she said, "What a character. He's all small and wrinkly and cuddly and the way he speaks - how on Earth can you understand him? I got about every other word, I mean, what's a "noggin" for example?"

"I think it must be a kind of hillock or rise. I'm only guessing, because my dad used to say "use your noggin" and by that he meant "use your head", so ... anyway, I reckon our old friend Jacob's given us a bit of a lead."

Across the road Bentley turned in the driver's seat of the parked Fiesta and slid down until they passed. He sat up and watched them walk back to the main road. His instinct told him to pay the old boy his respects.

FIFTEEN

LOUTH, LINCOLNSHIRE, 2021 AD

ALICE CLEARED SOME SPACE ON THE DESK AND THEY spread out the map. Heads together, they examined it for a moment. Jake traced his finger along Ings Lane up to a footpath across the fields.

"Look. The path was there in 1805."

His finger continued and stopped on woodland marked as *Bardsley's Wood*, behind it was a field with no particular labelling. He reached for a pencil, but she stopped his hand.

"Not a good idea, what if they break in here again?"

He looked at her and nodded, straightened up and stared at the map. Smiling, he jabbed a finger to the northeast of Covenham St. Bartholomew, pencilled a cross in a field and then wrote the word PRIORY and circled it.

"There's no mention of Monks Cote on the map," Jake said. "Mind you, I didn't expect there would be. I reckon it'd disappeared centuries before 1805 and remained as a reference point in local speech. Let's have a look at a satellite map of Earth and see what we can find."

The satellite image of Covenham St. Mary was sharp and Alice pointed at Rose Cottage. Jake took the mouse and zoomed out. Ings Lane was marked and he clicked on the arrowhead to move south. He found a public footpath running off to the left of Ings Lane; it was the same path as the 1805 one. Bardsley's Wood was bigger to the east in the nineteenth century, but its western edge seemed to be the same as in the past and behind it, he stabbed at the screen with his forefinger, marked in the green of the map was an almost unbroken oval shape.

"That oval would have been enclosed with dry stone walling and the small gap here would have been for a wattle gate. There's a good chance this is our sheepfold."

"We'll have to ring Mr Johnson," Alice said, already turning the pages of the directory. "This must be him, Johnson Edward, Brook Farm."

Jake rang and explained everything to Mr Johnson, including what he stood to gain. The farmer was rather taken aback by the whole thing, but when he ascertained that the search would be limited to the old sheepfold on the edge of his land, he gave them permission. He laughed off the idea of them finding anything of value, but as he said, if they turned something up, he *wouldn't look a gift horse in the mouth.*

"Tomorrow is Saturday, so we can go early and scout around. We'll have to be careful that no-one follows us. Have you got any boots? You heard what Jacob said, it'll be muddy along that trail and through the woods."

"When did he say that?"

" *'Tha"ll be clagged an" blathered clomping ower there"* don't you remember?" Jake laughed.

"Translate please."

"You'll get all muddy and spattered trudging over there. My granddad, a proud Lincolnshire man, still used some of these dialect words in ordinary conversation when I was little, that's how I know what he was on about."

"I've got a pair of hiking boots I bought when I was seventeen. We went on a school trip too when I was in the sixth form. Walking in the Lake District, up Helvelyn. We went over Striding Edge," she said, "it was scary, I'll tell you. I thought I was going to fall off; it made me so dizzy looking down. Anyway, the boots are still good. I'm starving, good grief, it's almost two o'clock."

They decided to set off at half-past eight the next morning. Each would take a separate torturous route to the road out of town, Jake by car, Alice on foot would meet him there, to avoid being followed.

Bentley's stomach rumbled in the Fiesta opposite the couple's flat. He lit another cigarette; he thought he'd be tempted to chew the next one if he didn't get a decent breakfast soon. He considered the situation: he'd driven here early without eating and goodness knew how long he'd have to wait. The door opened, interrupting his train of thought. *About time.* Copley, dressed casually, strode down the road, got in his car and headed out of town. Bentley tailed him as far as a roundabout and watched him take the second exit on the A157, whereas Bentley turned back to Louth. He didn't know where the fellow was going and didn't care. It meant he would have plenty of time to grab some food and to pay a visit to the music school, in that order.

Over a full English breakfast in The Mason's Arms, Bentley considered the facts. He flicked open a small black notebook. Just after he got back to Grimsby yesterday afternoon Briggs rang. It turned out the symbols on the bone box had a meaning and the barrister, quick to inform Bentley, had access to the best brains in London. Bentley should find out what he could about a vanished Benedictine Priory. He sneered as he thought: "Bloody careless if you ask me. How can you lose a whole ruddy Priory?" There was nothing much by way of a lead, but that was what Bentley was paid for, wasn't it? He snorted and gulped down a mouthful of sausage. It was much easier tailing an unfaithful husband than this wild goose chase for missing treasure. His eye savaged his cup of tea *'the bloody thing's more than half empty and I've only just sat down.* He could murder a pint of ale but they'd only serve non-alcoholic beverages at this hour; how he pined for the good old days before speed traps and breathalysers, when people were at drunken liberty to wipe out whole families. He told himself he needed to drive this evening too, so he'd better behave. The thought of whisky back at his rented house brought a crooked smile. He reminisced with regret about smoking in pubs:

This soddin' job must be getting to me.

He thought about yesterday afternoon when he tried to get something out of that old geezer at Covenham. He waited for the kids to drive away and then went to question him. It hadn't worked. The old codger wouldn't tell him anything. Bentley could still see those watery eyes boring into him as if weighing up his character. "Shrewd old bugger." He clammed up good and proper. Short of beating up a ninety-year-old, there was no way he could make him talk about what the couple were after. He finished the pie and the beer and made a note in his book. Something to do with the past; maybe they were on to this Priory caper as well. The more he thought about it the more this seemed likely.

Outside, in the Market Place, he lit up a cigarette and rubbing the back of his neck to ease the tension he felt there, Bentley headed for the music school. Having ascertained that the woman had gone out too, Stephen Bentley couldn't believe how naïve these folks were. The woman knew that he'd been in the building before, yet she'd taken no precautions to stop him breaking in again. It was true that there hadn't been much time to replace the lock, but she couldn't see it as a priority. Entering had been just as easy as before and now to cap it all, there was an old map of Covenham dated 1805 on the table. Next to it was a long cylinder bearing a Berkshire postmark, labelled with the company name. The postmark was two days old. *Look at this.* They'd even marked the old priory on the map for him. He was beginning to love his job again. There was a pencilled X with a ring round it to the north-east of Covenham St. Bartholomew and the word "priory" in block letters. The detective took a blank sheet of paper out of the printer, laid it on the map and copied the exact position. Well, he thought, this more than made up for yesterday. He would be ready for them tomorrow morning, but right now whisky called.

JAKE AND ALICE decided to fill their spare morning by going to a hypermarket to stock up on supplies. Driving into the large carpark, he easily found a parking bay. In the flower bed bordering it a gardener was raking the ground in preparation for the huge number of larkspur and delphinium plants lined up ready for planting. When they had finished and loaded their bags into the car, Jake said, "You wait here, I'll take the trolley back to the rack and get the coin back."

As he walked away whistling, Alice watched the gardener toiling.

Having left the trolley, as he rounded the building, Jake was still piping a merry tune. Before he could react, a huge hand clamped over his mouth and his right arm was forced upwards behind his back. The enormous strength of his assailant propelled him behind the building where plastic bins lined the wall. Alice, intent on the gardener, had seen nothing of this attack.

The wrestler threw Jake against the wall and he twisted to take the impact on his left shoulder. There was no time to assess the damage. A huge fist swung towards his face, but he increased his sideways momentum and solid brick took the full force of the blow. Shocked and hurt, off-balance, the Romanian was open to counter attack. Jake seized his chance. Pressing a foot against the wall for added power, he head-butted the man in his solar plexus, taking him off his feet. As the brute landed with a thump on his back, he kicked him under the jaw, but his trainers were light. The man grunted and sat up. Jake had seen enough. This was the gorilla that shot at him in Rose Cottage. One glance at those massive tattooed forearms and the iron pectorals under his skin-tight T-shirt was enough for him. It was no contest. He'd been lucky so far. He sprinted for his life round the building towards his car, the man's heavy steps pounding behind him. Jake was always going to be faster, but there was the problem of getting into the car, not to mention the likelihood of being shot in the back. No shot came. He pumped his legs even faster and fumbled for the remote control on his car key. He reached the car and pointed the device, forgetting in his panic that it was already open with his wife inside. There was no time to open the door. The man's rhino charge was almost on him.

Jake grabbed a gardening fork planted upright in the ground and, spinning round, thrust its prongs into the man's thigh as he tried to turn away mid-charge. The man screamed and blood spurted as Jake pulled the fork free and flung it to the ground.

He unthreaded his belt, threw it at the man sitting on the ground, bloody hands over a spurting wound. "Tourniquet!" he shouted and dialled for an ambulance. He refused to give his name and rang off. *Thank God for the gardener,* who was running towards him.

"I'll explain everything later. Stay with him and tighten that belt and hold it tight. Don't tell the police anything, trust me. This man is a Russian spy. Just say you were working and when you turned around, you found the man bleeding. If they ask, say it's your belt. Here, give me yours."

Impressed by Jake's manner, tone, and the Land Rover, the gardener, with just one state exam in art to his name, wasn't going to argue with this posh bloke. Open-mouthed, he obeyed and hoped he was doing the right thing. The Russian spy looked like a nasty piece of work and as an innocent bystander, he'd be only too pleased to do as the posh fellow had said. They could do nothing to him, could they? The Russian wouldn't blame him, in any case.

Jake got into the car and drove to Louth, clutching the steering wheel so hard his knuckles were white. He passed an ambulance with blue light flashing on the way. The gardener's last words were ringing in his ears "Thank God you missed the artery, he'd be dead in no time otherwise."

His shoulder was throbbing. "Thank God," indeed. As he told Alice, he didn't want a killing on his conscience, as opposed to these people, who it seemed would stop at nothing. He wondered why the gorilla hadn't shot him in the back. Another thing was clearer to him: these others were one step ahead. He and Alice needed to be far sharper to outwit them and come out on top.

He pulled into a layby and phoned Sir Clive, giving him an explanation. As he had hoped, his boss decided to phone the Lincolnshire Chief of Police so that the matter could be covered up.

Central London

It had been a very trying day for David Briggs. First, his driver had had an emergency operation in Lincoln County Hospital and although he had lost a lot of blood he was out of danger. He would have to manage without a chauffeur and drive himself for the foreseeable future. Then an important divorce case had to be put back a week, because the Lincolnshire Police needed all his attention.

He had faxed them Doganu's documents and assured them of his *bona fide* position as his chauffeur. It had been much more difficult persuading them that he had no idea what Victor was doing in Lincoln. He insisted that it was the Romanian's day off and whatever he did in his free time was his business and not that of his employer. And no, he couldn't understand why the driver wouldn't cooperate to help track down his attacker. Briggs suggested that the reason may lie in Doganu's communist past, perhaps a latent distrust of state police. This seemed to mollify the inspector, who, oddly enough, seemed eager to go through the motions and drop the case.

It had come as a relief to Briggs to learn that the police

unfortunately had no CCTV footage to help them. It was essential they learn nothing about Jake Conley and Briggs's involvement in the matter. That idiot Victor! Was it possible that everything he touched turned to sludge? Once back in active service he'd restrict him to simple dogsbody tasks. All that muscle wasted because he lacked a brain.

Briggs sat back in his plush leather chair. He sighed and reflected; it hadn't been a good idea. Better to leave things in Bentley's hands. He must learn to have faith in other people's abilities.

SIXTEEN

NEAR COVENHAM, LINCOLNSHIRE 2021 AD

Arriving early at the point on the road northeast of Covenham St. Bartholomew indicated on his copied map, Bentley's first move was to find a place to hide the Fiesta. That took some time, because there was nowhere suitable until he was about half a mile away, where he'd found a narrow lane with a lay-by. He locked the car there and went on foot to the place in a field marked with a cross by the youngsters. Bentley looked around confused. There didn't seem to be anything but grass in the field at that point. He shrugged his shoulders, double checked his copy of the map and went to the field boundary, where he jumped a ditch and found a break in the hedge beyond. He went through the hedge and stationed himself with a pair of binoculars and waited. Bentley became as one with the hedge life and, city man that he was, he had no idea of how much went on in a hedgerow. There was nothing to do except study the movement of small mammals, birds and insects. For him, this was comparable to watching paint dry. Give him a porn video anytime with a can of beer and a comfortable sofa—now that was wildlife—but this, no thank you. Ladybirds, wrens, hedgehogs, shrews, orange tip and peacock butterflies came and went as indifferent to the motionless Bentley as he was to them. He waited for two hours, smoked eight cigarettes, but by ten o'clock, stiff and disgruntled, it dawned on him that the couple wasn't coming and that maybe the two of them weren't as naïve as he'd thought. There was no sign in the field of any building either modern or ancient. Realising that the X on the map was a red herring and that he'd underrated them, he went back to his car, angry with himself, and resolved not to try anticipating their moves again. From now on back to the tried and tested methods: their shadows wouldn't be as close as he meant to stick to them.

SEVENTEEN

After the short trip to Covenham Jake crawled along, checking his rear-view mirror every few seconds. When he pulled up near the public footpath, he was certain nobody had followed them. He parked the Citroen just off the road and changed into his boots. Alice was already wearing hers.

They set off down the path. It was easy going at first, but further along it began to get slippery and they had to avoid some muddy puddles. On either side of them were open fields that had been ploughed in long furrows with wide sweeping turns at the end near the road. On the upturned soil the usual avian worm massacre was underway. The path began to rise and occasional stretches of hawthorn bushes bordered the fields. At the foot of the hedge, glossy yellow starred celandines and delicate violets added a touch of colour to an otherwise drab footpath.

Alice stopped him for a moment to look at three yellow birds ahead of them on the path. As they walked towards them, they flew ahead for another fifteen yards or so and landed with their tails bobbing up and down. The path was still rising and Jake pointed out that this must be the *noggin* Jacob mentioned. Ahead of them they could see a line of trees and before long the path led them into Bardsley's Wood.

Oak, ash, sycamore and maple dominated the dense bracken and bramble undergrowth. The track was still defined, but the going was slippery here, so they had to slow down. At one point a raucous jay flew, in a whirl of gaudy feathers, across their path. Birdsong filtered down from the trees and a few alarm calls sounded as they passed. Jake motioned his wife to stand still and listen to a woodpecker hammering at a tree. The trail began to narrow, hemmed in by thick, prickly undergrowth and fallen trees and branches patched with emerald green moss. The light was gloomy and he slipped, going down on one knee. He swore and straightening up, he cursed at a large, wet brown mark on his jeans. They continued along the way, with bramble thorns whipping across their jeans and low woody plants shedding their dew on to them. By the time they reached the far edge of the wood they were bedraggled and damp. Ahead of them lay a large ploughed field and as they broke out of the wood a flock of starlings wheeled up into the air. They looked around them and he pointed to the left.

"On the map, the sheepfold was towards the left-hand side of the woods. It should be about two hundred yards that way."

They skirted the woods and came to a halt at a low oval shape, buried in the grass bordering the ploughed field, defined by the long shadows of the early sun.

"I'm sure this is our sheepfold," he said, "look, here's the entrance."

"But what's happened to all the other stones above ground?"

"Carted off for building, I imagine. Too much trouble to dig out the stones used as foundation for the pen."

"But Jake, where do we start looking now? Do you think they buried the treasure inside the pen? I mean, we need a metal detector to cover the whole area."

"I don't think they'd have buried it in there, but we can't rule it out; as a last resort we'd have to pass a metal detector over it. They aren't cheap, as you know. Maybe they're for hire. But I think the treasure will be hidden under a stone."

He began to walk along the grassy hump of the pen outline and sighed, "There's a lot of stones to check. Let's try and get into our man's head. What would he have done? If you were going to hide a treasure under a stone, which stone would you choose?"

Alice had an idea. "I'd choose one that I could find again. Let's say one of the two stones either side of the gate. And, I'd mark the stone in some way: a sort of sign."

He felt the dull ache in his forehead and swayed on his feet. This was the right place— the ache confirmed it.

"You could be right. It's a start anyway. Let's go with that. What we need now is something to dig with."

He walked to the edge of the woods and found a small track, perhaps made by an animal. He plunged into the undergrowth and returned a few minutes later with two hefty sticks. Alice was already ripping away the grass to the left of the opening. He gave her one of the sticks and they started to remove the earth that had built up over the stone and no doubt over the centuries, working at opposite sides from one another. It was tiring work and soon they were both sweating.

"Why didn't we think of bringing a couple of spades?" she said, breathing hard as she took a break.

"Today was meant to be reconnaissance, sizing up the situation. But since we're here—"

He paused from his digging and gazed round in the early morning sunlight. In the distance over the ploughed fields he could see some farm buildings and hear the faint chugging of a tractor. There was no other sign of human life and he felt sure that they were inconspicuous with the wood so close behind them. The sticks were ineffective tools; still, after an hour or so, they'd managed to expose the whole stone.

"Clean your side and look for a carved sign," he told her, but he didn't sound very confident. They scraped the last of the earth away and examined the stone, but there were no marks. He went back to the woods and returned, jeans dotted with sticky burrs, carrying a log and a thick branch. He placed the log for a fulcrum and levered the branch under the stone. With little resistance he raised the long piece of limestone and Alice helped him turn it over. They cleaned the earth from the bottom, but there was no mark and nothing in the earth under it except many creepy, scurrying insects. The sun, as it rose in the sky, fleeting behind huge cumulus clouds alternated bright and dull across the landscape. They guided the stone back in its hole and turned to tackle the other stone on the right side of the gate but once again they were disappointed and now it was almost midday.

"I'm knackered," said Jake, "let's call it a day for now. We can't go on like this with every stone or we'll be at it all year."

Alice said nothing, but was happy to break off, she recognised that he had done the lion's share of the digging. His arms were glistening with sweat. So, somewhat discouraged, they retraced their steps to the car, wondering if they would have better luck with the correct tools. It still seemed a daunting task, because the two most obvious stones hadn't yielded a clue. She thought about the size of those two stones. On that basis there would be about sixty of them. She sighed. Even with good spades it would take days, if they found the sign on the very last stone, say, assuming such a sign existed.

They changed out of their muddy boots and set off back to Louth to buy the tools, each lost in their thoughts.

EIGHTEEN

Bentley had spent a frustrating morning driving around Louth and to make matters worse it was market day. He discovered that there was no sign of their car. They had given him the slip. Just as he was contemplating another visit to The Mason's Arms, he spotted the Land Rover drawing up to a red traffic light. Bentley got in the queue and followed several vehicles behind them. They were on the road to the flat. His quarry pulled up outside and, Bentley, parking at a safe distance, watched the young woman get out. His trained eye took in her boots as she trudged through the gate.

"They've been in the country all right—the priory." Bentley cursed.

A few minutes later, she was out again this time wearing pink trainers and a matching T-shirt. Then they were off. Bentley followed them out of town and had to be careful when they took a minor road into the countryside. Were they heading for the Priory? No...he dismissed that idea. She would have kept her boots on.

Their destination became clear as they entered the

village of Scamblesby and pulled into the car park of the Green Man. Bentley considered what to do. Neither of them had seen his face. No, it was quite safe; he'd be just another customer. He drove straight into the car park and saw that the couple had already found a table in the garden. He strolled with nonchalance over to a painted sign and read: ***Bind me you woodbines in your twines*** and lost interest: he'd had more than enough of nature for one day.

He found Copley at the bar ordering drinks and a meal and he did likewise. There was no eye contact. Bentley followed him out to the garden and took the next table. He kept his back to them, ears pricked like a hound, to snap up their every word. He sneered at Copley drinking bitter lemon.

"If I were hiding treasure there," Copley said, "I don't think I'd put it near the gate, after all. You know what? I think I'd do just the opposite. I mean, I'd put it opposite the gate."

"That's a possibility, I suppose. So tomorrow we can begin at the spot right opposite the gate and work our way sideways. It'll be a lot easier with the spades and the pick. Look at my hand it's full of blisters," she stuck it under his nose.

"Well, I hope whatever that psalm was referring to is worth a fortune after all this hard slog."

Bentley's interest was aroused. *What psalm?*

A waitress brought their food. Jake tormented Alice about how pretty the waitress was and the virtues of a single life.

Bentley's food arrived and just as he was losing interest in their stupid conversation, the young fellow said: "We'll head for the same place at nine o'clock tomorrow: it seemed to work all right this morning; it seems nobody followed us."

She bent over and kissed him and whispered in his ear. "After all that digging, you'll need a good rest tonight." She smiled and sipped at her beer with a roguish twinkle in her eye. "There are no parking restrictions on Sundays, so you can drive to the museum and leave the car there. It's further than I thought on foot. I was almost late this morning."

"All right, but remember to take a circuitous route. Make sure you're not followed."

A crooked smile, and Bentley finished his beer and left, snorting at the thought of bitter lemon, "Bloody fitness freak," he muttered under his breath, thinking, *give me a man who likes his ale*— which proved he didn't know Jake Conley at all. The detective smiled as he got in the car and set off for Grimsby. He just had to check out where the museum was and tomorrow, they'd lead him straight to the treasure and the beauty of it was, they'd do all the hard graft and he'd just help himself to the loot.

The next morning, when Jake pulled up on Ings Lane, Bentley, who had been following, drove past and pulled in by a field gate. He waited for twenty minutes and then drove back, to park just past the Land Rover. Focusing his binoculars his gaze swept up the public footpath until he spotted them in the distance. Just beyond a rise he could make out the treetops of a wood they were heading towards. Bentley decided to move at once for fear of losing them in the woods.

He was soon cursing the conditions underfoot. He should have remembered to get some boots; his suede shoes would never recover. The consolation of a fat cheque awaiting him didn't inspire the prospect of a wardrobe full of shoes, his crooked smile creased his face, but rather a cabinet full of fine single malts. Conditions could have been worse, last week it rained almost every day and this path would have been a quagmire. Instead, today, the sky was clear except for a few high wispy clouds: just the job for a country mud bath. Bentley took a deep breath–how he missed London's exhaust fumes.

Dense patches of cow parsley fringed the edge of the woods. Bentley sneezed, irritated by the pollen. Once in the woods he moved with care. He didn't want to crash through the undergrowth and alert his quarry. There was a strange timelessness under this canopy of leaves. Before long the ground was covered with dense ivy. Uncertain, and out of his natural habitat, Bentley stopped a moment and looked around him "I'm like a soddin' stag at Oxford Circus," he laughed at the thought and startled a chiffchaff perched on a nearby branch. Bentley saw its olive-green flash. Not that he knew what a chiffchaff was. He was visually illiterate as far as birds were concerned. He knew what pigeons and magpies were: there were plenty of those in London. As the detective tiptoed along the tangled trail, he reflected on his ignorance. What were those red berries and those brown fungi? He must make an effort when he got back to the Big Smoke. It was shameful not to know one tree from another. After all there were plenty of books on nature. Then he shook his head, no, let's be realistic, he didn't care a crap about nature. When he came to the end of the woods, he was extra careful; peering out from behind a tree, he scanned his surroundings. There was a large ploughed field dotted with crows and starlings. In the distance were some farm buildings joined to the woods by a public footpath. On his left, Bentley saw the youngsters each holding a spade. They seemed to be in an animated discussion. He decided that he'd have to get nearer without being seen or heard, so he ducked back into the woods.

Meanwhile, Jake and Alice were standing near the two exposed stones from the day before. He pointed across the sheep pen.

"That's about opposite the entrance," he paced across to a point facing her. "I'll start here, with this stone. You take the one next to me on the left and we'll work outwards in both directions."

She joined him without a word.

"But let's just clean up the outer side of each stone, because I reckon that he'd have left a sign on the outside of the pen, not on the inside. And that will halve the effort and the time."

She thought about this. "I'm not so sure. Maybe the sheepfold wasn't in use anymore when the treasure was hidden. It would have been too risky if there were shep—" she stopped short, "what was that?"

They'd both heard the sharp sound of a branch cracking in the woods. They listened in silence. There was just the sound of birdsong. Jake relaxed,

"I'm guessing it was an animal, a fox maybe."

"...I was saying, it would have been too risky to hide the treasure here if there were shepherds around. So, he could have marked a stone on the inside."

Jake nodded, "You may be right. But I think it was still in use in the seventeenth century. Look at it this way, if we clean up just the outside, we'll cover a longer stretch and if I'm right, we'll find the mark sooner."

"And if you're wrong, we'll find it later." she laughed, but then added, "come on then, let's get going, or we won't find anything at all."

The spades made it much easier to remove the grass

from the stones and to clean the exposed side using the paint scraper he had brought. The first five stones were disappointingly blank, but Alice squealed in delight.

"Look. There's something here!"

He threw down his spade and joined her. She was right. As she cleaned away the soil an incision appeared in the stone face. She scraped with vigour and soon, line-by-line, the crude carved form of a broken cup appeared.

"The symbol of the Olivetans," he whispered. "Alice. We've done it. We've found the treasure."

"Not yet we haven't. Someone else might have been here centuries ago."

"Well, we'll soon find out."

He ran over to the pen entrance and picked up the log and the thick branch he'd used the day before to lever up the stone. With little difficulty he prised the stone out of its hole. Together they rolled it over into the pen.

Jake went over to the pick and carried it to the hole. The moment of truth. Their faces were flushed with excitement as he swung the pick several times and loosened the soil for his wife to dig. There was a dull sound as she hit something solid. She threw down the spade, fetched the scraper and, removing the soil with care, brought a rotten wooden box to light. The earth around the box fell away as she tried to ease it out of the ground. One side broke off, revealing some dirty white linen. Alice used the scraper to push the box lid upwards and Jake wrenched it free, despite feeling sick from his pounding forehead and his spinning head. Alice lifted the object wrapped in linen and held it for what seemed an eternity to him, marvelling at its weight. Still squatting beside the hole, she spoke in an awed voice.

"Jake, nobody has seen this for more than three hundred and fifty years."

She unwound the tattered cloth and a flash in the morning sun dazzled them, a solid gold dove inlaid with a garnet-coloured stone lay in Alice's delicate hand. Its tarnished silver wing feathers glinted in the sunlight. The eye of the dove was a red jewel like a ruby, sparkling as if in joy of liberation. Mouth open in amazement, she turned it over in her hand. The back wasn't beautifully worked like the front, but there were some words inscribed there. She found her voice and faltered over the words: *lang dun* and below, the single word *treōw* and then *ac cyning*.

They straightened up and Alice said, "I've never seen anything so beautiful. It must be worth a fortune. It's Anglo-Saxon."

"You're the would-be archaeologist. Is that writing Old English then? From the Dark Ages?" She ignored the provocation. "We'll have to declare it, and it's up to the experts to tell us how old it is."

"But it *is* Old English and it's Anglo-Saxon, so at the very latest it's tenth century and perhaps earlier."

A harsh laugh followed by a raucous voice cut in, "I'm afraid I can't go along with that."

They spun round to face the sardonic grin of a man with a gun in his hand. Jake had heard the voice before and he recognised him as the man from the next table at the pub yesterday. His heart sank as he realised they'd betrayed themselves with careless talk.

"You!" Alice shrieked terrorised; she would never forget that voice either. Now she saw her ex-captor for the first time, a heavy man in his mid-forties, unshaven, a red, bulbous nose, his thick brown hair greying at the temples. The bottom of his trousers and his shoes were covered in mud, but his hazel eyes glowed with triumph.

"Put the birdie on the ground lassie and back off both of

you ...keep going...OK... now sit down." He stepped forward and without taking his eyes off them, bent down and picked up the dove. Bentley whistled through his teeth, "Somebody's going to pay a lot of money for this—to me." His laugh grated on their ears. "It was very kind of you to lead me to this little beauty," he said with a crooked smile, slipping the dove into his jacket pocket, "and so good of you to do all the hard digging, what with this hot weather and all. It's true that we're all alone out here and nobody can see us," he said. Alice's heart thudded fit to burst and she clutched Jake's hand, squeezing it tight. "But just to show you that I'm not an ungrateful person, you won't be harmed —on one condition. Listen. I'm going to walk away," he studied their faces, "and you don't move from here for twenty minutes. It's half-past ten now. You've got a watch," he pointed with the pistol at Jake. There's no sense in wasting young lives when I can make a clean getaway with a little cooperation. Understood?"

Jake nodded. Of course, he could have tried his mind-binding powers but why risk Alice's life? The man might be frightened of his penetrating stare and start panic-shooting. As matters stood, he meant them no harm. No ancient jewel was worth the risk to his wife.

"I'm glad you understand a kind offer when you hear it. Oh, and by the way, I wouldn't go trotting off to the police either. I can get to you before they ever find me."

Bentley backed away, slipped the gun in its holster and crouched down to get the pick and spades.

"Best to remove all temptation to silliness," his grating laugh rang out again and he turned and marched along the edge of the woods. Every ten paces he turned to make sure they were still sitting on the ground. He disappeared down the path among the trees. With some relief he dropped the spades and pick as soon as he was out of sight. His right arm was shaking from the weight. Bentley sped up; it would be a shame to blunder now. The couple, he reckoned, would be too scared or too sensible to make a move for twenty minutes. He smiled; his gun only was an embellishment in this case—nice people.

By the car, he cleaned the worst of the mud from his shoes with a twig and wiped them on the grass. He considered letting down the Land Rover tyres, but when he looked up the path there was no sign of life, so he got into his hired car and drove to London, where he completed the formalities of returning it to the rental company. Bentley congratulated himself on a successful operation concluded.

Jake wandered over to where they had found the treasure and absent-mindedly picked up the discarded, half-rotted piece of linen Alice had dropped. No sooner was it in his hand than the air around him vibrated and warped and he sank to the ground with his head spinning into blackness.

Alice gaped and rushed to him. He had confided his retrocognitive experiences to her but this was the first time she'd seen their effect. Sitting beside him on the grass, she stroked his head and waited, noting the disturbing pallor in his cheeks and the eyes moving under his closed lids.

NINETEEN

KINGDOM OF LINDSEY, 674 AD

JAKE ROSE GROGGILY TO HIS FEET AND LOOKED AROUND him in amazement. The landscape was different because he was standing in dense woodland at night with no sense of where he was nor with any idea of what era.

Skeletal oak branches beckoned in the form-changing moonlight and Werburgh made the sign of the Cross. Her stomach lurched, sick of the forest in the weird night: the flitter of bat wings, the barn owl's shriek. Bears and wolves and worse lurked among gaunt wayside trees. For sure, just as scudding clouds hid the stars, fiends and ogres lived hidden in the thick, black undergrowth; Werburgh prayed demons might not appear as suddenly as the North Star emerged against the ink-black sky. Her lips moved in a wordless prayer, imploring angels to save them from earthbound horrors: bands of thieves and cutthroats. Startled, she nearly dropped the reins at a wolf howl, too loud, too close. Eyes screwed up tight, she besought the help of St. Arilda, protectress of maidens.

Jake heard the same yowl and cringed. As far as he

could remember, in 2021 there had been no wolves in England for centuries. Here he was unarmed and lost— all he could do was pray that a wolf pack wouldn't sniff him out. He'd climb a tree at the first sound of onrushing paws.

Werburgh cursed herself for a coward and, rubbing her shoulder, groaned and shifted her slight frame. Her bones, jarred and jostled by the ox-cart pitching and creaking along the rutted track, ached at her every move. Her spirit near failed at the thought of Eldride lying in the box behind her. How she must be suffering. Poor Eldride, chosen from among the other nuns for her small childlike body; at her feet lay the treasure of the Abbey of Ely, wrapped with her, hidden in a winding sheet. However, this journey, this sacrifice, was to bury the treasure not the corpse of a young woman.

Jake froze on the spot, a crashing through the undergrowth and he was face to face, not with wolves, but with men: ragged, desperate-looking men with cudgels. They stomped straight towards him, but, as sometimes happened in retrocognition, they could not see him. It depended on the psychic potency of the place he arrived in. This was a forest and not a spiritually strong place. There probably wasn't any such for miles. If the scoundrels couldn't see him, nor would the wolves, he thought cheerfully, and he began to follow the rogues, sure to be outlaws. He was lost; they, at least, provided him with a sense of direction.

Werburgh glanced at Odelyna, lolling by her side, face white as a wimple. How she envied the older woman her ease of sleep. Her own nights were without end. Two nights and Odelyna, lulled by the plod of the ox wending through Mercia and into Lindsey, snored on. Yet, not even Odelyna was able to doze through Werburgh's nightmare-come-true

– men. Three of them, wielding heavy clubs, sprang from among the trees. The tallest grabbed the ox harness, forcing the beast to halt. Filthy, lank hair hung over his shoulders and the wan light hollowed his cheek, forming the half image of a grinning skull, gap-toothed and hideous. Unarmed, helpless to intervene, Jake looked on and heard the villain shout,

"Money, rings. Quick about it!"

Faint with fear, Werburgh scarcely found voice to reply. "God save your souls, brother, we have no coin. We are but two brides of Christ on our way to bury our poor sister at her place of birth," Werburgh turned and pointed to the wooden box on the cart. She prayed fervently that Eldride lie still and corpselike. One of the thieves neared the cart and peered over the side, while the tall one, the leader, leapt nimbly onto the cart and bent over Eldride. Werburgh held her breath, as did Eldride. The man studied the closed eyes of the nun and time stood still; satisfied, he made the sign of the Cross, jumped down next to his companions, then came around to the driver's side where they all stared at the two women in their grey habits. One of them, a stocky man with close-set eyes leered up at Werburgh.

"Here. This one's a rare beauty. I say we take her here and now."

He put one hand on the side of the cart, hauled himself up and grabbed at Werburgh. Odelyna, fast and lethal as an adder, thrust a knife into his face. It pierced the man's eye and brain. Lifeless, his body thumped to the ground. The nun screamed and sobbing flung the bloody knife into the trees. At the same time the shrouded Eldride sat up in her coffin and shrieked. Awe and terror contorted the faces of the other two thieves who fled like startled crows into the woods. Jake watched them flee with relief and mused: *The power of superstition.*

"Hush, hush," Werburgh hugged and rocked Odelyna and though older, she let her head fall on to Werburgh's breast, taking comfort like a child.

"Lie back down Eldride," hissed Werburgh, "you're supposed to be dead, remember." She glanced down at the real corpse. May God forgive them but there was no time to bury him. She urged the ox forward and the cart rumbled slowly away from the dead man. Invisible to them, Jake ran up to the cart and hoisted himself into the space between Elride's feet and the side-board. No point in walking when he could steal a ride. *In any case, I'm meant to be here, goodness knows why. I wonder what date? Since the cloth brought me here, and from their speech, these are Anglo-Saxon times.* Werburgh murmured a prayer for the dead man's soul and then begged forgiveness for Odelyna, whose tears wet Werburgh's woollen habit through to her skin. The danger was past and Werburgh began to tremble. The thought of what might have been, made her feel sick. She breathed in deeply and willed her body to be still, begging God, in His mercy, to forgive them. The older nun was numb with shock and Werburgh held her tightly; later there would be time a-plenty to talk of God's wrath and mercy, but now Odelyna needed peace and calmness.

Another thought struck her, the thieves were after their money and rings and yet unwittingly left riches beyond their dreams: all the treasure of the Abbey of Ely. Ah dreams. Her eyes filled with tears and she blinked them away. In truth, they were here now thanks to a dream. Four nights ago, God had shown her the men from north of the Humber and the flames and bloodshed to be wreaked on Ely. Afterwards, in His mercy, God had also shown her a place to hide their treasure. Werburgh's great-aunt, Aethelreda, her tutor and mother superior, one-time Queen of Northumbria, bowed to the will of God. She consented to her niece travelling into the Kingdom of Lindsey by night with a promise that all the nuns of Ely would pray for their safety and the safekeeping of the precious burden. Well, their prayers had not been in vain. The outlaws had fled. How could she doubt the Lord's will? Comforted, her body stilled its trembling and the menacing shadows seemed to slink deeper into the woods.

The cart rumbled on through the night and Werburgh's arm was on fire from the unnatural position of supporting Odelyna. It grieved her to wake the nun after her shock, but she was losing the struggle to hold the reins and cradle Odelyna at the same time. She wondered when this torment would end. The pain in her arm worsened, but she thought of Our Lord's sufferings on the Cross and bit her lip. Hours dragged by and mercifully the fire in her arm died down to a numb ache. Jake was not too comfortable either. His chief concern was not to roll against Eldride. He didn't want her screaming again. He dreaded to think what an Anglian nun would make of an invisible man. The ox followed the straight track along this flat land, so there was no need to tug the reins. Meanwhile Odelyna slept on and the beast plodded stolidly as the track began to rise slowly up a long, wooded hill. Then, at last, Werburgh saw it standing black against the mottled moon, as in her dream: a wayside cross with a tall carved shaft on a huge stone base. It marked the crossing of two ways slicing swathes through the dense woodland. As a girl, she had prayed here, folded in her father's woollen cloak, sheltered against the cold. Joyfully, she stopped the ox-cart and woke Odelyna and Eldride.

"This is the place, here." she called, and Odelyna jerked

upright, her eyes full of sleep. Werburgh shook her with her good arm, the other limp by her side. "Quick. Help me unwind Eldride." Jake leapt out of the cart and staggered, his legs stiff and numb from the uncomfortable cramping position of the ride. *At least I saved myself a long hike. What's going on here?*

She looked up at the moon, it was lower in the sky, but she thought there must still be two hours before dawn. Eldride groaned and stamped her feet against her stiffness, but obediently grasped the spade thrust into her hand. Odelyna's large hand grabbed another and Werburgh took the last one from the cart. She turned and glanced upwards to the top of the shaft with its huge stone cross towering above them. Her eyes ran down the carvings and there she read the Temptation of Adam and Eve before dropping her gaze to a winged devil whose hideous face, accentuated by the moonlight, made her flesh creep. The base of the shaft was an oblong with a carved border, made up of rounded shapes. Werburgh bent to study them and by the wan light of the moon, she made out the circles formed of odd long-legged birds, their heads arched back over their bodies and their beaks biting their tails. The moonlight cast heavy shadows in the carving so that the feathers stood out. Werburgh smiled at the cleverness of the craftsman and her gaze shifted to within the frame. Baleful carved eyes stared back at her and from a stone mouth tumbled entwined leaves and fronds.

"The Oak King," Werburgh murmured and shifted damp and rotting leaves with her spade, "we'll bury it here and he'll watch over it for us." *So that's what they're up to—burying treasure. That's why I'm here but how will I find the place again in our century?* It was heavy work to shift the clay soil and their delicate hands, used only to sewing, were soon blistered and sore. The wearing journey had taken its toll of their strength and, exhausted, they worked slowly. She thanked the Lord that she had brought the hefty Odelyna. Nearly an hour passed before Werburgh was satisfied with the depth of the hole—about five feet. It was almost beyond them to push and slide the oak chest lined with lead, in its crude coffin, down to the ground. Kicking feebly and levering with their spades, at last, they forced the end of the coffin away from its nails and, passing a short rope under the chest, Werburgh and Odelyna lowered it down into its resting place. *I wonder what's inside that baby.* He saw Werburgh throw the winding sheet on top of it and the three nuns said a prayer for the safekeeping of the treasure. *That looks like the same kind of linen that was around the dove. But that jewel was separate from this hoard.* Hurriedly they filled the hole and lifted the broken coffin back on to the cart before Werburgh led the other two some way off to load leaf litter onto their spades and carry it back to hide the freshly turned earth. They did this several times until they were sure that on the morrow no passing eye would see disturbed ground. Then they turned the cart round and made their long, slow way back to the Abbey of Ely. More uncomfortable cart riding did not appeal to Jake, who watched them disappear, silently wishing them a safe journey. He concentrated on Alice and was overcome by the familiar dizzy sensation.

ONE MOON LATER, 674 AD.

DAY SPEARED by Night bled slowly across the sky: thus, the heavens mirrored the blood seeping into the earth below.

The men of Mercia lay slain on the battlefield. Surrounded by his ealdormen, Ecgfrith, king of the lands north of the Humber, raised his gory axe above his head. A wild roar burst from the throats of the northern host. Lindsey was theirs and the way lay open to plunder Mercia...

TWENTY

LOUTH, LINCOLNSHIRE, 2021 AD

Jake's eyes flickered open and Alice peered down at him, concerned. His face was so pale and wan.

"Are you alright, my love?"

His weak gin was more like a grimace, "I've just watched three nuns bury a chest full of treasure."

"Where? Will you be able to find it?"

"I doubt it. All I know is that it was by a trail through a forest and they buried it beside a stone cross at the top of a long hill."

She looked pleased. "that's a lot of information, Jake. I think we can use it to start a treasure hunt. If we find your chest, it'll make the dove pale into insignificance." At last, the bitter bile of losing the jewel at the moment of their triumph left her.

Jake glanced at his watch and waited with his arm around Alice, in retrocognition time had no meaning. The journey with the nuns had lasted agonising hours, but here, he'd only been unconscious for fewer than three minutes. The overturned stones lay like an accusation in front of him. He was frustrated and resentful at the loss of the jewel, but he wasn't going to risk any harm coming to his wife. In any case, he was no match for a determined man with a gun. It was a few minutes before he spoke.

"I'm sorry," his tone bitter, "I should never have put us in this situation in the first place. Thinking about it, it was obvious he'd come after us. I just got carried away with the idea of the treasure. I should have waited a few months until things calmed down. I'd no right to risk your safety."

Alice snuggled closer to him, "Hey, what's all this it's my fault stuff? We're in this together and I don't remember being any less enthusiastic than you."

He summoned up a smile; she had a happy knack of making him feel better.

"Anyway, it's all over now," he said, "we should have taken more precautions, with hindsight, but I suppose that at least we can get back to normal life without any risk of kidnappings or threats and without any dreams of getting rich or famous."

She wriggled free of his embrace and gave him a challenging stare, "That's where you're wrong. You see, darling, we've lost the jewel, but we can still solve the riddle."

"What riddle?"

"I might be wrong, but those words carved in the back, I think they're a kind of clue or map intended to lead the bearer to something else— the buried treasure you saw."

He looked puzzled and thought about this for a moment. "They may be like a maker's mark or something like that."

"I don't think so; a maker would just put his initials or a date. Those words were like a message, I'm sure of it— a cipher to lead to the treasure. I wonder why the nuns were burying it? For sure they lived in troubled times."

He rubbed his forehead, "Oh well, even if you're right, don't you think that man, or whoever sent him, will think the same thing? You, more than anyone, should know how ruthless he is. He might not think twice about shooting us next time."

"So, you want to let him get away with *our* jewel? It's ours by rights." Her voice had an unusual shrillness to it, but now she forced herself to be calmer and her tone softened, "First of all, these people may not realise the importance of the inscription and even if they do, they might not be able to solve it—"

"We might not, either."

She ignored him, "...and second, they'll think that we gave those words no importance, all of which means that we could still get there before them and take the treasure first."

"What treasure? There's no proof there's any treasure." He was aware of the cynicism in his voice, most of it born from frustration. "And what about our track record at beating them? Anyway, even if we wanted to, we haven't got the words on the back of the dove." But he was forgetting that his wife was a secret agent and perhaps more expert than he.

"We don't need them. I can remember them and I'm sure they are a clue to more treasure."

Jake marvelled at her; she was so much cleverer than he. How had she entered the Secret Service? He must find out, he thought, glancing at his watch. He didn't say what he was thinking, judging it better to wait for a better moment; instead, he said, "It should be safe to go now, more than twenty minutes have passed." He hoped she would change her mind about the treasure—it was such a dangerous business—when she got over the bitter resentment of having the dove snatched away from them at the very instant of their success.

Their first steps were hesitant but they picked up speed as the path reached the wood. The spades and pick were just inside among the trees so they carried them back to the car, Alice thinking that they might prove useful for unearthing the main treasure. The immediate danger had passed, but tiredness and tension made them argue on the way home.

She wanted to start research on the words on the back of the jewel as soon as she got back to the flat. He was against it, saying that they were inviting more danger. This led to her calling him a coward and to him accusing her of being irresponsible. She left the car in stony silence and he parked feeling miserable.

She ran up the steps and noted the dark shadows under her eyes when she looked at herself in the wall mirror. She recoiled at the harsh expression that stared back at her, but the familiar flat soothed her in its cocoon-like embrace. She switched on the computer. Next, she filled the kettle and crammed a cracker out of the open packet into her mouth. Her anger with Jake had unsettled her stomach and although she regretted calling him a coward, she was furious that he wouldn't go along with her idea. She'd had the dove in her hands and, although she wasn't an expert, she'd felt its power. She could still see the intense colour of the ruby eye and its sparkle. They'd been clever to find it and it seemed like destiny that it should be theirs. It'd been stolen but she had a second chance, maybe to find something even more beautiful. Her eyes widened, her intuition told her she was right, but Jake Copley specialised in scorn and dampening her enthusiasm. She would show him.

The first inscription, she remembered, was *lang dun*. It

must be Old English and when she found an on-line dictionary it translated as *long hill* – and hadn't her husband spoken of a cross at the top of one such. The other inscriptions "*treōw*" and "*ac cyning*" meant *cross*—there—he'd said that, too. And *Oak King*. This, last inscription meant nothing to her, but the other two facts had proved to be exact. They were on to something important.

Alice sat back and wondered what to do. She typed *crosses* into the search engine and got a whole gamut of crosses: Huguenot, Carpathian, Celtic and even vampire crosses. She needed to refine her search, so she typed *Anglo-Saxon crosses a*nd found that these were often used to mark points where paths intersected, though they were later used as a gathering place for religious observance. She also found that wayside crosses might have been put up at sites already regarded as sacred in pagan worship. Jotting some notes down on a piece of paper, she leant back in her chair.

OK, but she was no further forward. Next, she put in *Oak King a*nd discovered that he was an old pagan god, the Lord of the Greenwood and golden twin of the waxing year, who rules from Midwinter to Midsummer. At Midwinter, he goes to battle with his twin, the Holly King, for the favour of the Goddess. He slays the Holly King, who goes to rest in Caer Arianrhod until they do battle again at Midsummer. The Oak King and Holly King are mortal enemies at Midsummer and Midwinter, but they are two sides of a whole. Neither could exist without the other. At Beltane, the peak of the Oak King's reign, he mates with the Great Mother, it's a sacrifice because dies in her embrace, and is resurrected. This is an enactment of the natural fertility theme of the season. The Holly King on the other hand, mates, dies and is resurrected at Lammas, in this way they fulfil their roles as fertility gods. She also found that carvings of the Oak King could be found in Anglo-Saxon churches and even on their crosses. What was this? An Oak King carved on a Saxon cross on a long hill. She sighed; even her enthusiasm couldn't take her any further. She was tired and realised there must be hundreds of thousands of long hills in England and hundreds in Lincolnshire alone. Should she begin to search the area around Covenham? She bit her lip and thought of Jake. Where was he? Was he sulking like a schoolboy? Marriage was no easy ride. She needed him to be here to talk this through, but in his present mood that wasn't going to happen. He most likely stomped off to get himself a coffee. She smiled and knew she'd have to apologise to him, but not straight away. She glanced at her watch and smiled– male pride.

She heard him whistling outside on the steps and the key turn in the lock. As soon as he grinned at her, she felt better, relaxed, and told him about her research on the web. She ended,

"We're looking for an Oak King carved on a Saxon cross located on a long hill. But there must be so many places in Lincolnshire with a long hill."

He took a folded sheet of paper from the back pocket of his trousers and smoothed it out on the desk. "I had a think in the café too. This is a photocopy of Psalm 68; we used verse 13 to lead us to the dove. But what if it is telling us something more general? So, I started to find out what the psalm means. Look at verse 12:

***Kings of armies did flee apace: and she that tarried at home divided the spoil*.**

It turns out that *she* was the prophetess Deborah. She

was a judge of Israel and the only woman to hold that office."

"Good for her! One of the world's first successful feminists."

"Not a feminist, because Deborah was used to staying at home and taking care of the family until she received a message from God." He glanced at his notes on the back of the photocopy. "At the time Israel was under the Canaanite King Javin and had suffered twenty years of oppression, so God told her to deliver Israel. The problem was that no men were willing to lead the tribes. When she appointed a certain Barak to lead the army, he was afraid. In fact, he refused to go unless Deborah went with him into battle..."

"And did she?"

"Oh yeah, she had great faith in God so she led ten thousand men to victory."

"Wow!"

"As the psalm says, she *divided the spoil* and vanquished their kings."

Alice looked impressed, "That's interesting, but I don't see what it has to do with what we're looking for."

"Maybe it hasn't. It's just an idea. I had in mind the period when England was invaded and under the rule of foreign oppressors..."

"What, you mean the Saxons?"

"I do. The dove is from the Anglo-Saxon period and those words on the back are in Old English. So, we'd be looking for troubled times when a woman led her people to victory."

He stood up, "Look, I'm exhausted. I'm going to crash out for a bit. Why don't you find me an Anglo-Saxon heroine in this area and maybe we'll start making progress." He kissed her on the cheek and flopped down on the sofa.

Alice twirled a curl around a finger, she wasn't sure. At first, his idea sounded a bit far-fetched. On reflection though, Thomas Manson was a priest and would have been very familiar with the history of Israel and the psalms. So, perhaps it was worth a try. She sat down at her computer.

A few websites later she found the story of Aethelflaed, the daughter of Alfred the Great, who when she was only a girl of fifteen travelled from Wessex to Mercia for her wedding. The Danes attacked her band in an attempt to kill her and so sabotage the alliance between Wessex and Mercia. Although half her company perished in the first attack, Aethelflaed used an old trench as a fortress and defeated them. For the next twenty-five years she helped her husband, Aethelred, in his struggle against the Danish enemy. When he died, she, then aged forty, became the Lady of the Mercians and, as political and military ruler, built a chain of fortresses to protect her lands against the Danes. She captured Derby and defeated the enemy at Leicester. In 918, the Danes in York offered their allegiance to Aethelflaed as protection against the Norwegians in Ireland. Some woman.

She had found her heroine, but she was uneasy. She couldn't see strong parallels between Aethelflaed and the Israeli prophetess Deborah; neither did Lincolnshire feature a great deal in what she had found about Aethelflaed. Her attempts to find another Saxon heroine proved to be frustrating. Link after link proved useless.

She sighed and waited for Jake to wake up. She gazed at him—love made her eyes twinkle. At least he wasn't as pale as when in retrocognition. How wonderful to slip back in time. She envied him, but it must be exhausting. At last, he stirred and she told him about Aethelflaed and after listening, he agreed that it was unlikely she was their

Deborah. He wanted to know what approach she had used to find another Saxon heroine and though he was impressed by her logic, he was disappointed at their lack of success. "It's the story of my life – clever, but not clever enough. Maybe it's not in our destiny. We weren't meant to find this treasure."

Alice winced but kept quiet. She wasn't going to give up without a fight and if she knew her husband—but did she?—he wouldn't either.

TWENTY-ONE

LONDON, 2021 AD

New suede shoes resting on the walnut veneer of his desk Stephen Bentley admired his handiwork. The jewel shone before him in all its magnificence. A little silver polish and a soft velvet cloth had worked miracles. The tarnish had disappeared and now he could appreciate the workmanship, the delicacy of the carving on the feathers, the sinuous lines of gold framing the blood-red stones, the exquisite double zigzag decoration around the dove. The bird seemed to dance as he moved it in the sunshine pouring in through his office window. He guessed it must be worth a small fortune, but the age of the jewel was what made it so priceless.

Bentley was tempted to keep it. All he had to do was say the kids found nothing. He took his feet off the desk and sat back in his chair swivelling backwards and forwards and thinking hard. If he kept it and later brought it to light, he would have a very dangerous enemy in David Briggs. Sheer folly to take on a silk. The barrister's callous words during their phone conversation had made an impression on him.

Apart from anything else, given the circumstances in which he'd obtained the jewel, he couldn't declare it and without declaring it he'd have organise a private sale and that would be a risky business in the unscrupulous world of art trafficking. He was only a small-time detective used to snooping on cheating couples. He'd be out of his depth. Far better to hand over the dove to Briggs. He looked at it with regret and mulled over his deal with the lawyer. One thousand pounds plus expenses guaranteed, rising to twenty thousand depending on consignment and the value of the treasure. But the situation had changed.

Briggs you have no idea how much this is worth.

Bentley made up his mind. Going over to a cupboard, he took out one of the tools of his trade. In his line of work, it helped to be an expert photographer. Setting the Canon to macro, he adjusted his desk lamp over the jewel and switched it on. A ten pence coin from his pocket would give an idea of size and he placed it beside the dove. Bentley took three photos from different angles and one of the reverse with its inscriptions. Satisfied, he slipped a USB adapter into his pocket and wrapping the jewel in the velvet cloth he put it into a large, yellow padded envelope and sealed it.

Half an hour later, he left a bank with a safe deposit key in his pocket.

CENTRAL LONDON

Pacing backwards and forwards in his London office, David Briggs couldn't keep his concentration. For the thousandth time he touched his fine worsted jacket. In the inside pocket was the mobile phone that never rang. It was the one that he dedicated to Bentley. Not a minute passed without some attention given to its silence: a silence that weighed on his spirit like a phantom millstone. The thought of being close to finding the family treasure had twisted his gut into a knot. He wasn't sleeping or eating well and was snappy with his secretary and Kate.

When the phone rang, startled, he fumbled it out of his pocket and almost dropped it onto the floor. He was angry with himself for being such a fool and his irritation showed in the harshness of his voice as he answered.

"Well? Have you got it?"

Stephen Bentley knew not to expect gentlemanliness from Briggs, but even he was taken aback by the curtness of the tone. It served to harden his resolve.

"Oh, yes, when can we meet?"

There was unmistakable avarice in the lawyer's voice, "As soon as possible. Where are you now?"

"Across the road from your office. Nero's coffee bar. I'll just finish my coffee then, see you in ten minutes." He closed the phone, not waiting for a reply. At this stage it was far better that Briggs got used to who was in control.

David Briggs's irritation exploded and he heaved a heavy reference book against the studio wall. That damned detective had the nerve to cut him off before he could ask the entity of the treasure. Now he had to wait ten minutes. It was exasperating. Fifteen minutes passed before his secretary announced Bentley. Briggs had him sent through at once.

The first thing he noticed was the expensive looking camera hanging round the detective's neck and then, his empty hands.

"So, where is it?"

"Here," Bentley tapped his camera.

"What do you mean?"

Bentley walked over to the barrister's computer, took the UBS cable out of his pocket and connected one end to his camera and the other to the computer. He loaded the four images on to the lawyer's hard disk.

David Briggs stared in rapt silence as the photographs flashed across his monitor. At last, he looked up at Bentley. "It's magnificent. Where is it? Do you have it?" His voice a mixture of anxiety and irritation not lost on the other man.

"Look at the inscriptions," Bentley clicked on to the last image again, "it looks like Old English to me. That would make it Anglo-Saxon or in other words, something like 1400 years old. I think you'll agree that it's worth the twenty thousand pounds we shook on."

The lawyer's cold, hard eyes stared into Bentley's and although they held a calculating expression, he said, "Of course. I'm not used to haggling." Briggs took a chequebook from his desk drawer.

"You won't be needing that."

"I beg your pardon?"

He looked at the detective with new eyes. In the past he'd taken the man for granted, looking at him without seeing the person, almost like an object that he could use and dispose of at will. Studying him, David Briggs observed with distaste the well-worn, stained sports jacket its shoulders sprinkled with dandruff. Distaste turned to aversion as he registered the sneer at the corner of the detective's mouth:

"The conditions have changed. Twenty thousand as agreed and £130000 for my silence."

Briggs's eyes widened, *Bastard!*

"What. You dare to blackmail me?"

Bentley unplugged the cable and clicked back to the sparkling image of the dove.

"Now *that*, if I might say so, is an unpleasant expression and uncalled for. I prefer to look at it like this, Mr Briggs, there's been a bit of a change, as an intelligent man such as you will be quick to realise. And a lack of understanding on your part could mean that you never get to hold this." He pointed to the screen, "In fact ..." his harsh laugh jarred on the lawyer's nerves, "... you can't get your hands on it at all, because it's in a bank vault. Now, I can't sell it, because I'd have to declare it and that could lead to serious complications. I suppose I can go and look at it from time to time..." the laugh was through clenched teeth, "...whereas you'll just have to look at the images of what might have been. Very sad for both of us. Bit of a stalemate, in effect."

Murder in his grey eyes, David Briggs's glared at the detective. That a nonentity of this type could hold him, an eminent barrister, to ransom was almost inconceivable. Briggs looked with distaste at the shabby jacket and stained tie of the other man before raising icy eyes to meet those of Bentley. "Let's suppose I have the money—"

"Yes, let's..." Bentley said laconically.

"...how do you know that it's worth more than the sum I'm paying you? And what guarantees have I got that you won't blackmail me again?"

"As to the first question, neither of us is stupid. Just look at it. The dove is solid gold. It weighs goodness knows how much. It's Anglo-Saxon and best of all, unlike me, you have a document that proves it's in your family—"

The lawyer shook his head, "You've seen the document and, as you know, the jewel went out of my family..."

"Yes, but nobody needs much imagination to work out that Sir Henry got it back off Thomas Monson. After all, it was the Civil War and Thomas was on the losing side. And you bein' a direct descendent of Sir Henry: it's your birthright."

"What about the couple you took it off?"

That irritating smile creased his face again, "Well, even if they go to the police, they have no proof either against me or against you. I was careful not to leave any traces linking me to the scene. And as for... *er*, blackmail...well, as I said before, that's a heavy word. I just want a fairer share of the spoils. After all, I was the one who took the risks and did the business."

The lawyer nodded and scrutinised the hard-set face in front of him.

"Very well," he said, picking up the cheque book again, "but if you double-cross me," his steel-grey eyes bored into the detective's and his voice lowered to a hiss, "I swear to God...I'll have you killed."

Bentley had no doubts as to that. He noted the *have you killed*, no self-respecting barrister would dirty his own hands, but he found the courage to repeat, "I don't want a cheque," adding, "you've got an account on line." He hoped that was true. Reaching into his inside pocket, he flicked through a small dog-eared notebook and laid it open on the desk in front of Briggs. "Those are my transfer details. Just pay into that account for £150000. Now there's no need to waste time." He moved round the side of the desk and stood next to the lawyer. Once the operation was concluded he held out his hand, but the barrister ignored it.

"When do I get the jewel?"

"Tomorrow morning at eleven o'clock, do I have to make an appointment?"

Again, the intolerable laugh made David Briggs grind his teeth. It was worth killing him just for that laugh.

With a forced smile, the barrister said, "Until tomorrow then."

The next morning, the jewel flashed and sparkled in his hand as David Briggs tilted it in the light of his desk lamp. Bentley thought he had screwed him for one hundred and fifty grand, but, as he sat and traced the gold decoration with his fingernail and admired the intense red of the semi-precious stone, he knew the money was well spent. He recalled an Anglo-Saxon pendant found with a metal detector a few years ago: £250000 that fetched. This would be worth far more. How he wanted to get the jewel dated and valued. First though, he had to show the dove to Kate.

Picking up the velvet cloth that Bentley had left him, he wrapped the jewel before placing it in his briefcase. Later there would be time to buy a dignified container. Then, he tapped out an e-mail to his home computer, attaching the images of the artefact that Bentley had put on his hard disk. When he switched off the computer, he left the room and surprised his secretary, Ms Lethaby, with a bright smile.

"Cancel my appointment with that young lawyer, the O'Connell woman, at four, will you, Helen? Tell her I've been called to Chambers and try to fit her in tomorrow morning if she's free. Lots of profuse excuses, you know the sort of thing."

"Will you be back this evening, Mr Briggs?"

"No, see you in the morning dear girl. Bye now."

Helen stared at the closed door with a strange smile on her lips, she wondered why such a good mood. Maybe he was having an affair. She tittered to herself at the thought and reached into her handbag and took out a small vanity case. Filing her nails for just enough time to make sure that her boss didn't come back, she took her mobile out of the bag, flicked it open and found a number, this she dialled on the office phone. She got the ringing tone and Helen smiled happily, while the cat's away...

TWENTY-TWO

EAST END OF LONDON 2021 AD

At his riverside apartment, Briggs opened the front door and climbed the narrow stairs. He called Kate's name two or three times as he strode through to the sitting room, but the only movement that met his eye was outside the window: the river traffic. The sight always filled him with pride at owning a property with a splendid view giving a sense of the passing centuries. The River Thames, a paradox of constant change and permanence, bustling with vessels of various sizes. David Briggs stood at the picture window and gazed down at the water. It was simple to imagine narrow-beamed Anglo-Saxon sailing ships moored to a wooden quay with longhaired, bearded sailors, cloaks around tunics, swords at the side, setting about various duties. Briggs smiled, if he could step back in time, he wouldn't understand a single word those sailors shouted. What a difference between the *Engla-lond* of then and England today. What would Hengist have made of the Shard spiking up to the heavens? Snapping out of his reverie, he went through to his study and put the briefcase on his grey oak desk. Taking his mobile phone from his pocket he quick-dialled Kate. He picked up a glass paperweight with the image of St. George spearing a dragon and enjoyed the sensation of cold weightiness in his palm.

"Hi darling, I'm not disturbing you, am I? ...... No, no, nothing urgent, I was just wondering when you'd be back ...... OK. See you then. A double surprise for you Katie darling," Briggs murmured "A stir-fry meal and then the bombshell, the inestimable dove. Six-thirty isn't so bad, it'll give me time to sort things out."

He took the jewel out of his briefcase and switched on his desk lamp and the computer. While it was booting up, he unwrapped the dove and gloried in its beauty. "Dark Ages," he thought, "what a misnomer. Such skilful craftsmanship. Sell it? Sad, but inevitable with all that money at stake; I shall add a Ferrari or a Lamborghini to my Mercedes." Briggs downloaded the photographs to his hard disk and flopped into his high-backed leather chair.

What he needed was an authority on the Anglo-Saxon period, an expert on jewellery, the greater the authority the better. He found a number for Oxford University and after a frustrating joust with a fussy man at the switchboard, was put through to the secretary of the History Faculty.

"Good afternoon, History Faculty, can I help you?"

"Ah yes, thank you. I do hope so. My name is David Briggs I'm a barrister. Now, bear with me, my family has been in possession of an Anglo-Saxon artefact for many centuries. Well, now after careful consideration, I've decided to reveal its presence and I'd like you to put me in touch with an expert on jewellery of the period. I think it would be in the best interests of the university."

After a short silence, the woman said, "I see sir, what kind of artefact are we talking about?"

"One of inestimable value, I mean both from an

economic and historical point of view. It is an exceptional piece of jewellery in the form of a dove, made of solid gold, with silver wings and inset with garnet."

"Yes, I see, that sounds quite exquisite. I'm sure the most suitable person for you would be Professor Buchan, Christopher Buchan. He's our Full Professor of Late Antiquity and the Middle Ages. Except that, I'm afraid he's in a departmental meeting at the moment and with these meetings I can't be sure what time he'll be free."

"Could you give me the Professor's email address? I can begin by sending him some photographs of the jewel and I'll include my various contact details, so that he can reach me if he so desires."

This arrangement was to the secretary's liking and Briggs jotted down the email address, thanked her for her help and rang off. He proceeded to write a short mail to the professor saying that he needed details of the jewel's date and value. Then he attached the photos and sent it off. Re-wrapping the dove in the velvet cloth and stepping behind his desk he unhooked a Delap painting from the wall, punched in a five-digit number, put the dove inside the safe and repositioned the artwork. It was time to do some shopping for dinner and, of course, the first item on his list was a bottle of Moet & Chandon for the celebration.

He shopped, popping shrink-packed meats and fruit and veg. into his trolley, without having decided what dinner would be. Back home, he selected a recipe, Chicken with Burnt Chilli Paste and Cashew Nuts and began chopping the meat and vegetables to the powerful, assertive *Te Deum* of Bruckner: a good choice, it reflected his own self-confident mood. It was a magnificent moment, so good to be alive.

When Kate came home, she showered and slipped into

a grey velour sweatshirt and jazz pants. She peered over the rim of her glass as she sipped the chilled *Lillet Blanc* and watched David busy at the wok.

"Have I missed something darling? It isn't our anniversary and it isn't your birthday. What are we celebrating?"

"Can't a man just make his wife a meal, without it being a celebration?"

With her free hand Kate lifted the hair at the nape of her neck and shook her head. Then putting down her glass, she wrapped her arms around him while he stirred the sizzling mixture in the wok. She kissed the back of his neck and laughed, "Not when there's a bottle of champagne in the fridge, my love."

"You don't miss a trick, my girl."

After dinner, carrying the champagne and two glasses, he led her through to the study. Placing the bottle and the glasses on his desk, Briggs opened the safe. Kate noticed the strange, almost reverential care with which he lifted out a stained piece of old, yellow velvet. By now her curiosity was aroused and she watched with a curious half-smile as David laid the cloth unopened on the desk and angled the lamp to shine on it.

"There." he said in an awed voice, "What do you think of this?"

"I think it's a dirty, old, yellow cloth."

"Come over here, darling and prepare to be amazed."

Kate moved around the desk and with her well-manicured left hand peeled back the velvet.

"Oh my God." she gasped as the jewel blazed its magic. "David, this is fantastic. Where on earth—?"

The barrister put his arm around her waist and bent his head, touching hers, over the dove. They stood in silent communion worshipping the ancient jewel. Kate broke the silence, "It must be worth a fortune," she added and bit her lip, "... David, where did you get this? Is it yours?"

"A man could kill for this," he murmured.

Kate pulled away from him and, alarmed, as he turned to face her, her stare was accusing, "David, you haven't—"

"Oh, good heavens no Kate, what do you take me for?" His steel-grey eyes flashed.

"You remember the letter I found in this desk? Well, this is my family's heirloom. I told you I'd get it back and I have done. It's cost me the small matter of £150000 in detective's fees, but it's worth much more than that. We stand to make a tidy sum out of this beauty, Kate." As he spoke, he unwired the cork on the champagne.

"Promise me you haven't done anything illegal, David."

He touched glasses and gave her a disarming look in the eyes, "I promise Kate." They drank to the family heirloom and to the prospect it held of a significant sum of money. David's good mood changed only when Kate quizzed him about how he'd found the jewel. He became nervy, speaking too fast, telling her that if the police ever asked her that question, she should say that a young couple from Louth had asked him to open a treasure trove inquiry with it. That would straighten possible problems out. With fierce determination David steered the conversation away from the subject of the finders and the expression on his face made Kate too uneasy to press the matter further.

He couldn't take his eyes off the glittering dove and they glowed with a strange expression of mixed admiration and cupidity. Kate herself loved beautiful objects, but this was something else. Kate sipped at her champagne and her blue eyes studied her husband as he peered, face glowing with self-satisfaction, down at the jewel. How could he bear to part with something so exquisite? Some things surpass money: yes indeed, a person could kill for that dove.

She shivered and the last traces of her good humour were swept away by a disturbing presentiment.

EAST END OF LONDON AND OXFORD

David Briggs whistled along to a Vivaldi sonata while he worked. In fact, his concentration on his case in hand was so intense that, at first, he was oblivious to the phone ringing.

"So sorry, I'll just turn the music down. Who's calling?"

"Christopher Buchan from Oxford, I received your email, Mr Briggs, and I thought I'd contact you at once. I must say, your dove is just the cat's whiskers."

'Eccentric professor?' Briggs asked himself, but replied, "Yes, indeed, quite so."

"And I understand it's been in your family for centuries?"

"I can be sure that it was in the family a long time before the Civil War, because I have a letter to a family member dated 15 March 1655, which states that the heirloom was, and I quote, *of thy family for centuries*".

The professor's excitement was evident, "And nobody in your family has ever brought this artefact into the public domain?"

"No. Let's say that it's been buried away for a long time and that I have decided to expose it to the light of day."

The professor assumed a business-like tone. "I cannot be categorical about this from the photographs, but if the artefact is genuine it looks like we are—"

"Just a minute. What do you mean *if the artefact is genuine?*"

Professor Buchan hastened to smooth the barrister's ruffled feathers, "Oh dear, I beg your pardon, it's a kind of professional deformation, you see. In my line of business everything has to be verified, you understand, before any definitive statement can be made, otherwise we'd leave ourselves open to the long knives. You wouldn't believe how vicious the academic environment can be at times—other than the *dreaming spires.* So, as I was saying, from the image, I'd say it looks like your dove dates from either the sixth or the seventh century. I can only be precise if the artefact is subjected to a detailed examination. Only at that point can any assessment be made of its age and value. Would you be prepared to let me conduct such an examination?"

David Briggs hadn't expected this and he thought for several seconds.

"Hello?"

"Yes, I'm still here. Well, I'd be prepared to let you examine the dove, but on certain conditions. First, I'm not prepared to let the jewel out of my sight, so I'd have to be present at your examination."

The professor chuckled, "No problem there, I do assure you. I'm sure you will find it most interesting. And what are your other conditions?"

"Just one, the jewel mustn't be damaged in any attempt to ascertain its age."

"Good Lord no. We aren't vandals up at Oxford, you know. My dear Mr Briggs, I can assure you that the examination will procure no damage to your magnificent heirloom. Now, when can we meet?"

"Just a moment Professor, I'll just have to consult my

appointments." Briggs looked at his week planner on the desk; he could not free himself for a week or so, given that he had the actor's case the day after tomorrow and that could last up to three days if things didn't goas expected, plus a series of other engagements. "I'm afraid I'm rather tied up this week and I expect you're a busy man yourself—"

"Well quite so, but I'll admit to being rather more than a little excited about your revelation."

"Very well, I can be free on Monday if that's all right for you Professor."

"Jolly good show, what time shall we say then?"

"Let's see, it's only an hour or so up the M40 from here, so I could be with you around ten-thirty, or any time after that may suit you."

"Splendid, let's say ten-thirty then. You'll find me in The Old Boys" High School in George Street, I wonder, do you know Oxford, at all?"

David Briggs laughed, "I should say so...a Jesus College man myself...I got my degree in Law at Oxford. Dear old *alma mater*, I suppose that's why I rang you today and not some other place"

"Bravo. See you on Monday then David."

David Briggs QC put the telephone back on its base and glanced in the general direction of his wall safe. His magnificent moment continued.

TWENTY-THREE

LOUTH, LINCOLNSHIRE, 2021 AD

ALICE LEANT AGAINST JAKE AND GAZED FROM THE window down to the street below. There was a long silence as each pondered the problem of the dove. After a while, she spoke.

"Instead of trying to find another queen or princess, perhaps I should try looking at events." She sprang over to the computer and typed *Anglo-Saxon battles* into the search engine. The seventh century was a turbulent period for Lincolnshire and it captured her attention. Among these events she discovered Werburgh, the daughter of Wulfhere of Mercia, the nun who hoarded away the treasures of the abbey of Ely, burying it in a place known only to her and two sisters to save it from the plundering Northumbrians. Alice gasped; she was on to something.

In 675 the West Saxons defeated Wulfhere at the battle of Biedanheafde and the land of Mercia was no longer a safe place. Wulfhere died in 675 and was succeeded by his brother Aethelred. Increasing Northumbrian demands for tribute oppressed the Mercians. It was then that Werburgh went to her uncle with the message from God that he should deliver his kingdom from the enemy. The armies met in 679 near the River Trent and the Northumbrians were defeated and Lindsey retaken.

Alice sat up,

"Jake, this is more like it. I've found a Saxon heroine with a message from God to deliver her people from an oppressor. I wonder what happened to Werburgh after the battle?"

Jake hurried over to her at the computer and made her go back to the previous pages. As she read them again, she grew more convinced that she was on to something interesting. She knew that Jake agreed, since there was a reassuring absence of any of his usual scornful comments. In fact, he was absorbed by what he read.

They discovered that Aethelred invited his niece home to assume control of all the convents in the kingdom. Werburgh reformed the existing convents and founded new ones at Trentham, Loundon, Hanbury and Weedon. She decided on Hanbury as her final resting place, but was at Loundon when she died on 3 February 700.

Jake scrolled down and read on:

By the year 708, her cousin Coelred had succeeded Aethelred as king of Mercia and decided to move her body to a more conspicuous place; in fact, he chose the parish church of Hanbury. Her body was found to be intact despite the passage of eight years since her death. This was taken to be a sign of divine favour and her tomb became the object of veneration and

> ***a place of pilgrimage. Coelred himself is said to have been so affected by this miracle that he decided to relinquish the throne and took holy orders. The shrine remained at Hanbury for the next 160 years, but in 875 owing to the threat from Viking raiders, it was decided to relocate the shrine to Chester, within the city walls.***

"Jake, look." Alice sat up and tapped the screen when the subtitle *The Treasure of the Abbey of Ely* appeared. They read:

> ***When Ecgfrith, king of Northumbria, invaded Mercia, Werburgh, advised by God in her sleep, obtained permission to move the treasure of the abbey to a safe place. In great secrecy she set off by night, accompanied by two nuns. After several nights' travelling they buried the treasure in the place indicated by the dream outside the confines of the kingdom of Mercia.***

"That was what you saw, Jake." They read on:

> ***Owing to political and military instability Werburgh chose not to recover the treasure before her death. One of her faithful companions passed away before***

> ***her and the other, twelve years later, whispered her secret on her deathbed to the abbess. It is thought that the knowledge of the treasure's whereabouts then remained secret owing to dynastic change. With the abdication of King Coelred the direct descent from King Penda ended. Aethelbald took the throne. The first few years of his reign were marked by struggles against two rival kings: Wihtred of Kent and Ine of Wessex. It wasn't until 726 that Aethelbald asserted the hegemony of Mercia, but by then the secret had again been passed on and the substance of the treasure's location had apparently become too vague for the bearer of the secret to understand. With the passage of time only the fact of the buried treasure remained, which is why the treasure of the Saxon abbey of Ely has never been found to this day***.

Alice clapped her hands together and whooped; they'd found the secret of the dove. She said out loud, "Wow. Let me read that again ..."

> ***the substance of the treasure's location had apparently become too vague for the bearer of the secret to understand...***

It seemed to her that it just had to be the dove. She reflected, the dove was part of the treasure and Werburgh had the location of the treasure inscribed on the back of it.

She frowned; something must have gone wrong. If the dove had been passed on as the key to the location of the treasure, it would also have needed an explanation. Without an explanation it was just a beautiful piece of jewellery with some words on the back.

"I know." Alice exclaimed, "One of the nuns must have passed on the dove, but maybe she died before she could explain the inscription. That must be it. What do you think?"

They discussed Werburgh and how there were similarities with the heroine of Psalm 68. Jake bit his thumbnail and he ran his fingers through his hair several times, then he smiled at his wife.

"Alice, you've done a wonderful job in such a short time, well done. The account says that the nuns travelled for several nights from Ely and passed the confines of Mercia, so I suppose they could well have come into Lincolnshire if they went north-northeast. It seems that the dove refers to the lost treasure of the Abbey of Ely. It's possible that the nuns buried it in the south of Lincolnshire, which would have been the kingdom of Lindsey at the time, in a place with a long hill and marked by a cross with an Oak King carved on it ... is that it?"

Jake took a piece of paper from the printer and in pencil wrote the words *Saxon crosses; Oak King; lang dun; Werburgh*. He looked up into Alice's attentive face, "We have to check out each of these and see whether they cross reference in any way. Then maybe we'll be able to find this place."

"I'll delete the search history now. We're going to that Italian restaurant we saw. I'm starving and we deserve a treat. If I don't have to prepare anything it'll save time. I think a nice spaghetti *alla carbonara* should do the trick washed down with a glass of red wine. That should calm the hunger pangs for me to come back here and sort out this little problem."

But he wasn't banking on what happened next. His head began to ache once more, and the air around him wobbled...

LOUDON, MERCIA FEBRUARY 700 AD

Jake watched them approach, sure they couldn't see him as this was forest.

The priest and abbess of Hanbury, riding stocky mares, led a score of grim-faced men through a wychwood. The men trudged along in silence armed with bows and staves; at the rear of the band four men pushed a large wooden handcart. Where the sky overhead could be seen through the canopy of leaves, it held a ghostly twilight dwindling into gloom. The wan light cast the wood in such murkiness that the beaten track could scarce be seen ten paces ahead. The trees seemed huge columns of darkness, yet darkness was the key to their plan.

Jake followed them, by now he was used to night-time Dark Age forests.

Even a strong man like blacksmith, Ryce Redknapp, was cowed into silence. He felt tightness between his shoulder blades and a prickling on his scalp at a sound from among the trees. Hereabouts people said the wood was haunted. He'd heard odd tales about it from his father, his grandfather and truth be told indeed from his great-grandfather, at a time when Ryce stood eye level to the sheepdogs. His hand clenched the haft of his biggest hammer and his massive muscled forearm knotted hard as iron. The air was cold and damp but sweat beaded his brow at the nagging thought that no hammer could harm a wraith. Judging by the set faces of his companions, they too were troubled.

The wood lay three miles west of their destination: the convent at Loudon, where sisters in the faith, Hilda, Edgyth and Glenna knelt, hands pressed together and heads bowed in vigil around a table bearing an open coffin. The wilting wildflowers in a plain clay vase on the altar had not been replaced. The natural decay of their beauty was in stark contrast to the corpse that had lain those same five days before them. Far from decomposing, intact, serene, the body smelt of fresh-mown hay. The oval face was no longer young, but its prettiness and kindliness seemed to mock Death. The nuns at Loudon all loved their Mother, Werburgh, for her piety and her strength of character. Her passing touched every heart, from the prioress, Kendra, to the youngest novice, Jetta, the daughter of a simple cowherd. Werburgh, the niece of the king of Mercia sparing a kind word and gentle smile for the child of a cowherd was unremarkable to those who knew her.

Kendra swore they would not be sundered from her. Apart from the love they bore in their breasts for the dead noblewoman, the prioress knew she had the body of a saint in her chapel. A saint meant pilgrims and pilgrims meant swollen coffers. For this reason, she had ordered heavy bars fitted to the doors and windows and waived the strict rule of no men in the convent. Now there were ten of the stoutest villagers from Loudon behind the barred door, ready to spill blood to defend the mortal remains of their saint.

Of course, the villagers weren't to know that Werburgh had several times stated that her last resting place should be in another of her foundations: the convent of Hanbury. Not was Kendra likely to enlighten them. Indeed, her need was such that she turned a blind eye to their cask of ale and their gaming. On the other hand, the men were edgy, wary of their choice of words, ever since Alwin the miller had served penance for a loud oath. A coin lost at dicing, his oath, and the sour prioress was down on him like one of his millstones on a grain of wheat. A night's vigil with dried beans under his knees cured the miller's speech if not his temper.

In the chapel, Edgyth, nodding toward the coffin, whispered to Glenna.

"She worked miracles do you know?"

"Miracles?"

"Well there's a farm near Weedon, not many miles from here as the crow flies."

"What, a crow like Kendra."

Glenna and Hilda giggled and looked round, guilt on their faces, but they were quite alone.

"Go on," Hilda whispered, "tell it as it was."

"Well, I got it from Edlyn," Edgyth said, pleased that dropping the name of the venerable nun made her tale gospel for her sisters. "She told me that on this farm near Weedon a flock of geese were ravaging the cornfield." She nodded toward the coffin, "Mother ordered the geese to be shut up for the night. They obeyed her meekly, but when she scolded them for destroying the fields and ordered them to go away, they refused. That's when they told her ... and here Edgyth paused for effect before lowering her whisper to near silence ... they told her that one of the gaggle had been caught the previous night, killed and eaten by the farm steward. Werburgh told the steward to bring out the bird's remains and then she brought the bird back to life."

Glenna gasped, "The Lord be praised." she whispered, making the sign of the Cross.

"The flock left with their companion and never came back. Edlyn says that everyone knows about it," she ended with a wise nod.

Hilda stood up, leant over the coffin and kissed Werburgh's brow. Eyes wide Edgyth crossed herself too. Hilda took her place on her knees again and it was then that the Miracle of Loudon occurred.

Hilda yawned, Edgyth's head slumped on her chest and Glenna's heavy eyes closed. In moments all three were stretched out on the cold stone floor in the deepest sleep. A runnel of ale from two overturned beakers soaked into Alwin's cloak and no snoring companion could warn him. Elsewhere, Kelda's grey hair lay on a table close to a guttering candle. The even breathing of deep sleep or grunting snores were the only sounds to be heard within the convent. No one heard the insistent knocking on the door.

Outside on the orders of Grindan, the priest of Hanbury, Ryce Redknapp raised his mighty hammer. His task was to break down the solid oak door.

Jake watched, fascinated, he was watching play out a minor episode in Anglo-Saxon history.

The hammer swung back over a broad shoulder, but before the smith could strike, the ringing sound of iron bars hitting stone halted him in mid-swing. At the same time the heavy doors swung back on well-greased hinges. The Hanbury men stared awestruck. No hand had opened the doors from within, as everyone lay asleep. The priest sank to his knees and crossed himself. His followers did likewise. There would be no blows struck in anger.

Jake, who was well used to the supernatural, still stared awestruck at the scene.

Wait till I tell Alice.

After muttered prayers and thanks to God, it was a simple task to pick their way past the sleepers, load the coffin onto the handcart and carry the body of the saint to the resting place Werburgh had willed.

LOUTH, LINCOLNSHIRE, 2021 AD

For Alice, this was the second time she'd seen Jake overcome by his psychic experiences; nonetheless, when he recovered, he found his wife rubbing the back of her neck and biting her lower lip, staring at him.

"Don't worry, I'll tell you all about it over dinner. Let's just say that we're on the right lines, without a shadow of doubt.

TWENTY-FOUR

LOUTH, LINCOLNSHIRE, 2021 AD

FRUSTRATED IN HIS ATTEMPTS TO FIND A LINK between the Oak King, *lang dun*, Werburgh and Saxon crosses, Jake was on the point of giving up. Eleven days had passed since Alice had suggested the possibility and there was precious little to show for his efforts. Whether his tenacity was a virtue or just pig-headed stubbornness, he still hadn't decided. He mulled over what he'd found out.

First of all, they knew that according to legend Werburgh had buried the Treasure of the Abbey of Ely. He didn't doubt the legend; it must be fact, because they'd found the dove and he, despite lack of solid proof, felt that the psalm pointed to the treasure. It was historical fact—and he's witnessed it—that Werburgh died in 700 at Loundon and that her remains were transferred to Hanbury.

As for the Oak King they knew that he was carved on various Saxon crosses and some days ago he'd found a Victorian classification of stone inscriptions in Lincolnshire. It was a painstaking task checking them all out, because the list was very long, but with his usual doggedness, he eliminated all carvings other than crosses from his list. Some crosses were now in museums and the locations or the places of origin bore no resemblance to a *lang dun.*

He sighed and stared at the keyboard. Something was gnawing away at the back of his mind. There was a link, he knew there was, but he couldn't quite grasp it. He bit his lip and ran the middle finger and thumb of his left hand together along his eyebrows. He picked up the list of Saxon crosses again and counted them. There were forty-six, so the Victorian historian with the striking name of Sirach Harrington, had been thorough. Irritated with himself, he realised he'd overlooked a simple procedure. He could cancel all the places that weren't in the south of the county. How strange that this hadn't occurred to him sooner. Werburgh and her companions wouldn't have travelled too far into Lincolnshire to bury the treasure, because in those days travel was slow, at best the speed of a horse, but they'd used an ox. He printed off a map of Lincolnshire and began to cross out those places he knew, like Barton-on-Humber and Crowle and, in the case of Marton, where there was a Saxon cross shaft embedded in the wall of the tower, he had to check the map. Finding Marton to be by the River Trent near Torksey, he crossed it off his list as well: too northerly. When he'd finished, the list was a manageable nine crosses.

He wasn't sure what to do next. He looked at the first on the list, Brant Broughton, St. Helen's Church. He typed the name into the search engine and read: ***Brant Broughton is a small village in the North Kesteven district of Lincolnshire, England, lying north of the A17 and west of Leadenham, where the A 17 crosses the A607 road. The name itself means "Burnt***

fortified settlement", implying the place was burnt down at some point...Jake's eyes skimmed down the article and rested on: ***the south porch of St. Helen's has an Anglo-Saxon cross shaft embedded, with a possible mother figure at the base***. He sighed; a mother figure wasn't what he was after. He needed the male figure of the Oak King. In any case, Brant Broughton was north of Grantham and as such, the most northerly of his nine crosses and therefore his least favourite. He struck it off his list *down to eight*.

The next on the list was Threckingham. He liked the location, near Sleaford and about the right distance for the nuns. When he entered the name in the search engine, it asked if he meant Threekingham. He clicked on the name and read: ***Dominated by its church, St Peter ad Vincula, the small village of Threekingham lies seven miles south of Sleaford. Folklore suggests that the village was originally called Laundon, but this was changed after the bloody battle fought near Threekingham, in either 869 or 870 between the Saxons (led by the earls Algar, Morcar and Leofric) and the invading Danes (during which three Danish kings and many of their followers were slain)***...Jake read it again, something was bothering him but he just couldn't pin it down.

TWENTY-FIVE

OXFORD, 2021 AD

A PERSON SELDOM FORGETS HIS WAY AROUND THE town where he spent his student years, so Briggs found himself in front of the hand-painted sign of the History Faculty of the University of Oxford without undue difficulty. When he was a student, he struggled to recall, wasn't this the Social Studies Faculty Centre? He shrugged his shoulders, they must have relocated, and stared up at the fine Ashlar front of the two-storey building. There he read the inscribed date of 1880 and the edifying *Fortis et Veritas* on the right. A smug smile twisted his lips since Oxford was teeming with these erudite messages: only an elite could interpret them, including himself. His eyes strayed to the blue and gold painted dial off the clock in the gable whose hands, emerging from a flaming sun confirmed what he already knew: as always, he was on time. Briggs couldn't resist checking the clock against his watch before entering the building and striding upstairs without acknowledging the servitor.

Professor Buchan was much as Briggs had imagined him, in his early fifties, a round-faced, pallid individual with thinning sandy-coloured hair. Briggs approved of the dark grey suit and understated blue silk tie, but his critical eye found the light brown suede shoes quite out of keeping. The professor greeted the barrister with a cheerful smile and didn't waste time with formalities, explaining that they'd have to transfer to a laboratory. This was only five minutes away or even less by car. It was taken for granted that they'd use Briggs's car, which, once ensconced in the passenger seat, met with the scholar's wholehearted approval and a series of questions about performance. Interspersed with his interrogation the professor gave directions to South Parks Road and Briggs pulled up by the side of the Dyson Perrins Building.

Professor Buchan greeted a guardsman-sized security officer by his first name and led the way to the stairs. "This building is full of alien smells," he smiled, "of course, nowadays archaeology is a scientific subject purloined from the humanities. We're doing our best to humanise our scientific colleagues, but it can be an arduous task on occasions. *Ha-ha.* We have one laboratory here, the majority of the building being dedicated to pure sciences like chemistry. But you know, in the last forty years, archaeology has taken giant strides forward thanks to technology... ah, here we are."

A sign informed Briggs that this was the *Research Laboratory for Archaeology and the History of Art.* They entered a place of hectic activity. In one corner a group of students were gathered around a young woman with long, wavy, red hair, who was holding a glass slide in one hand and explaining something to her audience. Glancing around, the lawyer observed people at various side tables peering through microscopes, cleaning pieces of broken pottery and taking notes or photographing artefacts.

A tall, thin man in his late thirties, too gaunt for good health, straightened up from over a microscope and gave Briggs an appraising look.

"Let me introduce you to our wizard of the stereomicroscope," Professor Buchan led the barrister over to the archaeologist, "Mr David Briggs QC, Dr Paul Hudson, expert in all things Anglo-Saxon."

The two men shook hands.

"What have you got for me?" the younger man asked.

"What we have got, my dear boy," Buchan said with a flourish, "is a *pièce de résistance,* something right up your street. I must admit I'm rather excited about what is about to be revealed to us. David, over to you."

Briggs laid his briefcase on the desk and unclasping it, drew out the yellow velvet bundle. He unwrapped it, conscious of the tension in the two men next to him. The jewel blazed under the neon lighting of the laboratory and the two academics gasped in unison. Briggs passed the dove to Dr Hudson, who turned it in the light. He ran his fingers over the surface of garnet, silver and gold and his forefinger rested on the cabochon ruby that was the eye of the dove. The archaeologist stood silent for what seemed an age, enthralled or incredulous, Briggs, satisfied by the effect, couldn't determine which.

"Quite magnificent." Hudson said in an awed voice, "and look how skilfully our craftsman has used the gold foils. See how he's selected different foils to emphasise the different features of the wing feathers. Then he's aligned the individual cell foils ... here and here ...", Hudson pointed with a long finger, "so, he's maximised the effect—"

"There are gold foils under the garnet?" Briggs interrupted.

Professor Buchan looked at him as he would at a slow

student and smiling said, "Quite so, David. The foils are about three millimetres thick or thereabouts," he turned to Dr Hudson for confirmation, who nodded, this gesture together with the archaeologist's hooked nose making him look like a raptor over its prey, "otherwise, you see, the garnet is rather pale. This adds depth of colour, life and brilliance to the gem."

"In fact," he added, "they used a fine-grained wooden stamp to create a crosshatched effect on the foil. What happens is that the high refractive index of garnet results in greater refraction of incident light rays by the setting and so a smaller critical angle for internal reflection, this causes more light to be bounced back and forth between the foil and the top surface of the garnet. The result of course," he moved the jewel with a rocking motion, "in simple terms, is to create more sparkle; an effect enhanced by the movement of the wearer."

"I'm no expert, of course," Briggs said, "but I don't see how this could have been worn."

"I beg your pardon?"

"Well, considering that there's no hole in it for a chain and there's no sign of its ever having had a pin or clasp."

The archaeologist turned the dove over in his hand and an eyebrow arched. "Good Lord." he looked at the inscription, "this is Old English."

The professor chuckled and rubbed his hands together, "Quite so, dear boy. Quite so. And that, if I'm much mistaken makes this artefact quite unique: apart from its splendid condition. As far as I know, there are no other examples of inscriptions on jewellery from this period either in Britain or in Europe."

Two or three people had abandoned propriety and gathered round Dr Hudson to stare at the source of wonderment. They only moved away as Dr Hudson walked over to a stereomicroscope and switched it on. The archaeologist seemed distracted, "What on earth can it mean? It's a long hill and a cross and *ac cyning*" means Oak King."

The professor took the archaeologist by the arm and looking round at the curious faces in the room, lowered his voice and said, "I rather think that's something to be discussed in private, dear boy. Now, onward. What can you tell us about the date of our feathered friend?"

Briggs smiled. *Who better than an aquiline archaeologist to work that out?*

Dr Hudson turned to Briggs and pointed to another desk, "Would you be so kind as to bring that lamp over?"

Briggs picked up the anglepoise and carried it over to the archaeologist. He took it and positioned it so that its light flooded the jewel under the microscope.

"The foils become visible if well lit," Dr Hudson murmured, concentrating on focussing the microscope. "Now if you look at the monitor, you'll see the cross-hatching, with clarity." He hit a couple of keys on a keyboard and a sharp image displayed on the screen. He entered another command and a measure appeared. The archaeologist adjusted it so that he could measure the distance between the spacing in the cross-hatching.

"We can be sure about the date from the spacing," he explained, "what happened with Saxon jewellery was that there was an apparent progression from finer to coarser spacing with time. This spacing is 3.5 lines per millimetre, which means that it is from the late sixth or the early seventh century. Later in the seventh century we find spacing closer to 4 lines per millimetre. To get a more precise dating, we have to use other techniques." Dr

Hudson removed the jewel from under the microscope and switched everything off. "This way please gentlemen."

He led them to a small room off the main laboratory.

"We need to do an x-ray fluorescence analysis."

"Jolly good show." Professor Buchan enthused.

Briggs cringed at the professor's jocose eccentricity.

"It won't damage the jewel?"

"No, no." Dr Hudson reassured him. "It's a non-destructive method used for the chemical analysis of solids. The jewel will be irradiated by an intense x-ray beam," he placed the dove inside a metal chamber, "and the lines in the spectrum of the resulting x-ray fluorescence are diffracted at various angles by a crystal with known lattice spacing; the elements in our jewel, and, we will concentrate on the metal not on the garnet, will be identified by the wavelengths of their spectral lines. By the way, their concentrations will be determined by the intensities of these lines."

Professor Buchan laughed and turned to Briggs, "Now you see what I mean about archaeology becoming a scientific subject. I'm just happy to have the results without all this gobbledegook."

It wasn't long in fact before they had the results, which were seventy-five per cent gold, twenty-two per cent silver and three per cent copper.

"So how does that help us date the jewel?" Briggs asked.

"On its own it doesn't, David," explained the professor, "that's where...and thank goodness, I say...a humanities technique comes into its own, the comparison of coins: numismatics."

"That's where I beg to differ, numismatics is a science," Dr Hudson chuckled.

Briggs looked from one to the other, but saw from their

wide smiles that they relished this bickering and there would be no arid debate about the classification of numismatics.

"We now consult a graph of coin analysis, which should determine the date of this little chappie. Of course," Professor Buchan warned, "we can never be one hundred per cent sure, but I'd say that there's every chance our jewel was made by melting down Merovingian French coins. There was a shortage of native gold in this period and that's what they did to overcome the problem."

The three of them left the room and re-entered the laboratory where Dr Hudson stepped across to a shelf and, taking down a slim volume, consulted it for a minute or so. David Briggs wrapped the dove in its velvet cloth and replaced it in his briefcase.

"Here we are," he showed Briggs a graph. "with the respective percentages of gold, silver and copper, that'd place your dove between about 610 and 620 AD."

The barrister whistled low between his teeth.

"Is there anything else you can tell us, dear boy?" the professor said.

Doctor Hudson pressed his fingers together and held them to his lips, "Not a lot more, but consider the niello decoration of the silverwork at the wing extremities. That double zigzagging technique is typical of jewellery produced at Tallington, near Stamford in Lincolnshire about that time. You will remember that a fine pair of locking tongs was found there: a kind of hand-held vice for metalworking," he explained, noting Briggs's puzzled expression, "apart from that I don't think I can say anything else. Mind you, I'm rather intrigued about the inscription on the back of the dove."

The professor cast a furtive glance around the room and

with a conspiratorial air suggested, "Let's go to your study, where we can have a little privacy, if that's all right by you?"

They left the laboratory and made their way upstairs into a neon lit corridor lined with name-plated doors. Dr Hudson unlocked his study and they settled back into comfortable green leather chairs.

"What do you intend to do now that you know the origins of the jewel, David?" Professor Buchan asked.

"I'll be honest with you; I'm not attached to it. In the sense that despite its being in the family for such a long time, I'm prepared to let it go: for the right amount, of course. You'll realise that's why I'm here today. I was rather hoping—"

"...to have some estimate off its worth?"

Briggs nodded. The professor glanced across to his colleague, "I imagine I'm not alone in thinking that the inscription changes that estimate somewhat?"

"Are you thinking what I'm thinking, Chris?" Dr Hudson said. His expression was wary.

"By Jove. I think we may be on to something here. My dear boy, I believe that you hold the key to a centuries-old mystery. The dating of the jewel coincides and so does its provenance. Without the inscription, the jewel would still fetch hundreds of thousands of pounds on the market, but with the inscription...well, we are no longer talking about the worth of the jewel, but perhaps of the value of a whole body of treasure."

The barrister looked from one face electric with excitement to the other.

"I'm afraid I don't understand."

The professor put a reassuring hand on Briggs's arm, "I'm sure you don't, dear boy. You see, through our research, we try to shed light upon the so-called Dark Ages. What's dark about the period is our knowledge of it. Our task is to remove the veil from the face of Time and I'm sure that we are succeeding in this endeavour." He sat forward in his chair and his eyes lit up, "What's so fascinating, David, is that so much remains hidden, mysterious, cloaked in legend. You see, from this period we have the legend of the Treasure of the Abbey of Ely. More than thirteen hundred years ago the daughter of the king of Mercia, a nun called Werburgh, who was later canonised a saint, by the way, buried the treasure of the abbey of Ely to save it from the invading Northumbrians. The fact is, that until today, it was just another legend. Indeed, if it ever existed, the whereabouts of the treasure remained a secret."

David Briggs sat up, "And you think that the inscription might be a clue to the location of the treasure?"

"It's a possibility. Your shrewd point was that the dove wasn't intended to be worn. I'd hazard a guess that it was purpose-made to bear the message on the back."

Dr Hudson's right fist punched his left palm, "The inscription on the back smacks of primitive geographical co-ordinates to my way of thinking."

TWENTY-SIX

LOUTH, LINCOLNSHIRE, 2021 AD

SOMETIMES *NOT* THINKING CAN BE MORE EFFECTIVE than pondering, as Jake discovered. After work, an on-line crossword presented him with an anagram that set him on the right track. He'd made no progress in the past few days because Threekingham had changed its name. The Victorian writer had called Threekingham "*Threckingham*" and only a hundred years had passed. Place names were anyway variable and it was gnawing away at the back of his mind. *Laundon*, the place where Werburgh died. They'd found it as Loundon, but in either case, Laundon or Loundon, and this was the thing that he'd missed, it must have derived from *lang dun*. There it was. Threekingham was the place of the long hill.

He clicked on a new tab;

surely that part of Lincolnshire is as flat as a pool table?

Clicking on his satellite map of Earth, he was delighted to find the slow rise of the land from Threekingham to the west. He hurried back to the search engine and typed in Threekingham Saxon Cross and read: ***The decorated***

base of a shaft of a Saxon wayside cross, damaged by the Puritans in the Civil War, believed to be from near Threekingham in Lincolnshire, is now to be found in the Usher Gallery, Lincoln. The base of the shaft is decorated on all sides, three sides with geometric patterns of vegetable vine motifs and interlacing zoomorphic motifs, while on the front there is an interesting head of a man, vegetation flowing from his mouth, thought to portray the Oak King...

"Yes!" Jake cried, causing Alice to rush over for an explanation. At last! He'd found the cross marking the place where the treasure was hidden. A reality check calmed him down since its being in a museum in Lincoln was not the same thing as finding out its original location. They decided they would have to go to the Usher Gallery and investigate.

LINCOLN

A TRUCK SNARLED up the long hill of the trafficked Lindum Road emitting a cloud of noxious fumes. Jake coughed and spluttered waving his hand in front of his face. With some relief Alice and he turned their back on the road and went into the garden of the Usher Gallery, an imposing, neo-classic building dating from the 1920s. He stopped at the columned door and checked his watch, before looking up at the balcony located below a long, wide window. He'd never met a museum curator before and he didn't want to reveal the motive for their appointment.

"We're on time, remember not to let him know what we're about."

"Yeah, you've already said that five times today." Alice said.

They entered the building and asked a young woman at the reception desk for the curator. She indicated a double door and Jake knocked.

"Come."

He didn't like that either, to be invited in with that single peremptory word. Inside, a man in his sixties with a goatee beard and a red and white-spotted bowtie was sitting behind a desk. He looked over his half-moon glasses and waved them to sit down.

Alice, overcoming inward laughter, bit the inside of her lip to make sure it didn't escape. He was a stereotypical figure; she couldn't have made him up. Worse followed as the curator spoke in an affected clipped tone, sounding like a nineteen-fifties announcer of the BBC,

God, he should be in black and white.

Turning a laugh into a cough, she covered her mouth with her hand.

"I was expecting you," he said in a discouraging tone.

Alice's eyes alight with humour sparkled at him, "It's very good of you to spare us some of your time, I'm sure you're very busy."

Her winsome smile had the desired effect. The curator made an effort, "Not at all young lady, your interest is gratifying. Now, it's about the Saxon cross, isn't that so?"

Jake took the initiative, "The one that was once in Threekingham. What we're interested in is its original location. You see, my wife's thesis is about Anglo-Saxon roadways in Lincolnshire." He nodded at Alice, who replicated her smile at the curator.

"Ah, I see. Fascinating, my dear. As you know, Anglo-Saxon routes developed as and when required, they weren't metalled and straight like the Roman roads, but winding to suit the landscape." The curator cleared his throat, "So, you see, Threekingham would have been one of the many new villages to appear that didn't lie on the existing road network. In practical terms, we're talking about tracks, running from village to village that weren't constructed, but that left an impression due to erosion. Do you see what I mean?" Reassured by their rapt attention he continued, "You'd have wheel ruts forming and becoming deeper over a period of time. Where they had to climb a hill, you could have multiple routes, changing according to the seasons and the weather." The curator's hands both bore three heavy rings. As he spoke, he turned his wedding ring around his finger, causing the stones of the rings on his right hand to catch the light and sparkle. "Of course, nowadays, owing to their transitory nature, little remains of these medieval routes."

Alice smiled, "The point being that they used wayside crosses to mark the routes and I think that the Threekingham cross was used for this purpose, but I'm having difficulty locating its exact position."

The curator warmed to his theme, "Well, of course, they were used more or less as route markers, but their main purpose was religious. Often, they were placed on old pagan sites of worship, in effect to cancel out or neutralise the power of pagan gods through that of the Cross. As such the Anglo-Saxon priests would have used them for open-air masses too."

Jake sighed and fidgeted in his seat, the curator was like a schoolteacher and they weren't getting any closer to finding the original location of the cross. Indeed, the curator sensed his impatience and gave him the sort of look he once received as a wayward schoolboy.

"Well now," he cleared his throat, "getting to the point," a second reproving glance over his glasses at Jake and he continued, "you want to know where the cross was situated." He stood up and walked over to a large bookcase. "Now, let me see," he looked over his glasses again at the upper shelves, "all the exhibits in the gallery are catalogued. It's just a question of...." His voice died away as he as he ran a bejewelled finger along the leather spines to the correct catalogue. "Ah, here we are, Anglo-Saxon period." He carried a thick burgundy-coloured volume to his desk and began turning the pages. He read down the page, muttering something inaudible and then turned the volume with a flourish toward the young couple. "That should answer your question, I think."

They read the entry for the Threekingham cross and Alice reached into her handbag and took out a pen and notebook. The curator bestowed her an approving grunt as she made notes.

Before they left, they accepted his invitation to inspect the cross. It filled the whole corner of an exhibition hall, since its base was about five feet square. The shaft was broken at about ten inches from the base. What struck them both was the head of a man carved in the frontal of the base, with vegetation flowing from his mouth. Alice couldn't resist blurting out, "Look. The Oak King," which inspired a monologue about the density of this image in the county. Politeness compelled them to pretend interest in the curator's infinite knowledge on the subject. The dull ache in his forehead, didn't help Jake's wandering concentration.

It was with immense relief that they left the gallery and

their high spirits restored, they turned off the main road and at a safe distance from the Gallery, began mimicking the eccentric curator until they were pink-faced with laughter. They approached a newsagent's board and the headlines had a chilling, sobering effect upon them.

TWENTY-SEVEN

OXFORD, 2021 AD

Professor Buchan nodded in agreement, "Yes, and if we can decipher the co-ordinates, they could lead us to the treasure: hence my reserve earlier, my dear boy. This has to be done with the utmost discretion, at all costs we should avoid an unwelcome and unseemly treasure hunt."

David Briggs looked uncomfortable. "Where does that leave me? I made myself quite clear, I think, I want to sell the jewel."

Professor Buchan leant forward, thought better about putting a hand on the barrister's knee and sat back in his chair again.

"Think about this David, if we of Oxford University can find this treasure that has been hidden away for so long, it will be a worldwide sensation. On the level of the Sutton Hoo ship burial or ... indeed...it might even eclipse it, who can say? You mustn't be in a hurry to sell the jewel, dear boy. Don't you see its value could skyrocket? Imagine taking the key to the discovery of such a treasure to an auction house. There would be no limit to what it would fetch."

The barrister looked straight into the professor's shining

eyes and his own revealed bewilderment caused by doubt and avarice clashing head on. "But what if you're wrong? What if the inscription has nothing to do with the lost treasure? Isn't it only conjecture at this point? To be frank, I could do with the money."

There was a moment's silence, then Dr Hudson said, "Mr Briggs, I'm sure that you can see the potential in all of this. Perhaps what's troubling you is the fear that we could waste a lot of your time trying to decipher the inscription, am I right?"

"I suppose so, yes."

"What reasonable amount of time are you be prepared to concede before going public with the jewel?"

Briggs frowned. His eyes wandered down to the bowl of a pipe poking out of Hudson's breast pocket like a periscope. He tossed the matter over. It was to his advantage to put the jewel up for auction as the key to the most amazing archaeological discovery of the century. On the other hand, they could be wrong. It could be a wild goose chase. He hesitated.

Professor Buchan prompted him. "What would you say to six months, dear boy? If we haven't cracked the riddle by the New Year, you can go ahead and sell the jewel. What do you say?"

Briggs stood up. He was used to snap decisions in out-of-court settlements. "Very well Professor," his smile cold, "six months it is, then, and as it's in my best interests that you succeed in your quest. I wish you all possible luck."

Buchan and Hudson exchanged a satisfied nod. The latter reached into his desk drawer "Here, let me give you my card. It's got all my contact numbers, should you need to get in touch...even in a hurry."

Briggs slipped it into his wallet and pulled out one of his

own, which he gave to Hudson. Briggs held out his hand and Hudson clasped it.

"I'm convinced you've made a very wise decision, Mr Briggs."

On the drive back to London, Briggs whistled along to a Divertimento by Mozart. He became convinced of his decision. For an investment of £150000 he could be a millionaire within six months, whilst, worst scenario, he'd still be able to console himself with a new Ferrari.

He wouldn't have been so happy if he'd followed Dr Hudson to the scholar's Senior Common Room. Had Hudson's box of matches borne the slogan common in the Second World War, *Loose Talk Costs Lives*, maybe the archaeologist would have been guarded chatting at the bar with a colleague about his excitement at the lettering on the reverse side of the dove. But then, who can resist a good archaeological yarn?

Not the shrewd-eyed fee-paying PhD student from the USA at the opposite end of the bar, careful not to let anyone notice him hanging on to Hudson's every word. The American jotted down the names Dr Hudson let drop. Then he finished his beer and strolled out of the Senior Common Room to the series of phones lining the far wall of the entrance hall. Making sure he was alone, he inserted a credit card and lifted the handset for an urgent transatlantic call.

MANHATTAN, NEW YORK, USA

CONTEMPLATING THE SIDE-LIT bronze statuette of *fin de siècle* dancer Loïe Fuller by Pierre Roche, the lamp accentuating its sinuous line and swirling drapery, Warren Lightbourne, half-closed his eyes to heighten the effect. His heavy greying head cupped in his hand, he gazed at the dancer's lithe body beneath the diaphanous robes swirling centrifugally above her head from her outflung arms. He'd paid a lot of money for this piece of *art nouveau*, but it was worth every dollar. He loved beautiful objects and, indeed, was surrounded by them, but his real passion was Anglo-Saxon art; those objects from so long ago in England, the land of his ancestors, were what he desired. He sighed. His melancholic mood brought on by the complications involved in his latest would-be acquisition.

Lightbourne slid open his desk drawer and reached for a wad of visiting cards. Shuffling through them he found the one that interested him: *Marcia Fells, Financial Consultant, Buffalo, NY.* He wondered, then, what her real name was, he guessed she didn't know much about finance, but at her covert profession she was the best. In the past he had used her services to procure his jewelled and inlaid purse containing 34 Merovingian gold coins. While it was always a matter of regret that two lives had been sacrificed to achieve his purpose, the thrill he got from handling 1400-year-old objects and knowing that he was the exclusive owner more than compensated for any ethical inconvenience.

His hand strayed to the phone, but then determined, decision made, he rang her number. He was gratified to make an appointment with her for the following morning at 10.30 in the *Girls' Exhibition* by Mark Schwarzenstein at the Gagosian Gallery on Madison Avenue.

The next day he found her standing in a corner, holding a pamphlet, next to a 1.5 x 2.0 m. black and white cartoon of a beautiful young blonde, forefinger to her lip, with a speech bubble saying *it's ... it's not for me, is it?* Lightbourne was instantly struck by the similarity between the looks of the fantasy cartoon woman and the real live Marcia Fells. Marcia was about forty, but looked years younger, defying the stereotype that blondes soon age. About one metre seventy-five centimetres and with the physique of someone who worked out, she was power-dressed in a dark grey pinstriped suit, befitting a financial consultant. As he joined her and grasped her outstretched hand, Lightbourne delighted in her discreet and expensive scent. The only inkling she betrayed of her profession was a subtle hardness in her deep, blue eyes as she smiled her greeting. He smiled at the thought that his first impression of her formulated years ago hadn't changed in the slightest: this lady was the real deal.

Lightbourne led her over to a leather viewing chaise and checking they weren't overheard, explained the nature of her commission. They discussed terms to their mutual satisfaction and twenty-five minutes later she left him with the fading tick-tack of her high heels and a lingering trace of ambergris.

He rose and wandered around the gallery for a while, not taking in the art, his thoughts far away, revolving around another artwork in London more than 1300 years removed from the striking cartoons lining the walls around him.

TWENTY-EIGHT

BOROUGH MARKET, LONDON 2021 AD

The blonde met up with Joey near one of the entrances to Borough Market. It was a damp morning but even so the place was vibrant with shouting, bustling people busy buying and selling, oblivious to the drizzle outside. They walked over to a corner behind a stall out of the eddy of customers searching for bargains. Joey was holding a small, black leather case.

"You got what I asked for?" the woman's steady, blue eyes searched the red veined whites of Joey's.

"Hey babe, ya got youse the King of Nines—"

"Cut out the *babe*," her cold eyes bored into him and Joey felt an almost physical danger slice into him. He was twice her size and had done time for GBH, but he suddenly felt lamblike in the slaughterer's presence; her eyes expressed an emptiness that Joey didn't care to dwell on.

"Is it clean?"

"Sorry lady, I forget the manners sometimes, but hey, sure it's clean as a whistle. Feels like a glove, a sleek little beaut—"

"Suppressor?"

"Blackside-40."

"OK," the woman reached inside her coat and pulled out a thick white envelope, "1K, as agreed."

Joey's face split into a wide grin and taking the envelope, he pushed it into an inside pocket of his leather jacket and handed over the black case. She appreciated his discretion at not checking the contents of the envelope in a public place and her eyes softened. She held out her hand,

"Pleasure doing business with you, Joey. Until the next time." She turned her back on Joey and leaving him with a lingering trace of ambergris, strode out of the market before taking a cab back to her hotel.

In the privacy of her room she snapped open the black leather case. The Browning HP-SFS felt good in her hand, she inserted the clip of 9mm bullets and attached the suppressor. She walked into the bathroom and pointed the pistol at her forehead in the mirror, holding the weapon with both hands. Her mirror image smiled back at her and she lowered the gun. "So far so good," she murmured, slipping the pistol and the silencer into her travelling bag.

She undressed and showered.

Throwing her travelling bag over her shoulder and carrying the black case, she took the elevator down to reception and checked out. She decided to grab some lunch and do a little shopping on Bond Street and then make her way to her destination. There was still a light drizzle and this suited her, it gave her the excuse she needed to pull the hood of her jacket over her head. On impulse she took a double-decker bus for Oxford Street. The view of the city was interesting from up there and she relaxed as far as the street of shops.

KINGSTON-ON-THAMES, LONDON

THE DULL ACHE in his left leg was almost unbearable. Victor should have been resting up, but his irrational need to return to work, caused by insecurity and a desire to please, meant that he was now traipsing around Kingston Market Place. His employer's wife had an important business meeting in Birmingham the next day and would spend the night there. Before taking an early evening train from Euston, Mrs Briggs had the sadistic idea of visiting the market at Kingston *"just to kill time"*.

Victor began to limp and he felt beads of cold sweat forming under the rim of his peaked cap. Kate Briggs stopped in front of a fruit stall and bought some dark red cherries. Victor rubbed his thigh. One day, he thought, the fucking smartarse would pay for this. His boss had placed an absolute veto on any contact with Copley. Victor had some unpleasant Romanian acquaintances in London who would be happy to reduce the novelist to a gibbering wreck, but Victor didn't want that. He wanted to feel ligaments snapping under his own hands, to break Copley's legs with the brute force of his arms. He intended to leave the writer a cripple for the rest of his life. His lips curled into more of a snarl than a smile. Shocked, the woman serving at the fruit stall stared at him wide-eyed. Victor wiped the expression off his face and his close-set, anxious eyes glanced at Mrs Briggs. She hadn't noticed anything, absorbed as she was in the music of two guitarists, a case open at their feet for coins of appreciation. Kate opened her purse and threw them a pound coin.

Mrs Briggs spotted another stall and strode off without a word. Sometimes Victor felt invisible and insignificant despite his bulging muscles. He limped after her. Kate loved the confusion of markets, the crowds, colours and sounds of people milling around and the anticipation of a possible bargain. Not that English markets were a match for the French ones she adored. Here, the goods were often displayed in shabby plastic crates or just tossed in a jumble. In France the market was a visual delight, she reminisced about the market in Uzès with its ordered tubs of spices and its colourful canvas awnings. She was dragged back to Kingston by a stall full of garlands that caught her eye. Still, these were attractive, with convincing artificial flowers woven in.

Kate was soon in conversation with the stallholder, a middle-aged woman with striking red hair. It turned out that the woman made all the objects on the stall herself. They were soon engaged in a long conversation and Victor excused himself to wander off and sit on the fourth step of the memorial statue to give his aching leg some respite. He passed the time ogling young women without the fear of Mrs Briggs's disapproval or indeed that of the gilded Queen Victoria with her orb and sceptre in front of the Old Town Hall.

Kate bought a pretty garland with a sunflower at the base and other yellow and orange flowers covering the rest. She also took the woman's business card with the promise of contacting her again in a professional capacity. The bell in one of the Italianate towers chimed the hour. Kate picked her way through the crowd with the intention of finding Victor, but a stall selling ribbons and threads soon distracted her. It also had some animal figures, including some charming little frogs. Kate was delighted, at one time she'd have bought any frog figurine, but she'd become more discriminating. Nowadays only an unusual attractive frog would be added to her collection of over four hundred frogs.

At dinner David often made the joke that it wasn't so much the cost of the frogs that bothered him, more the cost of the china cabinets to house them all. Now here was another superb little frog, grinning up at her. She was beguiled, it lying there on its stomach in its black jacket with one hand behind its head and a red rose in the other. On its head was a top hat with a dark red hatband and it was wearing a red bow tie under its white collar— irresistible.

After that she found a stall full of bric-a-brac where the stallholder had no idea about hallmarks. She snapped up a sterling silver English porringer made in London in 1686 by a maker whose initials were DG. Kate was pleased with her clever manoeuvre. Of course, she spotted the object at once, but feigning interest in a brooch, she asked its price. When the man said fifteen pounds, she shook her head and said she only wanted to spend ten pounds on a friend. She transferred her interest to the porringer and asked how much he wanted for that *old bowl*. It was in need of a good polish and didn't look much at first glance, but she couldn't conceal her delight when he fell for it. "Give us eight quid for it, darling." She tried for six pounds, just to cover up, but eight pounds was the bargain of the century and she hurried off with her trophy in search of her driver.

She found him sitting quite forlorn under the statue of a lithe woman carrying an amphora on her shoulder and holding the hand of a little boy. He stood to attention briskly and Kate smiled, "Sit down Victor. I'm going to call my husband." She needed to share her triumph right away.

"Worth around two-hundred pounds, it's 1686 according to the hallmark, guess how much I paid, go on?" Kate could hear the notes of Weber's Clarinet Concerto Number 2 in the background: one of David's favourite pieces.

"How much?"

"Eight pounds. Can you believe it?"

"Well, at least, you haven't been wasting your time. You'll have to go to Kingston more often, maybe we can make our fortune. Let's hope it's a good sign for the hotel contract. Have a good trip to the Midlands and see you tomorrow evening."

"I'll send the porringer and the other things with Victor. There's no point in lugging them to Birmingham. Bye, darling."

On the train out of Euston a listless Kate leafed through a glossy magazine. There was no accounting for her mood. It wasn't anxiety. That would be understandable given the importance of winning the contract for the interior designing of a new four-star hotel. No, this was more an unpleasant foreboding. And it was a feeling she'd had several times in the last few days.

TWENTY-NINE

EAST END OF LONDON, 2021 AD

THE SOARING NOTES OF WEBER'S CLARINET CONCERTO Number 2 swirled around David Briggs's apartment. He jotted down a few margin notes about a new case without fear of interruption, since Kate was on her way to new clients in Birmingham. He wasn't expecting visitors, so he was surprised when his entry-phone buzzed. Briggs stared at the small screen, seeing blonde hair framed by a hood, the voice asking for admittance on Oxford university business had a slight American accent; distracted and curious, but with no sense of danger, Briggs pressed the button and let her in.

She stepped inside and transferred the pistol from her travelling bag to one of her shopping bags, before mounting the stairs and pressing the inside door bell.

David Briggs opened the door and greeted her with a puzzled smile. He asked himself what Oxford could want.

Inside, she controlled her voice, her plan depended upon his ignorance of Old English,

"This morning Professor Buchan asked me to contact you..." she said before he could ask any questions, "... he said he was very busy and couldn't deal with it himself...and I just happened to be in London, so...it's about the writing on the back of the dove, the professor says he can't make out from the photo you sent whether there's an accent over the *a* of *lang dun* and guess what, those dudes been arguing about it. The professor says there's no accent and the archaeologist, what's his name?...Hudson. He says there is, even though it's faint." Her deep, blue eyes probed his, feigning a look of sincerity and she was gratified to see curiosity there, "apparently, the accent changes everything —no, don't ask, he didn't tell me. I'm only the messenger." She laughed and opened her eyes wide.

"Well, it's easy enough to check." They went through to the study and removing a picture from the wall behind the desk, Briggs opened the safe. He took out a yellow cloth and turned towards her. There was just time for his face to register shock before the bullet thumped into his forehead.

She stepped over his body and picked up the yellow cloth, unwrapped the jewel and whistled. Turning it over and inspecting the inscription, "Nope, there ain't no accent over the *a*", she said through clenched teeth to the face staring unseeing at the ceiling. She took the dove and the pistol to her travelling bag and placed them inside, but held on to the yellow velvet.

She had to hurry now; she didn't know whether the barrister was expecting anyone. Taking a screwdriver from her bag, she went to the computer. In a few minutes she removed the hard disk, replaced the casing and wiped off any fingerprints with the velvet cloth. Back in the lounge she put the disk and the screwdriver in her bag and then spotted Briggs's jacket hanging by the door. She checked the pockets and found his car keys and another set of keys. The wavy-haired blonde put the latter into her jacket pocket, wiped the car keys and replaced them. Next, she went back to the barrister's desk and checked his office address on his headed notepaper. She was ready to go.

Victor found the outside door by the entry phone ajar, which was so unusual it alerted him. He climbed the stairs, carrying Kate's purchases. Victor wasn't the quickest of thinkers. He stood, finger hovering over the doorbell.

Inside, Marcia Fells took one last look around, satisfied, she gathered her bags and opened the apartment door. The last thing she expected to find facing her was a mean-looking man-mountain. It was so unexpected that she didn't have time to mask her feeling of being caught red-handed.

Victor didn't like the expression on the woman's face at all. Suspicious, he reacted instinctively, thrusting the woman back into the room. She fell backwards, hitting her head on a slender ornamental table, upsetting it; its Bristol blue glass decanter shattered on the floor. Victor dropped Kate's shopping and pounced. He grabbed the blonde and hauled her to her feet spinning her round and forcing her arm up behind her back. He was surprised that she offered no resistance. She let him think she was a weak dame.

He marched her into the lounge and immediately noticed the open study door. Victor propelled her toward it, marvelling at the lightness and subdued compliance of his prisoner. He exulted at his strength and her total helplessness.

That David Briggs was dead was obvious even to Victor, but the speed of his realisation didn't save him. With her left hand the blonde snatched up the Saint George paperweight and using her pinioned arm as a fulcrum, spun on her heel, unbalancing the Romanian, with all the force she could muster she smashed the heavy glass ball into the side of his head. Victor crumpled and she was on him like a tiger, crashing the paperweight repeatedly at his temple until she was satisfied that he was dead.

Motherfucker. What did he have to show up for?

She hated a messy job.

Fells retrieved her bag from the hall and put the blood-smeared paperweight in with the other contents. She opened the door, wiped the handle and closed it behind her. She pulled her hood well over her face, opened the outside door with the velvet cloth and rammed it into a shopping bag. A hasty glance up and down the street told her that she hadn't been seen, so she hurried around the corner and crossed three streets before hailing a cab. One street away from Briggs's office she paid the driver.

MANHATTAN, NEW YORK, USA, LATER THE SAME DAY

At his desk Warren Lightbourne picked up his Victorian silver and ivory paperknife and tapped the blade against the fingers of his left hand. He studied the hallmark on the ornate silver over the hasp of the paper knife, *R. Favell & H. Elliot, London, 1890* he murmured like a mantra. Lightbourne was in reflective mood. He had just received a call from Marcia Fells in London and from her account it was clear that phase one was complete.

He thought back on events. A few days ago, he received a call from Oxford, where his nephew, Simon, was studying archaeology for his PhD. Lightbourne, not an envious man: he was far too successful to experience a similar base emotion, but were it possible to turn the clock back, which it wasn't, he would have loved to study Anglo-Saxon history at

Oxford. Whenever he had the chance he enjoyed sitting down for a long chat about history with Simon. That young man was as bright as a White House candelabra and he proved his worth again the other day.

He ruminated on the information Simon had given him. The boy managed to overhear the name of a QC from London whose appearance in Oxford with an exquisite Anglo-Saxon jewel had caused a stir. On the reverse side was inscribed a set of three words or phrases; these were *lang dun*, *ac cyning*, and *treōw*. Simon's tutor, Dr Hudson, had been excited over this find and it seemed that there'd be a special team set up to decipher the inscription that might just lead to the legendary treasure of the Abbey of Ely.

Warren Lightbourne knew all about St. Werburgh and the treasure, but until today, he always believed it to be nothing more than a fanciful tale typical of medieval hagiography. Now it seemed there was a real chance that the treasure existed and if so, he intended to be the first to lay hands on it...or to be precise, lay on it someone else's hands, working on his behalf. In his tousled head possibilities soared in clouds of imagination lit by shafts of garnet and gold light. Illuminated manuscripts, gold brooches and pendants: ah, seventh-century Mercia.

Thinking about England, well, London— where they had easily traced the barrister thanks to Simon overhearing his name; now they'd got the dove, but not without some complications. He laid the paper knife on the tooled leather desk and sighed again. Deaths were always regrettable, but the jewel was his. Certainly, his choice of executioner was impeccable. Marcia Fells was a reliable professional. The piece of artwork, the dove, was his now, it was safely in her hands and those English cops were chasing shadows. He permitted himself a broad grin: now for the big heist.

Warren Lightbourne poured bourbon and swirled it round in his glass, admiring the deep red through the crystal. He held it next to the Roche lamp and mused at the sparkling effect created by the cut crystal— like an Anglo-Saxon jewel!

CAMDEN TOWN, LONDON, LATER THE SAME DAY

Entry and exit from the attorney's office were swift and rewarding. Fells was back on the street after twenty minutes with another hard disk inside her travelling bag. She crossed the road and turned down a side street. Putting the length of this street behind her, she came to a main road, where once again she flagged a taxi. She chatted with the driver, making out that she was a first-time tourist in London.

He dropped her off at Camden Town, one of her favourite parts of the city, full of funky, punk shops and oriental aromas wafting from market stalls. She enjoyed the mouth-watering smells, the gaudy lights and the vendors" calls for punters to sample sizzling stir-fries.

She hesitated by a tattoo parlour and studied the range of stainless steel, titanium and gold piercing jewellery in the window. She wasn't into piercing, but a tattoo appealed to her, something discreet. But no, in her profession it would never do. Shame, she loved the Grim Reaper design.

A bald man came out the door and smiled at her gawping at his head. There were overlapping autumn-coloured leaves where his hair should have been. Nice. He was young and good-looking too. It made her think of Pan and woodland orgies: pity she had other matters to attend to.

Moving on and without lingering around the stalls, the hooded Fells climbed the steps to the canal towpath and strode away from the well-lit, hurly-burly of the market into the twilight gloom. A solitary jogger passed her, red-faced, his vest soaked in sweat. There was a notable difference in the temperature by the canal and that of the market below. Marcia Fells shivered and strode out for a couple of minutes until satisfied that no-one was watching, she unzipped her travelling bag, took out the screwdriver, office keys, hard disks and paperweight, wiped them all for prints and flung them into the canal. The blonde zipped her bag and strode back to the lock: next stop Oxford.

THIRTY

LINCOLN, 2021 AD

The Grimsby Evening Telegraph

THE HEADLINES LEAPT AT THEM:

QC MURDERED IN ANGLO-SAXON JEWEL THEFT

They hurried across the road and pooled some change to buy the newspaper. There on the pavement outside the shop they read the article.

Queen's Counsel, Mr David Briggs (43), was found shot in the head by cleaner Mrs Eithne O"Brian in the study of his luxurious riverside apartment on Saturday morning. Mr Briggs's Romanian chauffeur, Victor Doganu (48), was also found dead at the scene. Metropolitan Police estimate the time of the deaths at around 7 pm on Friday evening. The killer stole an Anglo-Saxon jewel, an object in the possession of the Briggs family for centuries. His widow estimates the jewel, in the shape of a dove, to be worth several thousand pounds although its exact value has not been established. Police have issued an artist's impression of the piece (see left) and Mrs Briggs has offered a reward of ten thousand pounds to anyone supplying information that will lead to the recovery of the jewel.

David Briggs, graduate of Jesus College, Oxford, was a prominent barrister, specialising in high society divorce cases. His most recent success was the celebrated case of the actor Michael Wynn, whose ex-wife, supermodel Anna Kuchaylova had filed for a three million pounds settlement, instead, receiving £750000.

Under the article was the artist's impression of the dove.

"Look, that's our dove."

"Family heirloom, by Freya." Jake growled.

"Do you think we should contact Double-A?"

"Let's get back to the car and think about it."

They began to stride towards the car park, each lost in thought. Inside the car they sat in stunned silence for a minute or two. Jake spoke first. "The guy that took the dove off us was no barrister, that's clear enough. He was too..." he searched for the right word....

"Seedy?"

"Yeah, seedy. No way he was a barrister. So, that means the barrister hired our guy to get the jewel for him – and now the QC's dead. And another thing, that geezer who attacked me at the hypermarket—"

"You were lucky, Jake."

"I didn't want to upset you by going into the gory details, but that bruise on my left arm, well, the hulk that shot at me in Covenham...he jumped me by the trolleys."

"And you lived to tell the tale? What happened?"

"You were sitting in the car admiring that young gardener, so you missed the excitement. He described the chase and how he'd saved himself with the gardening fork, ending by adding, "I shan't have to worry about him again, at any rate."

"You were brave, darling," she stroked his arm. "I remember the gardener bending over the brute, but with the Land Rover being high, I couldn't see much. Do you think we should phone Sir Clive, then?"

"Why? It isn't going to help find the killer, is it? And he'd only complicate matters by calling in other agents. No, let's leave him to think it's separate from the Sir John Robinson inquiry.

"There's a £10000 reward. We could describe the man who took the dove from us and pick up some spending money."

"What and blow our cover, for what? Some new shoes and other accessories? I don't think the seedy guy's the killer. His job was to deliver the jewel to the QC. Look, we're well out of this. These jewels are worth a fortune and people are prepared to kill for them. It's obvious we should give up this treasure hunt and go back to our normal lives."

"But we know where the treasure is now." Alice protested, the look of steel and the clenched jaw made her position clear.

"Sure. But we knew where the dove was and that geezer turned up out of the blue and took it off us. I still don't know how he found out about us. How do we know that we aren't being watched right now?"

She shuddered and looked around out of the car window, "You're right, we should give up for the time being at any rate: let things settle down a bit. We could be the only ones who know where the treasure is. Maybe we can make a move when they catch the killer."

"If they catch him. But you're right. It's the only sensible thing to do. We're out of our depth working alone."

They drove back to Louth intimidated; all their earlier exuberance forgotten.

LEWISHAM, LONDON, AN HOUR LATER

IT WAS past lunchtime and Detective Chief Inspector Ron Willis of the Lewisham Borough CID was fresh from an interview with Chief Superintendent Aalia Phadkar. Her earlier career, peaking with the dismemberment of the Paolillo organisation, was legendary in the Metropolitan Police. Despite her humanity, Ron Willis felt in awe and threatened in her presence. He considered her an attractive woman in a statuesque way, because there was hardness in both features and eyes that hinted of marble. Willis tried to imagine her at home, brushing her hair in a chemise before a mirror and failed: she probably didn't even go to bed. He snorted as he walked back down the corridor to his office.

It was bad enough that a killer had the nerve to murder a member of the Queen's Counsel on his patch without the added pressure of his boss leaning on him. She wanted him to keep as much as possible under wraps for fear of a media free-for-all. Of course, he couldn't agree more; what irritated him was that she felt he needed telling. He walked into his office and slammed the door, causing his right-hand man, Detective Sergeant Ron Meade, to grin and remark: "Iron Maiden again, boss?"

In the force they were known as "The two Ronnies", after the famous comedians, but only behind their backs. Willis was fifty-three with a lifetime spent in the Force. Everything about him was built on the grand scale, standing at about six foot-seven, large hands and feet, a big round head with short-cropped grey hair and bushy moustache and eyebrows running like a railroad across his face. His first uneventful years passed on motorway patrol, but his investigative talent soon emerged in the CID where, to date, his involvement in over a score of murder or manslaughter investigations had left him with a formidable track record. Nine cases solved with the general recognition of the brilliance involved two of these. One in particular, that of a fourteen-year old schoolgirl, left him and his team high and dry. That was the one that hurt most. Eight years had passed since her body turned up in woodland near Harrow. The killer had been thorough, leaving no trace to pin him to the crime. Hundreds of hours of intensive work had left them clueless and despite his enviable record, the image of Laura Gray's strangled expression was imprinted on his mind, a constant reminder of justice unfulfilled—it rankled. Willis enjoyed the ungrudging esteem of his colleagues, but his apparently assured manner belied a man self-tormented by the Laura Grays of this world, leading to achievement through fanatical precision and scrupulousness.

His means of unwinding and emptying his mind of whatever the current obsession happened to be was fruit of the same fanaticism of precision and scrupulousness. Willis built 1:8 scale models of eighteenth-century British warships. A fleet of men-of-war with their gun ports open and their flags signalling imminent engagement therefore graced the detached house he owned in the leafiest part of Stoke Poges. Mrs Willis, long since defeated, had hoisted the white flag and divorced herself from the wreckage of a sixteen-year marriage. Her solicitor explained the marriage as a systematic isolation, the result of demanding police service interspersed with interminable research visits to the National Maritime Museum and long evenings spent by

DCI Willis in his miniature shipyard: otherwise, the garden shed.

The chief inspector wasn't in the mood for flippancy, "Shut up Meade, unless you have something useful to say."

"The killer's a professional."

"Something useful, I said, Meade. Even with your degree in Advanced Backwardness you should know that nine times out of ten when there's a murder, it's someone in the family who's responsible."

DS Meade smiled, the idea of a bull, its neck pierced by a picador came to mind, but almost five years of daily contact bred deep respect and fondness for this old-school copper. It was reciprocal. Meade was forty-two and from Liverpool, his Merseyside accent still detectable, but only to the expert ear. In their five years together, Willis had come to appreciate Meade's sharp mind. He knew his colleague's somewhat sleepy expression and laidback manner disguised an imaginative operator able to make striking connections between apparently insignificant details. More than one key breakthrough in recent cases was directly attributable to these virtues.

"You don't think it's the wife? This has the hallmark of a professional. There's no trace of fingerprints and all the CCTV footage shows is a woman wearing a hood. What we know is that she's between 20 and 50 years old, medium height, slim and she did some shopping at *Miu Miu* on Bond Street."

"Expensive tastes." Willis rubbed his bull-like neck and Meade thought of a picador lance. When he spoke, it was with conviction,

"That fits perfectly with what we know about Mrs Kate Briggs. And don't forget, she's a clever lady."

Meade had a beak-like narrow face with a cleft chin, which he cupped in his hand.

"Well, it's a busy shop and they don't remember a woman with a jacket and hood."

"Let's go back over what little we've got."

"According to your number one suspect, the widow herself, we know that the victim had been entrusted with a precious Anglo-Saxon jewel in the form of a dove, which he was going to declare to a coroner but that was taken by the killer. The safe in the study was open, but nothing else in the house appears to be missing except the hard disk of the victim's computer."

"Now that's interesting," the chief inspector sat down at his desk opposite Meade and placed the tips of his huge fingers together, "what does that suggest to you, Meade?"

"That our killer had contacted him by email and she wanted to remove all traces?"

"Could be. But I don't think so. Setting aside my predilection for lady wife, let's analyse: one, it seems he let her into his apartment quite happily and two, he opened the safe in front of her. Now, given that she took his keys and swiped the hard disk from his office computer, it could be that she wanted to remove something that he had on both of them."

"Well, you can send an email to the various addresses of a contact."

"Fair enough," Willis said, tugging at his short grey moustache, "but what if she wanted to remove any traces of the jewel?"

DC Meade pushed a piece of paper towards him.

"What's this?" He grasped the paper with thick, well-manicured fingers.

"An artist's impression of the jewel as described by Mrs Briggs."

"Blimey. Must be worth a fortune. How much did she say he paid for it?"

Meade flicked open his notebook, "£150000. And that's odd too."

"Why?"

"Well, look at it, that's more or less actual size as his wife remembers it. I'm no expert, but it must be worth a hell of a lot more than £150000."

"Get onto somebody, an archaeologist or art expert, find out how much the bauble's worth. Bit of a rum marriage this one, eh, Meade?"

"Well, you'd know more on that score, sir."

Willis smiled and pointed a frankfurter-like finger,

"Your little nurse still proving to be a slippery eel, eh, Meade? No, what I mean is, what a strange story the Briggs woman came up with about where this valuable and ancient piece of art came from. Don't you find that curious? If we believe what Kate Briggs tells us they live parallel lives, each concentrating on their own career without sharing their interests. Convenient, wouldn't you say?"

"It's called a *modern marriage*, sir."

Willis grunted and scratched his thinning grey hair, "There's nothing to go on from his week planner, nor from his diary. His wife and his secretary can't help with this jewel business, but I'd risk my pension on this one, the key to the murder is the dove, Meade, and the murderer is the demure Katie Briggs, mark my words. As I said before, smart cookie." Again, he jabbed a finger at Meade, "Don't forget, her alibi isn't watertight. Those clients of hers from Birmingham cover her up to four o'clock and quite frankly, the fact that she says she was shopping until she went home and found the body cuts no ice. The couple of receipts she furnished show times of around five o'clock, so there was still time for her to get back home and do the deed. By the way, notice that she's clever enough not to furnish a *Miu Miu* receipt—"

"But that can work both ways," Meade protested, "the fact that she didn't have that particular receipt might mean that she simply didn't go there and *ergo* she's not our killer."

Willis ignored the remark, "And another thing...motive. No children, so she gets to inherit everything. Check out what that adds up to and stick on the worth of the dove stashed away somewhere. A tidy little packet, I'd say. See what you can do about finding its real value and if we're lucky, where it came from."

Meade sighed, his boss had made his mind up and his instincts were almost infallible. Meade wasn't so sure; he couldn't see any immediate benefit to Kate Briggs in disposing of her husband, unless she had a lover tucked away somewhere. We'll have to dig into her personal life, he thought.

Willis's mobile phone rang and to his disgust found it was a journalist from a tabloid who, to add insult to injury wouldn't reveal how he'd obtained his number.

"I believe the police are looking for a specific person. Can you confirm this?"

"I can't confirm anything at the moment."

"Then can you give us any idea when some hard facts will be released?"

"It's early days, there are no plans for a press conference just yet."

"Come on, Chief Inspector, just a little titbit to keep us ahead of the field: according to my source your suspect is a woman. Is that right?"

Willis snorted. The damned place leaked like an old Thames barge. "I can't confirm or deny anything. You'll just have to be patient and wait for the press conference." He snapped his mobile shut. He was blazing. Very few people had this number and those he'd selected to bestow it on were above reproach. So how the devil had this journalist got hold of it? He glared at his colleague and barked: "Why are you still here, Meade. Get your over-sized arse moving."

THIRTY-ONE

OXFORD, 2021 AD

Nodding in time to soft jazz music, Christopher Buchan reflected on the events that had brought him to the Mood Indigo Cocktail Bar. Right now, an attractive woman, an American archaeologist, was ordering drinks for them. She insisted on paying since she had *'dragged him away from his work.'*

Her call came early this morning when she introduced herself as Melanie Draper a Teaching Fellow at Harvard, attached to the Peabody Museum of Archaeology and Ethnology. Afterwards he checked her publications, which made impressive reading. Given that it was a Saturday he didn't have any teaching obligations before lunch, so the meeting was easy for him. She reeled him in by claiming to know the location of St. Werburgh's treasure and was prepared to divulge the location of the *lang dun*" in question on condition that she could be one of his excavation team. She enthused that she couldn't miss out on the most important archaeological find of the century.

He protested, outraged that an American had accessed what was supposed to be an Oxford secret. Fells defused the situation, saying that the seemingly fusty world of archaeology was a hotbed of intrigue. Irritated or not, Buchan, a single man, could not resist the lure of her information nor her charming femininity. Here he was then, waiting for a cocktail—of all things—real ale being more his tipple, and above all, anxious for the bombshell of her news.

Buchan poked his head round the edge of the cedar wood booth with its bright, brass trimmings. On the panelled walls hung a series of black and white art nouveau mirror pictures. The nearest to him was the *Toilette of Salome* by Aubrey Beardsley. Buchan liked it, in fact, he reminisced, when he was a student, he had that very same picture, a print though, not a mirror, on his room wall. He drew his head back and by association thought of Oscar Wilde's Salome and then about the attractiveness of women in general and more particularly about the irresistible Melanie Draper. Maybe it was destiny that had brought her to him from America. He smiled and adjusted his tie, before running his hand over his hair.

Still at the bar, the woman took her change and waited for the barman to serve his next customer. She glanced at the far corner booth, chosen deliberately so they couldn't be seen from the bar. It checked out. Quite sure that she wasn't being observed, she let a white powder flow from a small container in the palm of her hand into the cocktail, where it immediately dissolved. She slipped the container into her pocket, checked that no tell-tale powder had stuck to the glass and carried the drinks over to their booth.

The bar was well chosen. Designed for discretion and privacy, it was the ideal place for an illicit love affair—or to kill someone.

"Here you are Prof." she pushed the glass towards him, *cin cin*. She clinked the rim of her glass with his.

Christopher Buchan looked suspiciously at his glass, "What exactly is this poison, dear girl?"

Without so much as a flicker of her eyelids, the blonde smiled at the aptness of his remark, "It's called an *Almond Affair*."

"By Jove. Is that so? And what goes into it exactly?"

"Well, you take six slivers of almond, some sugar syrup, cherry brandy and peach brandy and a good dollop of gin and some dry vermouth and you stir it all up—oh, and I almost forgot, the main ingredient – potassium cyanide, of course." Her laugh tinkled.

Christopher Buchan shared the joke with a sociable chuckle, "Cheers then," he took a hearty swig of the drink. "*Mmm*. You know, that is rather pleasant." He drank again and began, "Tell me precisely how you found out—" He clutched his chest, a stricken look on his face and he croaked, slumping unconscious across the table.

The blonde stood up quickly, went around to his side of the booth and hauled the body back upright in the seat. "Well, to be fair, I did tell you," she whispered. She slipped her hand into the side pocket of his jacket and pulled out a set of keys. Rapidly she finished her cocktail, put the incriminating glass into one of her shopping bags, pulled her hood over her head and walked calmly out of the bar before mingling with the people on the street. Later she went into a shop and came out with a stationery knife in her pocket.

Shortly afterwards Simon Lightbourne at Oxford University received a phone call concerning Buchan's computer. His task was to eliminate the hard disk. Fells listed what he needed to do—a quick, clean job.

After the call Lightbourne smiled grimly, the woman was proving to be as smart as expected and soon he would have the pleasure of meeting her.

Soon after making the call, Marcia Fells entered a hairdresser's salon as a wavy-haired blonde and exited as a brunette with a half updo. The police would question the Mood Indigo barman and she wouldn't fit the description. She arrived at the Dyson Perrins Building where she satisfied herself that there were no CCTV cameras trained on the car park. Simon Lightbourne appeared at the appointed time. They were wary of each other for different reasons and their conversation lasted less than five minutes, with the woman's eyes in constant movement between doors and windows. Satisfied that the young man was clear on what he had to do, she gave him Buchan's keys and they parted after Lightbourne pointed out Dr Hudson's Audi.

It was the work of a few seconds with the stationery knife to slice the rubber brake fluid tubes on the A3. Then she slipped away.

In Professor Buchan's study, Lightbourne slid the hard disk into his jacket pocket and re-screwed the back on the computer. The surgical gloves followed the screwdriver into another pocket and, after listening for footsteps in the corridor, he used a handkerchief on the door handle as he slipped out. It was only when he was locked into his own study, that he realised how tense he was. He flopped into an armchair and stared at his trembling hands.

"Get a grip man. What a chicken-wuss." he scolded himself.

He didn't like what he was doing and he didn't admire himself for it. But he knew what he wanted from life and nothing was going to stand in his way. He didn't give a buck for any Anglo-Saxon treasure or for archaeology, even though he was studying his PhD in Oxford, England. He was far from home in this goddam morgue asshole place to ingratiate himself with his uncle-daddy. He only found out a couple of years back that Uncle Warren had nailed mom. They didn't know he knew, and uncle-daddy was otherwise childless and sitting on a fortune. He wasn't about to mess up. Simon Lightbourne looked at his hands again: the adrenaline levels had settled down. OK, time to move and trash the evidence for good.

About the time Lightbourne was leaving the Dyson Perrins an ambulance reached Mood Indigo and the Thames Valley Police took Buchan's cocktail glass for forensic examination. Within hours a full-scale murder investigation was under way. Soon the small world of the university was a-buzz with the news. When Paul Hudson heard, he was shaken, finding it difficult to imagine that there was no coincidence with this and David Briggs's murder and the theft of the jewel. The morning papers and the radio were headlining the QC murder. Dr Hudson guessed he too was in danger and, after a little reflection, decided that it was time to make himself scarce.

He eliminated all traces of the jewel from his computer and left work. He got into his Audi and distracted, forgot to fasten his seat belt. Hudson hurtled through the gears of the A3 and when he had to change down towards the end of the road, he didn't notice that the brakes were spongy, because he was too preoccupied with deciding where to hide.

He accelerated along the road and came to another junction with a stop sign but—*horror*—his foot went straight down to the floor and there was no response from the brakes. Now in second gear with the main road only yards away, Hudson cast a wild glance each way. To the left, a heavy goods vehicle was approaching and to the right, a couple of cars. Reacting quickly, Hudson accelerated, changed into third and jammed down on the accelerator. The powerful engine roared as the black car leapt like a puma. He heard the booming horn of the truck, the hiss of its air brakes, the scream of rubber on tarmac, but by some miracle he was in one piece, changing into neutral and hauling on his hand brake. The Audi went into a spin and smashed passenger side-on into the massive trunk of a roadside plane tree. Hudson, flung sideways, hit his head against the side window despite the airbags inflating. The window glass crazed and the archaeologist lost consciousness. In a kaleidoscopic mess of mangled metal, shattered glass and inflated airbags, Paul Hudson, lay pale as a corpse unaware of an anxious voice: "Are you all right, mate?" A passer-by with a cigarette dangling from his mouth, its inordinate length of ash dangling over his brown poodle, pulled out his mobile and called for an ambulance.

THIRTY-TWO

LEWISHAM, LONDON, 2021 AD

Ron Willis reached for the phone. It was the Thames Valley Police in Oxford who informed him that Professor Christopher Buchan had been poisoned by an almond cocktail laced with potassium cyanide. The latter, with its odour of bitter almond had been disguised. The barman furnished a description of the woman who entered the cocktail bar with the professor. She was long-legged and estimated to be in her mid- or late-thirties with wavy, shoulder length blonde hair and blue eyes. Unfortunately, the barman was unable to be more accurate. "One customer's like another," he shrugged. The police held out little hope of the photo-fit.

One detail that emerged was that the blonde had an American accent. But as Willis later pointed out to Meade that didn't mean a thing. Anyone with half a brain could fake an American accent: indeed, many Americans with half a brain spoke with an American accent, he jested. And he was quick to emphasise that the description, such as it was, fitted Kate Briggs.

The reason that Thames Valley had contacted him was

that Christopher Buchan's diary contained an appointment at 10 o'clock in the morning five days ago with the late David Briggs QC. Given that both men had died at the hands of a woman, it was reasonable to assume that they were dealing with the same killer. Now there was the additional complication of a car crash involving one of Buchan's colleagues: an academic by the name of Hudson. The archaeologist was an expert on Anglo-Saxon artefacts and lucky to be alive. His car was a write off, but was being examined by police technicians.

"Right-ho, I'll send DS Ron Meade straight up to Oxford. He should be with you in an hour or so depending on the traffic. We'll chase up on a few leads at this end. Thanks a lot, and obviously I'll keep you posted on any developments here...OK, will do...yep, "bye now." He glanced across at Ron Meade. "Have you got anything juicy on the Briggs woman yet?"

"Not yet sir, I've got a few contacts looking into her private life. Don't you think we should haul her in and find out about her recent movements?"

"Not yet. I'd like to have something to make her squirm, first."

Willis stood, well, he thought, no shortage of quality victims. He'd better get down the corridor and report the latest developments to her ladyship.

Chief Superintendent Phadkar was in company, but told Willis to come in and impart the latest developments. She listened and then, with a thin smile, said, "So we have a serial killer on the loose. All the more reason for Helen's presence here," she gestured towards a woman of about forty, "let me introduce you. This is Chief Inspector Ron Willis, Helen Skinner, criminologist."

An inward groan and Willis thought, *that's all I need, a*

shitload of highfalutin jargon with a killer on the loose. He shook hands with the criminologist and noted the shrewd eyes weighing up his reaction to her presence. He tried and failed to put on a pleasant expression.

"Helen will profile this killer for you Chief Inspector," the Super said. "Get your team together for a briefing in half an hour."

Twenty-five minutes later Willis and his team, with the sole absence of DS Meade, were assembled in the briefing room. Willis had time to fill them in on the Oxford murder and the usual banter died down when Chief Superintendent Phadkar came in and sat down in the front row.

Helen Skinner didn't look like an expert on anything. Sensible flat shoes and teal tweed skirt, hand-knitted cardigan and plain cream blouse gave the impression of the housewife from next door. In contrast, when she spoke, her voice was clear, confident and authoritative.

"Ladies and gentlemen, I think we are dealing with a hired killer. These types do not conform to a general psychological profile: in this specific case even less so. Statistics show that only 12% of serial killers are female and of course, our subject, let's call her "K" for killer, is motivated by personal gain rather than, let's say, sexual perversion."

CI Willis looked round the room and at a glance saw that Ms Skinner had captured her audience. His grey eyebrows drew together, was DC Tomlinson actually taking notes? Bright lass, but she'd soon learn that it was practice, not theory that made a good cop.

"K is between 25 and 35 years old," continued Ms Skinner, "I'd guess at the older end. A loner— ruthless, remorseless and efficient. She sees herself as a dominant, controlling, powerful figure, after all, she holds the power of life and death. In the case of K, however, she is cold-blooded and calculating, not a typical psychopath who cannot control her addiction. We have to remember that K's motivation is financial gain rather than striving to make her violent fantasies real."

She paused and looked around the room at the expectant faces. There were no comments, so she added, "Most probably K will be glib and superficially charming. She's a manipulative person and will have no problem about cool and easy lying. She's extremely convincing. The people around K are not people to her, but targets and opportunities. So, for K, the end always justifies the means and she won't let anything stand in her way. K. is incapable of love and is callous, with no empathy for her victim—that's about it. Now, are there any questions?"

Willis set aside his prejudice and asked, "You say K is a loner. Would you exclude accomplices?"

Skinner half-closed her eyes, looked down demurely and smiled, "No, I wouldn't. Most of her work will be done in isolation, but I repeat, she's manipulative and could easily make use of a person to further her purpose. I doubt very much that K would take anyone into her confidence, but it can't be ruled out."

A timid DC Tomlinson raised her hand, "Do you think there'll be anything in K's background that's led her to become what she is now?"

"Almost certainly there'll be a dysfunctional background of some sort, an isolated upbringing or an overbearing parent, maybe an alcoholic or drug abuser. But K is not an underachiever, quite the opposite I'd say."

There were no more questions.

Chief Superintendent Phadkar stood up, "I'd like to

thank Ms Skinner for her invaluable contribution. The victims are people very much in the public eye. It goes without saying that everyone should be on their toes. Expectations are high. Let's apprehend this woman before she can do any more damage and let's not lose sight of the fact that K is a tool, not the mastermind. Whoever's paying her I want behind bars, too. By the way, there's the not-so-minor issue of recovering the stolen jewel—what's it worth, CI Willis?"

"Our expert at London University values it upward of £500000."

"Very well, back to work everyone and good luck."

CS Phadkar took Helen Skinner by the arm and they left the room.

Willis raised his voice, "Just a minute everyone. He deliberately stood with his back to the whiteboard as if to obliterate everything on it and glanced round to make sure that Phadkar was safely out of earshot. "There is something else to bear in mind of course." He cleared his throat, "not wishing to undermine what our expert colleague has just outlined, but, and bearing all that in mind, and *er*...always keeping an open mind," he looked shiftily about the room at the expectant faces, some puzzled by this unusual hesitancy and repetition, "our killer, let's call her K," he smirked, "may not be a professional. In fact, she may be a highly intelligent woman close to home, as it were."

DC Tomlinson placed thumb on one eyebrow and forefinger on the other to shade her eyes. She didn't want Willis to see her dissent. She found the criminologist far more convincing. The troubling thing was that Chief Inspector Willis was rarely wrong. She tuned into him again.

"What little information we have on K tallies precisely

with our fresh-faced widow, so I want some effort made to trace her movements, contacts, possible love life and so on. Be discreet, mind you. We aren't ready to pull her in yet. By the way, K's responsible for the deaths of Briggs and Buchan and there's news just come in of a possible third attempted murder in Oxford. Right, that's it for now. Tommo, I'd like a word."

DC Christine Tomlinson jumped. Willis wasn't into mind reading now, was he? She remained behind as the others trooped out.

"Well, DC Tomlinson," Willis gave her a crocodile smile, "did you learn anything you didn't already know from that briefing?"

"Not really, sir, it was mostly common sense," she plucked up courage, "but I suppose hearing it all laid out gave me a clearer idea of our killer."

"Anyway, I want you to turn Mrs Briggs's Interior Design business inside out and see if you can get us any leads."

Christine Tomlinson stared at the broad back of her boss as it disappeared into his office and shrugged. It wasn't inconceivable that Kate Briggs matched the K profile and her respect for Ron Willis meant she would work on that theory for now.

OXFORD, 2021 AD

THE DISINFECTANT IN the Radcliffe Hospital irritated Meade's sinuses and the place triggered an unwelcome boyhood memory of a post-op blood-stained pillowcase. Nowadays it seems they weren't so keen to slice out children's tonsils. DS Meade fought to overcome his uneasiness and concentrate on what the softly-spoken, distinguished-looking doctor was explaining to him about Dr Paul Hudson's condition.

"...neuropsychological deficits in attention and memory in the early stages. There may be some exaggeration of cognitive dysfunction—"

"Sorry? What's that to a layman, doctor?"

The short-sighted neurologist peered through his stylish frameless glasses and smiled apologetically, he cleared his throat and tried again in simpler terms. "With craniocerebral trauma—sorry, concussion in other words—there may be deficits in memory and attention in the early stages. Then, the patient has to be monitored during the weeks that follow for signs of PCS, that is post-concussive syndrome. The symptoms range from the obvious headaches, difficulty in concentrating, irritability, noise sensitivity, depression, fatigue, sleep problems, nausea and drowsiness, inability to tolerate stress and alcohol to the less obvious, personality changes, aggression and poor judgment. There may even be depressed libido."

"What state is Dr Hudson in?"

The physician studied a clipboard for a moment or two and Meade studied him. A laminated nametag indicated that the doctor's name was Dr Mark Pearson, who was grey —short grey hair, unsettlingly pale grey eyes, grey trousers under his white coat and a grey tie, which grudgingly conceded a regular, thin diagonal red stripe.

"Conscious and stable. Given the impact, his wounds are superficial, slight facial cuts and bruising to the arms. As I say, our main concern should be post-concussional disorder of some kind. Dr Hudson will need a series of check-ups after being discharged."

Clear enough on Hudson's condition, Meade asked the question he had held back, knowing full well that doctors have to protect their patients from the stress of interrogation.

"May I interview Dr Hudson?"

Dr Pearson nodded cooperatively, with the briefest of recommendations,

"Just 5 minutes. Don't be surprised if he can't remember the details of the accident."

After an unsatisfactory few minutes with a barely recognisable Hudson—although Meade had never previously had the pleasure of his acquaintance—his handsome features compromised by swelling and bruising, Meade left him to convalesce.

Meade got on the phone to Willis.

"I'm in the Radcliffe Hospital, sir. The guy's in pretty good shape all things considered. Concussed and a little vague or evasive, depending on how you look at it. He's had a sharp blow to the head but sustained just superficial injuries from flying glass. Ah, by the way, I just took a call a few minutes ago from the local lads and they are certain it was no accident, it seems the brake fluid tubes were severed...yes, that's right...no doubt at all. Right sir, will do."

Meade closed his mobile and sighed. It looked like he'd be in Oxford for some time and the situation was very messy.

THIRTY-THREE

RANNOCH MOOR, SCOTLAND, 2021 AD

A camping holiday in Scotland was Jake's idea. Some years ago, with a school friend on a fishing holiday at Loch Eigheach, he had been impressed by the beauty of the wilderness around Rannoch Moor and above all by its remoteness: you couldn't even get a beer in the Rannoch Moor Hotel, only a scotch.

LONDON

The funeral of her husband and the trauma of the last few days had left an emotional Kate Briggs exhausted. Black suited her, but when she looked into the hall mirror, a drawn face with puffy eyes stared back. She turned away and went into the study. There was so much to do. One of her first tasks should be to put the flat up for sale. David's dream, she sighed, an apartment overlooking the river. She fought back tears and forced memories of the happy, early years out of her mind. The flat would always be too full of memories for her and too much his place. Instead, she planned to go ahead with conversion work at Monken Hadley. True, David had been born there, but so little time shared in his parents' house meant that it would be a new home. It was also better placed for her work. She sat down at the desk and stared at David's monthly planner. She'd sell the Porsche too. When all was said and done, Kate reflected, there'd be a tidy sum in the bank.

It was the thought of the bank that reminded her of something she'd put off until things calmed down. Kate opened the central drawer of the desk and found David's diary. He showed it to her once saying, "you never know..." She flicked through the final pages to the notes at the back, where disguised among other writing were his user name and password for his on-line banking. She tried to switch on the computer, but of course, that was useless, the hard disk was missing. She frowned and went upstairs to work magic with her makeup.

Two hours later she was sitting in front of David's bank manager. After his condolences they discussed practical affairs. When she left, she had a piece of paper in her handbag with a name written on it.

Back in the apartment she smoothed the piece of paper out on the desk and re-read the name: Stephen Bentley. So, David had paid this man £150000 for the ill-fated jewel. She opened the top left-hand drawer where David kept his visiting cards and began to shuffle through them. She found one with Stephen Bentley, Private Investigator indicating an SW 11 address and phone number. She dialled it and fixed an appointment for the afternoon. Strange she thought, the man had sounded as though he expected her to contact him. She wondered what he knew. Kate shrugged. The important thing was to discover whether he had any clue to the identity of her husband's killer. Kate screwed up the piece of paper and let go when she realised that her nails were digging into the palm of her hand.

Kate tottered up the stairs to the detective's second-floor office. She'd never met any of David's private detectives and had no idea what to expect. She couldn't have imagined such a banal scene. The windows of the office were closed and the air was stale with cigarette smoke. On the dirty, off-white painted walls were pinned a Chelsea FC scarf and a several seasons old team photograph of the Cup winners. The detective was sitting behind his desk and half rose to indicate a seat for her. Kate noticed the shrewd expression in his hazel eyes. Late-forties, thick brown hair greying at the temples, he had a well-worn sports jacket over a green shirt and a brown, woollen tie. A cigarette dangled from the corner of his mouth and he didn't take it out when he spoke to her. Fascinated, Kate watched its glowing end bobble up and down with his words, ash falling onto his shirt. At least he had the grace to sympathise for her loss, even if his respect fell short of not ogling her breasts.

When asked how he'd come into possession of the jewel, Bentley was evasive, saying there were some aspects of the affair that must remain confidential. But when Kate pointed out that she was happy to pay for this consultation and that she knew about a young couple in Louth, he became more cooperative. She found out about Jake and Alice and how they dug up the jewel in a Lincolnshire field. She got their details and Bentley printed his three colour photos of the jewel.

Even the cynical Bentley wasn't prepared for what came next. This attractive, harmless-looking woman with earnest blue eyes leaned forward across his desk and asked him to procure her a gun. At first, he was adamant that it was impossible, but when she took a chequebook out of her handbag and laid it on his desk, he changed his mind, but his natural cynicism surfaced. There was a pistol that he could sell her, but as he pointed out to her, she hadn't thought this through.

People just didn't understand that you couldn't just point a pistol and hope to hit the target. She would need shooting lessons.

"As a matter of fact," Kate smiled, "the left hand keeps the pistol steady and the right exerts even pressure on the trigger. The arm is an extension, like a rifle stock and if everything isn't perfect to a millimetre, you miss the target."

Bentley's jaw dropped, "You've experience of shooting?"

"As a girl," Kate stated without offering any explanation. She smiled at the memory of her father and his love of small arms.

"Well," Bentley said, "It'll mean having a firearms license. The license implies an all-clear from the police. In present circumstances they won't allow you a license, you can see that?" He looked at her with an air of challenge. "You'll need a false identity and two referees for the rifle and pistol club." He was prepared to be one and, yeah, he could get another. This all meant time and—as Kate understood from his vulgar thumb and forefinger gesture—money. The detective flicked the long ash of his cigarette onto the floor, took another long drag and, remembering what an ashtray was for, stubbed it out.

Kate had to swear that whatever happened, Bentley wouldn't be involved. Under his avid gaze she wrote him a cheque for four thousand pounds and he unlocked a drawer in his desk and slid a Glock 19 across to her. She picked it up, its perfect balance a pleasant sensation, then placed it in her Prada shoulder bag.

They went on talking and Bentley gave her a card bearing the name of a famous shooting club that had transferred from the Marylebone area. She was happy to leave his predatory eyes and harsh laugh, a promise to call her when everything was ready hanging in the air.

Outside, even the fume-laden London road seemed refreshing after the detective's office, Kate breathed in and considered the situation. She was no nearer to the identity of David's killer, but she had more on Louth. Kate hurried back to her car. There was an appointment in just less than an hour with a client from Reading to deal with.

LEWISHAM, LONDON

Ron Willis rang and found Meade in the Research Lab for Archaeology and the History of Art at the university. His call had interrupted something close to meditation on Meade's part. Dr Paul Hudson was setting the detective's instincts to red alert. They had come to this office together from the hospital, Hudson going against medical advice and taking responsibility for his own discharge by signing the disclaimer form. Hospitals gave Meade the creeps, he hated their odours of canteen food and disinfectant and nauseating colour schemes, which left him with a sense of vulnerability and unease. Yet he couldn't put his mood down to this, as he explained to his chief.

"Hudson's computer had no trace of the jewel. He denied ever having it there and when I asked him if he didn't want us to see a picture of the jewel, he became... how can I put it?—evasive, shifty, if you like."

"*Mmmm.*"

"I suggested that he didn't want us to see the inscription on the back and you know what he said? He claims that he can't remember what was written there. Clammed up when I pressed him. He's lying. I mean, an expert like him, trained to scrutinise the smallest detail to piece together the past isn't going to forget a clue as big as a barn door, is he? Unless it's this blessed PCS that Dr Pearson told me about. What? Oh yeah, PCS—post-concussive syndrome. It means you forget things. Damned convenient in this case, but the devil of it is, it might be true. The silly sod wasn't wearing his seat belt. No. Lucky it was a German car, if you ask me—"

"Where is he now?"

"The Oxford lads have moved him to a safe house. They made him aware—as if he needed telling—that his life is in danger. K went close and she will try again. He seemed stressed but co-operative enough."

"*Uh-uh*, well, see what you can turn up in the department there about Hudson and Buchan. About what happened on the day Briggs visited. There must have been quite a few people around someone will have noticed something. Then get over to the safe house and lean on Hudson, see what he's holding back."

"Will do. And I've already phoned through to the Oxford lads sir, to get them to see if there are any prints on the professor's computer casing, not that K's that careless. I'll keep you posted."

Meade flipped his phone shut and wandered out of the office into the laboratory. A young woman with long, wavy, red hair and a paisley print skirt showing beneath her lab coat smiled at him and Meade nodded. She was cradling a shard of glazed, dark red pottery in the palm of her hand.

"It's Roman," she ventured, seeing him looking at it, "Samian ware to be precise, look there's a little bear's head on this piece. Cute, isn't it?"

Willis turned the piece of pottery over in his hand. "Smashing. I'd like to ask you a few questions Miss...?"

"Mrs...I'm married. Emma Crawford, Lecturer in Roman Archaeology." She held out her hand, but instead of shaking it, Meade gave her back the shard, causing the archaeologist's blue eyes to sparkle with amusement.

"Detective Sergeant Ron Meade, Metropolitan Police."

"I suppose you're here about poor professor Buchan."

"Would you mind coming through to Dr Hudson's study, Dr Crawford?"

She nodded, pleased at the use of her title and followed him out of the door into the corridor. His mobile rang *Espionage* at high volume. It was Willis again.

"DC Tomlinson rang through; it seems that our Mrs Briggs is constantly on the move across county borders. She'd have had plenty of opportunity to commit these crimes. It may be time to have a word with the grieving widow...and another thing...maybe it's time for that press conference her ladyship has been rattling on about. Meanwhile, you see what you can find out from any of the other archaeologists in the lab. Oh, and I'm coming up to Oxford, we'll meet later."

"I'm doing just that, sir." He tried to keep the exasperation out of his voice and noticed Mrs Crawford's amused smirk.

Sometimes Ron Willis rang just for the sake of it, Meade thought, turning around and leading the way into Hudson's study, where he invited Dr Crawford to sit. He remained standing and thoughtful for a moment, seeming to make a decision and then said, "Bad news I'm afraid. Dr Hudson has been the victim of an attempted murder. He is unharmed and under police protection."

She gasped and put her hand to her mouth. She said: "But who would want to harm Paul? He's a lovely guy."

"That's what I want to talk to you about, Dr Crawford, "Meade said, "we think this case and that of Professor Buchan are connected and it has to do with their meeting here the other day. Can you think of anything that happened in the lab that could shed any light on this situation?"

Dr Crawford pursed her lips and looked thoughtful. "Well, I had a seminar with a group of students in the lab that morning. I should have been too busy to take any notice of anyone else, but the two of them were very excited about a piece of Anglo-Saxon jewellery. Paul had just analysed it for its metal content and I couldn't help overhearing that it was *quite unique* those were the professor's exact words. But something more than that, there was his tone of voice, he was so steamed up, that was what caught my attention."

"Quite unique?"

"Yes," she continued, "a few of us gathered round hoping to have a peep at it and I have to admit, I abandoned my students for a moment. Professional curiosity, I suppose. Anyway, that was when Paul–Dr Hudson–said that there was some Old English writing inscribed on the back. That's what made it so unique, you see. There are no other examples of inscriptions on jewellery from that period."

"And do you know what was inscribed on the back?"

"No, that's the funny thing, I remember Professor Buchan becoming very secretive and he insisted on Dr Hudson discussing it in private."

"Is there anything else you can remember that might be helpful?"

"No, I remember Dr Hudson saying that the jewel was made in Lincolnshire. At Tallington. Tallington's well known for its production of Anglo-Saxon craftwork. I'm quite sure about that."

"Well you've been very helpful. Here's my card," he took one from his breast pocket. "If anything else comes to mind, Dr Crawford, no matter how insignificant you think it might be, please give me a ring."

Meade drifted back into the Laboratory and discovered that among the researchers there was a Korean, an Italian and an American, the latter a guy called Lightbourne. Coincidence: the killer had an American accent. Willis thought it was put on. But what if it wasn't? It was a long shot, but he decided to follow it up. You never knew with small, insignificant coincidences. Lightbourne wasn't in the lab at the moment. He made a call to Tommo, and asked her to run a check with their American colleagues.

One of the other researchers, the Italian, confirmed that Hudson and the professor got excited about an inscription on the back of the jewel and that this was something quite unique for Anglo-Saxon stuff. He said one of them translated the inscription and he caught something about a hill and a cross and something else he "couldn't remember or didn't understand."

It was just after Meade finished with the Italian that a call came through from the Thames Valley Police. Hudson had slipped his guardians and left the safe house.

THIRTY-FOUR

RANNOCH, SCOTLAND

"The theory's simple enough, laddie, we call it a three-fly cast. That's because ye have a point fly, a dropper and a bob fly, that's the one farthest from the rod. But ye'll never catch a thing laddie, ye've never done it before." Alistair Stewart looked shiftily past Jake and Alice around an otherwise empty shop. He reached below the counter and dropped his voice to almost a whisper. He held up a piece of clear plastic shaped like a miniature flying saucer. "Bubble float," he said with a wink and a conspiratorial smile. "The trout think it's a bubble an" ignore it and go for the fly. Ye see the beauty of it, the bubble float keeps the fly up and ye just lob it out and pull it in.

"Sounds easy enough," Jake said.

"Aye, no doubt. But the hard part is not to be seen usin" it. Ye steer clear of other fishermen. As far away as ye can get. Not that there'll be many about at Eigheach in the week, mind. It's not permitted, ye see. I'll give you these Claret Pennels, they're a good fly an" if anyone asks ye, ye can tell "em that ye got "em from Alistair Stewart, but I'll deny all knowledge of yon," he nodded at the piece of plastic and touched his nose with his forefinger.

All of which accounted for Jake catching four brown trout on his first day out. But it didn't pass unobserved. He packed everything away at the end of the afternoon and, from his keep net, selected the biggest trout for dinner. He was just about to release the other three back into the loch when: "Hey. Over there. Stop."

Jake froze and lowered the keep net back into the water. A middle-aged man ran along the bank towards him, waving his arms.

"What do you think you're doing, laddie?"

Jake and Alice gazed at the man in astonishment.

"Sorry?" Jake glanced involuntarily at his tackle box, because he had a guilty conscience. But it was closed and there was no sign of his bubble float.

"You were about to throw them back," the man pointed at the net, his heavy Scottish accent between gasps for breath made him hard to understand for the English couple. "Don't do that, I'll buy them off you."

Jake relaxed. "Naw," he said, "I'll give them to you. You're welcome."

"No, no. I'll buy them. How much do you want?"

Later, cooking their trout by the tent Alice laughed and said, "I'll bet he went home and told his wife that he'd caught three trout in the loch."

"Well, apart from the sticky moment when I thought he'd spotted my float, it was quite a pleasant surprise," Jake pointed at the bread and bottle of white wine. "Courtesy of our friend the honest fly fisherman. His very good health and ours," he said raising his glass.

He savoured his wine, sooner or later they would have to leave this idyll and that thought bothered him.

"I wonder how far the police have got in their murder inquiries. It troubles me that sooner or later, our names will emerge. I mean, they've only to trace the dove to Mr Johnson's farmland and we're involved."

"You're right," she said, frowning, "Maybe we should contact Double-A – he'll have a hissy-fit if he finds out we're in Scotland and excluding him from our findings."

"True. But let's drive back down to Louth before ringing him and, I think we might ring our farmer friend to find out whether the police have contacted him or vice versa."

"Okay, but he might not know we found the jewel on his land. Neither of us breathed a word and that creep who stole it from us won't be in a hurry to contact the police."

"We can't be sure about that. He might want to clear his name and use us as an alibi. That's why we need Sir Clive to keep the police off our backs. Our trip to Scotland hasn't been a waste of time, it's kept us out of harm's way. I think it's time to drive south."

She agreed with him but didn't admit that she was excited about finding the Treasure of Ely Abbey. It was in her plans, risk or no risk.

OXFORD, THE SAME DAY

"WATCH OUT, sir, your boss looks like he's going for first prize in a bollocking competition." a young DC on the Oxford team muttered as he passed Ron Meade in the entrance to the police station.

"Yeah, he's entered for the World Cup next year."

If you didn't know Willis, there was no way you could

warm to the man, Meade thought. Those ferocious eyebrows alone were enough to scatter the faint-hearted. He tapped on the door of Detective Chief Inspector Graham Hicks's office and waited to be invited in. Inside, he found Willis in conversation with the chief inspector. Willis looked up and growled, "What kept you?"

It was obvious Willis was angry about Hudson's absconding. Even though Meade was a few minutes early for their five o'clock appointment, years of frequenting Willis cautioned him not to point it out. He smiled and sidled into the room.

Turning back to his colleague, Willis resumed the conversation, "...what do you think Graham?"

Meade raised an eyebrow; his boss was already on first name terms with his Oxford counterpart. That was a good sign. In his experience other cops were jealous of their patch and cooperated with reluctance.

"It looks like it's all falling into place. But if the woman had already got this valuable Anglo-Saxon jewel by killing the barrister, why the devil did she come up here and murder two university people?"

"To silence them; that's where Ron's inscription about a hill and a cross comes in." He tossed his head towards Meade as he said this in another familiar bull-like gesture. "If we can find out why it's important, we might get somewhere. My guess is that there's more valuable Anglo-Saxon stuff in the equation and that our avaricious murderess wants to get her pretty little hands on it. Well, for the moment that's all we can do here. I'll leave you to try and pin down this Hudson character, Graham. As for us, we'll get organised at the London end."

Getting organised for Willis meant hurrying back to base for a hastily arranged press conference. As far as he was concerned, there was no sense in calling it. They had nothing substantial to talk about, but of course, the murders were too juicy to expect the pressmen to behave themselves. What he had to do was to try to turn it to his advantage, but at the moment he couldn't see how.

LEWISHAM, LONDON, TWO HOURS LATER

Willis followed Chief Superintendent Aalia Phadkar into the police pressroom. The teak panelled floors and walls, witness to a time when local authorities borrowed money freely, looked dated but Willis loved the timeless sumptuousness of the glowing wood and precision of the joinery. A later more cost-conscious generation had acquired four-dozen uncomfortable red plastic and black steel stacking chairs. However, Willis liked these too, because the chairs combined with the infamous lack of hospitality of the Force, ensured that only the most assiduous or hard-bitten reporters lingered.

Willis hated being in front of microphones and cameras, each time was just as bad as the first time. He could already feel sweat under his moustache and damned uncomfortable it was. Out of the corner of his eye he noted that his raven-haired superior, instead, was at ease. He could imagine how much effort she put into that immaculate appearance, with just the right amount of eye shadow and lipstick, but he couldn't imagine where her effortless poise came from. She held up her hands and asked for everyone's attention.

"I'd like to welcome you all to this press conference and to apologise for the lack of notice in calling it. As you know we have two murders, one here in London and one in

Oxford and we'd like to share some of the information we have with you. For those of you from outside the London area, I am Chief Superintendent Aalia Phadkar, and this is Chief Inspector Ronald Willis of the Metropolitan Police CID who is in charge of the investigation. I will just read a short statement and then there will be an opportunity for you to ask questions."

C S Phadkar looked around the room and was gratified to see all the main TV channels represented as well as some crime reporters that she recognised from the major daily newspapers. The murders were sensational, involving as they did, two such prominent members of society.

"As you know, the first murders involved a member of the Queen's Counsel and his chauffeur some days ago and, as stated in a press release, a valuable piece of Anglo-Saxon jewellery belonging to the family was stolen. The victim died from a single shot to the head and his chauffeur, from a severe beating to the head; we have reason to suspect that the killer is a professional working on commission."

Willis darted her a poisonous look. He had no reason to believe it. Oblivious to this, Phadkar looked around the room at the expectant faces and noted that one or two journalists were already speaking into their mobile phones.

"The day before yesterday another murder, which we now have reason to believe was connected to the first two, took place in Oxford. An eminent scholar of the Anglo-Saxon period, Professor Buchan, was found poisoned in a café in the town." Phadkar glanced at Willis, we have evidence to suggest that the murders were committed by the same person."

Several people began talking at once and a voice louder than the others called out, "Have you got a suspect?"

Phadkar raised a ringed forefinger, "If you'd let me

finish my statement, as I said we'll deal with questions later. At this stage of our inquiries in order not to compromise the investigation we aren't prepared to divulge essential information, but what we can say..." She spoke for a couple of minutes, but it was all insubstantial waffle Willis concluded.

She passed the microphone to the Chief Inspector who swallowed hard and looked uncomfortable. There was an excited buzzing of voices in the air.

"Can you name this person?"

Willis looked at his Chief Superintendent and she nodded.

"It's a woman: she's about thirty-five with wavy, blonde hair and blue eyes. She is about one metre seventy tall with a slim build. We don't know where she is at the moment, but we believe that she is still in the country. We'll make a photo-fit available at the end of the conference and would appreciate the usual dissemination. We should like to appeal to the public. If anyone noticed anything suspicious around the time of the murders either in London or Oxford, we ask them please to come forward. Even the smallest, seemingly unimportant detail could prove vital in piecing together the events of the last few days."

"The Superintendent referred to an attempted murder, can you tell us about that?" shouted a reporter from a London paper.

"Our inquiries are at an early stage with this. All I can say is that the intended victim was attacked in Oxford, but that he is well, but shaken. Indeed, we have every reason to think that this latest attempt is connected to the two murders."

Several journalists started talking at once. Phadkar held

up her ring-decked hand and gestured to a reporter from the BBC who she knew and admired.

"You said earlier that you think the woman is a professional killer working on commission. Can we assume that she has been employed by a specialised collector?"

Willis shook his head; he was irritated that the Chief Superintendent had thrown out this suggestion in the first place. It was just the sort of red herring the press would make a meal of.

"No comment. Until we apprehend this woman the exact motive for the crime is only speculation." He fielded another two or three questions and then attempted to close proceedings, "We'll call another conference as soon as we have something more tangible for you." He avoided looking at Phadkar and parried several more questions before, to his intense relief the conference came to an end.

THIRTY-FIVE

LONDON, 2021 AD

After years of driving his feisty A3 Sportback, Hudson had to adjust to the Ford Fiesta but this silver-grey hire car was anonymous and it brought him down the motorway to the East End of London. He paid the congestion charge and turned into a side street to escape the procession of thundering double-decker buses making their way to the terminus at the end of the evening rush hour. There he consulted his A to Z of London to find Kate Briggs's apartment. He looked at her husband's visiting card again and back at the street map. It was only a couple of streets away.

He decided that the Briggs woman might be able to save him a lot of time and trouble if he could winkle out the whereabouts of the long hill with its cross. He pressed his hands to his temples. His head ached. It had been a constant ever since the accident. He wasn't sleeping very well either. Whenever he closed his eyes, he could see that truck bearing down on him. What was it he was thinking about? Oh, yes. Of course, there was no guarantee she'd know where the cross was or even that she'd be at home. He remembered from all those news bulletins that the widow had a career and was a busy woman. He chose not to phone her for an appointment, for several reasons: the police might have tapped her phone and he knew they'd be on the lookout for him, even if technically, he hadn't committed any crime; the radio account of the hooded killer had gripped his attention and though the general public had no idea, the police had confided that the killer was a woman, even hinting that they suspected Kate Briggs, Hudson wasn't so sure and in any case, both crimes and indeed the attempt on himself had been premeditated; without an appointment he'd be catching her by surprise and he felt that he could deal with her if things turned unpleasant.

He checked his watch. It was almost half-past seven, but few windows were lit, since not many professionals had returned home to have supper in their luxury flats. Would she be home from work at this hour? He felt restless and irritable with himself. Why couldn't he just wait? He glanced in his rear-view mirror and, focusing beyond the tiny spots of rain on the rear window, saw that the tree-lined street was empty.

Before he got out his eyes darted up and down the street. Was that movement across the road? He relaxed a little as he made out a female figure in the long shadow of a building. From an open French window, the quiet was shattered by the heightened volume and sentiments of a teatime soap opera. He was about to lock the car when his subconscious registered that the woman was wearing a hooded top. He spun round and saw her moving stealthily behind a lamppost. Hudson snatched the door open and flung himself inside, thrusting the key back into the ignition.

In seconds he was driving away, crunching gears, turning blindly down streets unknown to him, until he came to the East India Dock Road, which he drove along for several miles to where it became the A13. Only now did his speed slow to match the signs at the roadside. He blanched at the thought of the speed cameras he'd driven past, hoping that they were out of service. His head was pounding, aching fit to burst. Through the drizzle he made out a faint glow in the distance that materialised into illuminated letters, *The Fryer Tuck*, and he pulled in next to a battered white Transit.

A wiry trucker was standing just outside the door enjoying long drags on a thin hand-rolled cigarette. Hudson pulled his jacket collar up and darted out, past the smoker and inside to the strains of Presley's *Love Me Tender* and the heavy smell of frying oil. After ladling sugar, but without stirring, he drank his mug of steaming tea, trying to control his shaking hand. His nerves were frayed and he felt stupid. The possibility of the killer keeping an eye on the Briggs woman's flat was obvious with hindsight. The shadowy figure tallied with the police description: youngish, slim and hooded. He drained his mug, shuddering at the sweetness at the bottom. Feeling less shaky, he returned to his car.

Any doubts about the identity of the hooded figure dissipated: the rear window of the Fiesta had a neat bullet hole, with spidery tracery around it. He opened the car and looked for further damage. There was a hole in the upholstery of the passenger seat. Hudson got back into the car and thought for a few minutes. It was a lucky escape and he would have to be more careful from now on. Twice the woman had tried to kill him and he wouldn't give her another chance.

He decided to make for Luton airport. Waiting until the driver of another rental car opened the barrier to the hire returns, he sped through on its tail. He left the Fiesta in one of the Hertz bays and walked into the arrivals' terminus. At the Avis stand he chose a Class C car, a silver Toyota. Hudson calmed down as he typed *Llanfechain* into the Sat-Nav and drove out of the airport feeling sure it would be the next morning before the day staff found the damaged car.

He'd stop on the way before it got too late for a bite to eat, but above all, to let his father know that he was coming. He needed a break anyway; he was feeling lightheaded with fatigue.

Hudson settled down to enjoy the drive to Wales, where the fresh farm air would do him the world of good. Comforting, as they should have been, these reflections didn't slow his whirling thoughts. What had he let himself into? Why the impulsive and irrational behaviour? What were his motives? Was he a suspect?

Dr Paul Hudson realised he was hyperventilating. He slowed his breathing and concentrated on the traffic. No point in obliging that hoodlum by doing her job for her. Self-analysis could wait for Llanfechain and he would buy some aspirin there. His headache was getting worse.

LEWISHAM, LONDON, NINETY MINUTES LATER

WILLIS SNATCHED UP HIS PHONE.

"Sir, a call came through about Luton airport. A car rental company have reported one of their cars with a bullet hole through the rear window."

"Get to the point Tommo."

"Guess who hired it? Our man Hudson. Forensics have

retrieved the bullet from the passenger seat and I'm waiting on their report."

"No prizes for guessing who took that pot shot. Luton airport, eh?" Ron Willis drummed heavy fingers on his desk and looked quizzically at the far wall. "Where would our absconding archaeologist want to fly to?"

At her end of the line DC Tomlinson allowed herself a self-congratulatory smile. This was the opportunity to show her efficiency.

"He wouldn't, sir. That was the first thing I did. I checked out all departures for today and there's no Paul Hudson listed..."

"*Mmmm.*"

"...but get this, sir, Hudson hired a silver Toyota Avalon from another company," she consulted her notebook, "registration KB58 PJB and he's got it for a week."

"Good work, Tommo. Put out a general alert for Dr Hudson. What on earth would make an intelligent man run the risk of being shot at by our killer?" he mused more to himself than to his colleague. "Anyway, let me know as soon as forensics get back to you."

About the same time.

Kate crossed London Bridge on her way from the shooting range. The state-of-the-art, air-conditioned, six firing point, 25 metre range with its auto target changers was the key feature of her new daily routine. Motivated from the start, Kate was gratified that her instructor, Pete, described her as a "natural talent". But then, he had no idea of the hours Kate had spent with her father perfecting her stance and technique as a teenager. These sessions just served as a refresher course, but complete with soft plastic earplugs and hearing protectors that reduced outside noises to a dampened hush. None of the ringing ears of her youth.

While she played along with Pete's suggestion of competitions and trophies, she had one thing on her mind, finalised at a human not a cardboard cutout target.

Kate worried that the days were slipping by and the expected visit from the police still hadn't happened. She aimed to invert roles. The police should think they were interviewing her, but she'd squeeze information out of them. Kate Briggs needn't have worried, far from being below the police radar, at that moment Meade began to think Willis's fabled intuition was right after all.

"Sir, there's something Tommo turned up. She was checking Briggs's bank statement a couple of days ago and it seems he paid £150000 to a private detective a few days before he died. Tommo went to see him yesterday and he claims that the money was used to "acquire" the jewel on Briggs's behalf."

"Do we know this detective?"

"Yes, Stephen Bentley, you know the Battersea one. Well, Briggs used him through solicitors to snoop out the dirt in divorce cases, that sort of thing. His story is that he paid a young couple in Lincolnshire for the jewel and here's the juicy bit—the same couple that Kate Briggs said had given the jewel to her husband so that he could open a coroner's inquest for treasure trove.

"You're on to something there."

"Quite so, sir. I've sent DC Tomlinson back to Bentley to sort him out."

"*Mmm.* I'm waiting on Tommo too for the forensics report on Hudson's hire car."

Meade soon received DC Tomlinson's call. Bentley had admitted that the £150000 was his payment for stealing the jewel from two young people in Louth. However, he was adamant that Briggs had hired him to do that, which meant there was a contradiction in Bentley's and Mrs Briggs's stories. Willis thought about this for some time and his gut feeling was that Bentley was now telling the truth. So, he instructed Meade to go to Louth the next day, find the treasure hunting couple and get Tommo to find out why Kate Briggs had lied about the jewel.

Forensics also confirmed the bullet retrieved from the rented Fiesta had been fired from the same gun as the one that killed the London barrister. Willis pondered events; he was right from the start. The dove was the key and anyone involved with it was at risk. Time to turn the screws on the lovely Kate Briggs.

At the same time as Willis was patting himself on the back, Jake and Alice were driving back down to Lincolnshire. Reassured by the absence in the daily press of any further horrors associated with the Briggs case, they were convinced that they were out of the inquiry. In the beautiful Tayside surroundings, they had done little else except go over all the risk percentages. The guy who took the dove from them was not the murdered professor. They knew that for sure. So, he was still alive. No mention of him in the Press suggested that the killer wasn't bothered with him and he was the only link to them. Why had the killer eliminated the professor? Because the poor man knew where the treasure was, therefore so did the killer. It was logical that the killer would have no interest in them unless they tried to get to the treasure first and they agreed they didn't want to provoke a professional killer. On the other hand, Alice pointed out, the killer may not know where the treasure was hidden and just killed the professor for some reason like protecting her identity. In that case, their knowledge of the whereabouts of the treasure was theirs alone and there was no need for them to rush into finding it. Alice argued they could wait "even for years" but that was not her intention.

They crossed the Humber Bridge oblivious to the fact that they were of pressing interest both to the head of the Thames Valley Police investigation into the death of David Briggs QC and to his widow.

THIRTY-SIX

LOUTH, LINCOLNSHIRE, 2021 AD

After an appointment with two young women from Reading, Kate made a couple of phone calls and cancelled her engagements for the next day. She drove home from her office, crisscrossing her way through the traffic-calmed backstreets. Once home she changed into a pair of Armani jeans and fuchsia cashmere V-neck and drove the Porsche out of the city on to the northbound motorway. She marvelled in the smoothness of the gear changes and the power of acceleration. David had never let her drive his "baby", she smiled, maybe she'd sell her own car now, instead.

On the steps outside the modest flat in Aswell Street that Stephen Bentley had indicated, Kate heard the hesitant notes of a piano, then the same notes repeated in a more confident way. In the pause that followed she knocked and a striking young woman opened the door.

"Hello, you don't know me," Kate said, glancing over the young woman's shoulder where she saw a man seated at a piano, "and I hate to disturb you during a lesson. I wonder if we could have a chat when you're finished?"

Alice was intrigued by the posh accent and paused to study the lineaments, dress and accessories of the woman in front of her; she glanced at her watch and stepped back into the room.

"Come in. We were just finishing anyway." She turned to her husband sitting at the piano, "Jake, practise that exercise until you can play it without hesitating and prepare the Clementi piece for next time. I'll see you next week at the same time, OK? Say hello to your sister, won't you?"

Jake understood at once and played along with her.

When she'd seen him out, Alice gave her full attention to her visitor. She was amazed when Kate introduced herself as the widow of the murdered barrister: the man killed for the dove that she and Jake had dug up. Kate told her about the discovery of the seventeenth-century letter that had led to the two killings, about their research in Lincoln and their visit to Louth.

Listening to this self-assured woman with her home counties diction, and designer clothes, Maria was reminded of the upper-class students who had dominated her university, whose self-assurance had made her feel insecure and awkward during her first year there. As she matured, her confidence in her own ability had developed and Lamia-like she'd shed her anxieties, but an arrogant diner in the restaurant or a domineering colleague could still trigger unwelcome sensations. Despite her conditioning, she intuited a certain vulnerability in Kate and was drawn to her sincerity. Before long, she found herself liking her enough to recount her visit to Covenham with Jake, the find in the cottage, her subsequent kidnapping and the theft of the dove. However, there her story came to an end, because she wasn't prepared to divulge their latest findings. Instead, she began to ask Kate about her work and then about her home. Until, with a start, Alice realised that she was so enthralled by her new acquaintance that it was getting late and her husband would be irritated about hanging around killing time. She wondered where he was. They agreed to meet in the morning; Kate wanted to offer breakfast to the couple and, it seemed to Maria, continue their chat. They shook hands and Kate left for her hotel. Both of them unsure of the path they had chosen: a path hedged with mistrust and winding to what destination? Alice would have to explain everything to Jake and hope he would approve.

———

LEWISHAM, LONDON HALF AN HOUR LATER

As DS Meade was preparing to leave for Louth, a flustered DC Tomlinson intercepted him.

"What's up Tommo?"

The young woman was flushed and Meade could see she was bursting to blurt out something. He cast her an appraising glance— attractive lass, and a damned good cop into the bargain.

"Remember that American at the Research Lab, sir? Simon Lightbourne? Well, the FBI has come up with a link. Lightbourne is the nephew of a certain Warren Lightbourne of Manhattan. Seems this gentleman inherited the bulk of his estate from his father, a German immigrant, who began carrying vegetables to the City market in a three-wheeler van and ended up as the owner of trunk railways and vast sums of money. Well, the FBI reckons this Warren Lightbourne is an art collector. His place is packed with every type of masterpiece, but wait for it, here's the interesting bit... he's in the market for anything Anglo-Saxon, his real passion."

"Now, *that* is interesting."

"Then there were the two killings associated with an art robbery in Massachusetts. You remember that big Manet theft a couple of years back?"

"With the two art dealers shot in Boston?"

"That's the one. Well, the FBI suspect Lightbourne was behind it and that he hired a certain Marcia Fells to do the dirty work."

"Marcia Fells?"

Tomlinson displayed a row of even white teeth in a wide grin, "...and here's the beauty of it, they can't pin anything on her, but she's in her early forties, slim, over one metre seventy, wavy, blonde hair, blue eyes and so they say, quite pretty."

"In other words, a dead ringer for our K and for Ronnie's Kate Briggs for that matter."

Tomlinson exchanged a conspiratorial smile with Meade at the disrespectful reference to their chief.

"Exactly."

"...and you say that the FBI can't pin anything on this Lightbourne character?"

"Lightbourne, sir? No, he's a powerful man, friends in high places and all that. Any case, it's not the masterminds that get caught. It's the ones who do the dirty work. But in this case Ms Fells would appear to be a real pro., just like that criminologist woman said."

"Good work Tommo. Have you told the Chief Inspector?"

"Not yet, sir." Tomlinson looked embarrassed, "to tell the truth I thought it ...*er*, wiser...to broach it with you first."

"All right, leave it with me. *Ha-ha*, I'll break it to him, oh and get back on to the FBI, see if they can fax us a photo-fit of this Marcia Fells."

"Done it, sir." The policewoman chirped, "We're waiting for it to come through."

"Smashing, good work, Tommo!" I'll get the chief up to speed then."

THIRTY-SEVEN

POWYS, WALES, THE SAME DAY

ON A STRETCH OF DISUSED BRANCH LINE IN NORTHERN Powys Dr Paul Hudson walked his black Labrador, Duke, where steam locomotives of the Oswestry and Newtown Railway once belched smoke on their way to the Llanymynech Junction. Today Duke panted along the line as his pensive owner seemed intent on walking all the way to the next village of Llansantffraid.

The dog was four years old now and a ruthless ratter. Every end of winter, when the haystack was reduced to a few feet from the ground, the farm labourers with shotguns formed a circle around it. They threw a flaming brand onto the stack and when the rats fled the blaze they shot as many as they could. Four years ago, Duke, then a puppy, was outside the ring of men and copying the big dogs, went for a fleeing rat. The rodent's incisors inflicted a deep wound on the inexpert nose. Duke bore the scar together with a broody lifelong loathing of rats. Last early spring, according to Paul's father, Duke alone had killed more rats outside the ring of shotguns than all the men put together.

Now Duke bounded into the thick cowslips and St.

John's Wort with murder on his mind, little difference whether his victim was a rat or an innocent dormouse. Paul Hudson was oblivious to the Labrador's antics, because he also had murder on his mind. Unlike Duke, he wasn't thinking of committing one, but rather of how to avoid becoming the victim. His dog cavorted over and dropped a lifeless dormouse at his feet. Hudson stared at it and ignored Duke's fussy tail-wagging performance.

He felt safe on the farm. Llanfechain was a village of only 600 people and unusual movement was easy to spot. Yet, he thought, safety was relative, the killer was a professional and he was a walking miracle. He had survived her murderous assaults twice; but he looked around him taking in the total absence of human life on the ex-O&N line and what that implied, he couldn't expect to survive on luck alone. This, for example, was the ideal place to kill someone and here he was out walking his dog. Hudson shuddered and asked himself for the hundredth time why he had left police protection. He couldn't find a satisfactory explanation. That was it— on impulse. Underlying it was his desire to make his name as the finder of the legendary Ely Abbey treasure. That would guarantee him early passage from Lecturer to Full Professor. Irritated, he gazed at Duke pouncing and growling in the undergrowth of the cutting. He loved that dog. So why did it irritate him so much today? It must be this damned headache. The aspirins didn't seem to have any effect.

He grasped at the thread of his thoughts and pulled them back. There must be more to his motivation than ambition? The police knew he was at risk and soon they would trace him to his father's farm. Should he just let them protect him and deal with the killer? That was the logical course of action. So why then, was he so intent on risking his life? Why, even now, was he thinking of going back to the farm and departing armed with one of his father's shotguns? He knew how to handle one, that wasn't the problem.

A thrush called its alarm as it rose from among the weeds disturbed by the Labrador. He noticed the dog's fur full of burrs and dandelion snow. He would need a good brushing now, he grumbled. No, the problem was that he wanted to honour the memory of his friend and mentor. That was his real motivation. *Poor Christopher.* Chris Buchan had lost his life for St. Werburgh's treasure and Oxford University had the right to unearth it, not some random boffin chosen by the Home Office; if he went back into police protection that would be the inevitable outcome. He set his jaw: no way. Hudson heaved a sigh difficult to interpret. A sigh of relief to have his motivations clear at last? Or a sigh of awareness of the difficulties and dangers the task he had set himself would imply?

He whistled to Duke and turned on his heel. Back to the farm at all speed. He had to get away as soon as possible and pick up from where he had left off in panic the day before.

LOUTH, LINCOLNSHIRE, AT THE SAME TIME.

The waitress put two china cups down for Jake and Alice just as Kate, on time, walked into the café. Her understated Joseph separates, pale grey, cool wool trousers and silk and wool T-shirt hinted at the curves beneath. Jake stared for an instant too long and then recovered, calling the waitress to bring another cup and saucer. After summary introductions and a minimum of small talk, Kate came to the point. She needed their co-operation. Tentative, she broached the subject of what they could tell the police to justify David Briggs's possession of the jewel at the time of his murder.

"When the police interviewed me, I told them David had acquired the jewel, that he received it from the two of you. I didn't know who you were, you see, just a young couple from Louth. That was what David told me to say in the event of police making inquiries into the jewel. I kept quiet about the letter and the family heirloom. Just as well. If they retrieve the dove, in my opinion they won't hand it over until they're satisfied about how David came to possess it."

Alice realised what Kate was driving at, "You mean that the police would assume that your husband had somehow tried to stea...*umm*, I mean keep...a national treasure from the State?"

"Yes," Kate sipped at her coffee and pulled a face. She took a tube of sweeteners out of her handbag and popped another into the drink. "In fact, he stole it from you through that loathsome Bentley. Which makes it all the more important that I put you forward as the finders, so that there can be a treasure trove inquest. I have no interest in the money. I'm quite well off. David had a large life insurance that will come to me, apart from anything else. I'm much more concerned about keeping his reputation intact and by association, mine as well. You know, he was so well respected in his profession. I'm desperate that it stays that way." She lowered her voice, "Here's the problem. Will you help me? In any case you are the true finders of the dove and when the police have it back you will have an uncontested claim to it. Would you be prepared to help me invent something plausible for how David obtained the dove? I know it's a lot to ask after the way David treated you, but I'm blameless and..." She opened her eyes wide, looking straight at Jake, "...I don't want the truth to come out and I'm relying on you both for that."

"Easy, if we keep it simple the police will believe us..." Jake said.

Kate gazed at him wide-eyed while Alice was surprised that he was so willing to help.

He held Kate's eyes, "The police don't know that it took us ages to work out how to find the dove. We can say that we dug it up that same afternoon. Let's say that evening you and your husband had dinner in Alice's restaurant. It's Italian food, by the way."

"Italian food," she murmured languorously.

"...let's say we got talking and when we found out that David was a barrister, we asked him for advice. He told us about the treasure trove law and then offered to handle the legal side of things for us. He just didn't get around to it before," he hesitated, "...well, before what happened."

Kate tossed her hair back, "What about Bentley?"

"It's three against one and he won't want to go to jail for kidnapping."

Alice summoned a forced smile, "I suppose all that could work," she said, unconvinced and rankled; since when had her husband been so cooperative and quick thinking? She felt like the candle at a romantic dinner for two.

Kate nodded her appreciation, looking into Alice's eyes, "I suppose I'd have to explain why I didn't tell them this at the time. But that's easy enough. I can say that I didn't want to get you into any bother, whereas now that I've thought about it, I realise that they have to know everything. Mind you, they'll come and see you about it, so we'll have to be word perfect."

They ran through the story again and confident that it held up, finished their coffee and stood up to go.

"I'm so grateful to you both," Kate smiled and put her arms round their shoulders. "The least I can do is to invite you both to dinner this evening. What do you say?"

Alice was about to say that it was impossible because she had work, but her husband cut in.

"Alice, that would be lovely, wouldn't it? What time shall we meet, Kate?"

They made their arrangements and left the café, Alice determined to have this out with Jake as soon as possible.

Their story was still fresh in their minds when DS Meade, back at the flat, held up his ID for Alice some hours later. She racked her brain for a way of warning her husband who had stormed off for a coffee after a heated discussion. She thought it best to say,

"If you could give me a little time, I'll find Jake, my husband, he slipped out, for some reason, a few minutes ago. It would be better if he was with us."

"This is a murder inquiry, miss, but I suppose I could come back in half an hour or so..."

"Please, that'll give me time to find him."

As soon as the policeman had gone away, Alice rang Jake, who promised to come straight away. To her relief, at the mention of the police inspector, his tone had become conciliatory after his first snappy response.

Jake arrived three minutes before DS Meade. Grey-suited and very smart, carrying a shopping bag, Alice noted, wondering whether the look was dinner-date inspired. He gave her a lingering kiss, which calmed her resentment.

In response to Meade's question about how Briggs had

obtained the jewel, they related the story agreed with Kate and Meade took their statements. Apart from reproving them for not having come forward at the time of the theft, on other matters, the detective was inscrutable. They supposed he was satisfied with their account and were encouraged by his words before he left: "Of course, if we recover the jewel, there will have to be a coroner's inquiry. So as finders, you could be in for a pleasant surprise. Of course, you can't shed any light on the killer, because these events preceded the murder."

When he'd gone, Alice hugged Jake, any residual ambivalent feelings about Kate dispelled by their acting prowess and the prospect of the wealth they might receive.

"Well, that went as we'd planned, she said, "Let's hope the police catch the killer. We could be in the money big time."

"I hope they get her for Kate's sake."

Alice bit her tongue and stared out of the window hiding the expression in her eyes. She decided to give Jake the benefit of the doubt for the time being. She too hoped fervently that the police caught the killer and not just for the sake of the sophisticated Kate Briggs.

THIRTY-EIGHT

LEWISHAM, LONDON, THE NEXT DAY

MEADE WAS PLEASED TO FIND THAT THE CHIEF Inspector wasn't too discomforted by the disintegration of his pet theory. Quite the opposite, he was galvanised into action. He congratulated his sergeant on his fine nose for a suspect and then he phoned through to the Thames Valley police.

"*Mmm*. How are you fixed for manpower, Graham?"

"Same as everyone else, Ron, understaffed. Why?"

"I wondered if you could spare a couple of lads to keep tracks on a certain Simon Lightbourne."

He explained who Lightbourne was and his connection to the American of the same name, filling in his Oxford counterpart with details from the FBI.

"This Simon Lightbourne isn't a professional crook, but with a bit of luck he might just lead us to the Fells woman."

Hicks leant forward across his desk and his wrinkled face creased even more, "With a hired serial killer loose in Oxford, if I didn't spare you a couple of men, I'd be the psychopath." He picked up another phone and a few moments later two young detectives came in.

"What are you two working on right now?"

The taller one, replied, "The hit-and-run on Walton Street, sir."

"Pass it on to Sally Jenkins. I've got the Met on the line about the university killing."

Down the phone he said, "DC Mark Porter and DC Gavin Jones, they're solid enough."

He smiled at the two young policemen. His tone was approving. "Right, Ron, I'll pass you Porter and leave you to get him organised, Chief Inspector," and with that he ceded the line to his colleague.

There was a spring in his stride as Willis walked from the police station to grab a prawn sandwich for lunch. His instinct told him that they were closing in on Marcia Fells. He just hoped to get her before she struck again. The archaeologist, Hudson, was complicating his own survival. As he walked, he reflected that something righteous and vengeful in his psyche made him want to catch a foreign killer even more than a home grown one. There was no sense to this, he knew, and he didn't want to look into his motives too closely. He clasped his hands behind his back and began to whistle a folk tune he heard on the radio and couldn't get out of his head.

As he walked, he realised that he hadn't noticed what a lovely day it was. If it came to that he couldn't remember when he had noticed his surroundings since Briggs's body had been found. It was too bad. The pressure of work took him over body and soul. Willis sighed, what he'd give for a few hours to himself in the Maritime Museum. He crossed the road and walked into a churchyard. It was right next to a busy road, but screened by tall trees. Willis sat down on a bench and studied the pigeons vying for crumbs falling from a pastry being devoured by a man in a grey white-striped suit. Willis ignored his rumbling stomach for as long as it took him to relax, then he stood up and strode to the sandwich bar.

His mood was buoyed even further when he met Meade back in the office. True enough, Hudson was as slippery as a well-oiled pole dancer, in fact, the West Mercia Police in the form of the Llanfyllin constabulary had visited his father's farm. They missed him by some forty-five minutes and had no idea where he was heading. A general alert was out to all units, but so far, nothing. In any case Hudson was not a suspect and hadn't committed any crime. One disturbing development was that David Hudson, the father, had noticed a shotgun and cartridges missing. Even so, there was no offence involved, because his son had a regular shotgun license. Willis blew aside the grey clouds the archaeologist had brought to his otherwise clear skies and concentrated on the good news—the warrant to tap Simon Lightbourne's phone had come through and a team from the Met Special Branch were on their way to set it up.

"I want his Internet usage and his email intercepted as well as his mobile calls," he told Meade.

"The Internet might be difficult, sir, at least as far as the Laboratory is concerned, because there's a lot of sharing goes on there. His office shouldn't be a problem though."

Soon after this conversation, two Special Branch men arrived in Oxford with an unmarked white van full of interception equipment. Hicks filled them in on the latest developments in the case and in particular on Simon Lightbourne. He also called in DC Gavin Jones from surveillance, who reported on Lightbourne's movements in the last couple of days. All his contact with young, white females in this time had been checked out, but so far none of these had given any cause for suspicion: all five of them having some relation to his university work.

Hicks sent the three of them off to join Mark Porter with their equipment at the Dyson Perrins Building. They parked the van in the corner of the car park and began the patient work of monitoring the suspect's mobile phone. Jones watched fascinated as they sent a virus to Lightbourne's computer. In only a few seconds, it was transmitting back information about his emails and web browsing.

Simon Lightbourne, at that moment, was looking at a site about Anglo-Saxon carved stones in Lincolnshire. They discovered that in the last half hour he'd used his Earth satellite map to locate Threekingham, a village in south Lincolnshire and that he'd also clicked on two links about the Oak King. They phoned this information on to Hicks. After that, one of the Special Branch men opened a large flask of coffee and poured them each a drink in plastic cups. They settled down to their long, patient work.

LOUTH, LINCOLNSHIRE, AT THE SAME TIME

Kate ran a critical professional eye over the décor of the Stonebow Hotel restaurant. The hotel had a 5-star rating and was in the Michelin Guide, which was the reason for her choice. The fourteenth-century beams and windows were charming, but she'd have a chosen pastel shade, maybe sage green rather than this dull brown, which deadened the original features of the room. However, the food couldn't be faulted. A polite, relaxed waiter served a delicious onion consommé.

Between spoonfuls Jake updated Kate about the visit of the Metropolitan Police; like a child reporting to a parent or teacher, his eyes lit up with gratification when Kate squeezed his arm in thanks. Then she turned to Alice anxious to know her opinion as to whether the police believed the story. As the meal progressed Alice noticed that Kate was keeping pace with Jake's drinking and they were now halfway through their second bottle of Cotes du Rhône. This disturbed her. There was a red flush at Kate's throat and her cheerfulness seemed forced and her attempts to ingratiate herself clumsy and distasteful by her own very high standards. She didn't want Kate to drive in this state and began to worry about how to tell her. At the end of the second bottle, Kate delved in her handbag and pulled out a sheet of paper, "I've got something to show you." She held out a coloured print of the reverse of the dove, showing it to Alice but not letting go of it.

"I can't get this out of my mind," she said, "why kill him? She had the jewel, so why not just take it and have done?" Her lip trembled. "That's the reason, isn't it?" She swept her napkin from the table and held it to her mouth in an attempt to stem the tears. "Those words on the back of the dove, they're the reason she killed him and the reason why she took the hard disks from his computers, so that there'd be no trace of *those* words."

Jake stared at his wife and an almost imperceptibe eye movement told her to stay quiet. He held his breath, but Kate continued in a small voice.

"That's the clue to why he died." Her lower lip trembled, "When the police come to check on my alibi with you two, I'll show them this. Maybe they can work out what it means and it might lead them to the monster *th*-that took David from me."

"Yes, that's the best thing to do," Alice said, letting go of her corner of the print. "I'm sure they'll catch her, Kate. You must miss him terribly."

"When I'm not hating him for being so damned stupid." Kate burst out and buried her face in her hands.

Jake put his finger to his lips and nodding to Alice for approval first, leant over and put his arm round Kate. There was an awkward silence and the interior designer whispered an apology. He moved away but took hold of her hand. There was another interminable silence.

"What a meal. That dish was delicious!" he said, "What was that main course called, again?"

A somewhat forced discussion about the ingredients of a Tornedos Rossini and the best way to prepare the artichokes ensued. Kate recovered her composure, and in an altogether more cheerful vein asked them about their future plans and offered to help with the furnishings and décor when they finally got around to refurbishing their manor house.

They walked out of the hotel, the earlier crisis pushed to the back of their minds, a pleasant, satisfied glow of those who have eaten really well, accompanied them under the thirteenth-century arch of the Stonebow and Guildhall as they made their way to the car park, where Kate surprised Alice by asking one of them to drive.

"I'm sorry," she said, "I've behaved badly this evening. I'm afraid I still haven't come to terms with my loss – I shouldn't have drunk so much. To tell the truth I still feel rather tipsy." and she giggled.

Alice was pleased when Jake asked her to drive. Normally, he'd have insisted on being the driver, but he had drunk, too.

"It's the kind of car to attract police attention at this

time of night and you're the only one under the limit, Alice. You don't mind, do you?"

In cavalier fashion, he accompanied Kate and opened the door for her before taking his place next to his wife where he began tracing a line with his finger down the back of her neck.

Alice stuck to all the speed limits despite the empty roads, but even so revelled in the sensations transmitted by handling such a thoroughbred sports car. She got them back safe and sound to Kate's hotel, where they swapped phone numbers, said their goodbyes and promised to keep in touch.

In the taxi home, Alice snuggled up to Jake and put her head on his shoulder. Neither spoke. Lying in bed later she asked what they were going to do about the treasure.

"We haven't got much choice," Jake said. "If Kate goes to the police with that print, they'll use the same logic as we did and, sooner or later, they'll get to the treasure. If they're fast, they'll get there before us, because, let's face it, they'll have all the resources and the top brains on the job. We might not find it immediately and they'll put surveillance on any suspected location and get archaeologists in."

"Do you think that woman killer is looking for the treasure?"

"I don't know. If she is, it'll be about as safe as swimming past a cottonmouth snake."

"She might not realise that the words are important."

"Why kill Briggs then and why take the hard disks?"

"What if she hoped no-one else knew about the dove," Alice said.

"If we want the treasure, we're going to have to take the risk that the killer hasn't worked it out yet and we're going to have to cut Kate in, always assuming that she'll want to accept the risk."

"We can talk to her tomorrow morning before she sets off for London," he slurred as he drifted off to sleep.

The next morning Jake and Alice caught Kate in the hotel lobby. They found some inviting chairs in a quiet corner next to a window. She listened as Jake explained about their interpretation of the inscription on the dove, Alice interrupting to add information or clarify a point. Kate's reaction was tempered by caution.

"I knew there was something like this behind David's murder," she said. "There had to be more riding on this than the value of the dove alone." She frowned, "We'll have to be careful. We should be armed."

"I don't know how to get hold of a gun," Jake said.

"I wouldn't even know..." Alice began.

"You can leave that side of things to me," Kate interrupted with a determined light in her eyes. Now what else will we need?"

"We've got spades and a pick, but what we need is a metal detector. That could save a lot of time and effort. I've no idea how much they cost though."

"Don't worry about that. Leave it to me to sort that as well. Whatever it costs, I'm sure it's a good investment."

They agreed that if they had the good fortune to discover the treasure first, they would report their find to the authorities. There would also be an equal three-way split of any money made from the discovery. They decided to meet on Wednesday evening at seven o'clock in Threekingham. There was a motel on the A17, suitable for an overnight stay, Jake knew it from a business conference he'd attended, when he'd been directing the Red Horse Theme Park. Situated close to Threekingham, the motel gave them the chance to be up at dawn so ensuring plenty of daylight hours to search. Meanwhile Kate would see to the other arrangements as well as going to the police, if they didn't come to her first, to explain about the provenance of the dove. They shook hands as Kate left for London. None of them could imagine that they had just grabbed a dragon by its tail.

THIRTY-NINE

OXFORD, 2021 AD

HICKS WAS BROODING ON WHAT BEST TO DO ABOUT THIS American killer on the loose when his dated ringtone disturbed his train of thought. He must change it when he got a minute to himself. Jones from Special Branch had a hit.

"Lightbourne made a call on his cell phone sir. A woman answered. We got a number for her and the SIM card is in the name of Felicity Page. Our lads think it's the American using false ID. The accent's right and so is the content of the call."

"What did they say?"

"Cagey, sir, she didn't say much at all, but he told her he knew the location from the inscription. She more or less cut him dead and said they'd meet as arranged and closed the call."

"Stand by to follow Lightbourne. Be careful he doesn't catch on that you're tailing him - this may be the only chance we'll have of him leading us straight to the killer. And I don't want any heroics. This woman is a professional. If you find her, call in reinforcements, clear?

"Yes sir."

Hicks put the phone in his pocket and rubbed his hands together. Things were warming up. He made a call to Willis in London, who in turn called Professor Bryan Cox the Met's archaeology consultant at the University of London. The Detective Chief Inspector told him that Special Branch would forward the details from Lightbourne's computer. He impressed on the professor the urgent need for a solution to the inscription on the back of the dove. It's possible lives depended on this.

Willis rubbed his moustache with a clenched fist and thought through the latest information, he should get back to Graham Hicks and update him, because there might very well be the need for armed back up. Then he'd better see to the awesome Aalia: as usual, and quite rightly he grudgingly admitted, she insisted on being kept informed on all developments.

Soon afterwards, a photo-fit of Marcia Fells came through from America. The Superintendent summoned a press conference, this time with Willis's blessing and the picture was issued to the press as well as to all airports and ports, so with the net tightening on the American, Willis was where he wanted to be: in Phadkar's good books. He was too long in the tooth to draw comfort from that. Experience told him—no—bawled at him from close range, that ten minutes could be a lifetime in police work. The mixture of ingredients was volatile: something dark and unpleasant was brewing on the horizon.

At the same time, one of Willis's other worries was on the way from Wales to London. A double-barrelled twelve-bore shotgun lay in the boot of Paul Hudson's hire car. He worried that his father would notice the absence of the weapon from its cabinet. He'd selected the one at the end of the row, thinking that it was less obvious than from the centre. If his dad saw a gun missing, what would he think and how would he react? Fiddling with the knob of the car radio, Hudson sought a little distraction. But as soon as he found some pleasant music, he switched it off. It was as if he couldn't stand noise of any kind. He rubbed his forehead and concentrated on the road. By the time he pulled up in an East End street the sun was overhead.

The surveillance of Kate Briggs's flat was short, after twenty minutes he heard, before he saw, her Porsche roar out of the garage. Hudson followed at a discreet distance. What he didn't know was that a black car that pulled out, at the same time, was also following the Porsche. Kate, in any case, was too busy concentrating on the early morning traffic to notice her double tail. She was heading for Battersea. It was imperative to see Bentley and persuade him to change his version of how David obtained the dove to align with that agreed with Jake and Alice. He was expecting her for half-past nine. A traffic light turned to green and Kate shuddered at the thought of his grimy office hovel as she moved the Porsche away.

She was lucky to find a place to park outside Bentley's, because just when she arrived a white electrician's van pulled out. She took its place and the two following drivers passed by cursing.

Once again Paul Hudson was in luck. Marcia Fells found a parking space before he did, so that Hudson, driving round the block and passing the Porsche for a second time, saw the woman in her hooded sweat shirt stealing into a doorway opposite the one Kate Briggs had just entered. He recognised her as his would-be killer and whistled through his clenched teeth, then managed to park.

He dodged along, hugging the buildings on Fells's side of the road. Getting to within about ten doors of her before prudence halted him. He took up position in a doorway with a clear view of her hidey-hole and of the Briggs woman's destination.

Twenty-five long minutes passed before Kate Briggs, in leather jacket and smart checked trousers, came out of the building across the road. The archaeologist didn't dare move. His eyes followed her to the Porsche, but his mind was on red alert for Fells. Was she still in that doorway? In fact, the Porsche pulling away barely registered as he spotted the hooded figure emerging on to the pavement. Change of plan. Heart thumping, he watched the killer pause to look at something for a moment before entering the building Kate Briggs had left. Hudson glanced at his watch and waited. God, how he hated waiting. He'd never thought of himself as impatient before. About ten minutes, which seemed to him an hour, passed before the woman reappeared at the stair door, looked up and down the street, let a couple of cars pass, then crossed over and walked in his direction. Oh God, what now. Stepping out of the doorway and strolling past her was out of the question: too risky. Nor could he stay where he was, because she'd see him when she passed. Now there were only five doors between them. Hudson pressed the entry phone. He could feel himself sweating as a woman's voice answered.

"Good morning, my company is researching cable TV," he spluttered, aware that Marcia Fells was passing him right now. He kept his face turned to the grille. "Do you have cable TV, madam?" There was a sharp buzzing noise as the main door clicked open and he was inside. By the time he reached the window of the mid-floor landing, Fells was driving away in a black car. The woman, hair in curlers, peered down at him from her half-open door. She saw him looking through the window and noted his obvious relief. Her mouth tightened and her nostrils flared with suspicion.

Hudson looked up and could not fail to interpret the signs, "Please forgive me, ma'am," he said, giving her his most winning smile, "to tell the truth it was a bit of an emergency. I'm a private detective and I had to disturb you or my cover was blown."

The woman relaxed, raised her eyes, clicked her tongue and withdrew her head into her flat. Hudson stared at the closed door and his breathing returned to normal. His head was pounding like a pile driver. Grateful to be outside and free of danger and suspicion, he crossed the road, pausing in front of the building the two women had entered. A small, transparent plastic sign with neat black lettering informed him of the offices of

Stephen Bentley Private Detective
second floor.

He asked himself what the lovely Kate and the evil killer wanted with a private eye? He would soon find out. Taking the steps two at a time he knocked on the door. There was no reply. He knocked again but there was silence.

Hudson tried the door and it opened. What he saw there made his stomach lurch. A middle-aged man in an old sports jacket was slumped over the desk, where a crimson crescent had formed from a hole in his forehead. What made the scene even more grotesque was that his cigarette was still stuck to the lower lip of his gaping mouth, but its end was extinguished in the blood. Next to his head, still between his finger and thumb, was a cheque. The computer on the desk had been opened up. Hudson went over and saw that the hard disk was missing. Hudson lifted the cheque with the end of a pen from his inside pocket. It was for one thousand pounds with today's date and signed by Kate Briggs. Well, Bentley wouldn't be paying that one into his account. He wondered what she was paying for? The room stank of stale air and Hudson's eyes kept going back to the blood on the desk; he began to feel queasy. He decided to get out before anyone came.

Turning to leave, he noticed something on a cabinet by the wall. Unrolling it, a piece of paper fluttered to the floor. The archaeologist bent to pick it up, silver stars passed in front of his eyes, and with difficulty through half-closed eyes, read the name and address of a woman in Louth. He pocketed it and glancing at the map, he was thrilled to see that it was a reproduction of a part of Lincolnshire in 1800. Another lucky break? Could it show the location of the long hill and the cross? He rolled the map up and carried it out, closing the door behind him. There wasn't a sound in the building, so he went down the stairs and walked a hundred yards along the road then rang the police. An anonymous tip off about Stephen Bentley, deceased, soon reached the ears of DCI Ron Willis.

Sitting in the rented car, with shaking hands, Paul Hudson examined the map again and noted with a thrill of pleasure that the map had the name and address of the suppliers printed in the bottom right-hand corner. The mail order department was in Berkshire, a good hour's drive away. It was just after one now; he was feeling exhausted but high on adrenalin, so Hudson decided to pay them a visit.

After a stressful drive through heavy traffic he reached

his destination. He found the premises with little difficulty and sauntered in. The well-built shop assistant, a fussy, black-haired man with a pencil-thin moustache seemed gratified to have something to do. He was even prepared to call the mail order department to find out who had ordered a map of the Covenham area in 1800. With an air of self-importance, he informed Hudson that there was little request for that part of England, not like say, London. It was therefore easy enough to discover that it'd been ordered by a certain Alice Copley – "yes, the name and address on the gentleman's piece of paper,"— at the beginning of May.

Outside, in his car, Paul Hudson was thinking hard, a little too hard, the tension and the driving were taking their toll now. At first the thoughts went spinning in his mind like a crazy out of control merry-go-round. He tried to piece together what he knew. What had he got? An exquisite piece of Anglo-Saxon jewellery, made in Lincolnshire, a map of Lincolnshire in 1800; a woman in Lincolnshire who ordered the map; the jewel found in Lincolnshire; three murders and his own attempted murder (twice) connected to the dove; Kate Briggs connected to the private detective; her husband had the dove; the detective had the map. He forced his trained academic mind to slow the whirl of thoughts. His concentration wasn't what it used to be. Was it possible that Kate Briggs was on the trail of the Werburgh treasure? Now Fells was following her, so it was too dangerous to approach Briggs. Meeting her would be like signing his own death warrant with Fells lurking around. Was there an alternative? He thought furiously. Of course. He could drive up to Louth and find out what this Copley woman knew. That was altogether a safer and, possibly more rewarding, option. He could be in Lincolnshire in about three hours allowing for a quick, if very late, pub lunch somewhere just near the M1.

With this decision Paul Hudson casually tossed another ingredient into the mix whose explosive nature so concerned DCI Willis at that very moment.

FORTY

LEWISHAM, LONDON LATER THAT DAY.

Ron Meade followed up an anonymous tip-off to find Stephen Bentley in his office shot through the head. An appointment with Kate Briggs at 9.30 was pencilled in on his desk pad, which was more or less the time of death according to the police doctor. A routine check of his bank transactions showed a cheque for fifteen-hundred pounds paid in several days ago and drawn on Kate Briggs's account and his body was found holding another cheque dated today and again signed by the lady in question. Blackmail sprang into Meade's mind.

It didn't weaken his suspicions to see shock followed by relief rather than displeasure on Kate Briggs's face when he told her of the detective's death. Both emotions seemed genuine enough and on instinct alone the wily Meade tended to rule Kate Briggs out of the murder. He didn't think of her as capable of murder and hoped that this interview wouldn't reawaken his DCI's fanciful theory.

The interior designer was sitting at a table in the interrogation room with her solicitor, both opposite himself and DC Tomlinson. Chief Inspector Willis was on his feet in the corner of the room listening to the confident upper-class tone of her voice: "...about ten to ten when I left him. I know because I glanced at my watch. I had a half-past ten appointment in Shoreditch and didn't want to be late. Mr Bentley was alive and in good spirits when I left."

"And the £1500 paid to Mr Bentley a few days ago?"

The cool Kate expected the question and fielded it. "My husband didn't leave many debts Detective Sergeant, but Mr Bentley still hadn't been paid for his last assistance with a divorce case, so as a matter of correctness—"

Meade pushed a plastic envelope containing Kate's cheque of that day across the desk. He studied her face and was certain that she paled. But she remained unflappable.

"In fact, that was why I was there this morning. I hired Mr Bentley to protect the young couple in Louth. You see, I feel in some way responsible...I know it's silly...for their involvement," Kate seized the initiative and trotted out their new version. She ended by adding, "So, you see, after what happened to David and to poor Professor Buchan, I wouldn't want anything to happen to them, I thought it was the least I could do. The one thousand pounds was just a deposit. Mr Bentley was going to start later today by driving up to Lincolnshire—the poor man."

"I see. And that's your statement. There's nothing you want to change?"

Her blue eyes hardened, she glanced at her solicitor, whose shake of the head was hardly perceptible before she replied to DS Meade.

"What I've told you today is the absolute truth," she said, "Do you have reason to doubt it?"

DC Tomlinson spoke for the first time, "Mrs Briggs, before he died, Mr Bentley stated..." she paused and opened her notebook flicking through several pages, "'...Mr Briggs paid me £150000 to steal the dove from the kids in Louth.'" She smiled tight-lipped at Kate, "Now you've told us that your husband received the jewel from Mr Copley and his wife in order to open a coroner's inquest for treasure trove?"

"Yes, that's right. I repeat, by chance we met Jake and Alice in an Italian restaurant on the very day that they found the jewel. When they discovered that David was an eminent barrister, they thought it a splendid idea to entrust it to him."

"So, Mrs Briggs, how do you account for the £150000 and Mr Bentley's statement?"

Kate barely hesitated, her voice confident, "It would be untrue to say that I didn't know about the payment, since I have had time to study all David's accounts, but I assumed it was a regular payment for services rendered and I don't know why Mr Bentley should then lie about it...and we can't ask him, can we? What you can do, of course, is ask the young people in Louth. I think you'll find that I'm telling the truth."

"*Mmmm*," from the corner of the room.

"You travel around a lot in your work, I believe madam."

"Yes, I do, Detective Sergeant."

"Would you be kind enough to leave us your mobile phone number in case we need to get in touch with you when you are out of town?"

They let her go, but all three were convinced that she was lying. When she'd gone, they speculated on her statement and what she was hoping to gain from it. Of course, with Marcia Fells at large it was probable that she hadn't killed Bentley, because the bullet once again was from the same gun as those fired at her husband and at Hudson. Even Ron Willis confessed to his colleagues that he didn't now suspect her as a murderess. So, what was she hiding? What was the £150000 paid for if not for the dove? If her version was true, had Bentley been blackmailing David Briggs and consequently his widow?

For her part, Kate knew that they didn't believe her. However, as far as she was concerned the interview couldn't have gone any better, she was certain of that. With a light step, she headed off to another shooting session in the Marylebone Club. On the way home, she'd buy the metal detector that she'd seen on the Internet. If she had known that Marcia Fells had followed her to Bentley's office her step might not have been so carefree.

LOUTH, LINCOLNSHIRE, AT THE SAME TIME

While Kate was driving to her shooting session Dr Paul Hudson was saying to Alice:

"...you see, she's stringing you along. She's not the altruistic person she's led you to believe and it's not just to clear her family name. She wants the Werburgh treasure all for herself. Kate Briggs is a very clever and calculating person. You don't suppose her husband was acting alone? Now he's been murdered, her resolve is even fiercer. The Werburgh treasure is of national, no international, importance. I'm an archaeologist from Oxford University and you should know that the woman who killed Professor Buchan also tried to kill me."

"I don't believe that Kate would ever harm anyone." cried Alice.

"No, presumably not," said Hudson impatiently, "she didn't kill Buchan or try to kill me. You've seen the photo-fit pictures in all the newspapers this morning. That's another woman, even more dangerous...or maybe...not."

"What do you mean?"

"Listen, you should know that Kate Briggs was with that private detective, Stephen Bentley, this morning."

"My kidnapper." she blurted out, regretting it when Hudson said, "What? I didn't know that. Why did he kidnap you?"

"Never mind, it's a long story. Why is it important that Kate was with Bentley this morning?"

Dr Hudson, black rings under his eyes and contrasting with an unnatural pallor, rubbed the palms of his hands into his eye sockets.

She looked at him with concern, "Are you OK, Dr Hudson?"

"Fine. It's only a headache and tiredness. I've had a stressful few days. Anyway, you'll see it in the evening papers. I saw her come out of Bentley's office just before I went in. I found him shot through the head. The blood was fresh."

"Oh my God."

"I found your name on his desk pad and decided to come and warn you. You and your husband are in danger. Don't you see, Kate Briggs will do anything to get her hands on that treasure?"

Her mind was in a whirl. Was Kate capable of killing after all?

"Did you phone the police?"

"Of course, but I didn't give them my name. I wouldn't be here now if I had. I'll be frank with you. I want to be involved when the treasure is found, apparently on my own account, but really on behalf of the University. Even a part share in the treasure trove would mean so much for my faculty. If I can associate the university with the discovery, maybe I can stop another important find ending up in the British Museum. I've seen them grab the lion's share time and again," he said, with a degree of venom that surprised her. "If we can come to an arrangement, maybe we can find the treasure before anyone else."

"You are assuming that Jake and I know where the treasure is, though," casting a shrewd glance at Hudson. "Supposing that's true. What would we gain by cutting you in?"

Hudson rubbed his forehead and half-closed his eyes. He didn't answer and looked vague and distracted. Alice repeated the question, thinking that Dr Hudson didn't look at all well. He re-connected.

"Several advantages: let me list them for you. First of all, I have access to the best scientific equipment for finding buried treasure. Without it, even though you know the approximate location you could search for years and years and never find anything. Then, when the treasure is declared you will have the extra plausibility of being associated with Oxford University. Third, you won't be in danger of being double-crossed and killed by the Briggs widow and..." his voice took on a hard edge, "if you agree to work with me, I won't denounce you and Briggs to the police for trying to defraud the state. I feel sure that an arrangement can be made through the university for recompense."

There was no doubting the sincerity of the threat.

Alice looked at Dr Hudson for several seconds, scrutinising the handsome, but wan and restless face. He looked everywhere, except back at her, embarrassed by her gaze.

"Again, assuming that Jake and I know where the

treasure is, why would an archaeology professor, like you, come to us? You're the expert. You can work it out for yourself, always assuming that we've deciphered the inscription in the first place."

"It's a question of time. I've been too busy trying to stay alive: too many brushes with that Fells woman." He spat out the last two words with nothing short of loathing. Again, she felt uncomfortable. "I haven't had time to research the inscription. She's still after me, you know, and I have reason to think that she's after Kate Briggs, too."

She stared at the archaeologist, "It's like the frying pan and the fire, isn't it? If we associate with you, it's dangerous. If we associate with Kate, it's dangerous. Why should we take any risks at all?" She thought,

I wish Jake had allowed me to involve Sir Clive – it'd be so much easier for us.

There was a long moment of silence. At last Hudson met her eyes, "Of course you don't have to. But if you want the money—"

Alice, still holding his gaze, bit her lower lip and then added, "Don't get the idea that we're just after money. There's more to it than that. Remember, we were the ones to find the dove and we had it stolen from us. Look, I'll have to talk this over with my husband." She paused and thought, *where is Jake when I need him?* "I can't make a decision like this without consulting him. You'll give me until tomorrow morning to decide, won't you?"

"Of course, can you recommend a hotel in Louth?"

She told him about Belford House and said she'd meet him there after breakfast with Jake. Dr Hudson seemed satisfied with this and took his leave.

Alice felt wretched. Every time she and Jake took a decision, some other problem reared up to confound them.

She didn't know what to think. The Kate that Hudson described wasn't the Kate she knew. But, anyway, how well did she know Kate? Hardly at all. She caught herself biting her thumbnail and snatched it away. She was in a state. She decided that the best thing was to ring Jake straight away.

He came around at once. They sat on the sofa for an hour, not speaking, each running through the options in his own mind. They came to the same conclusion that Paul Hudson was the more reliable of the two. They both liked Kate: Jake too much for Alice's liking, as she was quick to point out. But setting petty jealousy aside, free of her dominating presence, they realised they might have been taken in by appearances. It wasn't as if they'd known Kate Briggs for more than a few hours. The same could be said of Dr Hudson, of course, so they had to consider the credentials of the two people: one was the widow of the person who had set in motion the kidnapping of Alice, the theft of the jewel, and who had got himself killed for his troubles, whereas the other was a university don, who had also been attacked. This fact was enough to explain the archaeologist's rather emotional state that had disturbed Alice. It seemed the choice was to go ahead with Dr Hudson or to deny all knowledge of the whereabouts of the treasure and take no risks. Then they would forgo all treasure trove rights. They stood to lose a fortune. They also wrangled over the opportuneness of involving Sir Clive. In the end, Jake prevailed because as he pointed out, failure would mean death and therefore, there'd be no comeback. Success, on the other hand, would mean completion of the task Double-A had called them in for. Their task had been to solve the Robinson family mystery – and that, he said, they had already done.

Finally, there was still the problem of Kate Briggs and

their previous agreement with her. This was getting contorted. Taking his wife's hand, Jake suggested that it was better to tell Hudson about their appointment with Kate Briggs in the morning. If they were going to trust him, he would have to know all the facts.

FORTY-ONE

BICESTER, OXON

SHE LOOKED UP FROM CLOSING THE FLAP ON HER handbag and the instant when their eyes met was enough to tell Marcia Fells that he had recognised her. He looked away but the damage was done. The man was young and he might as well have worn a neon flashing "I'm a cop": how he failed to blend in with the general public. She needed to act without alarming him, so she weaved through the standard sidewalk obstructions of the elderly and young mothers with pushchairs. She pretended to hesitate, glancing in a jeweller's window, gaining reconnaissance time. Sure, there he was in his grey sweatshirt and tight tracksuit pants, being a clever cop, following her and pretending to look at everything except his quarry. Seeing what she needed, she moved on, leaving the pristine façade of shops and offices for a narrow alleyway. She hoped it led to somewhere suitable.

The brick walls stank of urine. She picked her way through discarded condoms and rotting fruit, hoping not to soil her new white sneakers. Either side of her the walls hinted at imminent collapse staved off only by a crisscross of rusting drainpipes and half-detached cables like bindings around a battered parcel.

The alleyway opened up on the right to a paved area. No sunlight penetrated the yard. At the far end a low building stood like a dwarf next to its giant neighbour. She turned into the space and from the corner of her eye confirmed that the cop was entering the alley. She gave no sign of having seen him and turned into the yard.

She looked around. There were no CCTV cameras in this stinking hole. The surrounding buildings showed no sign of life. Most of their rear areas likely were storerooms and services, toilets and similar. The low building was boarded up. It's faded sign had something to do with turbines, but all that mattered to Marcia Fells was that the only living creature was a motionless black cat, its yellow eyes peering at her over the rim of one of six trash cans lining the back of the tall building. She opened her handbag and fitted the suppressor to the Browning.

PC Matt Johnson was off duty. That morning in the newsagent's he had taken particular notice of the blonde in the photo-fit on the front page of several daily papers. It caught his eye because the woman looked so much like his cousin Clare that he had to do a double take. Without bothering to buy the paper he read the article about the American woman wanted for questioning in connection with the death of an Oxford professor and was still thinking about Clare when he came face to face with the suspect outside the newsagents. She wasn't blonde anymore and had changed her hairstyle, but there was no mistaking her delicate features.

His first thought was to use his cell phone, but he didn't want to alert her. He wasn't sure whether she had noticed his interest and he didn't want to blow his first-ever glorious opportunity to impress his superior officers. He was overdue for a promotion. If he followed her, he might be able to gain vital information like her hideaway or the number plate of her vehicle. He tailed her along the high street past several shops. She looked in a jeweller's window and then, hips swaying, she turned into a nondescript alley.

At first Matt Johnson was taken aback. He wondered why such an elegant woman would step so confidently into a place fit only for down and outs and curs with the mange. He grimaced. There was an explanation: she was meeting an accomplice and he should get a description. He moved swiftly to the gap between buildings and was just in time to see her turn sharp right near the end of the alley.

He began to follow, but halfway along the alley, some concepts of police procedure began to curb the enthusiasm for the chase that had brought him this far. The woman was dangerous. He should be calling for backup and be moving with caution. Off duty, he was without his radio. He fished into the pocket of his tracksuit and pulled out his mobile. Time to let his sergeant know, but the suffocating buildings proved to be a problem. There was no signal except for emergency calls. Matt Johnson weighed up his possibilities. An emergency call would get him the switchboard. It meant losing time with explanations, time he didn't have. While he dithered, his suspect could be lost to him. He snapped the phone shut and strode on down the alley. It was the worst decision, as well as the last, in the young policeman's life.

LINCOLN

Professor Bryan Cox enjoyed cooperating with the Met; he didn't live in Baker Street, but it amused him to think that his aquiline nose and its unerring ability to sniff out hidden details made him worthy of occupying 221B. This however was the first time in his association with the police that Cox felt the thrill of an archaeological chase. Not that there was any need here for Holmes-like prowess. The connection between the Anglo-Saxon *lang dun*, Loudon and Threekingham was soon established and from there it was a short step using the links intercepted from Lightbourne's computer to the Threekingham cross in the Usher Gallery.

The implications of this information were destined to light a firecracker to rouse the most somnolent of his colleagues, so he rejoiced in his head start. It was imperative to make Chief Inspector Willis understand that his involvement was indispensable to the miraculous rediscovery of the Ely treasure. This was the gist of his conversation when he phoned his findings through to police headquarters.

As a result of his call, DS Meade wasn't thrilled when Ron Willis instructed him to go back to Lincoln. He might as well be a travelling salesman and not a copper he grumbled to himself at the thought of the miles driven this week alone.

"Go to the Usher Gallery. Find out what you can about the Threekingham Cross. Above all, its Saxon location and check out whether the Copleys have banked a sizeable sum of money."

Nevertheless, the drive cheered Meade because the weather was fine and the sunshine enhanced the beauty of the gentle, rolling scenery around Horncastle and its sleepy neighbouring villages. Already Meade could make out the majestic form of Lincoln cathedral on its hill, dominating the surrounding countryside. He promised himself a short break in this area if ever Ron Willis gave him the chance. As ordered, he went to Louth first to get information from the bank. Neither Copley had any new money in their accounts. He phoned this through to Willis and drove back to Lincoln.

Meade settled into the cerise damask armchair on the other side of the desk from a man in his sixties. This was what he expected a museum curator to be like. A white goatee beard and a dark blue striped bowtie, half-moon glasses and three pens clipped into the breast pocket of his jacket all contributed to confirming Meade's mental stereotype.

"So, you want to know about the Threekingham Cross, Inspector."

"Sergeant, sir. Yes *er*...what we'd like to know is the exact location of the cross before it ended up in the museum."

"Rather a coincidence, what?"

"Beg your pardon, sir?"

The curator looked over the top of his glasses. "It was only a few days ago that I was asked the same question. Of course, it's quite extraordinary. Nobody has asked a single question about the blessed thing in all the years I've been here and now it's the centre of attention."

"Might I ask who was interested in the cross, sir?"

"A young couple. She was a university student doing a thesis on Anglo-Saxon roadways. You see, the Threekingham Cross is a wayside cross, which marked the crossing of two routes in the Saxon period. That isn't to say it wouldn't have been used for open-air services..."

Meade almost growled, “Can you describe this couple. It might be important.”

“Oh dear, let me see. She was a pretty young thing. Blonde, wavy long hair, rather foreign looking, about thirty years old—well, she would be, she’s a student, so—”

“And the man, was he in his thirties, a wiry type with short, chestnut-coloured hair?”

The curator frowned as if the effort to remember caused him physical pain. “Yes, indeed. That would be a fair description.

“You didn’t by any chance get their names, sir?”

“No, it didn’t seem necessary for such a simple enquiry.”

“Of course not.”

He tugged at his beard. “Mind you, the young fellow did refer to the girl by name...Annette, I think. I distinctly remember imagining that the girl was of eastern-European extraction.”

“Alice?”

“By Jove that’s it! I remember now.”

“That’s very helpful, sir. If you can give me the exact location of where the cross stood in Saxon times.”

Pleased to have made progress and to have reduced the verbose curator to a subservient series of monosyllables, Meade stepped out of the gallery and decided to combine work with his own human necessities. This led him to the *Bel Paese* restaurant in Louth.

Appealing dishes and quite reasonable prices thought Meade as he peered at the menu inside the glass display case at the side of the door. With a bit of luck, he could interview the owner after a pleasant meal. Lunch of a pasta dish would go down a treat, especially because he could put it on his expenses.

Inside, Meade looked around, favourably impressed. The restaurant was pleasantly furnished, the tables laid out smartly with sage green tablecloths and napkins, with matching chairs comfortably upholstered in a green-patterned material. Strange how most English restaurants didn't use tablecloths, Meade reflected. It was a welcoming touch that made such a difference: inevitable laundry bill though. Just two tables were occupied, one by a couple in their mid-thirties and another by two elderly ladies, one waving a fork in animated conversation.

Meade walked over to have a closer look at a large photograph. It showed a white sandy beach next to the turquoise sea. A craggy rock rose up from the water topped by a baroque church. There was a deep blue cloudless sky.

"Ah, *signore*, that is my beautiful town in the toe of Italy. *La bella Tropea*."

Meade turned to face a short muscular man in a white shirt and black waistcoat. He grinned at his guest and said, "We are famous for our white beaches and for the red onion of Tropea."

"Onion?"

"*Sì, sì*. Our onion is famous in the whole of Italy. The whole of the world. It is sweet and we even make it into jam." He twisted his forefinger into his cheek. "It's delicious," he explained the gesture. "Table for one, sir?"

Signor Perri persuaded Meade to try a dish of homemade macaroni dressed with a lamb ragout and with a touch of spicy chilli. This, he told Meade, was a typical local dish of his area and should be washed down with a red *Cirò* wine. Meade allowed himself to be persuaded and was surprised when the man reappeared with a small plate of ricotta cheese and a jar of conserve.

"*Ecco*." he said, this is a little antipasto, eat the cheese with the famous onion jam of Tropea and a little bread. On the house."

Meade, feeling very satisfied, paid his bill and complimented Signor Perri on the quality of the food. Then he introduced himself and showed his ID.

"I needed a good meal, but I'm also looking for a couple who dined here, Mr Perri. Don't worry, no trouble for you, but you might be able to help us with our inquiries."

Signor Perri looked agitated, "Anything to help, officer"

He was able to confirm that two couples matching the descriptions had eaten in his restaurant. But Meade noted, not that he had seen them talking together.

"Thanks very much, Mr Perri, you know, I may just persuade my girlfriend to take a holiday with me in Tropea; especially if the food is as good as what you served me today."

"*Sì, sì signore* and the weather is so much better: always sunshine, every day sunshine."

Meade left the restaurant still savouring the aftertaste of the ragout, but he frowned. He reported his findings to Willis, who wanted him back in Oxford as soon as possible and his tone of voice suggested the moment of crisis was at hand.

FORTY-TWO

ABINGDON, OXON

His instructions were clear and Simon Lightbourne followed them to the letter. "You think you ain't being tailed? Behave like you are." Marcia Fells had told him the morning of Hudson's accident. "Essential phone calls only and keep them short."

At last her call came. It was time to move and to get their hands on the treasure. After leaving home through the back door Lightbourne strode away. As agreed, he was wearing a Leicester Tigers rugby top and blue jeans. He jumped on the first bus that came along, getting off after five stops, then changed buses twice to the high street. Strange—he found, he enjoyed playing the fugitive, even if he was convinced no one was following him.

In the town centre he went to the coach park and lingered over a cup of tea until the coach for Abingdon arrived. It filled up with shoppers and noisy schoolchildren in blue uniforms. He found himself sitting next to a woman with a tiny kitten for the whole stuffy ride. When they swarmed out in Abingdon, Lightbourne got off and wove his way through the busy shopping area. He passed under a medieval arch, through some bollards and hurried along a cycle path, swearing at a distracted youth who almost biked into him. Then he crossed a car park. He saw the paddling pool he had been told about and crossed a small bridge into the Abbey Gardens. There were the public toilets and the café. He checked his watch: half-past six. He was on time. All he had to do now was to stay near the café until Fells showed up.

She had selected a park bench in the shade of some trees where he couldn't see her from the café, but she could see him. In fact, she saw him arrive and look around. She waited. There didn't seem to be anyone following him, still, better safe than sorry, so she circled the area to take her to the paddling pool, tracing the path he walked earlier. There was no sign of anyone suspicious: a young mother with a toddler and a pushchair, an elderly couple each eating an ice cream. Satisfied, she walked across the grass and joined Lightbourne, who greeted her with a wide grin. She took him under the arm and they turned back towards the car park and the hired Punto. She opened it with the remote and revving the engine asked "Do ya know the way to Sleaford?"

For an instant Marcia Fells was just two metres away from Hudson. She and he were both blissfully ignorant of the circumstance since their cars were on the same road going in opposite directions. His car was on its way to Burton Acre Farm where, Hudson explained, the University had re-opened excavations begun there in the "60s and "70s. The site lay within an original land grant to Abingdon Abbey where a Saxon settlement provided plenty of information on the critical sixth century period.

The University hoped to find out more and needed to do this with urgency, because the farmer had permission to develop a few acres for residential purposes.

There was a proton magnetometer in a storeroom at the farm. Hudson had the key to the storeroom and nobody on the farm would see anything wrong if he took it away for a few days. The archaeologists weren't on site, because they had skipped to an emergency Roman dig at Bicester.

"Ah a proton magnetometer." Jake said, remembering that his ex-wife Heather had used one in the Red Horse Vale. Dr Hudson turned right down a farm track.

"It's an instrument that measures minute differences in the magnetic field of the earth, caused by ferrous concentrations in the soil." He explained to his wife.

"What if there's no iron in what we're looking for?" she said.

"No problem, Hudson cut in, the device can detect differences in the magnetic susceptibility of disturbed soils."

"You mean once somebody's buried something this machine can tell you that they've done it?"

"Exactly."

"Smart."

They bumped along the track until they came to a series of outbuildings.

"I'll just stop here," he said and opened the boot. Back in a minute."

Hudson put a pick and two spades into the boot along with some technical equipment, sensor, cable and staff. He disappeared into the building again and returned with a hard plastic, black control box in his hand. He got back in the car and placed the box on his knees.

"That it?" Alice asked.

"Yes."

"Wow. It's quite small. Somehow I expected—"

"Nobody saw me take this stuff," the archaeologist said.

"Better and better. Let's go." Jake clapped his hands together.

Hudson passed the box to her and drove back down the lane. Before long they were heading north. After two motorways, they joined the unwavering straightness of the A46, the Fosse Way, which led Hudson to discourse on Roman roads and their construction. The time passed without boredom as the archaeologist was a good raconteur even if he kept yawning and rubbing his eyes quite a lot; Alice would never have guessed that she would be interested in the military importance of Roman roads. Despite the large number of snarling heavy goods vehicles belching fumes and choking the route, in a little over a couple of hours they were almost in Sleaford. Paul Hudson checked his watch; it was a quarter past one. They agreed it was time for lunch and to decide what to do about Kate Briggs.

LEWISHAM, LONDON

A COUPLE of phone calls soured the day for DCI Willis. First, Jones and Porter had followed Lightbourne to his Edwardian detached house on Morrell Avenue, watched him park his car and go inside. They waited in a good vantage point with the Special Branch van nearby. After an hour or more without any sign of movement, Jones rang the doorbell, with an excuse ready, but there was no reply.

When he went around the back of the house, there was no sign of Lightbourne. He had given them the slip.

Willis was furious, his annoyance compounded by the anxiety of having to explain to his Super. Jones's lame excuse that Lightbourne had no reason to suppose he was being followed morphed his fury into impotent resentment. It was lucky for Jones that he wasn't one of the Met team or he'd be back on traffic duty in the blink of an eye. Basic procedure when tailing someone was to cover all exits. Thank goodness, thought Willis, it was Thames Valley's problem and not his. Controlling his ire with difficulty he told Jones to set the Special Branch lads in motion in the hope that a general sweep would pick up and locate any call coming from Lightbourne's cell phone. When he rang off, Willis slammed the phone down much harder than intended, only for it to ring immediately.

Willis snatched up the phone and barked at an unsuspecting sergeant in Bicester who informed him that the garbage collectors there had found the body of a young policeman shot in the forehead by a 9 mm handgun. According to the police doctor, he had been dead for less than twenty-four hours. The estimated time of death was about 15.30 the day before. Acting with commendable speed, the Bicester police had pressured the pathologist for rapid extraction of the bullet. Their computer matched it to the same weapon that was used to kill David Briggs. All possible help from Bicester was offered to get "the bastard" who had killed young Matt Johnson—a lovely lad and a respected colleague. Willis thanked the sergeant and this time, lost in thought, put the phone down.

When Meade walked into Willis's office around seven o'clock, he sensed a haze of discontent hanging unseen in the air. Meade soon found out why. He heaved an audible sigh of relief, making Willis give him a peculiar stare, when he learned that Jones and Porter were the culprits.

The latter came straight to the point.

"It seems the inscription on the back of the stolen jewel is crucial. SB intercepted Lightbourne saying that he knew the location of what we must suppose is *the treasure*. Willis said the last words gesturing speech marks with two thick fingers of each hand. We think he spoke to Marcia Fells and they have an appointment, God knows where." At this point Willis broke into expletives about Fells and purple in the face made it clear to Meade *off the record* that he wouldn't *care a toss* if they blew the bitch away in a *botched* attempt to arrest her.

Regaining his composure, he continued, "Lightbourne browsed sites about Threekingham on his computer. Threekingham was the site of an Anglo-Saxon wayside cross and our couple in Louth, who found the jewel, think its original location at Threekingham..."

Ron Meade dared to interrupt, "They were spotted with a woman who matches Kate Briggs's description and all three could be going to Threekingham."

"So, the young fools are looking for this treasure too. That's all we need."

"And at the same time Lightbourne and Fells could be going to Threekingham for the same reason. The only difference being that Fells is likely to wipe out anyone who gets in her way."

"Then there's the complication of Hudson," Willis squeezed his moustache between thumb and forefinger, "he's a wild card. He has a shotgun and it seems that he is following Kate Briggs, but he's a prime target for Fells. This needs careful handling," Willis said drumming four thick fingers on his desk, "we need to be there before anyone else gets hurt. On the other hand, we mustn't scare this Fells away with our presence. It's a messy business all right."

Meade flicked a tiny dead moth off the grey metal table, leaving a trace of gold powder on his finger, which he transferred to an Ordnance Survey map spread out on the desk as he pointed to a crossroads in the countryside just north of Threekingham. Taking a fine-tipped felt pen, he drew a red ring around it.

"This is the place where the cross stood in the seventh century—"

"Blimey! That long ago?" Willis said.

"Well, it stood there until Victorian times, but in the Civil War it was damaged by the Puritans. Then it was taken to Lincoln. I'm not sure how long it's been in the Usher Gallery."

The two men inspected the map. Willis took the pen from Meade and marked four crosses.

"Here, here, here and here," he said, "we'll station four of our units from 7.30 tomorrow morning. I can't see any of them moving before that time, Ron. Now we'd better let the Super know."

Aalia Phadkar listened to what Willis had to say without interrupting him. When he finished, she said, "We'll send you ten armed men to Sleaford for seven o'clock tomorrow morning. I don't need to tell you, Ron, if bloodshed can be avoided..." she didn't finish the sentence and added, "...now I'll get on to the Chief Inspector at Sleaford and get you fixed up with an operations room. Give him a ring in half an hour or so. Oh, and Ron, good luck for tomorrow morning. I'm counting on you."

Willis put the phone down and looked Meade in the eye, "We've got complete support from the boss. She's not a bad "'un when pull comes to shove...now, the ball's in our court, at last. Let's get that American son of a bitch."

"Daughter of a bitch, doesn't have the same ring, does it?"

"American bitch."

With circumspection, Meade looked at his chief, his tone was meek, "Sorry, sir. I'll get off to Sleaford then."

FORTY-THREE

SLEAFORD, LINCOLNSHIRE,2021 AD

THREE SILVER BIRCHES BORDERING A SWEEPING LAWN justified the name of *The Birches Bed & Breakfast* standing beside a main road leading into Sleaford. The house was plaster over brick and painted white, its grey roof tiles providing a stark contrast. The flare of red geraniums beneath the ground floor windows broke the harsh monochrome effect. All around the lawn were variegated bushes, hosting innumerable birds, all orbiting a wooden birdhouse standing erect on its pole.

"Oh boy, it sure is pretty," Fells drawled, "Be ready at eight o'clock tomorrow morning."

"What about you?" Lightbourne was surprised.

"Better we separate, honey. No hesitations, no contrasting stories. Oh, and your name's Clarke, you got that? They're expecting you. I'll be round tomorrow, Tom."

Lightbourne watched the car disappear down the road. He resented the lack of consultation. He felt like a parcel dropped off at destination and, he reflected, he still had no idea what his role in this treasure hunt was supposed to be. Just manual labour he thought, someone to dig up the treasure. The thought of finding the treasure of Ely Abbey heartened him and he looked round at the pleasant accommodation, trying to ignore the incessant sound of rubber on tarmac at his back. He hoped the traffic would be lighter through the night. He shrugged, and walked down the garden path lined with delphinium and peony. He rang the doorbell and a friendly, ruddy-faced woman with grey hair answered.

"Mr Clarke?" she said.

Lightbourne held out his hand, the unfamiliar name grating "Tom Clarke, pleased to meet you."

"Muriel Woods," the woman beamed, "American, eh? Is your luggage in the car?"

"*Er*, no. No luggage and no car. My company has a conference in the area. A colleague dropped me off just now and she'll pick me up in the morning at about eight. Her family live in the area: she's single, you see...old-fashioned family and all that," he improvised.

Muriel Woods did see. The elderly woman clearly approving of this moral stance ushered him in, "Do come in, Tom, I'll show you your room."

All the formalities dealt with, Simon Lightbourne picked up a leaflet for St Denys parish church and decided that wasn't what he wanted to do with the rest of the afternoon. Dumped here, he might as well have been a parcel. With Fells's instructions not to use his phone for any reason clear in his mind, he sat on the edge of the bed and wondered what the hell he was going to do in this goddam place till morning.

ELSEWHERE IN SLEAFORD, THE SAME DAY.

Kate Briggs studied her reflection in the hall mirror noting with pleasure the poise bestowed by a combination of self-satisfaction and self-assuredness. The self-satisfaction derived from her manipulation of Pete, her shooting instructor. She had persuaded him that it was time to show her the art of gun maintenance. With this pretext she had him clean and lubricate the Glock to perfection. Kate fervently hoped she would never have to put gun maintenance into practice after the next couple of days in Lincolnshire. Instead, self-assuredness came from possession of the weapon.

It was lying on a beige marble-topped coffee table and Kate picked it up once again appreciating its perfect balance in her hand. The pistol weighed six hundred grams including the fifteen rounds in its magazine. She tossed it into her travelling bag and closed the zip. A few minutes later her Porsche roared out of the garage bound for Sleaford.

Meanwhile at Bannerman's in the outskirts of that town, Hudson, Alice and Jake had ordered ploughman's lunches that came with chunks of cheddar cheese each big enough to feed a family of four. Alice wrapped her and Jake's leftovers into a napkin and deftly slipped it into her bag. Paul Hudson smiled and raised his orange juice. He said he was altogether off alcohol. Now they tackled the thorny issue of Kate Briggs.

"It's simple enough, just call Kate and tell her that you and Jake have changed your minds. Say that you've thought it over, you realise that it's too dangerous and you're afraid. She has to accept that, doesn't she?" The tone of the question was nothing short of impatient and Alice noted, not for the first time, that Paul Hudson seemed prone to moodiness.

"What if she decides to go ahead on her own?" Jake objected.

"I've thought of that," the archaeologist showed his perfect white teeth in something resembling a snarl rather than a smile. "A twelve-bore shotgun should dissuade her. I brought one from the farm and I know how to handle it if the worst comes to the worst...but it won't come to that," he added, noticing the alarmed expressions across the table. "In any case, let's see how she reacts when you call her." He went back to the by now familiar rubbing of his forehead.

Kate pulled into a motorway lay-by to take the call. She wasn't pleased. At first, she tried to persuade Alice to change her mind, pointing out that they could be throwing away their share of a fortune. Then she tried moral pressure, because they were going back on their agreement. When that didn't work, she appealed to their friendship and finally, brusquely, told Alice that she'd manage on her own.

"That isn't what we wanted, is it?"

Dr Hudson looked calmly at her, "Not really," he said unperturbed, "but it's what I expected. She isn't the kind to give up at the first obstacle. This means that she'll be there tomorrow morning and will expect to be alone, so we have surprise on our side. We should be able to overpower her... without hurting her," he said.

Alice felt sick with dread. This wider scenario of violence and death didn't seem part of her life, but of another strange, alien world—more appropriate to when she was an agent not under cover. It was closing in on her and she heard Jake's words as though from a long way off.

"Why don't we go this afternoon, so we can have a clear run at finding the treasure and avoid..."

"One can tell you are no archaeologist Jake," the lecturer smirked, "you're way too optimistic. It will take time to locate anything, even with the equipment we've got. Digging up the past is a long, laborious job. One needs a lot of patience and persistence. None of that glamorous Indiana Jones twaddle. There will be all sorts of hitches and we have to find some accommodation. We can't go to your motel given the circumstances. Imagine the possible outcome if we leave a half-dug site overnight. There might be unwelcome interest and the last thing we want is a showdown with some overexcited locals in an out of the way spot like that." Paul Hudson took a long swig of his orange juice and half-closed his eyes as if in sudden pain.

"You all right Paul?" Jake asked.

"Oh, I've been having headaches since the accident, it's nothing," he smiled, his face wan.

Jake picked up the discussion, "You're right, better to deal with Kate at that point," He looked at his wife and noticed her pallor.

"Are you all right, Alice?"

She nodded, not answering. He shrugged, at least *he* felt on top form. He sat back and dreamed of gold coins and bracelets.

After lunch they found a small comfortable hotel in the centre of Sleaford and spent the evening together in the bar, having decided that it was better not to risk an unexpected encounter with Kate. After all, the town centre was small. *Nor with Marcia Fells*, Paul Hudson added to himself, whom he supposed was still following Kate. It was a mistake ever having mentioned that fact in the first place. He just hoped Jake and Alice had forgotten. There was no point in frightening them more than necessary or they would pull out of the excavation and he needed the extra hands. He could sense that the woman was living on her nerves and on the point of quitting. She had to be soothed at all costs.

Hudson leant forward in his armchair and engaged her with what he hoped was a reassuring smile.

"You know I've been thinking. Maybe I've misjudged Kate Briggs. I don't know her at all. Would you say she's the sort of person with whom one could negotiate?"

He was gratified to get the hoped-for reaction. She clutched at the lifeline with the eagerness of a drowning woman. She put her drink down and leant forward to place her hand on his arm while her earnest expression forced him to conceal his cynicism. She said: "Kate's a kind and generous person not the calculating woman you spoke of yesterday. Deep down that description of her never convinced me."

Dr Hudson nodded as though he was weighing up her words. She took up her drink again and swirled the olive around in it by its blue cocktail fork. She studied the archaeologist over the rim of her glass, as he seemed to wrestle with the problem. Jake was about to speak, but she held up her left hand in a quick and unmistakeable gesture.

At last Hudson spoke. "Maybe you're right. You know her better. Kate may not show at the crossroads tomorrow morning, but if she does, we'll make every effort to get her on board. An extra pair of hands would be manna from heaven." He studied the effect of his words on the young couple and satisfied that they were much happier, added the clincher: "Of course, it will give Kate the opportunity to restore the good name of the Briggs family by cooperating with the University of Oxford. From what you tell me she cares more about that than about money."

Paul Hudson watched the couple head for the stairs at the end of the evening. A sly smile curled the side of his lips. He had managed to tranquillise them and they should sleep soundly enough. How he envied them. He was in desperate need of sleep, but it eluded him. He felt agitated and held his head in his hands. He must see a doctor as soon as all this was over. Now, where was he? Ah yes, in reality he had other plans for Kate Briggs if she had the courage to show up. And as for Marcia Fells, she had tried to kill him twice. An old Sicilian saying came to mind: "*vengeance is a dish best served cold...*"

SLEAFORD, THE NEXT MORNING.

LIGHTBOURNE HAD bacon and eggs in the dining room at seven o'clock while Kate ate grapefruit and then muesli in her motel room. At about the same time, Ron Willis walked into his operations centre at Sleaford police station. The first thing he did was to lift the phone to check out that the armed police had arrived from London. He was told they were ready and waiting, so he split them into four units and gave detailed instructions on how to arrive without alerting any of the suspects, and then on their respective positioning. He wanted them on the spot for half-past seven, which was the time that Kate got into her Porsche to drive to Threekingham.

At eight o'clock Fells was waiting for Lightbourne outside the B&B.

"Sleep well, honey?" she asked in an indifferent tone.

"Like a log. You?"

She ignored the question.

"Let's go. There's a road map in there. She pointed to the passenger door pocket. We're on the A17. I need to know where to turn off for this buried treasure."

FORTY-FOUR

THREEKINGHAM, LINCOLNSHIRE, EARLIER THE SAME MORNING.

The A17 dual carriageway linking Newark to Boston was busy at half-past six in the morning with tractors, trucks, vans and cars moving in both directions. Even though it was the end of June, the morning air had an edge and the weak sun, low in the sky, glimmered on finger-like steeples seeming to indicate the direction to follow should the star deign to brighten the place up.

Just before the village of Threekingham Jake indicated left and Paul Hudson turned into a narrow hedge-lined lane with a grass verge on either side.

A mixture of trepidation and weariness determined Alice's unusual quietness. Her night had been restless and troubled by bad dreams.

"It's such an insignificant road," she murmured "until you think that it was once an Anglo-Saxon track and that soon we might find a fortune buried here," the last two words were distorted by a yawn and she rubbed her eyes.

"There's the crossroad ahead," Jake pointed, "Pull onto the verge just after that gate."

Hudson parked the Avalon and said: "We've blocked

the entrance to that field. Let's hope the farmer doesn't come along with his tractor."

"I shouldn't think so," Jake said, "it's a barley field and at this stage there's nothing to be done except let it ripen."

"That's true Jake, and to think I'm the farmer's son."

They walked up to the crossroads with a huge sense of expectation, savouring the moment, aware of its importance in their lives.

"I wonder which of the four corners is the right one?" Alice said.

"If the cross stood in the middle of the road, we're wasting our time," Jake said, "the treasure will be under asphalt and stones. I don't think the local authorities would take kindly to us digging a huge hole in the middle of the road."

Alice looked at Dr Hudson for guidance and torn by her desire for the treasure and apprehension about Hudson's contingency plan. The sight of him propping his shotgun against the back of the car was disquieting.

The archaeologist grinned, "I don't think the cross would have stood in the middle of the road. The Anglo-Saxons had wagons and carts and they would have had to pass without obstacles. The crosses are called wayside crosses, so the name itself suggests they were at the roadside." Alice watched him as he turned towards the car boot. With his pallid features and dark-ringed eyes, she couldn't help but think that the archaeologist resembled a wraith from the period he had just described. Hudson half turned and called over his shoulder: "What we should do is to set up the magnetometer to read all four verges along the crossroad until we get the right kind of signal and then we start digging. Come on. What are we waiting for?"

They hurried back to the Toyota and Jake helped with the magnetometer.

"We'll use the portable gradiometer option," Dr Hudson said, "It's a little technical to explain, but it employs two sensors, samples and stores readings from each in quick succession, and uses the difference between the readings to locate shallow objects. Gradient information is useful for shallow searches because it can define the depth and location of objects without any need for a base station."

"So, you don't think the Saxons would have buried the treasure too deep?" Jake asked.

"Well, once you cover something, there's little difference between say, three or five feet, why make the extra effort? The important thing is that it's hidden. In either case this machinery will signal it."

JAKE REMEMBERED the depth he'd seen the nuns bury the chest at and his forehead began to ache, but only very slightly. Hudson took out a proton precession sensor, cables, special sensor staff, and the black carry case containing the magnetometer.

"The gradiometer has an accuracy of 0.1 gamma or 0.02 gamma per foot for sensor spacing of greater than 5 feet. When used in the gradient configuration, the system is capable of storing up to 2850 pairs of readings." Dr Hudson continued. Alice pulled a face behind his back and raised her shoulders. Jake winked at her.

Hudson and Jake crossed the road carrying the equipment to the far left verge, a two-yard swathe of weed-strewn grass still glistening with heavy drops of morning dew. Crows cawed their regular warnings as the rising sun peeped over the hedge.

"This is a fourth-generation magnetometer," Dr Hudson explained, "very lightweight as you can see. The first ones were impossible." he chuckled. He held a one-metre long vertical probe in his right hand, which was connected by a cable to the black box, this he held by a carry handle in his left hand. "It's a kind of specialised antenna," he said, "it makes a high-resolution scan of the ground, sending a signal with a two-second cycle time down into the earth and back. If the readout changes it emits an alarm." He began to walk along the verge, holding the black tube in front of him. There came a piping alarm signal. "There!" Hudson said, "Come and have a look at this." Jake and Alice peered down at the control box in the archaeologist's left hand.

"This box has a microprocessor that can transform the signals received into the 3-D image you see in the small screen. They gazed at the image. There was a green background and, in the middle, a small blue shape.

"What is the blue shape?" Jake asked.

"Nothing more than an old Cola can, judging by its shape. We're after something much bigger."

Alice looked up and around the scene, "I suppose the hedge wouldn't have been there in Saxon times," she offered.

"True, and the verge is only two yards wide, but I think the cross would have been right by the track. So, it would have been where the verge is today. It makes sense, to cover the other three quadrants after this one, before going into the fields or trying under the hedge." Hudson resumed his steady walking backwards and forwards, glancing at the mini-screen when the signal piped its warning. "Horseshoes and nails," he grumbled, ignoring them and moving on. Alice studied the archaeologist with interest. True, he didn't look well, but this morning he was energised, alert and less distracted. It must be the thrill of the search, she reasoned.

In the quadrant across the road Hudson moved backwards and forwards, holding the sensor like a monk walking and meditating in a cloister. After ten minutes he thought it best to move on to the southwestern corner since, apart from some minor signals, they had to accept that there was nothing buried there either. Eyes down, they crossed the road, noting here and there at its edge dandelions breaking through the asphalt, nature reasserting itself. They began to worry that their treasure might not be so easy to find, if it was there at all.

Her uneasiness at the sight of the shotgun had unnerved Alice. Her mind fluttered between a feeling that they were being unrealistic in expecting to find treasure and resignation to the fact that it wouldn't turn up and, then the opposite, expecting Paul Hudson's next reading to pinpoint it. She bit the ragged skin around her nails. A shrill alarm sounded, the archaeologist whooped that he had something and she felt not only surprise and excitement but also that this was what she had known would happen all along.

"This could be it," he said without looking up at them, "I've got a big, rectangular shape at a depth of five feet."

Alice jumped up and down a little unhinged, she blurted "The treasure! The treasure!"

"We don't know that for sure," Jake said. "Let's not count our chickens..." Nevertheless, he rushed over to peer at the solid blue rectangle on the small screen. The shape and depth were right.

They hurried back to the car and dragged out the pick and spades. The purr of a car coming down the lane made them hesitate. It slowed down for the stop sign as it passed, the driver glancing at them, but he didn't seem interested in what they were doing.

Jake used a spade to cut the turf of the verge back, exposing a rectangle of dark, brown soil about two yards long and half as wide. A couple of fat red earthworms wriggled back into the dark earth. Meanwhile Hudson carried the detector equipment back to the car and packed it away. Jake told his wife to stand back while he set about loosening the topsoil with the pick. They didn't notice Hudson bring out the shotgun and lean it against the hedge. He took Alice's spade and joined in digging away some of the loose earth.

Few vehicles used the lane and although the occasional curious driver stared at them, nobody stopped to question them as work progressed. Alice was the first to spot something.

"Look!" she said, "the soil's discoloured. There are threads. It's some sort of old cloth. There's lots of it. It looks like it must have been a blanket or something. It's almost completely rotted away."

Jake took up the pick again. When they were well down the dark topsoil became sticky, grey yellow clay that was difficult to budge. He swung the pick a few times but it was hard going. Hudson removed the little he managed to heave up. Jake's face was glistening with sweat and they worked for some time like this, ignoring their aching backs and their blistered hands until the hole was quite wide and deep. Suddenly the pick hit something solid.

"There's something hard here."

"Let's have a look." Jake handed the pick to her and soon he had scraped away the soil to expose the unmistakeable shape of a wooden chest. The iron bands around it were almost completely rusted away, but the dark wood was in good condition.

"It's oak," Hudson murmured, "My God. Do you realise what we've got here?"

It took several minutes of hard graft to dig the ends free from the surrounding soil so Alice could slip two lengths of rope around it. Jake took one side and Hudson and she the other and they began to haul. They tugged with all their might, but the chest wouldn't budge and just when they were losing hope, with a sucking sound, the oak chest moved slowly upwards. They redoubled their efforts, but in vain, because the lid wedged itself under a stone that was sticking out of the side of the hole. They slackened the rope and stared at the chest.

"Good grief, what's in it?" Alice blew out her cheeks.

"It's no use," Hudson said, "we'll never get it out like this. We'll have to use the car. He threw the keys to Jake, whose glance took in the new position of the shotgun without giving it any thought. Back it up to the hole and I'll make a ramp.

He placed the three spades with their metal ends face down under the near side of the chest and their handles resting on the edge of the hole. Quickly he tied the two ropes together so that the chest was secure and when Alice directed Jake so that the Toyota was at the edge of the hole, Hudson tied the rope to a point somewhere under the back of the car. He stood up and went around to the driver's side of the car.

"Pull away very gently Jake," he said, "if not we'll damage the chest. Alice, you stand next to Jake's window and tell him to stop if I give you the word. Let's try it."

Jake let the clutch out very slowly and the rope became taut. Paul Hudson watched, holding his breath, as the chest gradually inched its way up the spade handles. The handles flexed under the weight, but they didn't break. Soon, the chest was clear of the hole.

"Stop now." Hudson shouted as the chest began to gouge into the soil. "We've done it." He began to untie the rope from the tow bar.

Jake jumped out of the car and hugged his wife. She could not know that his forehead was aching fit to burst. They stared in awe at the chest that had been in the ground for so many centuries. Hudson struggled with the knot he'd tied around the top of the chest, because now it'd pulled tight under the strain of the hauling. He gave up and took a clasp knife out of his pocket. He grunted as he hacked through the rope.

Voice trembling with emotion and the palms of his hands rubbing his temples, eyes half-closed with pain, Hudson's use of the first-person singular wasn't lost on Jake and Alice, "The Ely Abbey Treasure and I've found it!"

FORTY-FIVE

SLEAFORD, LINCOLNSHIRE, HALF AN HOUR EARLIER

"Base to Unit One, have you got anything?

"White male, late twenties and white female, thirties, fitting suspects" descriptions in black Fiat Punto just turned into lane. Over."

"Base to all units, on standby wait for order to move in."

Chief Inspector Willis put the mouthpiece down and thought for a minute. So, Fells and Lightbourne had arrived first. There was no sign of Kate Briggs and the young couple nor of Paul Hudson for that matter. It meant he could wait ten or fifteen minutes while they began searching for the treasure. That way they'd be out of their car and distracted, making it easier for his men to capture them without any police film antics.

He reflected on the gap between art and reality and congratulated himself on how his expertise had denied him the thrill of the car chase and gunfire. Some of those younger coppers weren't smart enough to see that thinking things through and planning in advance were more important than manoeuvring cars and toting arms.

THREEKINGHAM, LINCOLNSHIRE HALF AN HOUR LATER.

AT THE MOMENT of Willis's reflections Marcia Fells took in the scene of the excavation and it was with pursed her lips that she saw three people and a car parked by the road. Two of them were bent over a chest, inspecting it. The other was reaching for a shotgun next to the hedge. What the hell was going on? Jeez. That jerk, Hudson. He got lucky once too often. Her lips became tighter. No way would she screw up this time."

"He's pointing the shotgun from his hip at the married couple. The son-of-a-bitch."

She slowed to a halt, put her finger to her lips in a message to Lightbourne to be quiet and gestured him to stay where he was. Fells slipped out the car and slunk nearer moving as soundlessly as a great cat. She heard Hudson say to the other two:

"Such a short career as archaeologists – what a shame."

Wide-eyed and trembling, Alice grabbed Jake and screamed. She cursed herself for ignoring Hudson's erratic behaviour. All the signs had been there, and she and Jake had ignored them, driven on my once-in-a-lifetime chance to find buried treasure. Now they were going to pay the highest price as the maniac raised his shotgun to his shoulder and peered along the barrels.

Jake's voice came out squeaky and unnatural,

"Dr Hudson, don't throw away your career. Think about it. We've been seen together this morning. You'll never get away with this."

"It's my career I'm thinking about. With you two out of

the way I'll have the treasure to myself for as long as I need to study it. Then I'll spring my surprise on the academic world and reveal its presence with my in-depth analysis and commentary. They'll be falling over themselves to award me a full professorship."

Jake, heart thumping, careful not to make any sudden movement, held up his hands palm outwards at chest height, "But listen, the police will hunt you down if you kill us. What about your career then?"

"You're forgetting they are looking for the American woman. They'll blame your disappearance on her. We've got a ready-made grave too."

Jake, with Alice moaning and trembling beside him, tried one last desperate throw of the dice.

"At least open the chest and make sure there's something in it that's worth killing for."

Lip curling, Hudson glanced sideways at the chest. It was the last thing he ever saw.

A sound like a hollow pop exploded behind Jake. Dr Paul Hudson died on the site of his last excavation. Alice and Jake stared in shocked horror first at the sprawled body and shattered skull, then spinning round, at the incongruous, attractive killer and at a young man running toward them from a black car.

"Well, lawdie, how considerate of you, guys. Saved us a lot of work there, yes indeed." Fells drawled nonchalantly, her eyes hard and pitiless. "Take it easy," the American sneered, "it's so much easier with a pistol. Shotguns make such a mess and we want everything neat and tidy. Now turn around and kneel down on the ground. That's right. Say your prayers like good little folks."

Jake felt Alice's knees buckle from under her and grabbed her under one arm taking her dead weight. He was thinking frantically, but there was no hope in his heart. He felt emptiness inside; death was certain...

Simon Lightbourne dashed between Fells and the couple, "Come on Marcia." he cried, "you can't kill them—they're goddam innocent, for Christ's sake!"

Fells raised the pistol towards Lightbourne's face, "Out the way Daddy's boy." she hissed, "Never leave loose ends lying around."

Lightbourne blanched, he could see nothing but icy determination in her eyes. He moved aside, "Marcia, I beg you. There's no need to kill them. Please we can tie them up."

"Cissy boy, your uncle pays me to do a professional job. Now that's what I'm gonna do. Neat and tidy."

Kate Briggs found the black Fiat and the Toyota parked one behind the other in the lane. As she moved in unobserved behind, she heard a dull pistol shot. She leapt out of her car and climbed the gate into the field. Hidden by the hawthorn hedge she calmly listened to the discussion between Fells and Lightbourne. Her hand was steady and her heart sure. Chilled with the ice of distilled hatred, she pulled the gun from the waistband at the back of her jeans. There was the woman who had killed David. Now she meant to kill her young friends. Kate stepped up to a slight break in the hedge so she had a clear view of the hit woman. Her left hand cradled the Glock and her right gently covered the trigger and safety catch. She lined up the two sights to the target's heart, the woman now out of focus, but it didn't matter. Her left arm as still as a rock just as Pete instructed her.

Lightbourne, who was facing Kate, suddenly spotted her and gasped. It was enough to alert Fells. Fast as a cobra, she spun round and fired all in one movement, the report of her gun blending with that of Kate's.

Kate felt an atrocious pain and blacked out, collapsing backwards into the field. Fells pitched forward onto her face and the pistol fell free. Jake and Lightbourne sprang forward simultaneously to grab it. Alice, feeling ill, head on her chest, sank to her knees. The American got to the pistol first, his hand closed on the gun and Jake kicked out. His thumb broken, the American howled and the gun spun into the air—the same air that carried the wail of police sirens and flashing blue lights from all directions.

Ignoring the arrival of the police, Alice staggered to her feet, and plunged through the thorny hedge towards Kate, scratching her face, while Lightbourne turned to run towards the Punto, but Jake leapt forward and brought him down with a rugby tackle.

The lane was crammed with blue and white cars and a forest of black clad, helmeted policemen sprouting firearms. Detective Sergeant Meade surveyed the situation. Disastrous—Marcia Fells was dead, with a bullet through the heart; Hudson, dead, a bullet to the brain. He ordered the handcuffing of Lightbourne and went to Alice in the green-whiskered barley field, where she was cradling Kate's head in her lap.

Alice looked up at him tears and trickles of blood mingling like a watercolour on her face, "She's wounded," Alice choked out the words, nodding at the red stain spreading at Kate's shoulder.

"Call an ambulance. And get me a van to transport that thing." Meade pointed at the chest, "...and where's the damned photographer?"

The oak chest was attracting a lot of attention from the policemen who'd arrived to deal with the situation, but as soon as the ambulance arrived, about seven minutes later, Meade cleared the scene of the task force. The regular police moved the Saxon chest into the waiting police van.

Meade looked at the radio in his car—Willis wasn't going to like this. The whole business had been a total cock up, but he had followed his orders to the letter. His radio message brought an end to the clamour of the last half hour, which was replaced by birdsong and the dull chugging of a distant tractor. The only trace of recent events was a filled hole in the roadside verge.

FORTY-SIX

"Meade, bring those gentlemen through now, would you?" Willis barked into the phone, "And tell DC Tomlinson to bring her photographic gear."

The door opened and DS Meade showed a tall, scruffy man with an aquiline nose, into the room. He was carrying a small cardboard box. A similarly middle-aged man and an older woman followed him in. Last through the door was none other than Sir Clive Cochrane accompanying the pretty, auburn-haired DC Tomlinson, who was carrying a digital Nikon with flash.

The chief inspector held out his hand to the tall man, "Professor Cox, nice to see you again. Have you all been introduced?"

The tall man chuckled, "Come, come, Chief Inspector, we are all specialists in Anglo-Saxon history, you realise how many conferences and dinners we've attended together."

Jake tried to keep his expression neutral and was succeeding better than his flustered wife.

Bloody hell, double-A's here. He would be with all these bigwigs.

Willis looked a little crestfallen and Jake noticed the sergeant wink at the policewoman behind his chief's back, relishing his moment of discomfort. Alice, instead, was now looking over the professor from head to toe. The shirttail hanging out under his jacket and his gabardine trousers a little on the short side over suede shoes that had never been brushed told her that he wasn't one to bother about appearances.

"Yes, of course," said a sheepish Willis, "then let me introduce Mr Copley and his good lady, they are two of the three people who found the chest." Jake glanced at Sir Clive and noted his ironical smile. He just hoped that facing the music would not be too harrowing. Meanwhile, the policeman continued, indicating the tall man, "Professor Bryan Cox, London University, who helps the Metropolitan Police in matters associated with archaeology and we're very pleased that Professor Valerie Keys has been able to dash up here from Cambridge, very kind of you madam..."

A slight woman wearing a grey plaited skirt to below the knee and a pale blue turtleneck sweater, her hair in a neat salt and pepper bob, smiled and nodded her head, "I wouldn't miss this for the world if it *is* what we think it is."

Willis finished the introductions "...and Professor Gary Kirwan, in charge of the Research Laboratory for Archaeology and the History of Art at Oxford University, who has also spared us his valuable time." Alice found him fascinating, because he had such a lived-in face and looked anything but an archaeologist. His thick, wavy black hair dragged back into a ponytail and his fingers laden with hefty rings. She could just imagine him in a rock band, with a joint in his hand.

The door opened and a dark-skinned woman in an important-looking uniform came into the room. She had a charismatic presence and Chief Inspector Willis introduced her.

"Chief Superintendent Phadkar," he said and repeated the names of the others in the room for her benefit.

"Well, let's get started," the superintendent said.

"Just a minute, Chief Inspector," Professor Cox said, "everybody must put on a pair of these latex gloves and masks." He pressed open the central oval of the cardboard box he had entered the room with and began to hand round the gloves and masks that covered the mouth and nose. "Standard procedure," he said by way of explanation. He pulled out a small tape recorder and pressed the record button before letting it fall back into his jacket pocket, then speaking into a small microphone attached to his lapel.

"An oaken chest, its wood in good condition, iron bands corroded... hinges sprayed an hour ago with releasing agent. I'm going to open the chest now." The professor unclasped the lid and pushed upwards. The lid didn't move. He pushed harder and, with a crack, the ancient hinges ceded. "Hinges too corroded to resist pressure, broken apart, am now removing the lid."

Everyone in the room craned forward to get a better look and the silence was almost palpable.

The professor's deep voice rumbled on into the mike, "The chest is lined with lead and...full of precious objects." His voice betrayed his emotions. He laid the lid down on the table.

"Lead. So that's why it was so heavy," Jake's whisper seemed to boom in the silence.

"Indeed, but what good fortune," Professor Keys said, beside himself with emotion. "The lead has preserved everything to perfection."

"I'm removing the first object, it's a book, oak boards, bound in leather, I'm opening the book, its pages are calf vellum." He moved his hands with extreme delicacy. Good heavens. The *Poems of Caedmon*." He stared at the book and turned its pages, commenting all the while into his microphone before putting the book down with reluctance on the adjacent table and anxiously motioning to Professor Keys to go gently: a completely gratuitous gesture. She glided across to examine it and stared in disbelief at the manuscript.

"They are indeed. The *Poems of Caedmon*." She whirled round in triumph towards the two bewildered young people and the police. Her voice became professorial, "Caedmon was a monk of Whitby, he lived in the seventh century and wrote a metrical paraphrase of both testaments, but until today, the oldest extant version of the poem, from the tenth century, is in our Bodleian library at Oxford. If the chest contained nothing other than this book, it would still be worth a king's ransom." She turned back to Cox, her voice tremulous, awestricken, "What else Bryan?" and as she spoke, she transferred the book to the table where DC Tomlinson was sitting prepared to take her photos.

Professor Cox stopped her, "Chief Inspector, I must object to flash photography, it could do irreparable damage."

Willis held up a hand to Tomlinson, move my desk over to the window, he said to Meade, "Do your best with natural light, constable." Jake moved over beside the policewoman and watched her set the camera without flash on macro and screw the camera body to a small tripod that she positioned with extreme care over the priceless volume.

Meade prepared an inventory of the objects and wrote *Item 1: Ancient Volume, The Poems of Caedmon.* Cox reached into the chest, "I'm removing the second object, another book, its cover is gilded silver on wood, with gold cloisonné enamels, pearls and semi-precious stones." He turned the pages and breathed in, "again it's written on calf vellum, the text is interspersed with large illuminated pages, animated initials, beasts, grotesque figures and brilliantly-coloured ornaments. Condition perfect."

"What?" Kirwan asked.

The resonant baritone voice resumed, unhurried, "An Old English version of the *Psalms* by Aldhelm, Bishop of Sherbourne."

"My God. This is the find of the century. No, the millennium. Well, well, well, so they even had a copy of Aldhelm in Ely," Kirwan clasped his hands together and shook them as in triumph.

"We can't jump to conclusions, Gary," Valerie Keys said cautiously, "without indisputable proof, we cannot state that this is the Abbey of Ely treasure."

Alice joined Jake beside DC Tomlinson as she took photos, a page at a time, of the *Poems of Caedmon.*

"Isn't it beautiful?" she said, admiring an illuminated illustration of an angel guarding the Gates of Paradise. "I'm having trouble getting my head round the idea that this is over thirteen hundred years old and we found it."

Time seemed to stand still as one after another the treasures were taken with reverential care out of the chest. Jake and Alice watched as the books, which also included *St. John's Gospel* by Bede and a *Gospel of St. Matthew* in Mercian dialect, were photographed. The dialect provoked the most excitement and discussion. There was enough material in that book alone to keep an army of scholars busy producing volumes of new learning to fill an entire library if the professors' reactions were to be believed. Alice thought they were way over the top, but the strange animal and bird figures, snakes, human bodies in contorted shapes and animals biting their tails and intricate scrolls all flashed before her eyes, forcing her to admit that maybe it was true.

"You know, a book like that," Professor Keys said to Jake and pointing to the Bede manuscript, "might have taken up to seventy-five years to complete."

"A whole lifetime?"

"Perhaps two lifetimes in those days."

Jake gave a low whistle between his teeth. Lined up ready to be photographed was a chalice, its lower part in the form of a lion of the purest gold with onyx stones on its back. Next to it was a gold censer surrounded on all sides by small heads. Also, there were sculpted crosses with ivory figures, which according to Professor Kirwan were carved from walrus tusks. Then there were several gold and silver reliquaries, some with ivory figures interposed, silver candlesticks decorated with gold, another chalice studded with topaz, onyx, beryl and jasper with the engraved bust figures of Christ and the evangelists, each in interlaced oval frames. Meade noted them down out one by one, but DC Tomlinson was way behind with her photography. Professor Cox reached back into the depths of the chest and pulled out a silver plate embossed with the bust of St. Peter. The others saw him stiffen as he peered at the raised letters inscribed in Latin under the apostle's keys. Slowly and dramatically he read out the words: *Donum Abbatiae Elyensia Wulfhere Rege Datum.*

"Hallelujah. Here's the proof we needed," Professor Keys exulted. "A gift to the Abbey of Ely by King Wulfhere. Without a shadow of doubt this is the legendary treasure of

St. Werburgh. And now we have a definite date for this plate and that is, at the end of the seventh century."

She turned to Jake and Alice, "Well, young man and you too miss, it would appear that you have made the archaeological find of the millennium...as my colleague would have it. Congratulations." Professor Cox came over and shook them by the hand. Then, he added, "Do you think we could have a word afterwards? There are one or two points I would like to clear up with you?"

He finished clearing the bottom of the chest of its loose objects of precious stones and amber votive offerings and then looked at his watch. "It's getting late," he said, "Chief Superintendent, it's absolutely essential that these objects be locked away with the maximum security."

Willis checked his watch and was surprised to see that it was half-past seven. "It's too late to get these into a bank vault this evening, but we can lock them in one of the cells with an armed constable on guard all night."

"Yes, and tomorrow, I recommend a high security transfer to a bank vault."

"I think I can do better than that Professor," Chief Superintendent Phadkar smiled, "a couple of strategic phone calls should see it all safely in the Bank of England vault within an hour."

The power of a Chief Superintendent, Willis thought to himself. The Bank of England—no less—"

Jake was mirroring his words in thought:

The power of people like Sir Clive is incredible.

"There's a very good restaurant in the town centre. You two young people will be my guests, if you agree," Professor Cox said cheerfully.

Jake nodded. He was really hungry and Alice said, "That's very kind of you." But both were tired and would have preferred to curl up in bed with a couple of take-away pizzas.

"Robert, Gary, ladies and gentlemen of the constabulary, would you care to join us?"

The police did not care to do so, except for Chief Superintendent Phadkar, because they had too much to do, but the two professors accepted the invitation. To the Copleys' dismay, Sir Clive agreed to join the party.

Professor Cox checked that the inventory corresponded to the treasure in the room and signed four copies. One he folded and put in his wallet, another he handed to Jake and the other two remained with DS Meade. The strategic phone calls were made and within half an hour an armoured van accompanied by a small army of armed police and outriders was on its way to the Bank of England.

Jake and Alice each signed his statement and left the police station in exalted company, wondering what on earth Professor Cox wanted to ask them and what Sir Clive's reaction would be.

FORTY-SEVEN

NOTTING HILL, LONDON

That the sequence of events leading to the discovery of the dove should have been triggered by an old ghost story turned out to be a winner at the dinner table. They were seated in the elegant surroundings of *The Fat Goose* in Notting Hill, a favourite haunt of Professor Cox.

Alice had overcome her intimidation at being seated next to a Chief Superintendent of the Metropolitan Police Force. Witty and charming, Aalia Phadkar, sensing the tension in the young woman, made every effort to put her at her ease. She also proved indispensable as a guide through the baffling delicacies offered by Elena Keppler, the world's most famous female chef. Basking in the pleasant glow induced by the costly Sauternes and her Roast Quail Breast with Apricots, Chanterelles and Dandelion, Alice marvelled at the self-confidence Jake displayed in this company as he retold their finding of the dove. She looked across the table at him now and felt the deep glow of love suffusing her. She realised that money would be coming their way and drifted off into long-term dreams of home, garden and family.

A gale of laughter dragged her back to reality. A claim by Professor Cox that he had seen the ghost of a Roman legionnaire at twilight on a dig at York was met by general incredulity and mirth. The more he tried to convince them, the more they tormented him. In exasperation he spluttered,

"So how do you explain the finding of the scroll in Rose Cottage?"

These words had a sobering effect on them all. There was no convincing explanation except that Roy Robinson all those years ago had seen the ghost of old Agnes Monson.

The evening passed pleasantly amid talk of the implications of the discovery of the Ely Abbey treasure.

Instead, Alice told Aalia of her certainty that Dr Hudson had never recovered from the blow to the head caused by the sabotage to his Audi. She described his appearance and behaviour in the days leading up to his death. The Superintendent promised to make sure that an expert neurologist would appear in court. For the sake of his family, Alice wanted everything possible done that might save the archaeologist's reputation. Hudson had tried to kill her and Jake, but Alice was sure that the monster with the shotgun wasn't the real Dr Hudson. She settled down to enjoy her passion fruit soufflé with Sauternes ice cream and wondered whimsically what Saint Werburgh would have made of it.

BRITISH MUSEUM, LONDON

Glossy gonfalons on gallery walls, exhaust-fume defying banners taut across suburban roads, buses bearing elongated adverts and tube escalator posters proclaimed the cultural event of the millennium. Even the most dismal days of winter could not discourage queues of visitors from forming, everyone awaited his turn to marvel at what seemed like a modern-day fairy tale: the Werburgh Treasure Exhibition at the British Museum. More than one told-you-so expert murmured that the expenditure on advertising was unforgivable.

In effect, public imagination, fired by the events surrounding the discovery of the Treasure of the Abbey of Ely, was sufficient to lure people in droves from all over the world; they came to wonder at the expressive power of the seventh-century craftsmanship and partly to relive the emotions surrounding the hiding and rediscovery of the treasure. Once the story broke, and it ran and ran, eager editors had little difficulty in repositioning the spotlight. After examining every possible facet of the Sleaford slayings, the popular tabloids moved on to the bizarre, sick and surreal. As for the interminable queue in the Museum, shuffling forward at gulag pace, only the occasional witticism, laconically delivered in a foreign (generally Australian) accent, shone like a shaft of sunlight through the dull grey clouds of media-inspired monotony.

The hundreds of thousands of paying visitors a month buoyed up the museum's finances, making the £600,000 outlay on the "Werburgh Dove" seem like small change. As far as the Museum was concerned, the angel sent from Heaven by Saint Werburgh had materialised in the unlikely person of the Secretary of State, who, making reference to Article 81 of The Treasure Act 1996, disclaimed the Abbey of Ely Treasure. The coroner at the treasure trove inquest quoted an extract: "...***Reward will not be payable***

when the find is made by an archaeologist or anyone engaged on an archaeological excavation or investigation. In cases of uncertainty, archaeologists are recommended to require any individuals for whom they are responsible, or to whom they have given, or for whom they have sought permission to search, to sign a statement waiving their right to a reward..." Since Dr Paul Hudson had been an archaeologist, the Werburgh Treasure, as it became known, was allocated in its entirety to the British Museum.

The *Werburgh Dove* was another matter though. As the coroner explained, it was legitimate treasure trove and all the conditions of the Treasure Act had been fulfilled. Alice Copley, Jake Copley and farmer "Ted" Johnson were each awarded one third of the proceedings from the sale of what became known as the *Covenham Dove*. This artefact, being the key to the Werburgh Treasure, was a most desirable acquisition and, according to the 1996 law, the British Museum had the option of meeting the valuation committee's £600,000 tag otherwise it would be open to auction. Such was the potential of the proposed exhibition that the Museum had no hesitation in purchasing the dove, nor in investing in additional sophisticated anti-theft security to protect it.

THE STALWART GUARDIAN of public security, Chief Inspector Ron Willis, passed through hell on earth for several days after the *Sleaford Fiasco* as Chief Superintendent Aalia Phadkar called it. She had demanded a bloodless outcome and Willis's error of timing produced the opposite. A thunderous and outraged grimace met the Chief Inspector whenever their paths crossed at police HQ and the menace of an impending internal inquiry hung over his head like a huge icicle dangling from a viaduct. When the thaw came the effects were not in the least disastrous, the icicle came down as an innocuous refreshing shower rather than an icy dagger.

Thanks to the media thirst for another hero, he was catapulted from the sty to the stars. The dogged Willis was the detective who had tracked down an American serial killer and saved the inestimable Werburgh Treasure for the nation. Without the infallible instincts of this humble upholder of the law, goodness alone knew in which secluded vault it might have finished up, never to be seen by the public at large. Aalia Phadkar was quick to grasp this. All talk of internal inquiries vanished while her face became nothing less than affable. Her scrupulousness wouldn't allow her complete forgiveness. She pushed Willis into as many microphone situations as possible, imagining with glee that for the recalcitrant detective each interview was a torment far worse than any disciplinary inquiry. The Sunday supplements, tabloids and Radio 4 profiled his entire career in a series of articles and interviews, so in the long run, the detective came out of the affair with his reputation enhanced. There was talk of an organisational role in the policing of the forthcoming Commonwealth Games, enough to convince him that it would give his career the boost it needed.

A High Court judge cannot be influenced by media clamour, but in any case, there were extenuating circumstances for Kate. When her case came to court it was a sensation. Kate was once again in fine form, looking radiant. She was acquitted of all criminal responsibility for the death of Marcia Fells, whose killing was considered legitimate self-defence. However, on the lesser charges of illegal possession of a firearm and false identity, she was given a two-year suspended sentence and reprimanded by the judge for her lack of co-operation with the police. She also had to bear the costs of the hearing. Press coverage of her heroics meant that her already thriving interior design business boomed and she was able to take on a carefully selected group of talented young designers. The twenty-eighth of June—the anniversary of the discovery of the *Werburgh Treasure*—was the date she chose for the launch of her new *Werburgh* range of fabrics and wallpaper, with a swirling design reminiscent of Anglo-Saxon biting beasts.

LONDON UNIVERSITY, 2022 AD

Biting beasts in all their intricate formations became increasingly familiar to Alice, who inspired by their adventure, enrolled for a degree course in archaeology at London University. She opted for Anglo-Saxon studies under Professor Cox. The discovery of such an important archaeological treasure, to Jake's delight, had awakened the latent scholar in her and aroused a profound interest in all things Anglo-Saxon. She felt drawn to manuscripts and after her honours degree she began a PhD. Her research led to a thesis dealing with *Computer-Assisted Linguistic Analysis in Anglo-Saxon Manuscripts.* Her detective work now consisted in analysing word forms copied from different archetypes, each stemming from a different scriptorium and datable to a different time. Of course, she remained, as ever, at the disposal of Sir Clive Cochrane. Jake, in the same situation as his wife, returned to writing novels. His escapade over the *Robinson Affair* gave him ready-made material.

USA 2022 *AD*

LESS SENSATIONALLY, almost unnoticed by the tabloid press, Simon Lightbourne, was sentenced to three years in a London prison for his part in the death of Dr Paul Hudson. After his release, two years and 47 days later, he wasn't allowed to go back to Oxford or indeed to stay in England. His Doctorate was transferred to Yale University where thanks to his uncle's influence Lightbourne's criminal record was overlooked.

At this point, he abandoned all interest in Anglo-Saxon studies, dedicating himself instead to the Mashantucket Pequot Indians. He began to make a name for himself in academic circles thanks to his specialised knowledge of seventeenth-century housing in the Wawarramoreke uplands.

The FBI, unable to find evidence of connection between Marcia Fells and Warren Lightbourne discreetly dropped their inquiries. The Washington press insinuated that not a great deal of effort was made. Whatever the circumstances, the millionaire spent many of his evenings browsing through the British Museum's lavish brochure of the Werburgh Treasure, sparingly sipping vintage 1998 *Chateauneuf du Pape*, while dwelling morosely on—the pinions of a dove.

THE END

Dear reader,

We hope you enjoyed reading *Pinions Of Gold*. Please take a moment to leave a review, even if it's a short one. Your opinion is important to us.

Discover more books by John Broughton at https://www.nextchapter.pub/authors/john-broughton

Want to know when one of our books is free or discounted? Join the newsletter at http://eepurl.com/bqqB3H

Best regards,

John Broughton and the Next Chapter Team

The story continues in:
The Serpent Wand by John Broughton

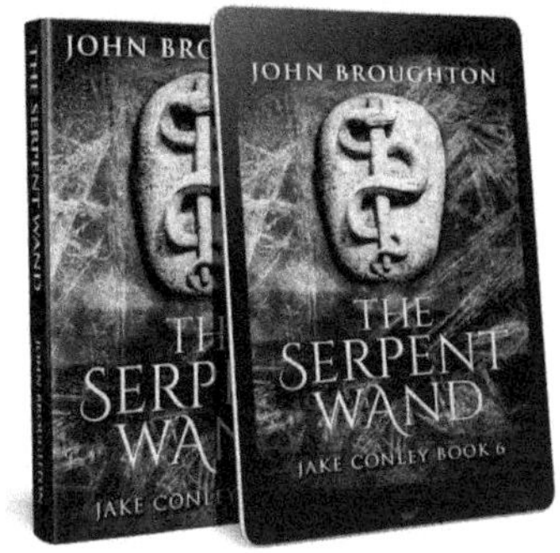

To read the first chapter for free, please head to:
https://www.nextchapter.pub/books/the-serpent-wand

ABOUT THE AUTHOR

I was born in Cleethorpes, Lincolnshire, UK, in 1948—just one of the post-war baby boom. After attending grammar school and studying to the sound of Bob Dylan, I went to Nottingham University and studied Medieval and Modern History (Archaeology subsidiary). The subsidiary course led to one of my greatest academic achievements—tipping the soil content of a wheelbarrow from the summit of a spoil heap, on an old lady hobbling past our dig.

Well, I have actually done many different jobs while living in Radcliffe-on-Trent, Leamington, Glossop, the Scilly Isles, Puglia and Calabria. They include teaching English and History, managing a daycare centre, being a director of a trade institute, and teaching English to university students. I even tried being a fisherman and a flower picker when I was on St. Agnes, Scilly.

I have lived in Calabria since 1992, where I settled into a long-term job for once, at the University of Calabria, teaching English. No doubt my lovely Calabrian wife, Maria, stopped me being restless. My two kids are grown up now, but I wrote books for them when they were little. Hamish Hamilton and then Thomas Nelson published six of these in England, in the 1980s. They are now out of print. I'm a granddad now, and happily, my grandson's parents named him Dylan.

I decided to take up writing again, late in my career. When you're teaching and working as a translator, you don't really have time for writing. As soon as I stopped the translation work, in 2014, I resumed writing. The fruit of that decision is my first historical novel, *Die for a Dove,* an archaeological thriller, followed by *The Purple Thread* and *Wyrd of the Wolf,* published by Endeavour Press, London. Both are set in my favourite Anglo-Saxon period. Currently, my third and fourth novels are available, too—*Saints and Sinners,* and its sequel, *Mixed Blessings,* set on the cusp of the eighth century in Mercia and Lindsey.

I began a new collaboration with Creativia/Next Chapter Publishing, who published *Perfecta Saxonia* and *Ulf's Tale* in 2019, followed by *Angenga,* a time travel novel bringing together the eighth and twenty-first century. They then published *In the Name of the Mother,* a sequel to *Wyrd of the Wolf.* A fifth historical novel, *Sward and Sword,* about the great Earl Godwine, is a forthcoming publication. My latest literary direction is a series of novels about psychic investigator Jake Conley, with the October 2019 release by Next Chapter Publishing, of *Elfrid's Hole,* to be followed by book two, *Red Horse Vale,* and this, book 3, *Memory of a Falcon,* which is scheduled for February, 2020. Book 4 *The Snape Ring* is due for publication.

Lightning Source UK Ltd.
Milton Keynes UK
UKHW022035180121
377284UK00012B/1034/J

9 781034 226222